Plaatu's Return

Plaatu's Return

Michael Merrett

Second Edition

To order additional copies of this book, contact:
Xlibris Corporation
1-888-795-4274
www.Xlibris.com
Orders@Xlibris.com
53611

CHAPTER ONE

The cacophony of sounds resonating inside the cabin of the little star-cruiser blended together to form a monotonous drone that caused Plaatu to become very, very sleepy. The steady pulsating hum of the engines and the soft-intermittent beeping of the ships on-board equipment had a way of lulling him into such a relaxed state that at times he would drift right off to sleep while sitting in his command chair.

As he snored softly with his head tilted to one side, the entire ship shuddered slightly as if being shaken by an unseen force. Plaatu shifted in his seat but resumed his cat-nap with his head now slightly tilted to the other side.

"Ion storm approaching," said the ship's computer in a monotone masculine voice. His command console was located just a few feet in front of his command chair. From this position, he could control every function on the ship. The myriad of dials and indicators were purely for informational purposes as most functions were carried out through simple voice commands to the on-board computer.

Plaatu didn't flinch. The ship shuddered again but with greater force this time.

"Ship entering Ion storm," the computer announced with no sentiment. It was merely a machine and not programmed to convey alarm or emotional duress. Plaatu had once quipped that no matter where he traveled in the universe, no matter which species he encountered, their machines were every bit as heart-less and soul-less as a pair of shoes.

Plaatu took no notice and continued snoring softly.

"Evasive action is strongly recommended," said the computer.

Plaatu shifted his weight again. He responded with a few indiscernible snorts and grunts, then he settled back into his comfortable chair. Visions of his home planet danced in his mind as he remained locked in a nostalgic state of reverie.

The outer edge of the storm hit the tiny ship with full fury. Plaatu was lifted right out of his seat and nearly thrown to the deck.

"What the hell is going on here?" he shrieked as he grudgingly returned to consciousness. He clutched the arms of the chair to steady himself. The craft was buffeted again as he was thrown forward onto the ship's computer panel. He tried to grab hold of the edges to break his fall with no success. He landed on his rump in a seated position against the side wall of the cabin. A panel flew open just above his head as packages of food rations rained down upon him.

"Damn! Why didn't you warn me about this?" he shouted at the computer.

"Warnings were issued but ignored," came the monotone electronic response.

Plaatu tried to regain his feet but another violent impact sent him sailing into the opposite side wall of the cabin. Another panel popped open as packets of medical supplies showered down upon him.

"Well get us out of here!" he shouted. "Evasive maneuvers!" The ship tilted to starboard and almost flipped. Plaatu grabbed on to a side rail and hung on for dear life. As the ship righted itself, he crashed to the deck striking his knees against the metal plating. The air temperature rose sharply from the increase in internal cabin pressure and droplets of sweat began to form on his brow.

"Damn it!" he shouted at the computer, "Reverse direction now!"

The ship started to roll again as he struggled to hold onto the metal rail, then he felt the engines surge as the computer laid in the new course. In a few moments the impacts ceased and the cabin went deathly silent. Plaatu slowly rose to his feet and staggered over to his command chair. He sat back and took a few deep breaths trying to clear his head. His knees were still throbbing with pain as he looked around the floor of the cabin at the debris that was strewn everywhere.

"Well," he chuckled, "that was invigorating, don't you think?" There was no response. "Check for structural integrity and any hull damage," he ordered.

"Complying," answered the computer.

"Guess that's what I get for dozing off on the job," he said softly. He walked around the cabin picking up the dislodged items and put them back where they belonged. He sat back down and breathed an enormous sigh of relief as his pulse gradually returned to normal. Then he stared out towards his main viewing screen. The large, three dimensional panel was capable of displaying a panoramic view of the galaxy that had taken Plaatu's breath away the first time he was introduced to it. These newly installed devices had holographic capability and the clarity was simply the best quality current technology had to offer. Despite his many years of service and millions of miles logged however, the limitless dangers that could virtually come out of anywhere out here in the vastness of space never ceased to amaze him.

Although it was a reality he had become somewhat accustomed to, every so often a gut-wrenching thought gripped him like an iron vice. The only thing standing between his frail ageing body and the crushing, deadly zero gravity environment of empty space was the three-inch thick cobalt-reinforced outer walls of his ship.

During his long career, he had covered a fairly large segment of the immediate vicinity which constituted "Coalition" space. While it spanned 31 solar systems, he was fully aware that it was nothing more than a tiny pin-prick in a universe that stretched beyond the imagination.

Plaatu got up and prepared a hot beverage. The ship's 'galley' was located to the right of his command chair. It was fully automated and any number of beverages or food items could be obtained in mere seconds with the wave of his hand. All he was required to do was keep the food processor stocked full of the small food ration packages that were loaded before every mission and the ship's 'vito-sequencer' was designed to prepare them automatically. As he sipped an amber colored vitamin-rich liquid, a nutritional supplement that resembled Chinese tea, he perused his next assignment which had been relayed to him via sub-space communications just prior to the storm. The communiqué was from his dear friend Em Diem. He could only hope that it would be far more pleasurable than his last assignment. He wasn't exactly sure as to the reasons why but it was beginning to feel like each new mission was exponentially more nerve-wracking than the one that preceded it.

He had been part of a six-member Coalition task force that was sent to the planet Terim to confront a notorious group of galactic pirates. They were engaging in the age-old practice of abducting young females and selling them into slavery. The sex trade throughout the galaxy was an increasingly disheartening problem and was one that struck a nerve in particular with Plaatu. He had a daughter and the thought of her being forced to endure such cruelty was simply unimaginable. Females from the planet Terim were known to have remarkably sensitive nervous systems and were reputed to have almost mythical levels of sexual prowess. They brought a huge sum on the black market but to Plaatu, it was one of the most heinous of offenses. The girls were wrenched away from their families to be abused on some alien world, then discarded like worn-out clothing once they outlived their usefulness. The task force had managed to rescue an entire ship full of terrified victims and Plaatu was moved beyond words by the looks of gratitude in their tear-filled eyes. He sometimes liked to think that over time he had become immune to all the suffering he encountered in his line of work, much like a doctor becomes numb to the emotions his wounded patients contend with. Deep down though, he was only fooling himself. Like most sentient beings, Plaatu had a reasonable tolerance level for most indiscretions accepting the fact that no one is perfect. Cruelty was where he absolutely drew the line. That was something he simply could never tolerate under any circumstances.

Plaatu ordered his computer to soften the lights in the cabin. Due to the fact that he was expected to live within the relatively comfortable but sometimes confining interior of his Class 3 Star Cruiser, a wide spectrum of lighting conditions were pre-installed to conform to daily cycles. Bright yellow was employed during work periods, soft blue for relaxation periods and blue-green for sleep periods. Plaatu was partial to the blue as it masked the somewhat cold, austere appearance of the gray metallic room he called home for much of his existence.

Plaatu reminisced about his friend for a few moments. He and Em Diem had attended the same university on their home planet Golon and pursued similar majors but Em had taken a different path than Plaatu after graduation. Rather than enter the CIPF (Coalition Interplanetary Police Force) which is the path Plaatu had chosen, Em seemed more attracted to the diplomatic side of inter-planetary affairs and had run for public office. He was a man of good will, an articulate and convincing public speaker and eventually rose to a high ranking position with the Council of Civil Affairs. It was their function to investigate and resolve disputes between member planets. It was the CIPF's job to enforce their rulings.

Like Plaatu, Em Diem was in the twilight years of his life. He had given many years of highly distinguished service to his planet and those around him knew that he was contemplating retirement. He was the kind of individual who would give you the shirt off his back and few members of the Coalition Council were held in higher esteem but he had one major flaw in Plaatu's eyes. He was far too trusting. By remaining back on Golon and confining himself to matters of diplomacy, he had not been directly exposed to the often seedy "underside" of the universe as Plaatu had. As a result, Em was far too willing to extend to all parties the benefit of the doubt when called upon to mediate interplanetary disputes. Plaatu had learned through countless experiences dealing with humanoids that the best approach was to immediately nullify every visible threat and ask questions later. Nevertheless, he was very fond of Em and trusted him implicitly. The two did have something very much in common that they each remained oblivious to, however. Age and years of sometimes very unpleasant experiences was causing them to become terminally cynical.

Plaatu glanced down at the electronic clipboard containing his new orders. As he read through the text revealing his next destination, his nerve endings felt like they had been struck by a mild electronic charge. He was instructed to head for "The third planet" in the distant system its inhabitants fondly refer to as the "Milky Way". The mere recollection of his previous visit there brought back a myriad of emotions. First off, he could never understand why the planet's inhabitants chose to name something as vast as a solar system after a chocolate candy bar that shared the same name. He had forgotten to ask someone of influence that very same question during his first visit. Then there was the infamous first encounter. No sooner did he step off his craft, he was fired upon by a nervous member of the planet's military forces. Fortunately it was nothing more than a flesh wound but then the distrustful buggers had the unmitigated gall to shoot him in the back during the latter stage of his mission. They seemed to harbor an inexplicable, downright primitive fear and distrust of alien life forms. If not for the quick response by his traveling companion, CIPF enforcement-robot Bort, he wouldn't be here today reading this communiqué. Bort had retrieved his lifeless body and placed him in the regeneration tube located in Plaatu's ship. Their advanced medical technology could restore life functions for an indefinite period of time. Plaatu was fully aware that as he sat there remembering the experience, it was now a half-century later. Most of his peers marveled at his astonishing resiliency and longevity. In Plaatu's mind however, he was painfully aware that he was living on borrowed time.

In fairness to the planet's incomparably irrational inhabitants, Plaatu grudgingly admitted that there were some fond moments during his visit to Earth. While the hairs on the back of his neck bristled with the thought of having to go back there, the idea did, on some level, intrigue him albeit in a distinctly apprehensive sort of way.

The primary purpose of his mission had been to inform leaders of planet Earth that the Coalition of Planets he represented wasn't trying to interfere in their affairs. However, if the planet's inhabitants insisted on developing weapons of mass destruction which in time could threaten their celestial neighbors, there would be dire consequences. On the surface at least, it seemed so ridiculously simple that Plaatu fully expected to rap up the entire mission in a single day. He was instructed to leave behind a monitoring device in a non-conspicuous location so that the Coalition could track their levels of progress, or lack thereof whichever the case may be. The good people of Earth would be given seventy five years before the Coalition would send another emissary. It was estimated that based on his planetary research, it would be at least 100 years before Earthlings would begin to send manned atomic-powered crafts to the outer edges of its solar system at their present rate of development. It had only been fifty years. So why the return visit, he thought to himself?

Plaatu felt the ship lurch in reverse causing him to spill his beverage all over his gray, one piece flight suit.

"What in blazes!" he gasped as he reached for a towlette and dabbed at his uniform. "Computer! What was that?"

"A passing ship has locked on to this vessel with a tractor beam," answered the computer.

"Didn't ship scanners notice its approach?!" he said still dobbing at his uniform.

"Ship was in sheer mode and scanners were unable to detect its approach," came the response.

"Sheer mode?" muttered Plaatu. The only ships that were equipped with such capabilities within the Coalition's sphere of influence were those used by the CIPF. Any member planet using ships with any kind of similar stealth-like technology were severely punished with economic sanctions and could even risk expulsion. Which meant that his ship was in the grip of a violator or . . .

"Hey there buddy!" said an affable voice through his ship's communication console. Plaatu recognized the voice immediately. It was his fellow officer and close friend Ecko Moov.

"You son of a Talon bog-beast!" snapped Plaatu with a smile. "You've spilled my beverage all over me!"

"Sorry about that old buddy," came Ecko's response from his ship which was now directly behind Plaatu's. "I just thought I would drop by and say hello."

"Is that your idea of a simple hello?" asked Plaatu whimsically.

Plaatu and Ecko had been classmates for the final two years of their CIPF training. Their class featured many outstanding cadets and it was widely considered to be one of the finest graduating classes in the academy's history.

Plaatu had developed a strong bond with Ecko and during the extensive training maneuvers; the two had become so familiar with each other's moves, tactics, and ways of thinking that they had developed a sense of confidence in each other's abilities that transcended mere camaraderie. Plaatu trusted Ecko with his very life and he was reasonably sure that the feeling was mutual.

The practice of sneaking up on a fellow agent and successfully locking onto his ship with a tractor beam was an age old prank throughout the force. It was a symbol of competence and any agent unable to perform the feat was considered a flunky.

"You're just angry that I sniped you so easily," responded Ecko. "I heard you were in this sector and wondered where you were going next?"

"You won't believe it . . ." answered Plaatu as he walked over to the laundry shoot and threw his towlette into the metallic bin. He pushed a button on the panel above it and the cleaning cycle whirred into motion.

"Do you remember that planet I told you about where I got shot with a lead projectile not once but twice in the span of one week? The one that makes my ribs ache every time I think about it?"

"I remember" said Ecko. "I thought they weren't scheduled for a return visit for another 25 years or so."

"They aren't," said Plaatu. "I am not sure what the reason is but I'm sure I will find out in good time. So, where are you bound for my friend?"

"Actually, I'm due for some R and R for a couple weeks. I've been working straight out for 4 months and I'm looking forward to just taking it easy for awhile. Wish you could join me."

"Yes, me too," muttered Plaatu remorsefully. He would have liked nothing better than to get away from the rigors of the job for a while but judging by the orders he had just received, the Council obviously had other plans for him.

An alarm sounded indicating another ship was nearby.

"Scanners are tracking ship of unknown origin three parsecs distance traveling at high rate of speed," announced the computer.

"Put it on screen," ordered Plaatu. He gazed at his ship's main viewing panel. In the distance, he could just barely make out the glimmer of a small craft. Whoever it was, they were in a hurry to get somewhere.

"Are you tracking that?" he asked Ecko.

"It is a Tilatin explorer according to my previous scans," answered Ecko. "They are elusive little creatures and I haven't been able to get close enough for a better scan. Now what the hell would a Tilatin ship be doing way out here?" In another moment it was gone.

"Ship has moved beyond scanning range," said the computer.

"That's odd," muttered Plaatu as he continued to search the viewing screen for any trace of the craft. "They have no business being in this sector."

"Oh well," said Ecko. "Don't worry about it, I'll see if I can pick them up on my way back to Central. Listen, check in with me when you get back huh? You still owe me that hiking trip, remember?"

"Yes I remember," answered Plaatu thoughtfully. "I'll give you a shout when I return. Justice be served."

"As always my friend," answered Ecko.

With that, Plaatu watched as Ecko's ship disappeared from his viewing screen. At its current location patrolling the outer rim of the Ceti Alpha system, Plaatu's ship was three days away from Earth at maximum speed. That would give him a few days to re-familiarize himself with the planet's geographic complexities. By tracking current radio and television signals, he could bring himself up to date on just how far Earth had progressed or regressed, whichever the case may be. He had, on occasion, glanced at the data being sent to the Coalition's monitoring center from the transmitter he had left behind on his previous visit but he had never had the time to study the data in-depth.

"Computer, lay in a course to designated new assignment," ordered Plaatu as he walked over to replenish his beverage. Then he ordered the computer to open a channel to Em Diem at Central Command to clarify the reasons for his return to Earth. The electronic servant complied and within seconds had made the communications connection.

"Plaatu?" came a voice over the intercom. It was the unmistakable tone of Em Diem. "Good to hear from you. I had a hunch you would be checking in. Are the Golon moons smiling upon your travels?"

Plaatu felt a deep sense of connection whenever he heard Em's voice. He confided in him often and would accept anything he told him without hesitation. In all his years of service to the Coalition, he had counted on Em's advice and guidance more times than he could count. Through all of their interactions, the bond they shared remained as strong as ever.

"The glow from our lovely planet's two moons is with me always," answered Plaatu, "But I am a bit perplexed. I didn't think we were scheduled to go back to Earth for another 25 years. What has changed?"

"There are two reasons, my friend," said Em. "The first is that we think the monitoring device you left behind is malfunctioning. It is indicating that the Earth inhabitants have accelerated their nuclear weapon programs to frightening levels. The numbers are so high we can only assume the information is faulty which will require you to merely repair the transmitter or replace it. You do have a few on board as standard cargo, correct?"

"Oh sure," answered Plaatu. "I have at least three in my inventory at all times."

"Good," said Em. "The first and highly more preferable scenario would not require you to make any contact whatsoever. They have already informed us that they have no desire to become members of our little Coalition of Planets and we respect their decision. We don't respect them enough to refrain from spying on them mind you as they still could represent a threat to our stability if they continue to pursue their present course but that is an issue for another day. For the present at least, try to get in and get out, no fuss, no muss."

"And the second reason?" said Plaatu. He knew that first scenario sounded far too easy. If there was one constant that seemed to dog him throughout his entire career up to this point, it was that few things ever came to him easily.

"The second scenario only becomes an issue if the signals we are receiving are accurate. Then . . . you will have to take action."

"What kind of action?" asked Plaatu, his nerve endings tingling with every word? He could still picture Earth in his mind. It was to the best of his recollection one of the most beautiful planets he had ever seen. He had thoroughly enjoyed his interaction with most of the planet's life forms, particularly the incredible assortment of birds and mammals, with the exception of humans of course. He grudgingly acknowledged that they possessed some moderately likable qualities, depending on one's perspective. Their culinary arts skills were without equal and they could spin a yarn with the best of bi-peds, a combination that often resulted in a reasonably pleasurable evening of dining and entertainment. But they could also, often with the slightest of provocations, be far more disagreeable than most species he had encountered over the span of his eventful career. "Perhaps they had mellowed with age," he thought, "but then again that might be too much to hope for." Plaatu was widely described by his peers as an incurable pessimist.

"It may require you," said Em earnestly, "to perform a far more extreme demonstration of the consequences they face if they do not cease and desist with their continuing efforts to build bigger and more destructive weapons. I fail to see why they cannot recognize the dangers this kind of shamefully aggressive policy poses to every living thing on their planet's surface."

"Well," said Plaatu. "Let us hope it is merely a faulty transmitter. We can always cross that other bridge when we come to it."

"Agreed," said Em. "Have a safe trip. Contact me again when you get there and have an update."

"Will do," answered Plaatu. Then he remembered his encounter with the Tilatin ship. "Oh, by the way, I scanned what appeared to be an explorer-class Tilatin vessel leaving this sector. Are you aware of their presence here?"

"A Tilatin ship?" said Em with genuine surprise. "They have no authority to be exploring that area. That would represent a serious violation of territorial mandates. I will check into it though."

"I just thought you should know about it," said Plaatu. "I too thought it was a bit strange. I'll get in touch with you again when I am on the ground. Take care my friend. Computer, end transmission."

Plaatu got up and walked around the ship's cabin to the empty alcove where Bort would normally be standing. All senior officers of the CIPF (Coalition Interplanetary Police Force) were accompanied by enforcement robots. Bort had been his traveling companion since Plaatu's very first mission after graduating senior officer's training at the police academy. The ship felt empty without him and somehow Plaatu felt vulnerable going off on any mission without him. Bort had been malfunctioning and was desperately in need of routine maintenance. He had dropped him off two weeks earlier with engineers and was told it would be another week before he would again be ready for service. His ship was equipped with weapon systems with a myriad of enforcement capabilities and Plaatu had nothing to worry about for the most part but something inside kept nagging him that it was bad luck to travel without his fellow officer, robot or no robot.

"Oh what the hell," he muttered to himself. "He would probably just scare the skin off the Earthlings again like he did last time."

Plaatu glanced down at the time piece on his wrist. It was time to consume nourishment. CIPF officers were required to adhere to a strict regimen of proper exercise and diet. Plaatu was a seasoned veteran of the force however, and the time allotment he was required to devote to each function had, over time, shifted ever so slightly. The required one hour of exercise shortly after each fifteen minute eating period had gradually morphed into a regimen that was a bit more to his liking. Fifteen minutes of exercise per day if he could find the time with four leisurely eating periods, each followed by a short nap. It was a regimen eminently more to his liking and far more suited to a man of his age he rationalized in his mind.

He got up and walked over to the galley. A daily menu was posted on the wall indicating portion sizes and daily items to be consumed in order to maintain proper weight and muscle mass. The CIPF standard-issue meals would bore a billy goat so everywhere Plaatu went he would pick up a healthy supply of contraband items to sustain him to his next destination. He was well aware he could be suspended and even fired for such rule violations but if the CIPF suspended every officer who had contraband food items on board, there wouldn't be anyone left to patrol the galaxy.

As he loaded up his tray with twice the allowed daily allotment of calories and filled a glass with a wine-like beverage compliments of the gracious families on the planet Terim, he retook his seat and a devilish grin came over his face. "It pains me to admit it," he said to himself, "but I have reached a point in my life where I am forced to confess I enjoy eating more than I do sex. How pathetic is that?" He flipped a switch on his command chair console and the cabin filled with the sounds of relaxing Golonian music. Plaatu's personal favorite was an orchestral piece titled "Flight of the Cybids" performed by the Fantara Orchestra based in Golon's capital city of Fantar. Cybids were the most plentiful of all the bird-like species on Golon. They were sky blue with white feathers and as they soared majestically through the Golon skies, their wings emitted a soft melodious shrill that was simply alluring to anyone within earshot.

He deftly cut into an 8 ounce filet of snarl-beast and popped a piece into his mouth. It had a similar consistency as the portion of cow he had once enjoyed on planet Earth all those long years ago. He closed his eyes and began to chew, savoring its natural juices.

"Ahhhhh!" he sighed, wafting in the culinary ecstasy of the moment. "It just doesn't get any better than this." He raised the glass to his lips and prepared to enjoy its contents.

"Ion storm ahead," announced the computer matter-of-factly.

"Of course there is!" snapped Plaatu. "You wouldn't have it any other way." He so loathed computers. He put down the drink for a moment and stared contemptuously at his command console. "Plot an evasive course."

The on-board computer managed to plot a course around the second Ion storm. Plaatu had noticed of late that these galactic phenomenon were occurring with greater frequency. There were some scientists in the Coalition's employ who insisted it was incontrovertible evidence of universal warming but there were many skeptics ready and willing to refute these findings. He finished his meal and put his head back for a few moments wafting in the orchestral magnificence.

Plaatu was grateful for the few days of travel time which gave him the opportunity to catch up on Earth Lore. As he monitored signals being emitted by the transmitter he had planted decades earlier, it did not appear, at least on the surface, that it was malfunctioning. The signal was clear and crisp but the data it was transmitting was nevertheless intriguing giving him much to digest. Time passed in what Plaatu often referred to as "the blink of a cosmic eye" and before he knew it, his ship had reached the outer edge of Earth's solar system. Pluto, the furthest planet from their sun was just off to his right. Approximately 1,475 miles in diameter, its icy lifeless surface appeared barren and uninviting.

"Computer," he said, "Scan for atmospheric readings as we pass each planet in this system. Transmit all findings to Command Central. Might as well conduct a little constructive research along the way."

"Affirmative," responded the computer.

Plaatu was fully aware that it would slow his progress a bit since the planets were not in straight alignment but conducting research was part of his duties as a CIPF officer. Besides, it was a great way to break up the day-to-day routine. In a few hours he had passed Uranus, Neptune, Saturn with its awe-inspiring rings, the mammoth Jupiter and was just shy of Mars. The "red planet" was reading little more than minute particles of bacteria at its lowest levels. Plaatu was fascinated upon his first visit here that of the nine planets in this system, only one was currently supporting corporeal life. That was very unusual and something he had not found anywhere else in his travels. Usually when he encountered a cluster of planets so closely aligned, a greater number of them would indicate some forms of life. In this group, eight of the nine were virtually dead planets.

As the afternoon waned, Earth loomed majestically in the distance. As his ship drew closer, the fog began to clear in his head and the hazy images that had faded with the passing of time all came back to him. He gazed intently at his viewing screen with renewed vigor as it grew larger and larger. It was like a big blue liquid bubble slowly rotating in the empty void of space. Plaatu recalled upon his first visit here how incredibly naïve the Earth's inhabitants were to the fact that they resided on one of the most valuable pieces of real estate in the galaxy.

His ship entered the atmosphere taking readings as it descended. After passing through the thinly layered exosphere, the ship entered the thermosphere and began vibrating slightly. Plaatu immediately noticed something very different from his previous visit. There were electronic satellites orbiting the planet in vast numbers. His ship's sensing equipment continued taking readings as it passed them by. He noticed that some were functional while others were not. Plaatu couldn't understand why the satellites that were no longer functional still remained in orbit. From his vantage point, the planet's inhabitants either lacked the technology to retrieve them or, they were content to just leave them there as floating garbage, a decision that would only come back to haunt them in the not too distant future as there orbits decayed.

A large craft came into view off in the distance. "What is that?" Plaatu mumbled in an intrigued tone.

"Craft is a manned exploratory vehicle of Earth origin," answered the computer.

"Manned craft!" said Plaatu. "Amazing! They really have progressed haven't they."

As the International Space Station grew closer, Plaatu was impressed with its size and complexity. It looked like a huge metallic butterfly floating in space. It appeared to be powered by solar arrays, a form of energy that did not exist when he had last visited here. He ordered his computer to give it a wide berth. He did not want to alert the good people of Earth to his presence just yet.

The ship entered Earth's stratosphere where the ride became a bit smoother. It orbited the planet and began scanning for changes in air quality, water quality and relative size of the ice packs at each pole. He would compare the readings to those he had taken five decades earlier. The ship was flying in sheer mode, unlike his first visit when he allowed himself to be tracked. There was no need to let anyone know he was here unless it became absolutely necessary.

As his ship soared above the continent of Antarctica, scanners picked up a large group of Emperor Penguins huddled together in a tight group. Plaatu watched his main viewing screen in amazement as a blizzard battered the defenseless creatures in what had to be intolerably cold conditions.

"Hover here for a moment," Plaatu ordered the computer. "What is the temperature down there?"

The ship was hovering about two thousand feet above the ice pack but the intense winds still pushed the engines to their limit as they struggled to maintain a stationary position.

"Surface temperature is currently -10 Celsius," stated the computer. "Winds are at 40 knots combining for a wind chill of -35 Celsius."

"Good God!" remarked Plaatu. He had never seen anything quite like this before. They were just standing there tightly huddled together in a desperate fight for survival.

As he continued to watch in amazement, the penguins at the outer edge of the circle appeared to be on the verge of freezing to death.

"Why don't they seek shelter?" he wondered. "This can't be some form of mass suicide can it?"

"A search of ship's records indicates the event is a normal occurrence which takes place in this region of the planet every 12 months," reported the computer. "Male penguins are required to keep newly formed eggs warm by shielding them for the entire winter."

Plaatu's heart ached for the defenseless creatures. "This is remarkable," he muttered. "What determination and sacrifice. A truly extraordinary species."

He continued to watch as two of the penguins at the outer edge fell to the ground. They appeared to have succumbed to the extreme cold and driving gusts of icy pellets.

"I can't just sit here and watch this," he said in anguish. "This is more than any living creature should be expected to endure."

Plaatu's mind raced in a desperate search for a solution. He was absolutely forbidden to interfere in the normal ecological progression of any planet. The Coalition had learned through many centuries of experience that even the best intentions to help a given species can have dire consequences when all factors are not carefully considered. Nature as a whole, regardless of the planet in question, had proven time and time again to require a very delicate balance in order to remain healthy and vibrant. If he had had the time, there were countless examples he could have studied where humanity had dealt with serious ramifications after introducing new plants and animals into areas of the planet where they had never existed before. Even on a planet as small as Earth, the inhabitants had managed to establish a strict set of rules regarding the transportation of potentially dangerous species of plants and animals across inter-continental boundaries.

But these were creatures on the verge of freezing to death, Plaatu thought. He wasn't going to move them which might upset the planet's delicate ecosystem. He just wanted to keep them warm. What could possibly be wrong with that, he thought?

"Computer!" he said with utter resolve. "Drop a thermo-pod over them. Set duration for 7 days. That should get them through the worst of the storm." A thermo-pod was a light-weight hovering device that generated a radiant heat over a designated area, then dropped harmlessly to the ground once its energy was expended. It could then be retrieved and re-charged for further use.

"Temperature setting?" asked the computer.

Plaatu thought for a moment. If he made it too warm, their body temperatures could rise causing an increase in metabolism. This would force their systems to burn more calories and they might not have access to food supplies until the conditions improved.

"Let's just make it more bearable," he said. "Set it at 0 Celsius. I would like to do more but it may cause them more harm than good."

The computer complied. As it dropped the device it descended to within twenty feet above the ground, stopped and began emitting a warm infra-red glow that would be uninterrupted no matter how strong the winds became. Its aerodynamically designed frame allowed it to remain in a synchronous position just above the penguin's snow-covered heads.

As Plaatu continued to watch for a few moments more, the two penguins that had fallen, gallantly trying to protect the others from the merciless forces of nature stirred to life. They floundered for a few moments, then staggered to their feet. Their heads bobbed side to side as if they were thinking, "Is it springtime already?"

"That's better," he muttered. "I just hope this doesn't come back to haunt me. Although a planet over run by penguins might be a refreshing alternative to one over run by humans. Computer, let's move on."

The ship proceeded north over Patagonia where he made a brief stop to pilfer some fresh coffee beans from the over-abundant jungles of South America. Coffee was a beverage he remembered thoroughly enjoying during his first visit. As every CIPF officer is fully aware, it is morally unethical to pass up on any opportunity to obtain contraband food items, just so long as no one is financially adversely affected in the process. Graft is definitely off limits. His ship then lifted off again and swung out over Brazil and the Equator. He crossed the Central Atlantic Ocean and decided to take some readings while flying over the Sahara, the largest desert on the planet. His ship's surveillance equipment was far more advanced than anything found on Earth. As his ship crossed over Nigeria and circled south towards Angola, Plaatu was stunned by the conditions that prevailed throughout the region. The entire area was riddled by political unrest and turmoil. Millions of residents had been displaced and were on the move. It was difficult to watch so many unfortunate victims desperately trying to seek refuge from the violence. Many appeared to be on the verge of collapse from malnutrition. The images were gut-wrenching. There were long lines of people of all ages, most of them barefoot, some carrying small children in their arms. An overwhelming sense of anguish gripped Plaatu as he watched in horror. This is not what he expected to find here.

"How can one region of this planet live in such lavish abundance," he thought to himself, "while just a few thousand miles away entire cultures teeter on the brink of starvation?" Once again, Plaatu's emotions were getting the better of him.

Judging by his readings, much of the African landscape was either too arid or underdeveloped to produce sufficient amounts of food to sustain its burgeoning population. He carried in his ship's hold high-yield grains and other food staples that could be used during moments of crisis. A quick scan of available inventory revealed that a hybrid, rice-like grain that had thrived in similar conditions on the planet Tarsa may prove equally vibrant here. Unlike many grains native to Earth which relied on an intricate system of roots and irrigation to draw up moisture from the ground, this grain required a minimal root source and derived its nutrients by absorbing necessary elements directly from the air surrounding it. Even under the driest of conditions, as long as there was a sufficient source of wind to provide a minimal supply of moisture, this alien grain should thrive and multiply. Two thirds of this planet's surface was covered by water, a statistic that was unsurpassed throughout the immediate galaxy. Humidity levels here were off the charts compared to those on Tarsa. When fully grown, the adult plant very much resembled the tumbleweeds that rolled across the American Southwest, only these were edible and quite tasty.

He got up from his command chair and walked around to the back wall of the cabin. He opened a panel, then descended three stairs that led into his ships storage compartment. He found the large sacks of seeds he was looking for, then placed them in the jettison tubes. Once they were properly positioned, he headed back up to the main cabin and returned to his command chair.

He once again gazed at the ship's main viewing screen and searched for a suitable location to drop the seeds.

"Unauthorized substance has been detected in jettison tube one," announced the computer.

"Is that a fact?" said Plaatu, still gazing at the viewing panel. "How observant of your little transistors."

"Unauthorized seed distribution in areas that have not previously been scientifically examined for suitability is expressly forbidden," said the computer.

"And I thank you profusely for pointing that out to me," said Plaatu impatiently. He waited a few seconds more until the ship was directly over an area that was devoid of any human life forms that may be frightened at the sight of seeds raining down upon them. Then he pushed the jettison button sending the seeds tumbling to the ground.

"Unauthorized distribution of . . ." said the computer but Plaatu cut it off in mid-sentence.

"Will you please shut up!" he snapped. He laid in a new set of coordinates and sat back in his chair. He could only hope that his action, which he was painfully aware, might pose a great risk to his career if discovered, would bear fruit. Or in this case, bear grain. His mind was momentarily awash in self-doubt as he had never done anything like this before no matter how severe the conditions. He had always adhered to the rules, just as he was taught to do. That doesn't mean he liked the rules however. There were many occurrences where Plaatu could have helped a particular species in need but was prevented in doing so by these infernal rules. Many of those missed opportunities continued to weigh heavy on his conscience. That was something he was growing increasingly weary of as the many years passed by. Virtually every action in the universe has a reaction, most of them unpredictable. He could only hope that this particular action's eventual positives outweighed its negatives. Either way, he was determined to never again sit idly by while innocent victims suffered through no fault of their own.

The ship again crossed back over the Atlantic and proceeded up the Eastern Seaboard of the United States, Plaatu's heart began to race a bit as a feeling of intense Déjà vu overwhelmed him. This was the same path he had taken upon his first visit when he landed in the middle of a baseball field in Washington DC scaring the bajeezes out of a good many unwitting little leaguers.

After completing the difficult mission, his departing flight path had taken him up over the Northeast section of the continent. Out of sheer convenience, he had decided to plant the monitoring device in the White Mountains of New Hampshire near Mount Washington. It was the highest point in the Northeast region of the United States. Its dense forestry which was protected by the government made it an ideal location. He imbedded it beneath the ground under the cover of darkness where it would hopefully never be discovered. The signal it was designed to transmit was light years beyond anything humans could trace or track. It was a highly sophisticated bugging device that tapped into radio and television frequencies, then relayed the signals to Coalition government agencies on the planet Obo in the Alpha Centauri system. The device and the readings it was transmitting were virtually undetectable. The only way it could be discovered is if the exact location, twelve feet beneath the ground at latitude 44° 16' N, longitude 71° 18' W was excavated. Because it was a National park, Plaatu knew the device would be completely safe high on that ridge and away from prying eyes.

But then again, Plaatu had never heard of condominiums, which didn't come into being until the 1980's. How could he have anticipated that a greedy developer would pay off the right politicians, allowing the construction of a ski resort that now sat right on top of his transmitter?

"Those Cretans!" he shrieked as his ship slowly circled the area scanning the ground below from an elevation of 10,000 feet. While his ship was virtually invisible to Earth's radar tracking equipment, it could be seen by the naked eye if he wasn't careful. He waited until the cover of darkness and found a suitable place to land just west of Mt. Washington. He chose a clearing within a state park that seemed to be totally deserted and closed for the season. As he approached he felt reasonably sure that the cloud-filled October night sky would offer him the kind of cover he would need to land undetected. The summer tourist season had ended and this was a relatively desolate, sparsely populated area.

It wasn't completely free of residents however. Tom Gibson's house was located on Pine Hill road just off of Route 302 and a few miles from the campground. As he sat in his living room enjoying his evening fix of "Wheel of Fortune", he heard a soft hum that seemed to be crescendoing outside his window. As he reluctantly tore his eyes away from the shapely, blonde-haired woman who was gracefully turning letters on the display board, he looked out into the darkness just in time to see the silhouette of Plaatu's ship sail by.

"Lucy," he said in an unconcerned voice to his wife who was baking an apple pie in the kitchen, "a flying saucer just flew by the house. It looked like it was coming in for a landing."

"That's nice dear," Lucy muttered, then she went back to her rolling pin.

Tom just shrugged and turned his eyes back towards the television set. If she wasn't going to worry about it, he sure as hell wasn't going to worry about it either.

Moments later Plaatu set the ship down and disengaged the engines. It was eerily quiet in the cabin of his ship but it felt good to be on solid ground again. He ordered the computer to do a complete scan of the surrounding area for life forms.

"No humanoid life forms have been detected within a two mile radius," said the computer.

"Good, good," said Plaatu. "This spot should work perfectly. I can plant another transmitter if necessary and de-activate the faulty one from this remote location. Hopefully I'll be out of here by tomorrow morning."

He got up from his command chair and walked over to the weapons rack. He removed a blaster pistol and strapped it to his waist. He was reasonably sure he wouldn't need it but the thought of traveling without Bort on board was still a bit unsettling to him.

"Then again," he thought to himself, "maybe it is just the memory of my previous encounter with these buggers coming back to haunt me."

"Extend exit ramp," ordered Plaatu as he prepared to leave the ship. The exit hatch opened and he stepped out as the long, smooth, gray-colored ramp slid to the ground before him. He filled his lungs with the cool invigorating air and walked down the ramp to the grass below shining his porto-light in front of him.

As he scanned the tree line around his ship, he surmised that the computer had picked out the perfect spot. The ship fit into this little clearing like a glove, the trees surrounded him in a tightly formed circle and the only access road from nearby Route 3 seemed totally deserted. He relaxed his guard and felt at ease as he walked around the ship and surveyed it for damage from the Ion storm. The outer hull didn't show a scratch and while he knew subconsciously that the shielding the ships were equipped with was time tested and of the highest reliability, Plaatu always felt more comfortable doing a visual inspection of the hull whenever he landed on solid ground. "'To hell with technology," he once told a colleague. Always trust your senses."

He paused and listened for a moment. He was miles from civilization and the only sounds the night was offering up was that of the slight breeze whistling through the trees, the incessant chatter of crickets and the occasional "hoot" of a nearby owl.

He bent to his knees and ran his hand over the cool green grass. It was a much-welcome alternative to the cold, lifeless metal of his ship's cabin that he had been exposed to for too many months. He walked slowly away from the ship and out onto the access road. The asphalt was cracked in many places from frost heaves and the extreme weather this area was prone to during the winter months.

He heard the sound of a babbling brook nearby, but rather than trying to find it in the unyielding darkness, he wisely decided to wait for daylight to explore it further.

The cool night air was intoxicating as Plaatu closed his eyes and drew it all in with unabashed glee. His lungs filled with the oxygen-rich air and Plaatu felt completely rejuvenated. He glanced around and continued to waft in the ambiance. "What a great place for a camp fire," he said to himself.

Plaatu went into the ship and retrieved a small heating device and a porto-chair. Then he returned to the grass below. He activated the heater and sat down to enjoy a short respite with nature. The porto-heater emitted a warm radiant glow as he rubbed his hands together and held them just above its metal casing. It wasn't the same as an open fire but foraging for the necessary elements to get one going was out of the question. This was still unfamiliar surroundings and in total darkness, wandering around might be unwise. "No," he said to himself as he carefully scanned the forest, "this will have to do."

He stared up at the night sky. The stars were only dimly visible through the thin clouds but he still visualized them in his mind. It always fascinated him how the cosmos appeared from the vantage point of each planet he had visited. The humans had given the constellations some very interesting names based on how they appeared from their vantage point in the universe. "The Big Dipper" and its younger brother, "Little Dipper". "Hercules", "Orion", and "Gemini". Most of the names were derived from ancient Greek and Roman mythology. From his home planet of Golon, Earth was part of the "Zepala Ta" system. 11 months earlier during his last visit to his home world, Plaatu remembers staring up at the Golon night sky and searching for some of the various planets he had visited. He had located Earth as well as a good number of others and had charted them as a personal diary. Here it was almost an Earth year later and he found himself looking back at Golon from the other side of the galaxy.

"This mysterious thing we call Fate is so full of wonder and surprise," he once read. He never could have guessed that he would be covertly re-visiting this species that was in the early stages of development. He imagined for a moment what it would be like when humanity finally reached that landmark moment when they would visit some other inhabited world for the very first time. The mere thought of that inevitable event made him chuckle for a moment. "When worlds collide," he mused.

Plaatu heard his sensor beep softly. He reached down and unclipped the small cigarette-pack sized device from his belt and looked for where the indicator needle was pointing. He was being scanned. He continued to watch as the needle pointed towards the night sky in a direction of approximately 1 o'clock. There were hundreds of Earth satellites in orbit around the planet but none of them were capable of scanning at a frequency level that would cause his sensor to activate. Then again, it had been a long time since his last visit. Perhaps their satellite technology had advanced to a sufficient level to cause such a reaction. He couldn't be sure. If it was an Earth satellite, he was reasonably sure they couldn't get a visual lock on his ship through that kind of cloud cover. The beeping stopped so whatever it was, it had either moved beyond scanner range or had shut down altogether.

"Curious though," he muttered to himself as he returned the sensor device to his belt.

He heard the haunting call of a Hoot Owl off in the distance. The wind continued to buffet the trees in a crescendoing, then decrescendoing "whoosh" of cool air. The hour was late and Plaatu gave a momentary thought to sleeping outside the ship for a change of pace. He decided against it however. It would be just his luck to wake up with a large hungry black bear staring him right in the face. They were indigenous to this region and not to be trifled with.

Plaatu felt a tinge of loneliness come over him. While he understood the CIPF's reasoning for employing one-man crews to patrol the galaxy feeling they could cover far more territory, it sure could foster a somewhat melancholy existence over long periods of time. There were missions when his job would require him to go days, even weeks on end without any human contact. Bort may have made him feel more secure but he wasn't much of a conversationalist. Plaatu wasn't one to wallow in self-pity though. He had learned through decades of experience that the best way to ward off loneliness and depression was to immerse himself in work. As long as he kept his mind active, it served as a much-needed diversion from the many pratfalls of his occupation.

He picked up his gear and returned to the ship totally unaware that a 350 pound black bear was watching his every move from thirty yards away just beyond the tree line. Fortunately for him, the bear had already had his supper that night compliments of the nearby brook and its ample supply of tasty trout.

CHAPTER TWO

Plaatu awoke the next morning and upon opening the hatch was greeted by bright sunshine and fair skies. He removed his uniform and stepped into the tubular sonic-shower chamber where a carefully mixed solution off water and anti-bacterial agents gently cleansed his entire body. Little effort was required as the spray jets were dispensed from every direction. The drying cycle engaged and in a few moments, Plaatu felt like a new man. He stepped out, got dressed and prepared a pot of hot coffee from some beans he had picked while surveying the Andes Mountains in South America the previous day. As he sipped the coffee, the robust flavor reminded him of how much he had enjoyed this beverage all those years ago. He recalled it as being one of the nicer aspects of his mission.

He descended the exit ramp and took a seat, anxious to take full advantage of the opportunity to waft in the soothing early morning breeze. As he pondered his dilemma, he concluded that getting at the transmitter to see if it truly was physically damaged would not be an easy task. The more he thought about it, the better the idea sounded to simply plant a new one. It was obvious that whoever had built the condominiums had no idea the device was buried there beneath the ground and chances are it would remain undisturbed for decades if not centuries to come. The entire area was covered with mid-level mountain ranges, vast acreage of dense forestry and locating an ideal spot to bury another would be relatively easy. "Get in, get out," he kept repeating to himself. He was determined to finish this assignment without making any contact at all. But then, the travel Gods are not always as accommodating as he would like them to be.

Plaatu was enjoying the coffee so much he re-entered the ship and poured himself a refill. He was in no hurry to go looking through his ship's storage compartment for the excavation tool he would need to bury a new transmitter so he walked back down the ramp and re-took his seat. The glare from the sun nearly blinded him so he removed a pair of tinted glasses from the pocket of his flight suit and put them on. "Ah," he said, "That's much better. Are my eyes becoming more sensitive or are they depleting their ozone layer since the last time I was here?"

He had slept well during thee night and felt thoroughly refreshed. There was just something about sleeping in a stationary ship as compared to one that is rocketing across the Universe that seemed to do wonders for his biological clock. Technically of course, the planet he was currently sitting on was traveling through space at approximately 67,000 miles per hour as it orbited its sun, but good old Mother Nature had her way of keeping the planet's inhabitants strapped in. Gravity is a wonderful thing, he thought to himself.

Upon exiting the ship, he had grabbed some charts he had made on his last fly-over, he took another sip of coffee. The caffeine was beginning to surge through his veins like a mild electrical charge causing his pulse to quicken slightly. Plaatu was a bit naïve to the chemical intricacies of caffeine and the negative effects it could have on a humanoid nervous system. He only knew the dark-colored, aroma-rich nectar stimulated his taste buds most pleasurably.

"A truly outstanding planetary offering if I do say so myself." He had enjoyed the beverage during his earlier visit while staying with an unsuspecting family who took him in as a boarder. He had never tried his hand with the brewing process and he was really quite pleased with himself. He made a point to "borrow" some more beans when his task was completed. He was reasonably sure the hard-working South American coffee growers wouldn't object.

He was beginning to feel more comfortable on solid ground and a bizarre thought came into his head. As he looked around at the incredible mid-October array of colors on display from the surrounding trees, he imagined that he could retire to a place like this. It really was a remarkably beautiful planet. "If only there were fewer human inhabitants," he chuckled to himself.

He studied his maps of the surrounding hill tops for a moment. "Mount Jefferson, Mount Madison, Mount Adams . . . they are all named after former presidents of this country," he remarked to himself.

"That is why it is called the Presidential Range," came a voice from his portable computer that he had brought with him from inside the ship.

"Hmmm," said Plaatu sarcastically as he scowled at the little micro computer, "Well then, that certainly explains everything now doesn't it."

Plaatu continued to scowl at the little electronic device. Computers had no sense of humor, they were totally inflexible and annoyingly never wrong. They irritated him to no end but he fully realized how much easier they made his life in more ways then he cared to admit. They could survey more accurately and at much greater speeds than any humanoid ever could. They were accurate to a fault and they never refused to do something they were told.

But just once he was going to prove one of these damn things wrong if it was the last thing he ever did.

"There is a ridge here high up on Mount Madison that would work well," he said to himself but loud enough for the computer to hear. He was looking for an analysis but didn't want to come right out and ask for it.

There was no response.

"Did you hear what I said," he snapped at the little metallic box.

"Are you presenting a question commander?" asked the computer.

Plaatu restrained himself for a moment and took a big gulp of coffee. He stared at the box for a moment and briefly contemplated the idea of burying it with the transmitter. "They'll never find you," he whispered. "Never!"

"You have visitors," said the computer suddenly.

Plaatu jumped to his feet and scanned the surrounding tree line. He saw nothing out of the ordinary.

"What kind of visitors?" he asked apprehensively. "Do they have fur?"

"There is a vehicle approaching from the southwest," said the computer.

Plaatu walked in that direction and stopped at the edge of the clearing. His ship was now directly behind him. As he listened intently, he thought he heard voices off in the distance. He rushed inside his ship and returned with a device that looked remarkably like a pair of Earth binoculars and a high powered listening device.

He peered through the dense trees and could barely make out movement in a camp site about a quarter mile away.

He put the listening device to his ear and stood motionless. He began to hear voices. They were faint but he could make out bits and pieces of what they were saying.

"Hey, who brought the dogs?" he heard someone say. They were male voices to be sure.

"They brought dogs with them!" said Plaatu nervously. "Tell me they are not hunting dogs."

He continued to listen but the wind was picking up making it difficult to make out complete sentences. All he was getting now were fragments.

"Who's job is it to . . . ." and "check out the ravine nearby . . ." as well as some references to "firewood" and "brewskies".

"What in creation is a brewski?" he muttered to himself.

Plaatu was fortunate that foliage season had arrived late due to an unusually long summer. The trees that separated him from the newcomers were dense and still held most of their leaves. He was convinced they could not see him from their vantage point but he wasn't going to take any chances. He would reposition his cruiser later that night once darkness set in.

"Just my luck," he said to himself as he walked back to his ship. "All my research indicated that no one camps here this time of year."

Plaatu's belt sensor began pinging again. He gazed skyward but could see nothing but blue sky and scattered puffy cumulus clouds that hung intermittently in the air like great big cotton balls.

"What in blazes is causing that?" he said to himself. "Could it be the faulty transmitter?"

He walked over to the entrance ramp to his ship and looked down at the remote computer.

"Continue to scan in that direction," he said pointing off towards the newcomers. "If they begin advancing in this direction I want to know about it immediately."

"Affirmative commander," it answered. "Planetary survey results are completed from readings taken the previous day. Where would you like to receive them?"

"I'll take them inside the ship," he said. Then he walked back up the ramp with his cup of coffee in hand and sat down in his command chair.

"Ok, what have you got?"

"After correlating readings and comparing them to those taken during previous visit," the computer began, "Results are as follows. Air quality has diminished 37%, fresh water availability ratio per life form has diminished 29%, and humanoid population has increased 123%, levels of sea life forms down 47%, number of life forms in danger of extinction up 73%."

"Alright, that's enough," said Plaatu in disgust. "That is most disheartening. They are consuming their natural resources faster than the planet can replenish them. They are fouling their environment faster than its ability to recover but it's their planet. They can do what they want with it. What about weapons numbers? That is all I am concerned with."

"Number of nuclear warheads detected during prior visit to this planet . . . 224. Number of nations with nuclear capability totaled 2. Relative strength of warheads equaled 10 megatons."

"And now?" asked Plaatu as he braced himself for the only really important number that would affect his visit here.

"Number of warheads . . . 27,397. Number of nations possessing nuclear weapon capability . . . 13. Relative strength of average warhead . . . 250 megaton."

Plaatu almost choked on his coffee. "That can't be right," he said aloud. "No civilized people would possibly be foolish enough to build so many dangerous weapons knowing the potential consequences."

His mind reeled for a moment. He went over the numbers again in his head. 27,397? That is nothing short of madness.

Plaatu wasn't completely naïve. Many nations throughout the Coalition possessed various types of weaponry. Many of them were far superior to Earth's, technologically speaking. Bort, for example was an eminently more formidable weapon and could devastate a planet if called to do so with greater efficiency than any of Earth's nuclear weapons. What frightened Plaatu and Em Diem was the reckless and completely arbitrary way in which these types of weapons killed indiscriminately. Coalition weaponry could be focused so accurately that the loss of innocent bystanders was no longer an issue. Only wrongdoers suffered in the event that force was required. That is not the case with weapons of mass destruction such as those found in the hands of this planet's leaders.

"Run a complete system-wide diagnostic to determine if you are working properly," Plaatu ordered. Normally he only ordered such an action when he wanted to upset the computer or castigate it in some vengeful way. In his mind he imagined that running a complete diagnostic must be an exhausting task for a machine and he equated it to ordering an underclassman to drop and give him fifty push-ups. It was a completely warped view of humanoid to machine relationships but Plaatu was, sadly getting older. He remained completely unaware that old man senility could be lurking around the next bend in the mystical road of life. He was unwilling to accept the fact that computers have no emotions and no feelings, therefore you cannot upset or insult them. No matter how many times he watched in relative self-content while the computer worked feverishly carrying out some insignificant task he had given it, to the machine it was nothing more than another routine function. On this particular occasion however, his request was not of a punitive nature. He was simply unwilling to accept such staggering numbers.

Three minutes passed when the computer responded with its findings.

"All systems are running properly, readings are accurate."

Plaatu sat back in his chair and tried to assimilate the troubling statistics. It was, of course, no concern of his or anyone else in the Coalition how Earth managed its own affairs. At its present rate of development, he had estimated that it would only be a matter of 50-100 years before they began sending manned spacecrafts to the outer reaches of their solar system. Their unmanned probes were already reaching Pluto and beyond.

The naivety of this planet's inhabitants was really quite startling, however. Did they really think they could continue to conduct themselves in such a reckless manner and not eventually attract unwanted attention to their little jewel of a planet? Humans seemed to have no idea that in their continuing attempts to explore the solar system, they would eventually come under the scrutiny of envious out-worlders. Some of these distant neighbors just might desire to take a closer look at this water-rich sphere that was bursting with natural resources.

Plaatu decided to relay the findings to Em Diem on an encrypted channel. It was with his help that Plaatu had been able to deceive the other Coalition members as to the real value and condition of this planet. With Em's assistance Plaatu had fabricated a galactic sized fib in an effort to give humanity time to develop intellectually and spiritually. Perhaps, given the opportunity he thought, they would achieve a greater level of maturity and come to their senses. Plaatu had downplayed the planet's significance in an effort to protect it from envious predators. Predators that, despite the restrictions placed upon them by Coalition mandates might try and make a case for taking it by a form of "eminent domain".

Such precedents had already been established elsewhere in circumstances where a planet's inhabitants seemed on the verge of rendering a perfectly healthy ecosystem unlivable due to their own folly. The number of worlds capable of sustaining humanoid life was always an issue in the galaxy and every measure was taken to maintain current stock.

Earth people had to this point only been exposed to one extraterrestrial and that was Plaatu, a genuinely nice guy as extraterrestrials go. They had no idea of how tenuous their situation could become if other more hostile species became involved in the mix. There were members who wouldn't hesitate to make a case for sterilization and recolonization of Earth if they knew how badly its inhabitants were treating its ecosystem.

It was true that Plaatu had developed a luke-warm impression of humans. After all, they shot him twice no less, and hunted him the entire time he spent on the planet. He was only trying to perform a simple task like delivering a message from the Coalition threatening them with total annihilation if they didn't wise up. Now what is so provocative about that, he mused? He grudgingly admitted however, that they deserved the right to develop just like any other planet. He was one of the staunchest opponents of recolonization. Plaatu knew that on each and every occasion that the issue had come before the Coalition, it was merely an attempt by some greedy party to use loopholes to steal something that didn't belong to them. Plaatu had learned from experience that as commodities, greed and envy were not the sole possession of Earthlings.

As the computer transmitted the data to Em Diem, Plaatu's nostrils filled with the aroma of something he had never experienced before. He had left the door of the ship open to the autumn air and the cabin had filled with the smell of something he simply had to investigate further.

As he walked down the ramp of his ship and out into the air, the scent became even stronger. It was coming from the direction of the newcomers. Plaatu approached the tree line and decided to take a closer look. He slowly began to weave his way through the trees but at all costs he had to remain unseen. His suit would give him ample cover as it was designed with a "chameleon-like" chemical that adapted to any surroundings. The dead leaves beneath his feet crunched slightly with every step however, so he was forced to move slowly, like a hunter sneaking up on its prey.

As he reached a point where he was 50 yards from the clearing he crouched down and watched intently. There were six adult men in all and they were performing a variety of activities as he observed them intently. There was a large beige canvas tent set up off to the right. The clearing was a good deal smaller than the one his ship was occupying. A blue van was parked near the entrance to the site just 10 yards or so from the access road. Fortune was on Plaatu's side. If they hadn't stopped where they did and proceeded further down the access road they would have ran smack dab into his ship.

He could hear their conversations clearly now.

"Hey Spike!" yelled a stout man in a red plaid shirt. "I'm still waiting on that fire wood buddy! I can't keep this going forever!"

He was crouched near a formation of cement cinder blocks. They had been set up to double as both a fireplace and a cooking area. A metal grille was placed over the top of the blocks. They were stacked two blocks high on three sides with the front left open to allow for the insertion of combustibles such as logs, newspaper, and just about anything else that would burn.

Plaatu could now see what was smoking up the entire area and causing red alerts with his sense of smell. Sizzling on top of the metal grille was a large assortment of various types of meat. If they were trying not to attract attention you wouldn't know it by the plume of billowing smoke that was wafting up from the cement enclosure. Then Plaatu remembered that there was really no need for them to be discreet. His readings indicated there wasn't another soul around for miles. They were out here in the middle of nowhere and something told him that is exactly why they chose this time of year and this particular location. If his guess was correct, they were looking for solitude, peace and quiet. If they had wanted to immerse themselves in a sea of humanity, they could have opted for any number of more popular vacation destinations this planet has to offer.

Plaatu glanced off to his right where he could see a man in a green shirt and grey vest rummaging through the bushes for kindling just beyond the tree line. He assumed this was "Spike" and he was one of the shorter members of the group.

There were two men, both thin but one taller than the other, who were putting the finishing touches on the large rectangular tent. It was apparent that they were planning to be here for more than just one day, giving Plaatu even greater reason to move his ship that night.

The taller man in a gray hooded sweatshirt took a lantern and what appeared to be a small heating device from the van and walked towards the tent.

"Brad, before you set that up, is this tent vented for a Coleman heater?" asked the shorter of the two. He was wearing a black long sleeve shirt with a large letter "B" on the front. Plaatu had no idea the "B" was a Boston Bruins Hockey logo. All the men were wearing dungarees and outdoor boots of various sorts.

"I don't know. Does it have to be vented?" answered Brad chidingly.

The final two men who appeared to be the youngest of the group had been emptying the van of other items such as folding chairs, sleeping gear and clothing. One had a "Boston Celtics" sweatshirt and sported a small goatee. The other was stockier and had dark curly hair. He, like the man tending the grille, had a red-plaid long sleeve shirt.

"You better check for a vent before you use that bad-boy," said the man with the goatee. "I'm not sleeping in that tent if it's gonna fill up with carbon monoxide fumes. I hear that stuff is bad for your health."

"It is?" said Brad. "Tommy boy," he said to the younger man in the red plaid shirt. "You and Chris can both sleep out in the cold tonight if you're gonna start complaining about some sissy fumes. I hear it gets down to about 20 degrees this time of year."

"Ryan," said Tommy to the other man working on the tent, "Talk to him will you?"

"I'll check for a vent," said Ryan as he unzipped the tent and walked in to examine the interior. After a few moments he came back out.

"Ok, you can all relax," he said. "It has a vent."

"I figured there would be," said Brad. "These tent manufacturers think of everything. Besides, how much fumes can this little thing give off?" The metal heater was twelve inches high and was powered by a twenty ounce can of propane fuel.

"Enough to asphyxiate you I bet," laughed Chris. "If you care about us at all, you'll keep that vent open tonight."

"I wouldn't think of putting your health at risk," said Brad. Then he placed the small Coleman heater on the ground to quell the uproar.

Mikey was still poking at the assortment of meats sizzling on the grille. As he looked up, Spike was walking towards him with an arm full of wood.

"It's about time," he said good naturedly. "I was about to call the park ranger to go out looking for you."

"Relax!" retorted Spike, "Gathering firewood is serious business." He dropped the wood next to Mikey and brushed off the splinters and any remaining small fragments of brush from his shirt. "Damn, that shit smells good."

Chris overheard his remark. "That shit smells good? Hmmm. isn't that a bit of a contradiction in terms? Because we all know shit does not smell good."

"Hey Chris," said Spike chidingly, "I got your contradiction in terms right here." Spike grabbed his crotch with his right hand.

"Mikey," said Tommy, "Don't go burning those steak tips like you did last year."

Mikey stopped tending the assortment of meat for a moment and smiled up at Tommy. "Do you expect me to believe that you remember how I cooked steak tips one year ago? I bet you can't even remember when you got laid last?"

"Yes I can," answered Tommy. "It was last night. It was just an inflatable doll but that still counts right?"

"Oh, you are disgusting," said Chris as the campsite erupted with laughter.

The men placed folding chairs around the fire to relax for a few moments. Brad took a chair to Mikey's immediate right and watched him languidly as he tended to his duties as camp chef. There was no need for constant conversation. Brad could scan the faces of each of the other five men sitting around him and knew them well enough to know exactly what each of them was thinking and what they were feeling. They were at least an hour's drive from anything that even remotely resembled a "big city". They lived within minutes of each other in the city of Stanford, Connecticut, five hours to the south of their current position. They had all grown up in the same neighborhood and developed a lasting bond which had remained strong despite the different directions their lives had taken after each graduated high school. Ryan had gone on to achieve his degree in psychology, having worked his way through college via the military's ROTC program. Tom became a master electrician, Mikey an auto-mechanic. Spike went to work for the phone company while Brad became an insurance claims specialist. Chris had ended up as a computer software engineer. They were all in their twenties and although they were still single, the freedom that came with bachelorhood allowed them to undertake annual camping getaways like this one. There were definitely some unique advantages to being unfettered by marital and family ties.

No matter how involved their lives became, no matter how consumed they became in their jobs, they were determined to make this annual attempt to escape from it all a regular event. It was a much-needed chance to just sit around a campfire, an escape from the ubiquitous noise that plagued their daily lives living in the city. No buses, no trains, no jets flying overhead. No angry motorists flipping each other "the bird" and the incessant honking of horns. No cell phones, (only Ryan's was left on for incoming emergency purposes), no radios, no television sets with their never-ending updates of who was at war with who, which corporation was screwing it's investors or who made the police 'rap' sheet the night before. For a few brief moments, they were determined to be allowed their God-given right to be "at one" with nature, or as close as they could get to it.

While they were relatively sure they would have the area completely to themselves, they were also not foolhardy enough to go anywhere in America completely unarmed. The New Hampshire-Canadian border was a popular entry point for illegal immigrants and not all of those trying to sneak into the country were non-criminals. The possibility that they might cross paths with a band of illegal aliens bent on ill-intent was very real.

Mikey threw some more logs on the fire. There was a glowing bed of hot ambers at the bottom of the neatly piled stack of wood and a radiant intense heat emanated from its center.

Tommy walked over and stabbed one of the hot dogs with a fork, then he gingerly bit into it. "Yep, they're done," he announced.

"Do you have to do that?" asked Mikey with a scornful look. "You know how much that annoys me!" He didn't like anyone touching the grille until he gave the go ahead. He was a very anal chef.

"Of course the dogs are done," snapped Mikey. "You can practically eat them raw right out of the package. This other stuff has another five minutes or so. Poke anything else and no soup for you!" He choked back laughter.

They all knew he was one hundred percent talk and zero percent action in situations such as this. None of the men had a bigger heart than Mikey.

He and Tommy had always endured a bit of a tit-for-tat relationship and it never failed to rear its humorous head when they were in each other's presence. To a man, the others knew that Mikey saw Tommy as the younger brother he never had. He was privately very fond of him and would give his life for him if ever called upon to do so. When not called upon to do so however, he never missed the opportunity to razz the poor guy mercilessly.

"You know what they say," quipped Tommy. "You can pick your friends and you can pick your nose, but you can't pick your friends' nose."

There was a prolonged moment of silence. Then Chris blurted, "What the hell does that mean!?"

They all broke out in laughter and Tommy looked around at them with a juvenile grin on his face.

"I have no friggin' idea," he said, giggling incessantly.

"Hey Ryan," said Brad. "How about I line up some empty beer cans along those trees over there? It looks like a nice upward grade behind it."

"Sure," said Ryan, "Looks like a good spot to me and this stuff isn't going to be ready for a little while longer."

Plaatu noticed Brad walking right towards him with a handful of what appeared to be empty cylinders. He continued to watch as he began hanging them from tree branches at equal intervals. When Brad was finished, he returned to the van and removed two long yellow bags with handles.

"Now why would they hang empty cans from branches like that," Plaatu wondered to himself. He felt a tinge of guilt that he was spying on these unsuspecting visitors but the aroma wafting his way from the grille was simply too much to resist.

Mikey and Spike cracked open cold beers as they watched Ryan and Brad remove .22 caliber rifles with four-power scopes from the yellow bags. Brad inserted a cartridge containing ten rounds. Then he pointed the rifle in the direction of the beer cans, and unknowingly right at Plaatu.

"Oh no!" Plaatu hissed and he turned to run when Brad began firing. The first two shots were direct hits on the defenseless aluminum cylinders. The third shot missed entirely, but instead it struck Plaatu in the left leg. He fell to the ground with a loud thud and shrieked in pain.

Brad lowered the rifle from his shoulder. "Did you hear that?" he asked in subdued alarm. The six men turned in the direction of Plaatu who was still writhing in pain.

"I think you shot somebody," said Chris incredulously.

"How could I shoot somebody," snapped Brad, "there isn't supposed to be anybody in these woods."

"Mikey," said Ryan. "Slide all that stuff to one side so it doesn't burn. The rest of you follow me."

Ryan, Brad, Spike, Tommy and Chris rushed into the trees in the vicinity of where they had heard the cries of alarm. Plaatu did not want to be found but the pain in his leg wouldn't allow him to rise to his feet to make it back to his ship. In a few moments, Ryan spotted him.

"Over here!" he shouted to the others and they all converged on his position. Plaatu lay there holding his leg which was oozing blood.

He looked up at them with scornful eyes.

"Damn humans!" he shouted, "why do you always feel compelled to shoot at everything everywhere you go!?"

"Damn humans?" said Brad with a puzzled look.

"Yeah," chimed in Spike defiantly. "Who are you calling damn humans?"

"I'm a medic in the National Guards," said Ryan softly, "let me look at your wound."

"Don't bother!" snapped Plaatu. "I'll treat it myself. Just help me up please so I can get to my ship."

"Your ship?" asked Chris. "Buddy, are you alright? The ocean is a few hundred miles away."

"I think he's delusional," said Brad.

Ryan looked closer at the wound but Plaatu refused to remove his hand which was now covered in blood.

"Chris," said Ryan, "grab the first aid kit from the van and bring it here."

"Got it," said Chris, then he ran off towards the van.

"Will you just let me look at it for crying out loud!" said Ryan harshly.

Plaatu reluctantly pulled his hand away. Ryan pulled up the leg of his uniform and wiped away the blood with a clean handkerchief he had in his pocket, careful not to touch the entry point.

"It looks like it just grazed you," he said finally. "You are fortunate that it didn't strike a bone. I can treat this with no problem."

Ryan looked directly into Plaatu's eyes and still detected anger but his temper tantrum subsided somewhat with the news that his wound didn't appear to be all that serious. Ryan was fully aware however that even a mere flesh wound like this could hurt like the dickens.

"Ok," said Ryan to the three other men, "help me carry him out into the clearing where I can move around. Let's get him out of these trees."

With Ryan and Brad each taking a leg, Spike and Tommy grabbed Plaatu under his arms and they gently carried him out into the opening, then over to the lounge chairs. They set him down as Chris arrived with the first aid kit. Plaatu breathed a little easier and realized that these men were merely trying to help. He sensed no threat from them and as they stood around him staring down at his leg, he sensed a collective feeling of remorse that they had caused him any pain. He scanned their eyes and read in each of them something he had almost completely forgotten about this planet's inhabitants. It was something he had experienced upon his first visit but in time, the recollection had blurred and become a distant memory. It was their ability to show compassion when faced with adversity.

"I'm . . . sorry . . . to have snapped at you like that," he said finally. "It's just that every time I come here it seems like I am always getting shot at."

"You've been shot in these woods before?" asked Ryan as he opened an antiseptic wipe and cleaned the wound. Plaatu flinched a bit but then relaxed again.

"Maybe you should try hanging out in some other woods," said Spike.

Plaatu gave him a dubious look.

"He's just trying to be helpful," remarked Mikey who had just walked over from the grille. He extended his hand. "How are you?" he asked. "Under the circumstances of course."

Plaatu shook his hand and said, "I am doing reasonably well, under the circumstances as you put it."

Each of the men introduced themselves in turn as Ryan applied a large gauze bandage and then prepared to tape it securely.

"Just a moment," interrupted Plaatu. He removed a small tube from his uniform pocket and handed it to Ryan. "Could you put some of this on the wound before you close it up?"

Ryan examined the tube. It had writing on it which he did not recognize. "Where did you get this stuff? Zimbabwe?" he asked as he removed the cap and applied some of the ointment.

"Not exactly," said Plaatu with a wry smile.

Ryan finished taping up the wound then handed the tube back to Plaatu. His leg was beginning to feel better already.

"There," said Ryan rising to his feet. "Good as new."

Plaatu's face again assumed a dubious look.

"Well, almost," said Ryan timidly.

Plaatu sat straight up in the chair and put his foot flat on the ground. He put some weight on it and while it increased the level of pain somewhat,

Ryan's assessment did seem to be correct. He felt comfortable he could walk on it if he had to and there was no skeletal damage. The bullet did in fact just graze him.

Plaatu took a deep breath and exhaled. The men were all still staring at him and that was beginning to irritate him more than the wound itself.

"Alright, gentlemen," he said finally, "At ease. Enough with the gawking, I forgive you, is that what you are waiting to hear?"

"Well, not really," said Brad. "I mean, it's not like I did it on purpose. What the hell were you doing hanging out in these woods at this time of year? And what was all that business about 'humans' and my ship? Have you, uh, escaped from somewhere around here? An institution of some kind perhaps?"

Plaatu clutched the arms of his chair and tried to stand. Tommy and Chris responded immediately and helped him to his feet.

"You really should stay off that for a while," remarked Ryan.

"I'll be fine now," said Plaatu. He limped over to the grille where the assortment of tantalizing smells reminded him of why he was in the woods in the first place.

"I smelled your cooking," he said with a smile. "The aroma was wafting all the way over there to where my camp site is and I was merely curious as to what you were cooking up over here. That is all. I didn't mean to spy. My remarks are just my way of spouting off. I guess it did come across as a bit unorthodox."

Plaatu stared down at the grille which was packed with sizzling meats of various shapes and sizes. After suffering through months of predominantly boring space-food in the way of rations and "nutritional supplements" with only an occasional treat from his withering stores of contraband, he was looking down upon Manna from Heaven, at least from his vantage point. As of three nights prior, his supply of illegal goodies had run out.

"I must say, I haven't had anything quite like this to eat in a long, long time," he muttered as if he were in a trance.

"Oh, the institution you live in is strictly vegetarian huh?" asked Chris.

Plaatu just smiled at him. "I do not live in any institution my good man, I can assure you."

"Well, enough of this," said Mikey, trying to break the tension. "This stuff is ready, why don't you join us for a bite Mister . . . . uh . . . what was your name again?"

"Mr. Carpenter," answered Plaatu. "Carpenter will do and I think I will take you up on your invitation."

"Hey, that's a hell of an idea," said Brad. "It will make up for any discomfort we caused you."

They each grabbed chairs and made a semi-circle around the opening to the campfire. It was approaching mid-morning and the sun was shining brightly overhead. There was still a cool breeze however and the warmth of the fire was inviting and almost magnetic.

Chris and Tommy passed around heavy-duty paper plates. Then they handed out plastic knives and forks as Mikey in turn loaded up everyone's plate with as much succulent steak tips, buttery corn on the cob, juicy cheeseburgers, hot dogs and Italian sausage as they could handle. From his very first bite, Plaatu was in culinary euphoria. So much for remaining faithful to a CIPF-sanctioned vegetarian diet, he thought but every once in a great while, the urge to indulge himself was simply too irresistible to overcome.

Mikey noticed Plaatu's look of content. "I marinate everything in my own secret sauce before grilling it up," he said with a smile. Seeing others enjoy the fruits of his labor brought him great satisfaction. "I don't give the secret out to anyone," he added. "Not even these hobos."

"One of these days," chimed in Spike, "We're going to tie you down and force it out of you."

"It is quite delicious," said Plaatu.

As he continued to savor the hospitality, he knew that he would have to be prepared to deflect questions. He could sense by the look in their prying eyes that they remained suspicious as to what he was doing in the woods. Plaatu was a master at reading people merely by studying their gaze. The Earthly expression "the eyes are the gateway to the soul" was not only popular on this planet. It was a truism that prevailed throughout the entire galaxy. He had many years of experience during which he had learned to size up almost any group and with remarkable accuracy, determine the group's dynamics and the hierarchy that existed within it. As he had watched closely at the reactions of each of the men thus far, he already had determined how each of them lined up in the proverbial pecking order. Humans were very much like other mammals in that respect, at least from what he had observed. Put them in a group and in a relatively short period of time, the dominant figures would exert themselves while others would assume positions of less authority and be totally content to follow rather than lead.

As he casually glanced at Chris with his elfish face and Tommy with his dark bushy hair and wide-eyed expression, it was clear that they took a much less serious approach to life than the others. They were apparently the youngest of the group but their roles were clearly not dominant, a detail that didn't seem to be borne strictly out of the fact that they were the youngest members. Plaatu guessed that they were every bit as competent in their chosen occupations as Brad and the others but they're exhibited personalities were simply less exertive in nature.

Mikey and Spike on the other hand were of a much hardier stock and seemed tailor-made for the outdoor life. Mikey was the most broad shouldered of the group. He had a softer gaze but it was nevertheless uncompromising and steadfast. He seemed to be the type of man who, once his mind was made up, would see a task to its conclusion with undeterred determination. Spike, he surmised, was the oldest of the group. He had a well-trimmed beard and showed the early signs of male-pattern baldness which was still premature for a man his age. He had a warm smile but he seemed to have nerves of steel. Plaatu could only guess, but he doubted that Spike was the kind of man who became unglued very easily.

Brad and Ryan appeared to be the brain center of the group. Plaatu seemed relatively sure that these were the two the others turned to more often than not for direction. Brad was the tallest of the six men. He had well-cropped dark brown hair and intelligent eyes. His gaze was piercing and was one that seemed to convey he was constantly trying to unravel a puzzle. Of the six men, it was Brad's stare that was capable of instilling the most fear but Plaatu was not fazed in the least. Ryan was a few inches shorter than Brad and less stocky. He was of dark complexion and his sensitive eyes implied that he was far and away the most analytical of the group. He was less impulsive than Brad and seemed to be the kind of man who moved to act only after careful deliberation.

While his assessment of the dynamics and hierarchy may not have been one hundred percent accurate, one other fact seemed undeniable. The bond they shared seemed strong and true, a characteristic Plaatu had learned to respect over the years.

"So," he said finally trying to gain the high ground, "What brings you men out here at this inhospitable time of year. It gets down to below freezing at night, why would anyone want to go camping out here so late in the season?"

Brad was still a bit on edge. He genuinely felt badly that he had shot Plaatu. He had never actually fired a weapon at another living thing in his entire life. He always quipped when in the company of his fellow campers, "if a can of beer is worth drinking, it's worth shooting afterwards." Inanimate objects were one thing, a living creature was quite another. He had done a stint with the United States Army but merely as a member of their correspondence corps. He had fired weapons during shooting qualifications but he had never been put in the position of having to shoot at live targets.

Part of him was still seething a bit too. His guilty conscience kept telling him that he wouldn't be feeling so bad about himself if this nut case hadn't been hiding in the bushes.

"We come up here every year," said Mikey as he set his plate down on his lap for a moment. "And that is exactly why we choose this time of year. When we want to get away from civilization for a while, why come up here in July and August when you are surrounded on all sides by the exact element you are trying to escape. Have you ever seen some of these summer weekend camper types? Downright scary people if you ask me."

"We've been doing this for, what," said Chris, "8 years now? We all graduated high school within a few years of one another. What better way to maintain friendships than by getting together for an annual long weekend in the barren wilderness. I love coming up here, even if it means putting up with these guys not showering for a few days."

Tommy put his hand on Chris's shoulder. "The feeling is mutual my friend," he said with a smile.

"So what are you doing up here this time of year?" asked Ryan, still skeptical of this stranger calling himself 'Mr. Carpenter'.

Plaatu was determined to make every effort to keep these men in the dark as to the reasons for his presence on Earth. There was nothing to be gained by involving them in something that was probably much bigger than they were prepared to handle. The issues confronting this planet were much larger than they could imagine and something told him it would be much more advantageous to keep his identity from them a secret. "Get in, get out," was the objective that kept running through his mind.

"I look for the same things you men do, Master Ryan," Plaatu answered. "Solitude, peace and a little respite from the toils of everyday life."

He gazed around the area taking in all of its beauty and serenity. Then he remained quiet for a moment. He empathized with these men and felt he could actually see inside their minds and feel exactly what they felt for these glorious surroundings. The tranquil gurgling of the brook nearby, the occasional chirping of the few remaining birds that had yet to fly south for the coming winter. The cool breeze gently caressing the leaves of the trees, it all came together to have an almost hypnotic effect and it reminded him of trips he had taken like this back on his home planet. Those days are gone forever he thought, over a long time ago.

"Well, gentleman," Plaatu said at last, anxious to get back to his ship and away from discerning eyes, "I don't want to overstay my welcome so I really must be getting back."

The six men all rose to their feet ready to assist him in the event he seemed the least bit unsteady. The salve Ryan had used to cover the wound appeared to be working splendidly however, as Plaatu showed no sign of requiring any assistance. The pain in his leg was nearly gone.

"What do you do with the remains?" Plaatu asked holding up his empty plate.

"I'll take the utensils," said Spike. "The plates are paper and we dispose of them right in the fire." Spike politely took Plaatu's plate and flung it under the grill. It burst into flames for a moment and then was gone.

"Well, thank you again for the meal," said Plaatu with a forced smile. He couldn't help but notice that the eyes of each and every man were still filled with suspicion.

"You really should stay off that leg for a day or two," insisted Ryan again. "It was only a flesh wound but it could become infected if you are not careful."

"I appreciate your concern," said Plaatu warmly. "Thank you again for your hospitality." He began walking towards the entrance to the site where he could more easily get back to his ship by way of the access road rather than returning through the woods. He was walking normally now and his limp had virtually all but vanished.

As he cleared the camp and turned left up the access road, the men watched him disappear behind the trees; the sound of his footsteps grating on the pebble-covered road diminished and then was gone.

"Was that the damndest thing you ever did see or what?" asked Spike to no one in particular.

"Damndest isn't the word," muttered Ryan. "Call me a monkey's uncle but his name isn't "Carpenter" and he isn't out here camping. Did you take a close look at that outfit he was wearing? Nobody goes camping in gear like that. That was some sort of military uniform although it wasn't like anything I've seen before."

"Did you see how fast he recovered?" remarked Chris. "One minute he couldn't get up and 20 minutes later he is walking like nothing ever happened. What's that all about?"

"I say we go out on bivouac," said Brad. "I think this calls for some good old fashioned, down-in-the-dirt, sneaking and conniving. Let's return the favor and go spy on him! What do you say?"

His suggestion was first met with reluctance. It was clear that the men were wrestling with the notion that they had merely come up here to relax. Something told them that agreeing to Brad's suggestion could cause their much-awaited camping trip to spin hopelessly out of control.

"The guy was spying on us for chrisakes!" Brad added vehemently. He turned to Ryan knowing that if he agreed, the others would follow suit.

"I'm in," said Ryan finally. Brad was right, something didn't add up here.

"Me too," said Mikey. "This guy is spooky."

Chris and Spike both nodded in the affirmative. They all turned towards Tommy who was still chowing down on a hot dog. He stopped in mid-bite to stare up at them.

"We're waiting?" said Mikey. "Are you in or what?"

Tommy glanced over at the grille.

"There is one more burger left," he said finally. "Anybody want it?"

"He's in," said Chris. "Let's clean up and grab the binoculars."

"And the twenty-two's," added Spike.

They all stopped dead in their tracks and glared at him.

"Hey, the guy already got shot once," said Ryan in earnest. "I really don't think it would be wise to shoot him again. Are you trying to land my ass in jail?"

"You really think he's a threat?" asked Mikey. The thought had never really entered his mind. This 'Carpenter' character certainly seemed harmless enough but maybe Spike was right. They were up here at a time of year when few if anyone was supposed to be camping. They were miles from any law enforcement assistance. They were just minding their own business when they find some guy spying on them while hiding in the trees. How did they know he was alone or for that matter, what his true intentions were? For all they knew he could be an escaped sex-offender, a peeping Tom or some other form of human degenerate up to no good.

"Hey," said Chris in a grave tone. "Haven't you seen the movie 'Deliverance'?"

Tommy was listening intently to the exchange and his eyes grew wider with every word. He had never seen the movie, had never even heard of it. Spike noticed the look and decided to have some fun with it.

"You know what happened to those guys in the woods?" he asked eerily, looking directly at Tommy.

"No, what happened?" asked Tommy, trying to conceal his increasing apprehension over the prospect of spying on "Mr. Carpenter".

"It wasn't pretty," said Spike with a devilish grin. "They only found parts of their bodies."

"Alright, knock that shit off!" said Ryan who was standing near the van. "For chrisakes, I thought we all outgrew the ghost stories."

He hung a pair of binoculars around his neck and paused for a moment looking down at the pair of rifles resting on the floor of the van. Brad walked over and stood beside him. It was a familiar picture. Of the six companions, they had remained the closest of the group.

"All bullshit aside," Brad said softly, "we really don't know anything about this guy. You and I are the only two with any military training. What do your instincts tell you?"

Ryan pondered the question. He looked over at his comrades and debated the wisdom of getting them involved in something he wasn't even sure they were prepared to handle. He really had no idea how they would react in a genuine crisis. For the most part they had all led charmed lives. None of them, including him and Brad had ever been in a real combat situation. He and Brad had been fortunate to serve during peace-time. They had all lived under the comfortable umbrella of protection that the United States military had provided its citizens since the day they were born. Even their old neighborhood enjoyed a relatively low-crime rate throughout their childhood. Lady luck had always seemed to smile upon them and none of them had ever been forced to face real-life tragedy.

All of which didn't add up to all that much as he stood their pondering the moment. They were not in the city anymore. Out here a totally different set of rules applied. Spike might have been joking but he was absolutely correct. When you are this far away from aid, you don't take any chances.

"Bring 'em," he said to Brad. "They may not be M-16's but they should be enough to get us out of any trouble in the event any should arise. This guy snooped on us once, how do we know he won't do it again? If nothing else, I want to know what he is doing out here and let him know not to mess with us again."

"I concur," added Brad. "Better safe than sorry right?"

Tommy watched from a short distance as Ryan and Brad hoisted the rifles over their shoulders. "Dun, dun-DUN-dun," he mumbled to himself. There was just something about the sight of a firearm that made his pulse rate quicken beyond normal parameters. "You guys go on ahead," he said aloud. "I just want you to know that whatever happens, I'm right behind you."

CHAPTER THREE

Private first-class Jim Forde admitted he had enjoyed a few cocktails before reporting for his evening shift as radar-technician. He aggressively asserted however, that his judgment was not impaired in the least and adamantly insisted he did see something on his radar screen at approximately 2200 hours. He had reported it to his superior officer but upon closer investigation, Lt. John Farrell, as well as Forde's fellow shift-mates could not substantiate it.

Loring Air Force base in upstate Maine was once a bustling, fully staffed military facility. It once served as a vital link in America's expansive defense network but that was years earlier when the "Cold War" was still an issue of national security. Since the fall of the Soviet Union, base closings had become very much in vogue with the Pentagon and Loring soon became a victim of military downsizing.

It had a huge impact on the region and cities like Presque Isle quickly saw its economies suffer dramatically.

The only purpose the base served now was the little radar tracking center in the northwest corner of the facility. It was a relay station more than anything else with a compliment of just 24 Air Force personnel. Much of the country's security surveillance was done by an intricate network of satellites and the readings were monitored on the ground by people like Private Jim Forde. It could be very monotonous work as America was not "officially" at war, other than its involvement in the Middle East a conflict which some pundits had difficulty labeling. The Air Force was reasonably sure that terrorists lacked the resources to fly supersonic jets that could threaten American soil.

Much of his time he would wile away the hours reading comic books or watching TV. Last night however, he had been riveted to his monitoring screen because he was receiving signals he had never seen before.

"I tell you sir," he said nervously as he stood in Captain Lansing's office the following morning. "It was like a hole soaring through space. The radar was sending back a very weak ping but there was nothing there. Nothing visible I mean."

Captain Lansing had investigated a few previous complaints by Forde's immediate superiors in regards to his imbibing before reporting for duty. He had been forgiving up to this point but his patience was wearing thin. Lansing was an imposing figure. As the senior officer of the base, it was no easy task maintaining discipline during peacetime, especially when one factored into the equation the relatively young age of his subordinates. Few if any of the men and women presently stationed there had ever seen real action under stressful conditions.

"You mean," said Lansing, "there was something there, but there wasn't anything there?" The sarcastic tone did not escape Forde who winced a bit, knowing full well that his credibility was sinking faster than a hooked large mouth bass.

"I can't explain it sir," he said, totally frustrated. "I have never seen anything like it before so I have nothing to compare it to."

"Maybe it was the Silver Surfer," chided Lt. Farrell who was also in the room. "I notice a fair amount of "advanced" reading material around your work station every night."

"Alright, that's enough," said Lansing as he rose to his feet. "Look, if I get one more report of you coming on duty half in the wrapper, you're gonna spend some time in the brig. You got that soldier?"

Forde stiffened at his tone but more than anything else, he remained totally frustrated that no one believed his claim that he had actually seen something out of the ordinary. He was at the same time aware that this is what followed a pattern of "indiscretions" and having lost one's credibility with his superiors. Prolonging this was futile and he knew it. Take your lumps and exit stage left, his mind told him.

"Yes Sir," he answered respectfully, "Understood sir."

"Now get the hell out of here," snapped the Captain.

Forde put on his cap, then saluted and turned to leave the room. As the door closed behind him, leaving Farrell alone with the Captain, the lieutenant turned more serious.

"He may have a drink on occasion," he said, "but he has never been prone to seeing hallucinations before. I'll check the records again from last night and see if I missed anything."

"Do that," ordered the captain. "As extreme as this example may be, you remember what happened when they ignored a radar technician's observations right before Pearl Harbor."

"That I do," said Farrell. "But that was all part of a deliberate conspiracy by President Franklin D. Roosevelt to goad the Japanese into attacking us so that he would have an excuse to enter the war."

"Don't start that bullshit again!" snapped the Captain. "You've been spouting that nonsense ever since I met you."

Farrell just ignored the remark. "Oh by the way, we got a report that some old geezer over in upstate New Hampshire claims he saw a flying saucer fly over his house last night. He thinks it may have landed somewhere nearby."

"Jesus H. Christ," sighed Lansing, "was there a full moon last night? Maybe I should start drinking again just to keep up with these whackos."

Plaatu hurried back inside his ship and went immediately to the medical cabinet. He set his left leg up on his bunk and lifted his pants. The bandage was well applied but he tore it off just the same. As he examined the wound it had already begun to close so he applied some more salve, then he covered the wound with one of his own dressings which would allow the wound to heal more rapidly.

"Damn nuisance, that's what it is," he mumbled to himself. "You order your on board computer to find a remote area where you won't be disturbed and in no time, you are disturbed. Damn nuisance."

"There is a message coming in from command central," he heard the computer's voice say. "Do you wish me to patch it through?"

"Well, I certainly wouldn't want to put you out or anything," said Plaatu sarcastically. "You're fragile little circuits must have been working very hard today."

"Non-sequitor," said the computer.

"Just put the message through," snarled Plaatu. It was times like this when he greatly missed the old days when computers were designed to accept input and responded in non-verbal form. Plaatu had sworn, on more than one occasion, to track down in the after-life the scurrilous mongrel dog that invented the means for machines to communicate through speech. He could only hope and pray in his mind that torture was not frowned upon in the realm of the un-living.

"Is everything all right?" came a voice over the intercom. Em Diem's image appeared on the main viewing screen. He was dressed in his traditional blue and grey jacket with the white sash that was indicative of his rank with the Council of Interplanetary Affairs. Plaatu studied his face. There were bags under his eyes and his long gray hair seemed a bit disheveled. Plaatu sat down in his command chair and exhaled heavily. So far everything had gone anything but alright.

"I had a little run in with the locals," he said. "Shot me again they did."

"Shot you?!" said Em Diem in alarm. "Again?"

"Yes, but I'm alright. Just a flesh wound. I did everything I could to find a spot near the transmitter where I could work in secrecy but as usual these ever-dependable on board computers failed me again."

"Humans are very unpredictable creatures," said the computer defensively.

"Oh shut up," barked Plaatu. "Nobody asked you."

"You sound very testy," interjected Em. "Are you sure you are alright?"

"I'm fine. I am going to have to change my location tonight when it gets dark. I am too close to a group of campers who appear to be planning on staying for a few days."

"Well, I'm afraid you might want to re-enter Earth's atmosphere again in order to kill some time and remain unnoticed," said Em. "That data you sent us regarding Earth's present condition has raised a few eyebrows. It seems to have confirmed that the transmitter isn't completely faulty after all, and that the humans have, in fact, apparently lost their collective minds."

"I thought we agreed to screen the data before presenting it to the other members of the council?"

"That is no longer possible my friend," said Em remorsefully. "The proverbial cat is out of the bag I am afraid. There are newly admitted members to the Coalition who are clamoring for the information about "the third planet". I cannot keep them at bay any longer."

Plaatu watched Em's demeanor closely. He couldn't quite put his finger on it but something was obviously weighing heavily on his mind. The galaxy had enjoyed a remarkably long period of sustained peace, unlike anything ever seen before. Granted, much of the reluctance to show aggression on the part of member planets was very likely directly connected to an inescapable realization. Any outward sign of aggression was guaranteed to invite a response by Bort or one of his fellow enforcement robots. The sight of any one of these 8-foot, vaporizing-beam-emitting giants was enough to make even the most unruly of perpetrators tremble in fear. Something was amiss here though, Plaatu was sure of it.

"What is troubling you my friend?" he asked thoughtfully.

Em paused for a moment as if stumbling for words.

"My heart is heavy," he answered. "The Coalition, in its blind ambition to expand and increase its sphere of influence, has granted membership to some new species that seem motivated by ill intent. Something tells me there are dark days ahead and I feel powerless to stop it."

"My sensors have detected the possible presence of alien ships in the vicinity of Earth Em," said Plaatu. "Are there unauthorized others prowling this area? You're not telling me everything and it's not like you to withhold information. Not from me that is."

Plaatu hated to admit it but for the very first time in their relationship, he got the distinct impression that his long time trusted friend was not being completely above board with him. It was a very distasteful sensation indeed.

"There is only so much I can tell you as of yet," Em answered, "Because the jury is still out on how the Council intends to proceed. These numbers in regards to nuclear weapons is particularly disturbing. This may require you to alter your mission and do more than merely check on a transmitter."

The hairs on the back of Plaatu's neck stood straight up and his nerve endings began to tingle. He wasn't a youngster anymore and he had been through so many crises over the years, he was beginning to grow weary of them. A hierarchy had been established within the CIPF where the more stressful assignments were being given to the younger members of the force. Plaatu was 73 years old when he first visited Earth, a relatively young age for his species. Now he was 123. As one of the most experienced members of the force, the rigors of the job and the many miles of travel being shut up in a ship for long periods of time were taking their toll on his health. This was supposed to be an easy assignment. "Get in, get out." Plaatu mumbled to himself. "Sure."

"Humans are approaching," the computer reported softly.

It didn't even register. Plaatu was deep in thought.

"Plaatu," interrupted Em Diem. "Are you still reading me?"

Plaatu sat up in his chair and tried to regain his mental focus.

"Yes, I am still here," he said finally. "What kind of additional action are we talking about?"

"Humans are still . . ."

"Stop interrupting me!" shouted Plaatu. "Now, what did you say Em?"

"I am not sure yet as to how to proceed," he responded. "When I receive the decision of what action we intend to take, I will contact you again. It shouldn't be more than a few hours."

"Well, I can't lift off until nightfall anyway so I will wait to hear from you. Give me a shout when you can."

"Will do," said Em. "Take care of yourself my friend." The main viewing screen went blank.

Plaatu got up from his chair and walked over to the hatch which he had left open to the refreshing mountain air. He decided to retract the ramp and prepare the ship for lift-off as it would only be a matter of a few more hours before darkness fell.

As he glanced down the ramp to the ground below, there were six figures staring up at him. Two were pointing guns right at his head.

"Is there something you would like to tell us?" asked Ryan in a commanding tone as he continued to train his rifle on Plaatu.

Plaatu was speechless for a moment. This was damned sloppy of him and merely served as further proof that he may be overdue for retirement. In his younger days he never would have allowed himself to be caught in this kind of predicament. The last thing he wanted to do was become re-involved with the most highly developed and equally notorious species on this planet. Preventing an army of penguins from freezing to death was one thing, dropping grain to assist starving refugees was another. If previous experience had taught him anything, it was that direct contact with humans with their annoying propensity to point guns at him could be very hazardous to his health. Finally, he regained his composure.

"Computer . . ." he said softly through gritted teeth. "Were you aware of the approach of these humans?"

"Affirmative," it responded.

"And you were going to tell me when?" asked Plaatu, still seething.

"This device attempted to notify the commander on two occasions. This device received no response the first time and was scolded harshly during second attempt."

"Infernal contraption," he muttered.

"You gonna come down out of there or what?" Ryan asked more harshly.

Plaatu needed to defuse this situation quickly. He was in no mood for a confrontation with anyone let alone armed humans whose reputation with firearms preceded them.

"Gentlemen," Plaatu said in as reassuring a tone as he could muster. "Please, lower your weapons. I am of no threat to you I can assure you."

Plaatu could have, with the wave of a hand, vaporized the six men where they stood. Despite Bort's absence on this mission, his ship was still equipped with offensive weapons. Such an action would only become necessary as a very last resort however. To be fair, they had in fact fed him rather generously after using him for target practice earlier that morning.

He started walking slowly down the ramp towards the men. Then he stopped abruptly when he noticed that Ryan and Brad had not lowered their weapons. Plaatu was well-known throughout his travels as one of the more reasonable, well-intentioned and forgiving members of the CIPF, but even he had his limits.

"I will ask you one last time to lower those weapons," he said sternly. "I can assure you I am quite capable of lowering them for you and I warn you, you may find my methods a bit unpleasant."

Ryan and Brad both glanced at each other. This guy was possibly from somewhere other than Earth so it was safe to assume he was also a member of a species much more advanced than humans. Following faithfully along that same line of thinking it was reasonable to assume that his ship was equipped with hardware that was a good deal more imposing than .22 caliber rifles.

"How do you know this guy can't just melt us down into little globs of goo if he wanted to?" muttered Tommy nervously.

They both nodded to each other and lowered their weapons.

"Thank you," said Plaatu as he again proceeded down the ramp and stopped when his feet met the soft layer of grass surrounding his ship. He stood there for a moment and tried to size up the mood of the men. It was obvious by the looks in their eyes that they were brimming with uncertainty and apprehension. But he did not sense overt fear. That was another characteristic he remembered about this species: they were of hardy stock. They did not back down easily and that was something that could serve to their advantage in the days ahead. They were under greater scrutiny now and something told Plaatu that could only mean turbulent waters may be looming on the horizon.

"You derive a sense of security carrying primitive firearms don't you?" he asked thoughtfully but without sarcasm or bitterness.

"They can prove to be good equalizers on occasion," answered Brad. "Since you seem to be curious about the subject, if I had my way, I would eliminate every damn gun on the planet. Until the government can guarantee me that the bad guys won't have access to them however, I'll be damned if I'll let them deny me my right to carry one."

Tommy and Chris continued to stare at Plaatu's ship as if in a trance. There stares did not go unnoticed.

"It's merely a prop," said Plaatu. "The film crew will be here soon. We're shooting a brand new sci-fi film called 'Invasion of the bogy men".

"Yeah," muttered Spike. "And I'm Mr. Spock."

"Look," interrupted Ryan impatiently, "Mr. Carpenter or whatever your name is. I only get to come up here for a few days out of the year and I sure as hell don't want to spend it standing here jawing with you over lies and fairy tales! Now who are you and what are you doing in my camp ground?"

Plaatu was unprepared for such directness. He felt a tinge of guilt that he had interrupted a seemingly significant event. It was clear that these men looked forward to getting away once a year as a much needed escape from the trials and tribulations of their everyday lives. He really felt badly that he had crashed their party but the damage had already been done. Perhaps it was time to stop being evasive and merely tell them the truth. Or at least part of it. If his fears were correct, they would find out soon enough that his attempts to protect this planet's inhabitants from the prying eyes of potentially hostile extraterrestrials had failed.

"Alright Master Ryan," Plaatu said softly, "you are correct. I am a visitor here. My name is Plaatu and I have been here once before many years ago. From what I gather, the governments of your world have allowed the details of my first visit here to fade into obscurity. I give you my word that I am not here to cause you or your planet any harm."

He noticed that the unyielding skepticism in their eyes persisted. That did not surprise him, however. He would be skeptical too if he were in their shoes.

"Come now gentlemen, think about it for a moment," he continued as he further endeavored to put them at ease. "Did you really think you were all alone in the universe? You have been attempting to solve the answer to that riddle for centuries with nothing to show for it. Well, I just solved it for you. You can shut down your SETI program now and put the money towards something more productive."

Their skepticism gradually turned to awe as the reality of the situation began to coalesce in their collective consciousness.

"Holy shit!" said Chris. "You mean you're the real deal?" His heart rate increased with every word.

"As real as it gets," answered Plaatu.

"Holy shit!" repeated Chris, his voice starting to shake.

"Yes," responded Plaatu with a terse smile. "You said that."

"Can we see inside your ship?" asked Tommy, still goo-goo eyed.

"I'm afraid not," said Plaatu. "Earth is not yet a member of the Coalition I represent and it is therefore denied access to any exchange of technology or other privileges." Plaatu waved his hand over a small panel to the left of the entrance ramp and it slowly and without the slightest sound began to retract into the ship. In a moment the craft was sealed up tight as a drum.

"Well that wasn't very hospitable," said Mikey nervously.

"I am sorry but the Coalition is very strict about such matters," said Plaatu.

The six men slowly approached the ship as if it was quicksand that would gobble them up if they drew too close. When they first saw it upon walking into the campsite, something in their minds told them that it just couldn't be what it appeared to be. Now that the remarkable truth had been revealed, their minds became awash in a sea of confusion. Plaatu claims to be an alien, But he can't really be an alien. UFO's don't exist. How could this be possible?

"I always dreamed I would actually see a UFO some day," said Tommy as he continued to stare in amazement at the dull grey hull of the ship. He reached out his hand to touch it. Then he hesitated as an inherent fear of the unknown gripped him.

"What will happen if I touch it?" he asked apprehensively.

"You will be instantly vaporized," said Plaatu with a grin.

Tommy cringed and took a step back. "For real?" he asked tenuously.

Plaatu just chuckled to himself. "No, not for real," he said warmly. "Go ahead and touch it if you like."

The first time he had landed here he found himself surrounded by a throng of frightened civilians and military personnel. The soldiers were ready and willing to shoot on sight. As he watched the campers continue to gawk in amazement and saw the sense of wonder in their eyes, he found it eminently more appealing than his first encounter. Granted, Brad and Ryan had in fact pointed their low caliber weapons at him, but he was convinced they did so purely out of self-defense and not out of ill-intent. Good and evil are forces that are constantly at odds throughout the universe but he felt reasonably sure that these six men were not in evil's camp.

"Look, why don't we sit down back at your little campfire and I'll explain everything. It's much more comfortable over there and I will be happy to answer all of your questions."

The men seemed unable to tear their gaze away from the bubble-shaped craft but Plaatu had many miles to go before he slept. There would be time for sight seeing in the days ahead. These men were still completely unaware that their lives and the lives of virtually every person on their planet may change in a truly profound way in the not too distant future.

"Shall we go?" he said politely.

As they turned away from the ship and began walking, the conversation remained intense but non-confrontational. Plaatu was impressed by their sincerity and levels of curiosity. The questions came at him so rapidly that he almost had trouble keeping up. The sound of their voices resonated through the woods and faded gently away in distant echoes. All that could be heard during the occasional breaks in conversation was the soothing sound of the cool breeze blowing gently through the forest. He was becoming acutely aware that the more he saw of this area, the more he enjoyed being here.

When they took their seats around the camp fire however, the tone grew much more serious. Mikey tried to put everyone at ease by handing out ice cold beers. Plaatu declined but instead opted for a can of soda. He proceeded to disclose the purpose of his visit but did not go into every last detail. He was also careful not to reveal the exact whereabouts of the transmitter he had left behind after his first visit. The men were quiet and attentive and for that matter, very respectful, but they were far from completely at ease. It was clear that they were having great difficulty digesting this incredible new revelation. It was as if their collective minds were asking the question, how could a seemingly innocent camping weekend all of a sudden turn into a close encounter of the third kind? The more he interacted with them, the more he began to recall his first encounter with this species. As he did, the occasional fog that had shrouded some details of the encounter seemed to dissipate. He paused momentarily and reflected on his initial perceptions of Earthlings upon interacting with them for the very first time. Humans were indeed aggressive, and in many ways they were prone to the same annoying characteristics Plaatu encountered with other species throughout his duties as a member of law enforcement. In contrast to some of their extraterrestrial neighbors however, they had this inherent sense of decency and good within them that, when tapped, was really quite admirable. Few other species that he encountered were as willing to give him the "benefit of the doubt" the way these men were. It wasn't very often that he felt this at-ease when outnumbered six to one.

"So, you are saying that you spoke with our government leaders fifty years ago and warned them against nuclear proliferation," asked Ryan, "and here we are fifty years later wrestling with . . . nuclear proliferation? As the details of what you are telling us becomes clearer, I vaguely remember reading about your visit. It ranks right up there with the "Area 51" incident as the greatest of urban legends, but I have always written off such events as nonsense."

"That is unfortunate," said Plaatu. "Why your government leaders would make such a decision and proceed under the assumption that they would never hear from us again is unfathomable. We may not be concerned with how you handle your internal affairs, but when you reach a point in your development when you begin launching probes reaching out to other celestial bodies and you possess nuclear capability, you become a potential threat. Then it becomes our business as your neighbors to present you with our concerns. We are well within our rights to do so."

The air was beginning to feel much cooler as the sun dipped below the tree line in the western sky. The ice cold soda Plaatu was holding all of a sudden didn't seem so inviting. He placed it on the ground between his feet.

"How's that leg feeling by the way," asked Brad.

"Oh, don't worry yourself over that," answered Plaatu. "By tomorrow it will be as Ryan put it, good as new."

"So you were intending to merely check on this transmitter, replace or repair it and leave quietly?" asked Mikey.

"That was supposed to be my assignment, until I substantiated the data it was gathering. Then I encountered you men," said Plaatu. "That does complicate things a bit. I may have to take you all with me and incarcerate you in one of our internment camps."

They all looked at him dubiously but without any fear in their eyes.

"I feel it is only fair to warn you," said Mikey, "that if you unleash Tommy here on a defenseless alien inmate population without properly inoculating them beforehand, you may find yourself in the middle of a prison uprising, the likes of which you have never seen before."

Tommy thrust out his chest and sat upright in his chair feeling highly complimented. "Gee, thanks Mikey!"

"I'm joking," Plaatu added. "That isn't going to happen. We don't have internment camps but I must ask you to please keep this visit between us, at least until I tell you otherwise. It could prove very detrimental to my efforts if you attempt to gain any kind of notoriety through this encounter. The government will merely discredit you and the most you can expect is a footnote on page 16 of the National Enquirer."

A gray squirrel scurried into the woods to Plaatu's' left. He watched it as it ascended a large maple tree and disappeared into a hole in its bark. Gathering nuts for the coming winter, he thought to himself.

"It is easy to see why you men choose this place to escape to every year," he said warmly. "I have to admit, I am quite taken by it myself."

"People who spend the vast majority of their time neck-deep in the madness of the inner-city just don't know what they are missing," said Spike thoughtfully. "But then, if they did all come up here, it wouldn't be the same now would it?" He got up and threw another large log on the fire. It was absolutely essential to feed the campfire's insatiable hunger from the moment they arrived until the moment they were prepared to call an end to the annual getaway.

"I still have one nagging question though," said Brad. "What if the governments of the world refuse to change? They have already, according to you, told your "Coalition" to go pound sand so what happens if we stay our present course?"

"I'm afraid that will invite the kind of attention Earth is not quite yet ready to handle," answered Plaatu.

"What do you mean?" asked Spike as he sat back down and cracked open another frosty.

"I mean there are species out there that would not hesitate to take advantage of an opportunity to lay claim to a planet as beautiful as this one. As unpleasant as it sounds, they wouldn't hesitate to exterminate every living thing on its surface in the process."

"For real?" said Chris in disbelief.

"For real," answered Plaatu. "In many respects, Earthlings are no different than many of the other species I have encountered throughout the surrounding solar systems. You are supremely arrogant, no offense intended. You are consumed by your own self-interests, and you delight in the mistaken belief that you are the most highly developed life form within a hundred parsecs. The notion that there might actually be another species out there that would look upon humanity the same way you look upon the lowly cockroaches beneath your feet is unfathomable. But I can assure you, there are species out there who would wipe this planet clean of every last one of you if given the chance. That is what concerns me more than anything."

The very idea of such a scenario seemed to cast a pall over the six men. Being hit square in the machismo with the cold hard reality that they were in fact as fragile as Plaatu was suggesting was sobering indeed. All this talk of doom and gloom was making them feel a bit vulnerable.

"Gee," muttered Tommy to no one in particular, "I never really thought of myself as a cockroach before."

"Awww, don't take it to heart," said Mikey, "I've thought of you as much worse things than that."

"And just how would they go about 'eliminating' us?" Chris asked sheepishly, drawing uneasy glances from the others as if they didn't want to know. "In the event such a thing came to pass which of course I pray it doesn't," he quickly added.

Plaatu wasn't trying to frighten them. He had probably already told them more than they needed to know. But something deep inside him kept nagging him. He had already confirmed with Em Diem that other ships were in fact traveling throughout this system and had scanned Earth. His attempts to shield this planet from others who would certainly covet it dearly had failed. Plaatu and his Em Diem would have to come up with a new strategy and do it quickly.

"There are many ways to "sterilize" a biosphere such as Earth without actually harming the planet itself," said Plaatu, trying not to sound morose. "More often than not the species interested in re-colonizing the planet would merely introduce a pathogen that would, in a relatively short period of time, infect every living organism and simply destroy it. The pathogen of course would be of no danger to them since they would have the antidote or in many cases would be resistant to it. Some of these agents are incredibly effective and fast-acting. Your scientists and medical establishments would simply not be able to find an antidote in time since the pathogen would be of an alien nature."

"You have seen this done before?" asked Ryan in disgust. He was leaning forward with his elbows on his knees and listening intently to every word.

"Do not draw your conclusions too quickly Ryan," said Plaatu. "You have to understand, there are fewer and fewer planets in the immediate vicinity that are capable of sustaining our kind of life. Look at your solar system. You are the only planet out of nine that is still healthy enough to support life. We cannot just sit back and allow Earth's inhabitants to have their way if it appears that the health of the planet is at stake. Look at your toxic waste dumps. What do you do when they become a risk to the surrounding area? You go in and you clean them up. This is no different."

A slight chill came over Plaatu as the sun continued to set.

"Well, gentlemen," he said at last, "I think I will return to my ship. I am not dressed for these dipping temperatures. I appreciate your hospitality and again, I urge you not to report my position or talk to anyone about this meeting. I can assure you if I meant you any harm, I could have already administered it. I actually am very fond of this planet and would like nothing better than to let it develop without outside interference. That is the goal towards which I will continue to work."

They all stood up as Plaatu prepared to leave. There was hesitation in the air as the men continued to weigh the sincerity of this enormous bulk of information they had just been given. Their perceptions of their place in the universe had just been shattered, their sense of collective invulnerability and security had been stripped away but as they looked at Plaatu standing there in a wrinkled uniform, a relatively unimposing man in the elder years of his life, something told them that he was, as he stated, no threat and no enemy to them. If this "Coalition" he spoke of was in fact intent on taking over their planet, they were reasonably sure they would have sent a massive army and not a one-man craft with an occupant as amiable as Plaatu.

They were still a bit on edge and genuinely nervous to a man, but as Ryan stared into Plaatu's eyes searching for some glimpse of sincerity or deceit, he saw only sincerity. Every bone in his body told him this man was telling the truth. He stepped forward and faced Plaatu.

"If someone had told me before I left my apartment two days ago that I would soon be standing in the presence of a genuine alien being in the middle of the White Mountain National Forest, I would have had them committed," he said firmly. He extended his right hand. "But you have my word that for the time being at least, we will remain silent. The purpose of your visit will not go any further than this campfire. I am convinced that if and when the time comes, you will let us know if your involvement here needs to go any further."

Plaatu shook his hand with genuine relief.

"Thank you," he said, "thank you very much. Your silence will make my job much easier and much quicker. Say a prayer that I am successful in my efforts and you can go back to coming up here every year without interference."

The men watched him once again as he traversed the ground separating the two camp sites.

"You think he is telling the truth huh?" asked Brad as he turned towards Ryan.

"I think he's the advance scout for an invasion force of Bogey-men that are bent on destroying our planet!" said Chris. "I think we should run for our lives."

"Quit fooling around," snapped Mikey. "Do you think this guy is legit or what."

They stood there staring down at the fire which was still burning brightly. For a few moments they seemed lost in collective thought. They had never experienced anything like this before. All their notions of whether or not there was life on other planets were just obliterated. The gravity of the situation was nothing short of mind-blowing.

"Do you realize we could be being watched right now as we speak by some other entity up there?" said Spike.

They all gazed skyward as the thought really spooked them. Clear to the horizon the sky was dominated by dark clouds that began to roll in from the west. Rain was coming, no doubt about it.

"They can't see us through those clouds can they?" muttered Chris pensively.

"How do you know they don't have a death ray pointed at us right now?" asked Tommy.

"I'll tell you what I think," said Ryan in earnest. "I think the jig is up. All these centuries, we have occupied this planet locked within an atmosphere of naivety and isolation thinking we are the only ones out here and now we are finding out differently. We're not the only show in town and we should be very grateful for this piece of real estate because it's a pretty nice place to live. I don't know about you but my gut tells me this guy, regardless of where he comes from is sincere when he says he cares about what happens down here. Hard as it might be to believe that some elderly alien claims to give a shit about what happens to humanity, I say we help him in any way we can. Something is coming, there's no doubt about that now. We can only hope that whoever or whatever follows is half as friendly as Plaatu."

"OK," added Brad. "So are we together on this or what?" He looked around at the faces of the others and saw extreme uncertainty. Hell, he wasn't even sure in his own mind as to the proper course of action. Elements in his brain screamed that he should notify the authorities and bring on the armored tanks.

Mikey seemed to be having the most difficulty of them all. "Hey, we're talking about aliens for chrisakes! And you want me to just let this guy prowl around down here and not notify anyone? You want us to just give him Carte Blanche to our whole planet, no questions asked?!"

A jet soared by overhead at a very high altitude, then it disappeared beyond the horizon.

"Maybe they know about him already," said Spike as he glanced up at the heavens.

Ryan knelt by the fire and began poking at the dwindling pieces of wood. He placed two more logs on top of the burning ambers and watched as the flames immediately began to feed on them. They all drew a little closer, eager to bask in its ambient heat as the temperature continued to drop.

"I don't care what you say," remarked Ryan after a long pause. "I say we give this guy the benefit of the doubt. We're not talking about eternity here. Hell, he only asked us to keep quiet for a short time. Is that too much to ask?"

"48 hours," said Mikey abruptly. "I'll give him that. Then I'm calling the cavalry. This is our planet godamit. I'm not going to just stand around like a spineless Democrat and let some alien run amok uncontested."

"48 hours it is," said Brad. "Now, how about a shot of tequila? Are we not men?"

"We are DEVO!" the others answered amusingly in almost perfect unison. Like the dark clouds that continued to mass in the sky above however, apprehension still hung heavily in the air.

Plaatu returned to the isolation of his ship and retracted the ramp, not wanting to be disturbed again. He had also heard the sound of a high altitude jet passing overhead just before entering the cabin but he felt comfortable that the ship was well-concealed and virtually undetectable.

Then the thought entered his head that he had already been careless on more than one occasion since he touched down. He had always lived by a simple rule. "Never assume anything," a universally accepted notion that had saved his hide on more than one occasion in the past. Something deep within the recesses of his mind continued to trouble him however. He was slipping of late. There was no denying that he was not as sharp as he had once been and he feared one of these slipups could eventually cost him dearly. He walked over to the medical station and took out a bottle of "vitamin supplements. He removed a blue and red capsule and popped it in his mouth, washing it down with some H2O. It was a compound of natural herbs and vitamins from his home planet of Golon. Plaatu was convinced that these so called health aides did little more than line someone's pockets but he always held out hope that he may benefit at least in some small way from the time honored "Placebo effect".

As the hatch sealed shut behind him he heard the computer's annoying voice once again.

"Communication from Council member Em Diem has arrived and is awaiting your attention." Plaatu gritted his teeth at the very sound of the baritone, masculine voice. "Why can't they program these things to speak in a sultry feminine tone?" he often thought to himself.

Plaatu walked over to a compartment near his bunk and removed two small clear tablets. This was going to be a multi-pill night, his mind told him. He popped them into his mouth and washed them down with more H2O. They were ant-acid tablets and after the carnivorous fare he had consumed while visiting the men, he was relatively sure that he would need them if he was planning on getting any sleep that night. Consuming anything other than vegetable matter had often wreaked havoc with his digestive system but what is life without an occasional indulgence or two, he mused?

He returned to his command chair which, despite its age and length of service still felt remarkably comfortable. He loosened the collar of his uniform and sat back to listen to the incoming communiqué.

"Activate message," he commanded.

As he watched his main viewer, Em's image appeared. He was wearing his dress uniform this time which usually meant he had just come from a meeting with the other planetary leaders. He was always a stately looking fellow but the responsibilities the position carried with it were taking their toll. Plaatu had learned to read Em's facial expressions over the years and as he watched intently, he saw tension and concern.

"Plaatu," the pre-recorded message began slowly. "I hope all is going well with the natives." A forced smile came to Em's face but quickly vanished. "The Council has examined your findings and I am afraid their decision is to take a much harder stance on the third planet's situation."

Plaatu wasn't surprised but his heart still began to beat a little faster in his chest. Something told him this assignment was not going to be as simple as "Get in, get out," and now he was about to find out just how lacking in simplicity it was going to be.

"We need you," Em continued, "to make contact once again."

"Well," chuckled Plaatu, "at least that directive is out of the way."

"We need you to once again, extend an invitation to Earth to join us," said Em in a calculated tone. "They must cease and desist their weapons production immediately and begin dismantling their nuclear arsenals. Only this time, they do not have any choice. If they refuse, the Council has decided that a sterner example must be made to convince them of their folly."

The computer interrupted the previously recorded message.

"Incoming live communiqué," it announced.

"Put it on viewer," said Plaatu.

It was Em Diem only now Plaatu was able to engage in a two-way conversation which he eminently preferred.

"I was just watching the Em Diem Show when you called," said Plaatu in a cheerful tone. "How nice of you to appear in the flesh, virtually speaking of course."

"Well, I wasn't sure when I would be able to get back to my communication console to re-contact you so I sent you that message as an update. How far did you get?"

"Up to the point where you want me to make them an offer they can't refuse," said Plaatu.

"Ah yes," said Em. "Doesn't that sound familiar? Haven't you noticed that over the last few decades the more extreme elements of the Coalition are beginning to gain greater influence?"

"That does seem to be an annoying trend doesn't it?" said Plaatu pensively. "Then again, maybe you and I are just getting too old for this never-ending madness. Think about it Em. Has there ever been a point in our careers where everyone just got along? A time when there wasn't some crisis or catastrophe that needed addressing somewhere? I can still remember vaguely when I first addressed the humans and I told them that we had found a system that worked. By giving authority to our robots to police the galaxy we had found a solution to the inherent aggression humanoids seem prone to throughout the universe. When in fact, we still have so many other foibles that continue to haunt us."

"It can get frustrating," replied Em, "but don't let it get you down my friend. You have done a great deal of constructive work throughout your career and you have made a positive impact in so many ways."

"As have you my friend," said Plaatu. "But perhaps it's time we both took a nice long vacation."

"Once you finish this assignment," said Em, "I would very much like to explore that thought further, believe me."

"Now, as for the task at hand," said Plaatu. "What is this demonstration you speak of?"

Em Diem leaned forward at his console and hesitated for a moment trying to gather his thoughts. It was apparent to Plaatu that the meeting he had had with the other Council members was perhaps, more contentious than usual.

"During your last visit," Em began, "you threatened humanity with the prospect that if they did not change their ways, we would reduce the Earth to a "burned out cinder'."

"I said that?" asked Plaatu in a surprised tone.

"Yes you did," answered Em with a chuckle.

"Not very friendly now was it?" said Plaatu. "No wonder they chose not to join us. Perhaps I need to work on my rhetoric?"

"Well, this time I was able to convince the Council to allow you to demonstrate some of the benefits to membership in the Coalition. Use some of those anti-bacterial agents you keep on board in a creative manner for example. Use your imagination, we are granting you some leeway here."

Plaatu gave the idea some thought for a moment. He did, in fact, have on board his ship the means to improve life on Earth immeasurably if humans would just show more willingness to co-operate. They must agree however to a mutually beneficial relationship. Time had proven that a system of give and take was the only way to effectively maintain a healthy rapport between planets. If one for example, always found itself in the role of "giver" and another the "taker", resentment eventually ensued leading to inevitable conflict.

"I must tell you my friend," continued Em, "I had a difficult time convincing the others to go along with this approach. I am quite tired from the ordeal but I fervently hope your efforts are successful. The Tilatins, in particular are lobbying strongly for a much harsher approach. I don't have to remind you that they have been dealing with serious, potentially catastrophic problems with their home world and are desperately looking for a suitable host to re-colonize. Earth would suit their needs quite nicely, sans its present humanoid inhabitants of course."

"Of course," muttered Plaatu. "Is that why they are orbiting this planet as we speak? And isn't that a violation of Coalition directives?"

"Not any more," said Em. "I had to compromise a bit in gaining support for this softer approach. The Tilatins demanded the right to monitor your progress. They suspect that someone, and they didn't mention any names, has been secretly trying to deceive the Council as to the true conditions currently existing on Earth. You wouldn't know anything about that now would you?"

"Not me!" said Plaatu with a wry smile.

"Damn Tilatins," he thought to himself. "Thugs of the Galaxy they are." He had experienced more problems over the past few years investigating complaints about this species than any other. The thought of them orbiting just a few miles above his ship's present location was something he did not relish in the least.

"They have no authority here however," stated Plaatu. "Am I correct?"

"Yes," answered Em reassuringly. "They have no authority, nor have they been authorized to interfere in any way."

"You are absolutely certain of that?" asked Plaatu. He was still unwilling to accept the notion that the Tilatins were going to just sit obediently in orbit and not meddle into his attempts to negotiate with this planet's inhabitants. The mere thought of such a scenario was downright preposterous, at least in his eyes. Plaatu had studied up on Earth history prior to this second visit. The parallel he saw between the way in which the Council was pandering to the Tilatins aggressive tendencies was not all that much different from the way the nations of Earth pandered to Hitler leading up to World War II.

"I give you my word," said Em, "that I expressed to the entire Council in the harshest of tones that your work was not to be interfered with."

Plaatu did not derive great comfort in hearing Em's response. Something told him there was more involved here. He had been employed in this capacity for 103 years and no other species had been given permission to "monitor" his activities before. The CIPF was the unchallenged authority throughout the galaxy and this new revelation that any species, least of all the Tilatins, were now being granted the ability to oversee their progress was downright unprecedented. Plaatu was painfully aware however, that it would serve no purpose whatsoever to protest the decision. Voicing his concerns to Em Diem would be a waste of time; the Council had already made its decision, much as he didn't like it. Not one bit.

"Em," said Plaatu.

"Yes, my friend?"

"I'd like you to do me a small favor," asked Plaatu in a slow thoughtful cadence.

"Name it."

"Could you get a message to Commander Moov and ask him to check on the repair status of my escort-robot Bort," he asked. The more he pondered his present assignment and all of its parts, the more the anxiety levels increased. Knowing that the Tilatins were already in orbit was beginning to feel like someone just poured itching powder down his back. This was supposed to be a simple mission to repair a faulty transmitter, an act of child's play. Something told him it was about to take on the full-blown gravity of a super nova. Not having Bort to call upon could leave him in a very tenuous position. He felt vulnerable and that was a condition no member of the CIPF ever wanted to find themselves in.

"I will be happy to get him that message," said Em. "As well as the status of your present situation."

"Thanks, I owe you one."

"Good luck my friend, contact me if you need me, or when you have completed your mission and hopefully have good news. I'm afraid we have reached a point where the only thing that is going to save this planet's inhabitants is for them to agree to our terms."

"One final thing," said Plaatu. He paused for a moment as the gravity of his situation continued to weigh upon him. Mandates, ultimatums, Tilatins, no-Bort, and now heart burn from the camp fire feast, were all combining to give him the distinct feeling that there was no place he would rather be than anywhere but here.

"Have you heard from Nara?" he asked sullenly. It had been far too long since Plaatu had seen his only daughter.

He stared directly into Em's eyes on the view screen and saw hesitation. Em was her Guardian-in-absence, an equivalent to Earth's godfather, whenever the biological parent was unavailable. If she wanted to get in touch with Plaatu, she always knew she could reach him through Em Diem.

"Not recently," said Em sadly. "But don't despair. I have it on good authority that she is healthy and doing well at her teaching assignment on the planet Obo. I will attempt to contact her again and see if I can get her to contact you."

Plaatu's spirit sank. He had not heard from her in months and he missed her dearly.

"Thanks Em," he replied with a heavy heart. "I'll be in touch."

The view screen went blank as Plaatu sank back in his chair. The silence of the cabin enveloped him in an almost suffocating cloud of nothingness. The only sensory input was that of an occasional beep from one of his various on-board monitoring devices and the soft lighting of the ceiling lamps. Part of his emotional being wanted to just sit there in the comfort of his chair and let someone else take on this task. Part of him wished, out of anger, that each and every member of the "High Council" be forced to venture out from the security and lavish surroundings of Command Central and experience first hand what it is like to carry out their difficult mandates. He doubted that any of them had ever been forced to put their very lives on the line for the sake of the "Coalition" as he and his fellow officers were so often asked to do.

It did little good to complain, he was painfully aware of that. For most of his career he truly believed in what he was doing, he remained staunchly devoted to "the cause". The CIPF played a vital role in maintaining order throughout the galaxy and his actions, on more than one occasion, had saved lives. In a few of those cases his actions had quite possibly saved thousands, even millions of lives. Anyone else would be proud of such a track record, even jubilant after achieving such worthy accomplishments, but for some reason all he could muster was self-doubt and apprehension. Part of him, an increasingly large part wanted nothing more than to reunite with his daughter and go away for a very long time. Escape to a place where they could be together and enjoy each other's company and make up for all the time they had lost because of the demands of Plaatu's chosen profession. Retreat to a place where there were no inter-planetary conflicts, no illicit drug activity, no hostility, and no CIPF.

His troubled thoughts continued to magnify until he felt compelled to get up and exit the ship. He needed some fresh air so he walked over to the hatch and pressed the button to open it and extend the ramp. When it was fully extended, Plaatu began walking down its long metallic length. When he reached the soft grass he walked out beyond the edge of the ramp and he noticed it was raining slightly. It was a cool night, the temperature had dropped considerably but the cold droplets of rain on his head revitalized him. He tilted his head back so that the little drops of water hit him square in the face. It was a sensation he rarely got to enjoy and even though his body began to shiver slightly, it felt remarkably invigorating. He gazed around at the tree line. It was extremely dark and the only light was from the very dim glow emanating from the open hatch of his ship. He could not make out any details but he could hear the sound of the rain hitting the leaves of the trees and then cascading to the ground below. It was a steady, softly pulsating sound and it had an almost hypnotic effect as he stood listening to the rain continue to descend from the heavens.

He glanced over in the direction of the campers. Their fire had completely expired and he heard no sounds from the six men. They must have retreated to the shelter of the tent.

As he stood there for a few moments more the rain had an unexpected effect on him beyond invigoration. Standing there outside his ship with his feet touching the ground of this planet, feeling the rain drip down upon him with the trees just a few feet away suddenly filled him with a new sense of resolve. All the troubling thoughts he had been wrestling with seemed to melt away and were replaced by an unshakable new sense of commitment. This was a beautiful planet, one of the most valuable pieces of real estate in the entire Galaxy. Granted the humans were turning it into one big cesspool, but damn it, it belonged to them. He was determined to do everything he could to prevent the Tilatins from getting their filthy mitts on it. Humans were an annoying lot, to be sure. They had already shot him three times, but the more he thought about it, they had never tried to kill him out of pure evil. Once it was an accident, another time it was out of nervous fear and a third time it was because they simply didn't understand his motives. On no occasion was it done to forcibly take anything from him, on no occasion was it done out of an inherent sense of evil. The humans had always proceeded under the mistaken notion that they were alone in the universe. The stark realization that this was not the case was a bit much for them to handle. They needed time to digest the concept and in time, Plaatu felt reasonably sure that they could become a valuable member of any Coalition.

The Tilatins on the other hand were the exact opposite. They had found out very early in their existence that they were not alone. And once they had discovered this, they immediately set about concocting ways in which they could exploit their neighbors. They were the most ruthless and unyielding players in the galaxy, a species consumed by their own self-interests. While they outwardly endeavored to display attributes which would be palatable to the Coalition, a ploy which successfully won them membership, Plaatu saw right through this facade. In his experiences, and he had many with them, they were as inherently evil and despicable as any species he had ever encountered.

The rain began to fall more heavily so he went inside his ship and returned with an umbrella-like device. He opened it above his head so that he could continue to enjoy the pleasure of the audio portion of this experience for a few more moments. Under warmer temperatures he could have stayed there for hours but the sun had set taking with it its radiant warmth. Being cold and wet was not a condition his body could endure for very long without suffering ill effects. He closed his eyes and strained with all of his senses to absorb each and every soothing sensation when suddenly he heard the sound of a helicopter's rotor blades overhead. He continued to watch as it passed directly over his ship and disappeared beyond the tree line.

Plaatu glanced over in the direction of the campers. He hoped and prayed that they had not given him up to the military. It would only make his task that much more difficult. Besides, he genuinely felt in his heart that they were men of honor and would hold true to their word.

He turned and walked up the ramp of his ship and closed the hatch. As he re-entered the cabin he turned towards the control console to address the ship's computer.

"Extend a communications dampening field in all directions surrounding the ship," he said.

"Affirmative," the computer replied.

That would prevent any communications signals from working within a 20 mile radius surrounding his current position. It would at least give him time to get a good night's sleep before beginning the difficult task ahead. He would once again have to re-engage humanity in an attempt to convince them of their new situation. He only hoped he had a sufficient supply of antacid tablets on board because this time around, Bort was in abstentia. Plaatu feared there would be some serious bouts of indigestion in the days ahead.

As he prepared for sleep, he gazed at the photo of his daughter Nara that he kept next to his bed. A myriad of emotions rushed through him as he lay in his bunk staring at it thoughtfully. She was all he had left now. His wife Kutrel had succumbed to a rare form of heart disease three years earlier. Nara still harbored some underlying anger towards Plaatu for not being there for her during her mother's final days. She was completely unaware that her mother had kept the severity of the disease to herself so as not to cause Plaatu additional stress. She knew only too well how difficult the demands of his occupation could be. Her love for Plaatu was so strong that she repressed the anguish and suffering she endured right to the very end.

Golonians are a very spiritual people, very much like humans in some respects. Kutrel had prayed that during the final weeks the three of them could get away for just a few days and escape to their favorite hide-away at Glistening Lake. When Nara was young she and Plaatu had made it a point to go there at least one week out of the year to spend quality time together as a family. Her wish had been granted as Plaatu just happened to have several days of leave time at his disposal and he too felt an inexplicable need to just get away.

The memory of that trip still remained vivid in his mind. The evening of the final day was spent sitting on the cool pink sands of the beach looking out at the moon glistening across the surface of the water which gave the lake its name. It was surrounded on all sides by lush green forestry and majestic mountains and at times, Kutrel wondered to herself if that was what heaven would look like. Plaatu remembered how tightly she had held him that night and it wasn't until three days later that he understood the reasons why. Plaatu had left on a mission the following day that would keep him away from home for two weeks. When her condition had reached the critical point, Nara had driven her mother to the local medical facility where she succumbed two days later.

Plaatu had never known that kind of emotional pain before. He tried desperately to console Nara but he feared she would never forgive him for leaving on that mission. Plaatu wasn't sure if he would have been able to go on with his life if not for Nara's presence. His grief-stricken mind kept wrestling with the gut-wrenching dilemma that once you have lost what means most to you, what reason is there to go on?

He had been required to make far too many sacrifices as a result of his chosen profession. Missed birthdays, missed anniversaries, his inexcusable absence when the woman he loved most lay on her deathbed. His conscience would never forgive him and he was growing increasingly weary carrying around such a heavy burden of guilt.

Plaatu lay the photo back down next to his bunk and tried to sleep. "So much lost time," he muttered. "So much lost time." The dim lights emitted an eerie glow and for some strange reason, the interior cabin of his ship felt more desolate and terribly empty than it ever had before.

CHAPTER FOUR

The hours had passed slowly and Plaatu had tossed and turned all night. It was one of those evenings when he felt like morning would never come. After preparing his morning nutritional supplement, he lowered the ramp to the ship. The rain had stopped but the grass was still wet and dark clouds continued to hang ominously overhead. He heard a mockingbird in a tree nearby and for a moment he wondered whether he was the target of the bird's sardonic tone. As he pondered his next move, he endeavored to call upon all his previous experiences to guide him.

Humans had some truly wonderful qualities but they could also be as stubborn as any species in the galaxy. He discovered upon his first attempt to make contact that they could be impertinent as well. They didn't take kindly to his dire message of 'severe consequences' if they refused to curb their aggressive tendencies and had sent a message via primitive radio waves that they chose to decline his offer to join the Coalition. They could benefit greatly through membership but they simply didn't appreciate being intimidated by outsiders. The true reason was more likely that the possibility of getting every nation on Earth, or even a two-thirds majority of them to agree on anything was remote at best.

Perhaps it would make sense to approach this from a different perspective, he pondered. No threats this time, no ultimatums, just straightforward diplomacy. Maybe that would work. There was just one problem. Plaatu wasn't exactly a diplomat. He was a member of law enforcement and he did not have a great deal of experience to draw upon in this area. He wasn't a complete fish out of water. Diplomacy did factor into his line of work in a limited capacity but this could become very dicey if he wasn't extremely careful.

As he continued to breathe in the morning air and enjoy what would possibly be his last moments in these incredibly beautiful surroundings, an idea popped into his head. It was a long shot, but it just might work. He turned ruefully in the direction of the campers. He could not see their site through the trees which separated them, but he could barely make out sounds of activity. They were up and about and from the aromas that were beginning to waft in his direction, it was clear that they were preparing a scrumptious breakfast. Difficult as it was to resist, he was determined not to indulge in human culinary offerings again after the heart burn he had experienced the previous night. It wasn't merely his troubled thoughts of home that had caused him so much difficulty falling asleep. His digestive system had paid dearly for the previous days' indulgence.

He decided instead to return to his ship and his regular diet of Coalition-issued meals. They may not be as flavorful as grilled cow but they were much easier on the organs.

After breakfast, he rummaged through his ship's supply of anti-bacterial agents and scanned through the ship's library to match them against known pathogens that were found in Earth's eco-system. Then he ascertained which would work best and against what elements. There were a number of demonstrations he could call upon to convince the people of Earth of the benefits of entering into a mutually beneficial relationship with their neighboring planetoids. But this time, he would prefer to make contact in a slightly different manner.

He showered and donned a clean uniform, then he prepared to return to the camp site of the six men. Plaatu knew full well that he had no right to ask them to get involved, but then, they did have a vested interest in the outcome whether they liked it or not. For better or for worse, their fate, like the fate of everyone else on the planet depended directly upon the success or failure of Plaatu's efforts.

For all intents and purposes, failure was not an option.

Plaatu again exited the ship and closed the hatch behind him. He had inadvertently left the hatch open the previous day only to return to find a raccoon rummaging through his belongings. Stubborn little buggers too he discovered. It took some serious persuasion to coax the oversized fur ball off his ship.

As he began walking towards the campers, he could hear the nearby brook gurgling at a higher level than the day before. The runoff from the previous evening's rain had obviously raised its level considerably.

He reached the opening to their campsite and saw the six men apparently enjoying breakfast and conversing among themselves. As they saw him approach, they all rose to their feet and turned towards him. Their posturing was not out of alarm or of a defensive nature. To the contrary, he sensed it was more out of simple courtesy and respect.

"Good morning," said Mikey as Plaatu approached. The men were all dressed and while they appeared to be unshaven, they were for the most part, reasonably well groomed and presentable considering the limited resources at hand.

"Good morning!" answered Plaatu in a cheerful tone. "I trust you all slept well?" He stopped a few feet from the camp fire which was burning nicely and generating a radiant heat that was simply irresistible.

There was a bit of awkwardness in the air. It was apparent that there was still a bit of a divide between them but Plaatu completely understood their apprehension. He would react the very same way if some stranger had arrived upon his home planet unannounced and uninvited. Regardless of any suspicions they were harboring however, he needed to gain their confidence.

"I would have slept a lot better if Chris didn't snore so loud," said Tommy.

"Don't start with that again," said Chris harshly. "I wasn't the only one. It sounded like an army of crazed lumberjacks leveling the forest in there last night."

They all laughed over his remark but it was still a bit forced. Plaatu needed to ease their suspicions but one little detail needed to be resolved first.

"Well, I am sorry your slumber was interrupted Master Tommy," he said. "By the way, I heard a helicopter flying over our location on more than one occasion last night. You men don't know anything about that do you?" Plaatu was a master interrogator and would know instantly if they were lying or not.

"Yeah, we heard it to," answered Ryan. "But I have no idea what they were looking for. If you are wondering if we had anything to do with it, the answer is, absolutely not."

He sensed the truth and Plaatu felt both relief and renewed confidence that he could trust them at their word. That would be of tremendous importance if they agreed to his request for help.

"Now how about a question for you?" said Brad with an air of slight defiance. "Our cell phones aren't working and they were working just fine before you arrived. Does that have anything to do with you?"

Plaatu was accustomed to directness and confrontation in his line of work but rarely was he put in a position of having to defend his own actions. It was a fair question however, and it deserved an honest answer.

"I jammed communication signals last night because I was concerned that you had put a call in to your military people when I heard a jet, then a helicopter," said Plaatu. "You will find that they are working normally again as I have shut down the device."

"Fair enough," said Spike. "Now, can we offer you some coffee or some of Mikey's fine cuisine?"

"I wouldn't say no to coffee," said Plaatu. "But I have already eaten my morning meal thank you." Clearing the air seemed to ease the tension between them considerably and once again, honesty had proven to be the best policy.

Ryan pulled up a chair so Plaatu could sit down. As he did, Spike handed him a cup of steaming coffee and as Plaatu wrapped his hands around it, it warmed his fingers and helped calm the shivers he had been trying to stifle since the moment he left his ship. It was still colder than he would have liked and the air was damp and raw.

They all sat quietly for a few moments as they stared down at the fire. Tommy was still working on a second helping of scrambled eggs and bacon. As the fire hissed and popped, its warm glow provided a much needed diversion from the imperceptible awkwardness that still lingered in the air. It was as if the six men were collectively pondering the moment from the standpoint; "It isn't every day you get to sit around a camp fire with a genuine, down to the boot straps alien."

It had not been easy for them to maintain their positions of non-interference the previous night. They had spent a good deal of time in introspective thought as to whether or not to abide by Ryan's commitment and honor his word not to give Plaatu up to the authorities. Their cell phones may have been rendered inoperable but there was nothing stopping them from driving to the nearest police station and blowing the whistle.

Plaatu finally broke the silence.

"I have received new instructions this morning from the people I answer to." He hesitated for a moment; once again his mind was mired in indecision. He hardly even knew these men. Trust was such a fleeting commodity, almost as difficult to hold onto as time itself. Once it is gone, there is no bringing it back again. Did he dare place his confidence in them? This was unfamiliar territory to be sure. He had always relied on his own abilities and those of his metallic travel companion and the success or failure of every mission had rested entirely with them. But after all, he kept telling himself, it was their planet. "I'm afraid I find myself in the uncomfortable position of asking you gentlemen for assistance," he said sincerely.

The men looked at Plaatu with puzzled eyes. Then they looked at each other apparently not sure how to respond to such an out-of-the-blue request.

"You need *our* help?" said Spike finally. "With what?"

Plaatu could sense reluctance in the air. He had no previous experience dealing with humans when they are in vacation mode. If he had, he would have known that you never ask anything that requires a significant expenditure of energy when a human is in vacation mode.

"My superiors have advised me to take a more conciliatory approach to convincing the people of the Earth that they need to join our Coalition. They must also foster a drastic departure from their aggressive tendencies and begin to dismantle their nuclear arsenals."

"Or else what?" asked Chris innocently.

"There is no longer any 'or else' my friends," Plaatu responded remorsefully. "If they refuse this time, your fate could very well be sealed."

The clouds overhead began to break allowing a ray of sunshine to pierce through. It seemed to have an immediate effect on air temperature and it lit up the campsite in a radiant brilliance.

"I'm sorry Plaatu," said Brad, "but this is all a bit much to swallow. I came up here yesterday to have a nice time being at one with nature and hang out with my closest friends and here it is 24 hours later and I'm learning my planet could be doomed. What would you think if you were in my shoes?"

"I understand your skepticism," he answered, "but I can assure you what I am telling you is true and accurate. As I speak there is a Tilatin ship in orbit and if I am not successful, they are poised and ready to act decisively. There are species out there even more frightening than the Tilatins that covet this planet. I have tried to keep its condition a secret for all these years but I can no longer do that. The word is out and there are many eyes upon you now. I am not asking you men to put your lives on the line but I would be grateful if you would accompany me on a mission to your United Nations building in New York where I can address your world leaders once again. That is all I ask. On my previous visit here I was shot on sight the moment I stepped off my ship. I am convinced that if I bring you men along as companions, this will go much more smoothly. First contact is always an extremely delicate matter. You and I have already overcome that obstacle. Now will you help me?"

Plaatu watched their reactions and tried to discern what each of them was thinking. He suspected that they were engaging in the common initial human reaction of trying to discover the easiest way out of a dilemma. It wasn't that he had found humans to be unusually lazy compared to other species he had encountered, but they could, when faced with a seemingly insurmountable challenge, be very shifty creatures indeed.

"Are these Tilatins friendly?" asked Ryan.

"Anything but," answered Plaatu. He reached over and picked up the stainless steel pot of coffee that was sitting on the grille. He refilled his cup, then set the pot back down again.

The men paused to digest his answer.

"Do you think they would become hostile if our leaders resist?" asked Mikey.

"Without hesitation," answered Plaatu. He casually sipped his coffee. He was in no hurry. He was willing to give them time to study all the angles and weigh the potential consequences that could ensue if they chose to become involved.

Again there was a pause.

"What about their women?" added Tommy, feeling the need to interject a little levity. To those who knew him best, he was the undisputed king of flatulence and frivolity, the life of the party, the court jester of joviality when called into service. "Are they . . . cute?"

"I guess that all depends on one's perspective," said Plaatu matter-of-factly. "I haven't heard too many complaints from the Tilatin men."

"That is significant," said Chris with a devious grin.

"Significant enough to influence your decision?" asked Plaatu. "I wasn't aware that the allure of an alien female had so much influence on human thought processes."

"In case you haven't heard," said Tommy, "Very few decisions are actually made by human males without first consulting human females. Then the hopelessly outmatched male weighs all the possibilities and carefully considers how he should proceed. When all his calculating is done, he foolishly presents his case in a ridiculously futile attempt to sway said female, then he watches helplessly as she makes the final decision and does the exact opposite of what he suggested in the first place. So the prospect that alien females might be, shall we say, a bit more submissive than human females does have some interesting possibilities."

"I think I see where you are going with this," answered Plaatu, but he really had no clue and was just being polite.

"I don't think you do," said Brad, growing a bit weary of the exchange. He knew Tommy and Chris were just trying to make light of the conversation as a coping mechanism. In their defense, they were merely frightened and had never been faced with a scenario that even remotely resembled this, but it was time to return the conversation to solid ground.

"It is our planet," remarked Ryan finally.

"We can't let him risk his life and not at least give him a hand," added Brad.

Mikey tossed his plate into the fire. It burst into flames and disappeared.

"So much for this camping trip," he muttered.

The other men followed in turn, each throwing his paper plate into the fire in an almost ritualistic gesture of solidarity; each plate in turn exploded in a fiery burst, then was gone.

All except Tommy who was still holding his on his lap. "What if I'm not done eating yet?" he said. They all glared at him and it only took a moment for him to submit. He hurled his plate into the fire and watched as the flames consumed it instantly.

"Guess it's time for a road trip," said Ryan.

"Road trip!" they all shouted in unison.

"Does that mean you will help me?" asked Plaatu.

"We'll get you to New York," said Ryan. "We'll even get you in to see our congressional representatives who can get the ball rolling. I went to college with one of them and I'm sure she will be willing to meet with you."

"Wouldn't it be easier to take your ship?" asked Chris.

"I would rather not attract that kind of attention if I can help it," said Plaatu. "It didn't go over well last time. I would prefer to seal it up and leave it here. I can bring what I need in a simple carrying case."

"Well then," said Mikey, "we might as well get packed up and ready to go."

The men stood up and closed up their lounge chairs. Then they took one last look at the fire.

"Hell of a fire Mikey," said Brad.

"Thanks man," answered Mikey with genuine pride. Then he poured a large bucket of water on it and watched as a huge cloud of smoke billowed up and the flames were gone.

Brad took Ryan aside for a moment. He needed to clarify a few minor details before they embarked upon the journey south to the Big Apple.

"Just how are you going to get us in to see your congressional lady friend?" he asked. "Are you just blowing off steam here? I didn't think you were in that tight with her."

"What are you talking about?" answered Ryan, appearing genuinely put out by Brad's insinuation. "I went out with her in college," he said. "Almost."

Brad turned away impatiently, then swung back towards his friend. "How does one 'almost' go out with someone, exactly?" he asked in a frustrated tone.

"She dug me," said Ryan flippantly. "She would have gone out with me in a heart beat."

"But?" said Brad impatiently.

"I just never got around to asking her," responded Ryan sheepishly.

"You're a pissa," laughed Brad. "You better not screw this up 'cause I will kick your . . ."

"Yeah, yeah, yeah,' Ryan interrupted as he turned and walked towards the van.

Plaatu returned to his ship and packed up a small briefcase-sized container with all the "tricks" he would need to put on a convincing show. Then he exited and sealed the hatch behind him. Even if his ship was discovered by the military, they would not be able to gain entry with the current technology that existed on Earth. The metals used to construct the ship were still light years ahead of anything humans were working with at that time.

He returned to the camp site and the six men had already taken down the tent and were nearly finished with breaking down the camp site.

"You gentlemen work fast," he remarked.

"When you have a job to do, you do it," said Ryan with a smile.

He took Plaatu aside for a moment while the other men continued to pack their gear into the large Dodge van. There was something he needed to know before they headed anywhere. As the unspoken leader of the six men, he somehow felt responsible for their well-being. It had always been his position to be over-cautious rather than accepting a given situation at face value.

He gently led Plaatu to a sufficient distance where their conversation would not be heard.

"Listen," he said earnestly, "I need to know right here, right now if you and all this talk about more aliens is on the level. Because if it isn't and you're yanking my chain in any way, I don't care where you're from . . . I WILL kick your ass."

Plaatu paused for a moment. He was somewhat insulted by the remark but he was also respectful of the fact that Ryan was speaking out of genuine concern for his comrades. While his choice of words may have left something to be desired, his intention to protect his friends was commendable so Plaatu felt obligated to grant him a little latitude . . . for now at least.

"You gave me your word yesterday and you kept it," said Plaatu, "Now I will give you mine. I am being totally honest with you. Further, I can assure you that what happens in the next few days is of the gravest importance to your planet. If I fail, life on Earth is going to become extremely unpleasant for you I'm afraid. If you care at all about your families and your species for that matter, it is in your best interest to help me in any way you can."

Ryan tried desperately to get an accurate read on this slender aging man who seemed to be carrying a huge weight on his shoulders. If nothing else, he sensed in Plaatu's voice a sincere tone of concern for the fate of this planet. Could Ryan and the other show any less?

"OK," said Ryan. "I just had to know. I'm trusting you. Don't let me down."

They walked back over to the van where the others were already sitting in their seats and waiting to go.

"Plaatu," said Mikey from the drivers' seat, "why don't you sit up front so you can appreciate the ride."

"Into the valley of death rode the six," said Brad.

"Hundred," added Plaatu. "Rode the six hundred."

"You've been studying up on Earth poetry I see," said a surprised Ryan.

"It's a great poem," said Plaatu as he closed the door behind him.

Mikey threw the van into reverse and backed out onto the access road. Then the van lurched forward and headed for the highway south. During the six hour drive, Plaatu was vividly reminded of how aggressive human drivers can be. He prayed to every God he had ever heard of to deliver them safely. At one point after a close call with a tractor trailer, he even revisited the wisdom of not taking his ship.

Ryan had placed a call to Congresswoman Stacy Randell's office as soon as the van left the camp area. She was their district representative so he asked if she could meet them at the UN. It wasn't an easy task to convince her executive aide Philip Agnetta to pass the details of their mission along to her but Ryan had attended classes with her at the University of Connecticut just a few years earlier. He also had a few previous work-related experiences with the congresswoman and members of her office staff were familiar with him and knew he wasn't just another over ripe fruitcake. They were probably rethinking that opinion however after hearing his wild story about bringing an alien with him.

When they reached the United Nations building, Mikey found a parking spot after circling the block no less than eleven times. With the completion of each unsuccessful pass, Mikey muttered with greater determination, "I hate this friggin' city!"

They all got out and began the long walk up the street towards the front entrance. There were a number of protests occurring all over the plaza. One group was protesting world hunger, another global warming, and yet another chanted loudly against religious persecution. They were collectively making so much clatter in their attempts to be heard, they were accomplishing little more than contributing to a wall of indiscernible noise. Brad thought to himself if there was some way of harnessing all the wasted energy that is expended at protests around the world and channeling it into planting food, their wouldn't be any world hunger to protest in the first place. "Why don't these assholes go and join the Peace Corps if they are so concerned about everything," he remarked to no one in particular.

They had wisely decided to leave all metal objects in the van so as to make it through the security check-point without difficulty. Plaatu wanted to bring his case but Ryan felt there was no way they were going to let him enter the building with it so he reluctantly agreed to leave it in the van. He would not need it until it became time to set up the demonstrations. Plaatu's concern was whether or not it would still be there when he got back. He wasn't completely oblivious to the reputation of a certain segment of New York's inhabitants and their propensity for taking things that don't belong to them.

None of the six men had ever been to the United Nations building before. As they navigated their way across the plaza and through the throngs of clamoring protestors, it all seemed a bit surreal. They had awoken that morning to the quiet tranquility of the White Mountain National Forest and here they were just a few hours later in the heart of one of the most densely populated cities on the planet. It was as if they had just stepped into another dimension. As they walked slowly towards the main entrance, they passed the colorful flags of all the nations of the world. The UN building loomed ominously in front of them like a gigantic wall of glass. The surrounding buildings reflected off of its thousands of windows forming a breathtaking urban mosaic. Plaatu didn't appear to be the least bit intimidated but Mikey had to urge Tommy along at one point upon noticing he had stopped dead in his tracks, apparently gripped by overwhelming apprehension. They walked through the sliding glass doors and got in line with scores of other visitors and apparent dignitaries waiting to be scanned by the security personnel. Fortunately, the line moved quickly and once inside, they walked down a long hallway and took the elevator to the third floor where the United States Ambassador's office was located.

The United States Ambassador to the United Nations at that time was Joseph Henderson, a relatively amicable fellow who had served two years as governor of the proud state of Pennsylvania. He didn't get to finish his first gubernatorial term as he was called into emergency service by the president to replace the previous ambassador who was still among the missing after embarking upon a diplomatic mission to Tibet. The Dalai Lama steadfastly insisted that the Ambassador never arrived but he promised to let the president know if he happened to bump into him. Rumors abounded as to the reasons for the ambassador's disappearance. Some alleged that he became involved in an ill-fated attempt to climb Mount Everest. Some suggested he ran off with a 12 year old Tibetan girl he had purchased from her parents. Either way, he had not been heard from since getting on the plane in New York.

As ambassadors go Henderson had, during his short tenure, earned a moderate reputation as an individual held in relatively medium regard by his peers, mildly compassionate to a degree and almost trustworthy to a fault. The government of the United States, and for that matter most governments around the world, were led by men and women who had to bend a few rules in order to obtain their positions. It is simply impossible to win an elected office or be appointed to a high ranking position as Henderson was, without kissing many asses along the way.

None of this came as any surprise to Plaatu. He had been monitoring radio and television transmissions for the past few days and had discovered, much to his dismay, that not all that much had changed since his first visit in regards to the way in which human political affairs were being conducted. Morally and spiritually, Earthlings were sure doing everything they could to slow the advancement of their species in this particular regard. Plaatu had concluded that their evolutionary development was pretty much at a crawl, at least from his vantage point.

As they reached the door leading into Henderson's office, the six men looked around at each other and Plaatu could sense they felt a bit underdressed for the occasion. They looked like a walking poster board for LL Bean's Outdoor Wear.

"This guy is gonna think the city has been invaded by an army of crazed woodsmen," chuckled Tommy. He was feeling a bit more at ease now that he was inside the building. He quickly came to the realization upon clearing the security checkpoint that as imposing as the structure appears from outside, once inside it looks just like any other building. Bland colored walls, polished elevators, dull carpeting and pictures of distinguished people all along the corridors. He felt reasonably certain that they were important people in someone's eyes, but he didn't recognize a single portrait.

"He'll be happy to know we checked our axes at the door though," said Chris.

"Don't worry about it," said Spike. "We'll be out of here in no time. Besides, did you see how some of those Pakistani guys were dressed? They looked like a bunch of football faggots in those long white robes. I wouldn't be caught dead in outfits like that."

They walked into the outer office and were greeted by Henderson's receptionist Penny Gwynn. She stared up that them from behind her desk with a cold stare and a truly repulsive air of complete indifference.

"Can I help you . . . gentlemen?" she asked with impertinence that did not go unnoticed by Plaatu. He ignored it however, knowing full well that this was going to be no easy sell.

"We should be listed in your appointment book for a meeting today with the ambassador," Ryan said politely. "My last name is Shanahan."

Plaatu was willing to grant the campers some latitude with the course of action they had suggested. It was under their advice that he meet first with Henderson and Randell who would then, if all went well, arrange an audience with the General Assembly.

"I don't see anything on today's agenda," she said glibly. She began flipping through a calendar book. She stopped at the month of June the following year.

"We can get you in on . . . . June 13th," she said. "Would you like me to schedule you in for that date?"

"I called ahead of time to Congresswoman Randell in order to set up a meeting," said Ryan. "Are you kidding me?"

"I don't 'kid'," she snapped. "Did you think you were just going to walk in here and we would roll out the red carpet for you?" Her tone was dripping in sarcasm.

"I have an idea," said Chris. "How about if we schedule you for a facial tomorrow. Have you looked in the mirror lately?"

She slammed the calendar book shut and picked up the phone to her right.

"How about if I call security and have them throw your asses out the door," she said angrily.

Plaatu gently put his hand on the phone. This was going nowhere and he really didn't have time for frivolity.

"Ms. Gwynn," he said as respectfully as he could. "Please accept my apologies for barging in here like this. I can assure you that if my business was not of the utmost importance, I would have called personally to make an appointment. Please, put down the phone."

His manner was so convincing, the look in her eyes changed to one of utter submission.

"Can you teach me how to do that?" quipped Tommy.

"I really need to see the ambassador," continued Plaatu, "and I need to see him right now. The fate of your entire planet is at stake."

"*My* planet?" she asked, now looking a bit confused.

"He's not from around here," said Tommy as he continued to stare down Ms. Gwynn's blouse. She was wearing a low cut floral number that left nothing to the imagination.

"Too bad she has a face that would stop a charging African elephant in its tracks," he thought to himself.

Ambassador Henderson had heard the commotion from his office and stepped out into the waiting room. He was a short, rather round man with wire rimmed glasses and thinning brown hair. Ryan guessed he was 55 if he was a day.

"Is there a problem Ms. Gwynn?" he asked tentatively. The sight of what appeared to be six unruly woodsmen in his outer office seemed to unsettle him a bit.

"These men are demanding to see you," she said.

Henderson stepped towards the men hesitantly. Before he could speak again the outer door to the waiting room opened and it was Congresswomen Randell. She had brought along two other United States representatives who turned out to be John Stevens of the 11th district of Alabama and Jennifer Hall of the 51st district of Colorado. The three of them stopped dead in their tracks, not sure what to make of the six men.

"What is it about red plaid shirts that have such an intimidating effect on everyone?" asked Brad.

"Yeah," said Chris. "Maybe we should send our soldiers off to battle in these things. They can kick butt while the enemy is trying to figure out why they are dressed like red-necked huckleberries."

Ryan stepped forward to greet Ms. Randell.

"Hello congresswoman," he said, shaking her hand. "Thank you for coming on such short notice."

"How could I refuse a request of such an alien nature, pardon the pun?" she answered. "Is this your friend?"

She turned to face Plaatu who was the only member of his group who didn't look like he had just come from a John Deere tractor convention.

"Yes," said Ryan. "Plaatu, meet Congresswoman Randell."

"How do you do," said Plaatu politely. Her hand was warm and soft but her handshake was firm and confident.

Ryan and Ms. Randell finished with the introductions as Ambassador Henderson joined the group, seeming a bit more at ease now that some of his government colleagues had come to his rescue.

"So you are the gentlemen Ms. Randell called me about earlier?" asked Henderson. His eyes were filled with curiosity now that the situation had become a bit clearer.

"Yes," said Ryan. "This man asked us to bring him here. We only met him yesterday but he claims to have visited Earth 50 years ago."

"That is correct," added Plaatu. "Privately, your planet contacted the organization I represent in response to the message I delivered but publicly your leaders tried to explain away my visit as a publicity stunt. I have only recently learned that a mere handful of people knew the truth regarding my visit. I can tell you now that it is imperative that I be given the opportunity to discuss issues of extreme importance with your world leaders once again."

The government officials stood in awkward silence, not sure who should respond first. They were experiencing the same emotions the men had wrestled with the previous day upon hearing this perfectly normal looking human claiming that his living room is actually millions of miles away.

"Could you excuse us for just a moment?" asked the ambassador.

Plaatu took Ryan aside as the three congressional reps spoke privately with the ambassador. It wasn't difficult to ascertain by the expressions on their faces that they were more than a bit dubious.

"Do you really think I should be meeting with people at this level?" asked Plaatu. "How much influence do they wield? Are they intelligent?"

"Intelligence?" said Ryan. "You never said anything about intelligence. These are members of congress. If you want intelligence you came to the wrong place."

"I don't understand," said Plaatu.

Ryan glanced over at congresswomen Randell. She had her long blonde hair tied back nicely in a ponytail. She had sky-blue eyes, a pert little nose and well-defined features with just the right amount of lipstick and makeup so as not to appear cheap. She was wearing a navy blue business outfit with a nicely fitted skirt hemmed just above the knee and a perfectly tailored jacket to match. She was, at least in his opinion, the most strikingly attractive female politician he had ever seen. He eyed her from head to toe as she conversed privately with the ambassador, completely unaware of his lustful gaze. He had always wanted to ask her for a date during their time together as college classmates but he had never quite found the courage to pop the big question. Ryan's dominant thought at that moment was that she should definitely have those incredible legs insured.

"When you can look like that in a skirt," he said to Plaatu, "you don't need to worry about anything else when it comes to getting elected in this country. We stopped electing people based on intelligence a long time ago."

Ryan continued to stare at her longingly.

"You pig!" interrupted Brad.

"What?" said Ryan sharply?

"I see that look in your eye," said Brad softly. "You want her. Well forget about it, she's not the type to get involved with hobos like us."

"Speak for yourself," said Ryan.

"You could have called on any one of the other members of the Connecticut congressional contingent, now I know why you picked her," added Brad. "You disgust me."

Spike was attempting to distract Ms. Gwynn so that Tommy could raid the candy dish on the corner of her desk. She wasn't falling for it as her eyes darted back and forth between the two men.

"Gentlemen!" said Plaatu in total frustration. "I have work to do. Can we keep our attention on the task at hand please?"

Ryan took his eyes off of congresswoman Randell's legs for a moment and looked at Plaatu. There was a sense of urgency and purpose about him that was impossible to ignore. For a moment, he felt genuinely sorry for him. It was as if Plaatu was more concerned about the fate of Earth's future than he was.

"Sorry Plaatu," said Ryan. "They don't mean to make light of this whole business. I think we are all still in a state of denial. Please forgive us and leave everything to me."

Ryan walked over to Mikey, Spike, Chris, and Tommy who were still standing near the desk. Ms. Gwynn continued to watch their every move with venomous eyes. They looked as out of place as sumo wrestlers at a weight-watchers convention.

"Guys," he said, "there is really no need for all of us to hang around here now. Brad and I can handle things from here. Why don't you guys head downstairs and wait at the van. We'll rejoin you as soon as we're finished here."

"Great idea," said Mikey. "My van was probably towed already but if it wasn't, I'd like to get down there to keep an eye on it. You know how they love to tow in this city."

"Grab some candy on your way out," whispered Spike.

"Yeah, good idea," added Tommy.

"I'll be downstairs charging up my ray gun and preparing for the coming alien invasion," said Chris as he turned and left the room

"Don't worry," said Mikey who was the last to leave and always the voice of reason. "Spike and I will keep an eye on tweedle dee and tweedle dum. Do what you have to do and take your time."

"Thanks man," said Ryan. "This shouldn't take long."

Ryan closed the door behind them and once again approached congresswoman Randell and the others. The closer he got to her, the more intoxicating the scent of her perfume became. "For duty and humanity!" his conscience shouted inside his head. "Stay focused!"

"Excuse me for interrupting," he said. "Can we sit down somewhere where we can talk privately?"

"Of course," said Ambassador Henderson. "Step into my office."

They each went in and sat down at a conference table on the right hand side of the room. Brad and Ryan were still feeling a bit underdressed but they were determined not to abandon Plaatu until they were reasonably sure he was in good hands.

Ambassador Henderson sat at the head of the table and was the first to speak.

"So Mr. Plaatu," he began, "we were just discussing what Ryan conveyed to congresswoman Randell over the phone and your remarks in the waiting room. I have to admit I remain a bit skeptical about all of this. Would you mind elaborating on who you are and what you are doing here?"

Plaatu was not the least bit impressed with this individual and was beginning to regret asking his camping neighbors for help. They had gotten him to New York however, where he could connect to almost every nation on the planet by way of the General Assembly so he tried to contain his apprehensions. They had, after all, merely been out for a leisurely camping trip when he had interrupted their annual soirée and asked them to help him save their planet. In all fairness, it was a difficult segues for anyone to handle.

Plaatu calmed himself and proceeded to inform the group of his earlier visit. They were all familiar with the "event" of 1950 when a space ship had landed in Washington DC. The government had, as Plaatu discovered, subsequently proclaimed it a publicity stunt to demonstrate Earth's vulnerability in the event alien life forms ever did in fact, visit this planet. Plaatu learned that only a few high-ranking members of the president's cabinet at that time were involved with contacting the Coalition and informing them that the nations of the world were not interested in accepting his invitation to join them. That bothered Plaatu that they would attempt to trivialize the purpose of his mission and the gravity of their situation.

"I can assure you," he said directly to the ambassador, "your planet will not be able to ignore the situation any longer."

"I am having a hard enough time believing I am sitting here with someone who claims to be 'not of this Earth'," said Henderson. "No disrespect intended sir but what proof do I have that you are speaking the truth?"

The three congressional representatives waited for a reply. They were content, at least for the moment, to let the ambassador serve as their spokesperson.

"He's the real deal alright," said Brad. "We've seen his ship. It's sitting right now as we speak in . . ."

"Yes!" interrupted Plaatu. "Let us just leave it at that." He didn't feel it necessary to reveal the whereabouts of his ship knowing full well that the area would be crawling with military personnel in a matter of minutes. Earthlings had already clearly demonstrated on one occasion how distrustful they can be and how quick they are to flex their military might, paltry as it might be in galactic terms.

"Plaatu," interrupted Representative Randell finally. Her voice had a calming effect that he was unable to resist. "I came here because I have learned to give my constituents the benefit of the doubt. It has always worked for me in the past and I hope it continues to be the right approach in the future. But if I am going to go to the president with this, I need a little more than your word that you are from out there somewhere and that our planet is in grave danger. Please try to understand how this would look if you were on your home planet, where ever that is and someone came to you claiming to be an alien life form bringing dire news that your planet was about to be invaded."

"I can assure you," answered Plaatu, "that if I was on my home planet, we get visitors from other worlds all the time. To me, it is quite routine. What you people need to grasp is the reality of the situation that you are not as alone as you have always believed. There are other planets out there with humanoid life forms. Some of them are the nicest beings you would ever want to meet while others are, shall we say, not so nice. Much like your planet here. I will reiterate for the benefit of those of you who I have just met. We are not here to dictate how you run your internal affairs. It is essential however, that I convince you and the leading nations of the world that it is imperative that you cease in producing large-scale destructive weapons or there are species who are much more advanced than you who are ready, willing, and fully preparing to come here and eliminate humanity. They would lay claim to this planet without hesitation and are prepared to re-colonize it. You do not have much time."

Hesitation still hung in the air as the government officials tried to absorb all that they were hearing but it was clear that they remained unconvinced.

"Look," said Brad who had been sitting patiently and trying to remain anonymous. "This doesn't have to be all that complicated. Ambassador Henderson, why can't you just call a meeting of some of the most influential leaders and get an audience with them so Plaatu can state his case?"

"Actually," said Plaatu, removing a slip of paper from his pocket. "I have prepared a description of a few demonstrations I can put together to illustrate some of the benefits Earth can enjoy if they choose to become members of the Coalition." He slid the paper in front of Ambassador Henderson. "Take a look at it and let me know your thoughts. But do not deliberate for too long my friends. Time is an issue here and while I don't want to arouse any undue alarm, you need to act quickly."

Henderson looked at Plaatu and his uniform, the likes of which Henderson had to admit he had never seen before except on some of those Grade B science fiction movies he had enjoyed as a child. Then he looked at Ryan and Brad who hadn't shaved in a few days. He just couldn't fully accept the authenticity of what was being presented to him.

"Would you gentlemen mind waiting in the outer office for a moment while we speak privately?" asked Henderson.

"Sure," said Ryan. "Come on Plaatu."

The three men got up and walked out into the waiting room where Ms. Gwynn gave them another look that was anything but friendly. They sat down against the far wall and a collective wave of frustration passed over them like a solar eclipse.

"I know what you are thinking," said Ryan, turning to Plaatu who was sitting next to him with his head lowered. He seemed momentarily lost with a forlorn look on his face that made Ryan feel as though he had disappointed him badly.

"We couldn't just charge into a meeting of the General Assembly and start screaming the sky is falling!" said Ryan. "I know my people. I have lived among them all my life, you haven't. We can be a bunch of vindictive sons of bitches when we want to be. They would have locked us up and thrown away the key. We needed to do this in a well-thought out calculated manner and I still think this is the best approach."

"Bullshit!" said Brad. "You were thinking with your dick again. If it were me, I would have gone to members of the scientific community. Isaac Asimov, Carl Sagan, those kinds of people. Not "Lacy Under alls" Randell in there."

"Asimov and Sagan are both dead," said Ryan sharply. "And nobody takes the scientific community seriously, you know that. Look at all this talk about global warming. The so-called experts have been screaming about it for years but is anyone listening?"

"I'm only going to wait for a few moments more gentlemen," said Plaatu. "But fear not. I do appreciate your motives here. Of course if this fails, I will have to incinerate you both with a death ray."

"You really have a death ray?" asked Brad.

Inside Henderson's office the three congressmen and women continued in their attempts to gauge the sincerity of what they had just heard. Congressman Stevens got up and helped himself to a glass of water. He really just wanted an excuse to stare at Randell from an unobtrusive position where he wouldn't be noticed. The refreshment table was located on the other side of the room. He walked slowly back towards the table, his eyes never leaving her slender legs.

"Pretty outlandish story if you ask me," he said as he returned to his seat next to Hall. "Do you really expect me to believe that the 1951 incident was a government cover-up? Yeah, sure, and the CIA was behind the Bay of Pigs invasion too right? Preposterous."

His remark received little more than confused silence.

"The CIA *was* behind the Bay of Pigs invasion," said Henderson.

Congresswoman Hall turned to Ms. Randell. They had been friends for just a short time but she had developed a tremendous amount of respect for the way in which the Connecticut rep conducted herself. She found herself voting in favor of many of the legislative bills that Randell supported and from an ideological standpoint, she saw her as an extremely valuable ally.

"You are the one he contacted," said Hall. "You are the only one who knows this constituent of yours. What does your gut tell you?"

"I have only known Ryan for a few years or so, and purely on a superficial level," said Ms. Randell. "I attended classes with him in college but I can tell you with a reasonable degree of certainty that he is not some random crackpot who just stumbled in off the streets of New York. If he believes this guy is genuine, I can't think of any evidence or indications from our previous dealings that he would have any reason to lie."

"I can't go to the General Assembly with something like this without authorization from the president," said Henderson. "And I am not going to even breach the subject with the commander in chief if you three are not in total agreement."

"He obviously doesn't want us to know where his space ship is," said Stevens, "either because he is concerned for its safety or because it really doesn't exist which would prove beyond any shadow of a doubt that he is in fact, nuttier than a bag of Peanut M and M's. Why don't we do this? Let him conduct his demonstrations and see if he is legit? These look like pretty lofty demonstrations he has presented us with so why not put him to the test. Invite a few leaders of the government and scientific community to validate his results and then we can go from there."

"In the meantime," added Congresswoman Hall, "I overheard one of them say they were camping in the White Mountains of New Hampshire. Why not have the military conduct a covert search and see if they can find his ship?"

"Do it quietly though," said Ms. Randell. "I don't want him to think we are trying to deceive him."

"Alright," said Henderson. "I'll contact the president's people, inform them of everything we talked about and give this Plaatu guy a chance to prove himself. As crazy as all of this sounds and even if there is only a remote chance he is telling the truth, it needs to be explored. If what he says is correct, we may be in jeopardy. Very serious jeopardy."

Henderson got up from his chair, then walked to the door leading to the waiting room and opened it. He poked his head out and motioned the three men to join them once again.

As they walked in, he closed the door behind them.

"Alright Mr. Plaatu," said Henderson. "I'm going to speak with the president first. Then I'm hoping to set up an audience for you to conduct these demonstrations of yours and if successful, we can approach the other nations for a meeting of the General Assembly. One step at a time if that is alright. You said you traveled here once before. If you have any recollection of what it is like trying to deal with a group of representatives from all nations, you are no doubt aware of the astonishing levels of irrational behavior we are capable of displaying. We humans are not always known for being remarkably reasonable beings."

Plaatu couldn't help but smile. That is an understatement, he thought to himself. "You surprise me Mr. Henderson," he said aloud. "That was very astute." Plaatu stifled an impulse to reach out and pat the little man on top of his head. "I accept your proposal. How does tomorrow morning sound?"

"I will try and make all the necessary arrangements," said Henderson.

"That is a good start," said Plaatu as he shook hands with the ambassador.

Ryan thanked congresswoman Randell and the others. He shook her hand and for a moment locked eyes with her. A moment of awkward silence passed as the others waited for him to let go of her hand. Ryan didn't let go. Brad cleared his throat but it did no good.

"Thank you again," said Ryan feebly.

"Yes," said Randell blushing slightly. "You said that. It's my pleasure." She gently pulled her hand away and stepped back, fully aware that her colleagues were observing every nuance and every move. "Well!" gotta be going gushed Brad and he grabbed Ryan by the arm and dragged him out of the office.

"What was that all about," asked congressman Stevens, attempting to conceal his jealous rage. He was secretly infatuated with Randell. She on the other hand had no romantic interest in him whatsoever.

"I have no idea," Randell answered softly. Deep down inside, she thrived on such attention and wasn't the least bit troubled by the incident.

Out in the hallway Brad let loose on Ryan.

"Don't you ever embarrass me like that again!" he barked. "I have a reputation to uphold you know."

"I couldn't help it," responded Ryan lamely. "When I gazed into her eyes, it was like staring at a goddess. I couldn't move or look away."

"Just goes to show you Plaatu," said Brad as they reached the elevators. "You can dress him up but you can't take him anywhere."

When the doors opened, Plaatu followed them into the elevator and stifled the urge to laugh. He wasn't entirely sure if Brad's temper tantrum was genuine or feigned. The car lowered to the first floor and the three men exited and hurried down the hall to the main exit doors. Brad was still fuming but Plaatu could now see that he was stifling laughter as well. He had only been in their company for a solar day but he was already beginning to understand the chemistry that existed between the six campers. It was, at least from what he could gather, a very special chemistry indeed. They rode each other relentlessly, they addressed each other at times in the harshest of terms but the thread that bound them together was simply unbreakable. It seemed to be that rarest of relationships where they could literally say anything to one another without fear of hurting each other's feelings. It was the kind of camaraderie some people can only dream of.

They walked out onto the plaza where the protestors were still fully engaged in trying to out-shout one another. Plaatu had been to many such gatherings throughout the galaxy and had come away with the regretful conclusion that freedom of speech could sometimes come back to haunt a society in more ways than one. Freedom of speech often leads to freedom of assembly which usually results in little more than a migraine to anyone who is forced to listen to the ensuing, sometimes mindless banter these gatherings can produce. Plaatu was willing to bet that many of those protesting at that very moment were "screamers for hire", out of work individuals who would hold a sign that read "Treat me like a farm animal" if you paid them enough money.

As they reached the van, Mikey and the others were just hanging out with the side doors wide open. Spike was sucking down a beer.

"A little early for that eh Spike?" asked Brad.

Spike looked at his watch. "It's after noon," he said with a broad grin. "Plus, by my watch I'm still on vacation."

"Yeah," added Mikey, "but keep it down and out of sight huh Spike? The boys in blue are not far from view."

Devilish grins took shape on the faces of Tommy and Chris. It was clear that a profound sense of calm had returned to their demeanor. Perhaps it was borne out of the assumption that their role in this bizarre adventure was over and they could go back to their more comfortable, insular lives.

"He drinks a beer but shows no fear," said Chris.

"Let's close the van and hide the man," said Tommy. He and Chris started giggling at each other.

"You had to start didn't you," said Ryan.

"It was an accident," said Mikey. "I'm a victim of circumstance."

"Plaatu," said Ryan, "why don't you sit up front in the passenger seat. I don't think you will be able to stand it back here."

They all climbed into the van and closed the doors, shutting out the protesters and their unceasing chatter. Mikey turned the ignition key, then threw the shifter into drive and pulled away from the curb. Just as he did, Chris started up again.

"The doors are shut, to Connec-ti-cut!"

Tommy began laughing hysterically. "That was hideous!" he guffawed. The others tried in vain to stifle their impulse to laugh knowing full well that it would not be wise to encourage them.

"Time to leave this city, it's really big and shitty," said Tommy.

"Oh sure!" snapped Chris, "And that one wasn't hideous right?"

Brad had quite enough. This could go on indefinitely and usually regressed beyond all boundaries of sanity. He searched the floor for something to throw at them but everything within arms reach had too dense a molecular structure. Flashlights, a crowbar, baseball bats . . . he needed to silence, not maim.

"I've got one for you,' he said giving up the search for something a little softer, "One more word and I'll throw your asses out!" The remark was followed by confused silence.

"That doesn't rhyme does it?" asked Chris.

"No, it doesn't rhyme at all," protested Tommy. "You can't use that one."

"Yeah," said Brad, "but while you are bouncing along the highway after I toss you out, it really won't matter much will it?"

Plaatu just sat quietly in the front seat taking it all in. He was not accustomed to spending this much time in the company of beings that seemed

to possess a truly limitless capacity to make light of any situation, even under
the shadow of impending doom. Something in his mind told him that none
of the humans he had encountered thus far, the campers, the congressional
representatives, the ambassador, fully grasped the magnitude of their situation.
He was the only alien they had interacted with thus far. They still remained
oblivious to the forces that were beginning to prowl along their celestial
borders, forces that were chomping at the bit to wipe that collective impish
grin off the face of the human race. The dangers they faced were quite real
and somehow that message wasn't getting through to them.

As he continued to listen to the languishing levity inside the van, he felt
reasonably sure that bringing the conversation back around to one of a more
serious nature would be futile so he struggled to suppress his frustration.

"Do they ever get along?" he asked Mikey in a hushed tone.

'Don't pay any attention to them," Mikey answered. "When push comes
to shove, any one of them would be there for me if I needed him to be."

The mid-afternoon traffic was relatively light as Mikey pulled down Main
Street in Stamford's west end with its rows of stick-built single family houses.
Each had a moderately-sized tree out front, mostly maples and sycamores.
He continued up Griffin Street and dropped off Tommy and Chris. Then he
continued along, taking a right onto Millis Avenue then pulled onto Argyle Street
where Spike called home. He lived in a second floor apartment that overlooked a
small playground. It gave Spike a great vantage point from which he could enjoy
watching the children play from his living room window. Spike loved kids and
he hoped that someday he too would have a son or daughter he could take there.

Mikey then dropped off Ryan and Brad at their apartment building on
Jefferson Avenue. Plaatu accompanied them and they all agreed to regroup the
next morning to assist him in any way they could with his demonstrations.

The interior of the six story red brick building was quiet as they walked
down the dark blue-carpeted hallway to Ryan's second floor flat. Halloween
was coming and many of the doors they passed were adorned with brightly
colored decorations. Ghosts, goblins and witches seemed to glare at them
eerily as they passed each entrance. Most of the residents were middle-aged
professionals and were most likely at work. There were few if any stay-at-home
residents throughout the building.

As Ryan unlocked the door to his apartment Plaatu looked a bit
uncomfortable.

"Don't worry," he said, noticing his awkwardness. "I'm straight."

Plaatu wasn't sure what he was talking about, then the relevance of his
remark clarified itself in his mind.

The three men began laughing which eased the tension.

"I'm going to head upstairs to my place and grab a shower," said Brad. "Maybe we can grab a bite to eat in a few hours. You hungry Plaatu?"

"Now that you mention it, I could eat something," he said. "Thank you."

"Ok," drop back down when you are ready," replied Ryan. He and Plaatu entered his living room and Ryan closed the door behind him.

It was agreed that Plaatu would stay the night at Ryan's since he had the largest apartment and had a spare bedroom. As Plaatu looked around at the furnishings and the wall hangings, it became apparent that Ryan took a great deal of pride in the way he maintained his residence. Everything was meticulously neat and tidy. There were pictures of his mom and dad on the wall along with various prints of French Impressionists.

The bedrooms were adjacent to the living room on opposite sides.

"You can put your stuff in that room," said Ryan. "Would you like something to drink?"

"I'm all set for now," said Plaatu. "Thank you. You have a very nice place here. How long have you and Brad lived in the same building?"

"We've been here for over two years now," answered Ryan as he took two white towels out of a small closet. "Brad actually found this place when we went apartment hunting after graduating college. It was clean, reasonably priced and close to downtown where we both knew we could find jobs. So it worked out great. It's a bit less rural than I would like but it will suffice for the time being."

Plaatu walked into the second bedroom and set his case down on a walnut textured bureau against the wall. He had brought with him a change of clothes in the event that they were going to spend the night in New York.

"I'm going to hop in the shower," yelled Ryan from the other room. "You're welcome to do the same once I get out. Help yourself if you want to catch some television."

"Television?" Plaatu repeated in his head. He had been monitoring television signals for days in an effort to bring himself up to date on Earth's progress since his last visit. It didn't take him long to come to the unarguable conclusion that progress may not be the appropriate term and that perhaps regress may be more fitting. He had already absorbed a sufficiently unhealthy dose of daytime TV and came away with a humorous thought. Perhaps humans were actually far more clever than he gave them credit for. Could it be that they were purposely airing incredibly atrocious and completely mindless programming? Were they hoping that potentially dangerous aliens would tap into their frequencies and be so appalled and disgusted they would be frightened off by the utter debauchery that seemed to permeate this species? Humans were capable of being remarkably devious creatures. Such a ploy would be downright ingenious, Plaatu thought to himself.

He sat on the edge of the full-sized bed and just looked around the room for a moment. The blue and white floral comforter covering the bed was soft and inviting. Flashbacks of his previous visit to Earth flooded his mind. Vivid images of the home in which he had stayed rematerialized in his consciousness. He remembered that humans had a remarkable knack for decorating a domicile. Many of the things he could see as he panned the room were strictly ornamental and could be done without but they were at least, not overly ostentatious and were in fact, somewhat aesthetically pleasing. There were colorful pictures on the cream-colored walls, assorted knick knacks, and what appeared to be an artificial flower arrangement on the bureau. They all represented an attempt, he assumed, to make the room feel what humans referred to as "homey". Totally illogical as far as he was concerned but he had to admit, it did give the room a certain warmth and ambiance.

He heard the water being turned on in an adjacent room. As he continued to sit there, trying valiantly to take in all that had transpired over the past few days, he shuddered slightly. The pangs of loneliness continued to haunt him. He had been in space far too long. More and more in his mind, he was beginning to come to terms with the harsh realization that he should have taken an assignment like that of Em Diem. This jetting around the galaxy stuff was for the younger folk. Retirement could be a very scary prospect, but an increasingly strong sense of resolve was beginning to grow in his mind. This would be his last mission. He had had enough. The thought of enjoying a nice long rest in the company of his own people was beginning to take on an irresistible appeal.

He was determined to locate, then re-connect with his daughter. He had not seen Nara in far too long. While he wasn't sure if she would be willing to forgive him for being absent from her mother's bedside when she needed him most, he simply had to find a way to bring her back into his life.

The fact that he was back on Earth should have been proof enough that he was beginning to spin his wheels. He had already gone this way before. Yet here he was, once again trying to convince yet another species of the error of their ways. The pressures of such missions which oftentimes carried with them dire consequences were beginning to weigh on him as if an enormous invisible ogre had climbed onto his back. An increasingly loud voice inside his head kept telling him he didn't want this anymore. Pass the gauntlet to the next CIPF cadet who would be called upon to take his place.

He stretched out on the bed. It was firm but comfortable. Without intending to, he drifted off into a troubled slumber.

Ryan went into Plaatu's room and shook him gently as the clock approached 4:30.

"Hey," he said softly. "We're going to have supper in a half hour or so. Just thought you might want to freshen up beforehand."

Plaatu was a bit startled and rose to a seating position. For a moment he forgot where he was. Then it all came back to him. He rubbed his eyes gently and tried to get his bearings.

"I must have dozed off," he said, still dazed a bit. "Didn't mean to."

"It's OK," said Ryan. "You probably needed it. It's not like you haven't traveled a ways to get here."

"Yes," said Plaatu, "Quite right. Maybe I will take that shower now. Hopefully it will revitalize me a bit."

Ryan heard a knock at the door. It was Brad. As he let him in, he noticed that he was carrying a large white bowl of pasta in his hands.

"I knew I was coming so I baked a bowl of pasta," he quipped, as he walked through the door.

"Next time, bake a cake," replied Ryan as he shut the door behind him. "I have all the pasta I need."

Brad set the steaming bowl down on the dining room table.

"Well now you have even more than all the pasta you need. How's our guest doing?" he asked.

Just then Plaatu emerged from his bedroom carrying a towel. He looked a bit disoriented.

"Ah, Master Brad," he said, "nice to see you again."

"You look like you just woke up," said Brad.

"That's because I did," said Plaatu. "What do you humans call it? Catching a few Z's? Which way is the shower facilities?"

"The shower is right through here," said Ryan as he directed him towards the bathroom. Then he went back into the kitchen to finish preparing sauce and fresh bread. Ryan was a man of many skills and cooking was one of them. It was something he inherited from his mom who was of Italian descent. He and his four brothers grew up in a household where the evening meal was always something special and worth looking forward to. Even something as relatively simple as spaghetti and meatballs was a major-league culinary event not to be missed.

In his youth, it was customary for families to sit together around the dinner table and converse with one another. Topics ranged from his dad's day at work to homework and after school play. The dinner hour usually allowed his family precious time to cover the full gambit of what had transpired earlier that day. All that had sadly changed as the days of the one-working-parent morphed into a new era in American life. As both parents were gradually forced to enter the workplace out of financial necessity and the dramatic increase in the cost of living, the time-honored dinner hour had seemed to fall victim to the need to put more bread on the table. Ryan missed those days and was painfully aware that they were in all likelihood gone forever from the national landscape.

At 5 o'clock, the three men sat down to an old fashioned Italian supper, complete with red wine and Tiramisu for dessert. Plaatu was increasingly aware of how fond he was becoming of Earthly cuisine. If only there were no side effects after the fact.

The conversation was light and jovial. Unbeknownst to Plaatu, Ryan and Brad were still having trouble accepting the fact that they were sitting down to dinner with a non-human. On an almost sub-conscious level, it was still freaking them out more than just a bit.

"The timing of this worked out very well," said Ryan. "We still have four days of vacation left so we can help you out until you have completed your mission. It shouldn't take you more than a few days right?"

"I should be able to conclude everything in two to three days," said Plaatu as he raised his glass. "Here's to a successful mission."

With a gentle clinking of glasses they acknowledged his toast respectfully.

"What will you need to pull off these demonstrations of yours?" asked Brad.

"The first two will be relatively simple," said Plaatu. "I'll need a body of water, a pond or a lake; it doesn't matter how big or small."

"Why don't we start small," said Ryan. "Just to be on the safe side." Plaatu remained oblivious to the nagging cloud of doubt that was continuing to plague Ryan's thought processes.

"As you wish," said Plaatu, "as long as it has relatively high levels of harmful bacteria. It will make for a more convincing demonstration."

"Oh, you won't have any trouble finding bacteria in our water," said Brad. "Frog Pond is only about ten minutes from here and it's the next best thing to toxic sludge."

"Then, I will need a research facility of some sort where medical experiments are conducted on lower life forms," said Plaatu. "I believe such facilities still exist on Earth." He buttered another piece of bread and dabbed at the remaining sauce on his plate.

"You mean lower life forms like mice and rats?" asked Brad. "Because I am personally familiar with some humans who fall into that category too."

Plaatu wasn't quite sure how to take his remark. Then again, he seemed so pre-occupied with his meal that Brad wasn't even sure if he was paying any attention to him at all. "Rodents will do," said Plaatu. "Although nothing I am going to do will cause them any harm."

"There is a facility out on Route 89 that I know of," said Ryan. "It should suffice quite nicely."

"Very good," responded Plaatu. The plate was so clean in front of him Ryan could have just put it back on the shelf as is. Both he and Brad marveled at Plaatu's appetite but apparently even he had his limits. With a well-suppressed belch, Plaatu backed himself away from the table. "If you will excuse me, I have some calculations to make prior to the morning. Thank you for the tasty dinner. It was much appreciated."

"It was our pleasure Plaatu," answered Ryan in a sincere tone. "Judging by the way you handled my pasta and meatballs, I wouldn't be surprised to find out that you have some Italian in your family lineage."

"That would indeed be a miracle," responded Plaatu.

He got up from the table and returned to his room. Ryan and Brad watched him intently as he closed the door behind him.

"Quite an eventful week so far," remarked Brad.

"To say the least, if not less," replied Ryan. "I really didn't give it much thought until just now but what are the chances?"

"What do you mean?"

"There are over six billion people on this rock," said Ryan. "What are the chances that of all those people, we are the ones who just happened to be hanging out where this guy decides to land his ship? I just think it's freaky."

"I never really thought about it much until now," said Brad.

He popped one last meatball into his mouth and swallowed it down.

"Great meatballs," he said. "You must have worked all afternoon on these."

"Of course I did," said Ryan. "What do you think I was doing?"

"Uh-huh," said Brad. "And I bet if I checked your trash I wouldn't find a discarded "Mama Leone's frozen meatballs" bag right?"

"You stay the hell out of my trash," said Ryan. He got up and started clearing the plates from the table.

"Turn the news on will you?" he said, motioning towards the TV.

"Sure," said Brad as he walked over and turned on the 26-inch set against the far wall of the living room. In a few moments, an image appeared on the screen as Brad sat down on the couch. "You sure you don't want some help with those dishes?" he asked.

"No, I'm good," answered Ryan. "Besides, I like things done right."

"Up yours," said Brad. Then he picked up the remote control and clicked the channel selector.

"Elsewhere in the news tonight," said the anchorman from CNN, "A fifth body was found in the woods of Virginia. Police believe there is a serial killer on the loose but they have few leads in the case. Each victim was found decapitated, then buried in a shallow grave."

Brad's stomach churned as he switched the channel to Fox News.

"Great Britain intends to enforce a new law that makes it a criminal offence for anyone to force women to undergo female circumcisions." reported an attractive brunette in a tastefully low-cut blouse. She was displaying just enough cleavage to hold Brad's interest. "According to Doctor Elaine Wilson of the London General Hospital," the reporter continued, "She claimed to be seeing more cases of this barbaric procedure than ever before."

Brad again turned the channel as a shiver shot up his spine. "Serial killers, circumcisions?" he said to himself. "Woof!"

"In other news," said a channel five newscaster, "143 people died when a suicide bomber blew himself up in the middle of a densely populated market in downtown Baghdad. Rescue workers are still digging through the rubble for remains of victims . . ."

"How about if we skip the news tonight," said Brad as he switched to the Boston Bruins channel. The pre-game show was just about to start. "Let's watch the hockey game. At least there's no violence in that sport."

Ryan finished doing the dishes, then he joined Brad in the living room just in time for the opening face-off. It wasn't more than a matter of minutes before Brad looked over to see Ryan sitting with his head tilted back and snoring softly. He wasn't sure what caused it exactly but there was something about a plate full of spaghetti and meatballs followed by the steady drone of a televised hockey game that seemed to lull him to sleep. He gently whacked him on the arm and Ryan's head lurched upright.

"What? What's the score?" he stammered.

"Nothing to nothing," answered Brad.

"Oh," said Ryan sluggishly. "But who's winning?"

I'm heading upstairs to my place," said Brad with a smile. "Why don't you get some sleep? We have a big day ahead of us tomorrow."

"That's cool," answered Ryan. "Maybe I will. It has been anything but an ordinary day, huh?"

"Yeah," answered Brad pensively. "It was literally out of this world." He got up and headed for the door. "I'll see you in the morning."

Ryan got up and locked the front door behind Brad, then he walked softly over to Plaatu's room. The door was closed but he couldn't hear any movement from within. He too was apparently succumbing to the sleep aide of a home cooked Italian dinner.

"Gets 'em every time," he chuckled, then he headed for his room.

CHAPTER FIVE

Ryan turned on the radio while he prepared breakfast the next morning. Plaatu emerged from his room and Brad knocked at the front door almost simultaneously. The coffee was hot and the bagels and cream cheese ready for consumption but the news that the country had raised the terrorist alert level to its highest point put a damper on the collective mood.

This was certainly not the first time terrorist alert levels had been raised to their highest stage. It was just that Ryan and Brad had sat around the camp fire a few days earlier discussing a very frightening inevitability. They were both convinced that it was only a matter of time before a fanatic element smuggled a dirty bomb into a major US city, most likely New York or Washington DC. Everyone knew a big event was coming, the country just didn't know where or when. Consequently, when alert levels were increased, the two men felt an elevation in their anxiety levels as well. Knowing it was inevitable didn't make it any easier to deal with the emotions that were aroused by the mere thought of such a cataclysmic event.

Discussing politics was a favorite pastime of the two friends. They knew they were in no way, shape or form possessed of the ability to do anything about the myriad of issues that troubled them deeply. Brad had remarked on more than one occasion that there was no reason for them to feel the least bit inadequate. The richest billionaires on the planet lacked the power to stop wars or end poverty around the world any more than he and Ryan did. Or at least the upper-class didn't seem to have any such inclinations.

"This Muslim-Christian conflict has been going on now for centuries, has it not?" asked Plaatu. His tone was not one of arrogance, nor was it condescending. Brad still couldn't help feeling a little paltry in the eyes of this man from another world when put in a position of answering any questions regarding human conflict. Something just made him feel small in Plaatu's presence, but this couldn't be farther from the truth. This was nothing new to Plaatu. In his travels, he had seen more strife and conflict than most men and for every reason imaginable, some justifiable but more often to the contrary. Plaatu sensed Brad's embarrassment.

"My friends," he said warmly. "There is no need to feel self-conscious in my presence. You humans are not alone in your petty differences with one another. This is not something that is unique to planet Earth. We may have eliminated war throughout the Coalition, largely because no one would be foolish enough to risk the wrath of our robot enforcement corps. But we still are prone to the same frailties you are. We are not perfect by any means. Greed, jealousy, intolerance . . . these distasteful humanoid tendencies can be found throughout the galaxy. Do not ever feel the need to lower your heads in my presence."

Ryan locked eyes with Plaatu for a moment. He couldn't put his finger on it exactly but there was just something about him that was more, for lack of a better word, genuine than most people he knew.

"You're alright Plaatu," he said. "I don't care what they say about you."

"Someone has been talking about me?" he asked innocently.

"It's just an expression," said Brad as the phone on the kitchen wall rang loudly.

"Jesus!" said Brad, "How many times have I asked you to turn that ringer down? I can hear your phone ringing when I am upstairs in my apartment."

"Relax," snapped Ryan, "it's not that loud."

"Actually it is," said Plaatu under his breath to Brad.

Ryan picked up the receiver before it could clang a third time. It was in fact, annoyingly loud but he wasn't going to let Brad get the upper hand on the subject. That would be simply uncivilized. It was congresswomen Randell's office. He quickly briefed her executive aide Phillip Agnetta on what they had discussed the previous night regarding Frog Pond and the medical facility they had suggested. Agnetta agreed to pass along the information and informed Ryan that the congresswoman had already organized a contingent of hand-picked government and scientific representatives who could meet them at the pond at 9 o'clock.

Ryan thanked him, then hung up and walked back over to the table where Brad was pounding down his second bagel.

"Save some for the starving people of the world," he kidded. "Damn, you are one incredible eating machine." He looked at the clock on the wall. It was 7:30. They had an hour and a half to kill before meeting the government officials.

"How much time will you need to set up over there Plaatu?" Ryan asked.

"Not more than ten minutes or so," he answered. "But it would be nice to check out the area for suitability ahead of time. Would you mind?"

"Not at all," he answered. "I'll give Mikey and the others a call and let them know that we won't be needing their assistance though. I know they will be anxious to be involved but it will be crowded enough as it is. We can get together with them later on. Besides, there are going to be some VIP's there and I don't think it would be wise to expose them to the Chris and Tommy show. Wouldn't you agree?" he asked turning to Brad.

"Indubitably," said Brad. "I'm going to run up to my place and grab a light coat though. You might want to do the same. It gets a little cool over there this time of year."

Plaatu returned to his room to organize his case of chemical agents. He wasn't unusually nervous which surprised him a bit. The outcome of his mission could quite possibly alter the course of this planet's inhabitants for centuries to come. Yet, it wasn't weighing all that heavily on his mind. Most men would likely crumble under such pressure. His years in space were many and the assignments too numerous to count. Perhaps he was simply becoming numb to the constant anxiety and stress the job brought with it.

The three men met downstairs outside the front door. The sun was shining and it appeared that the weather would be very much to Plaatu's liking. They decided to take Ryan's Honda SUV which was parked in the lot right next to the building.

As the three men approached the vehicle, they noticed a group of teenage youths lingering in the parking lot. One of them was leaning up against Ryan's SUV. He had a look on his face like he had just been caught with his hand in the cookie jar.

"Can I help you?" asked Ryan sharply. His car had been vandalized twice before and it was beginning to annoy him to say the least.

"Just looking around," replied the youth. He was as tall as Ryan but much thinner. He couldn't have been more than 17 years old. He was wearing jeans with worn out knees and a light blue winter vest. His red baseball cap read 'Born Killers' on its brim. As they squared off face to face, the youngster wasn't sure which way to turn and was still blocking access to the driver's door. Brad stopped in front of the vehicle with Plaatu and watched as several more youths approached.

Ryan glanced down at the youngster's hands and noticed that he was holding a slim-jim, a device used for breaking into cars.

"Just looking' around huh?" snapped Ryan. Now he was really pissed. With a three hundred dollar insurance deductible, some despicable asshole had already cost him a total of six hundred dollars over two previous vandalism claims. He couldn't be sure that these were the responsible parties but it didn't matter. He was going to take out his frustrations on this punk anyway. For all he knew this upstanding young lout could have been related to whoever had performed the two previous acts of unconscionable malfeasance upon his defenseless vehicle. Guilt by association was a perfectly acceptable justification for doling out suitable retribution to all culpable parties thereof. Such a law had to appear in a law book somewhere, he thought to himself and if it didn't, damn it, it should.

"Hey," he said cajolingly, "that's a pretty cool tool you've got there. Can I see it"?

The defiant youngster wasn't intimidated, or at least he did not appear to be. That was one thing Ryan had noticed about these new young thugs as compared to years ago. They seemed to have no fear or respect for authority. 'Brass balls' he called it.

As the youngster lifted his hand, Ryan grabbed his wrist with a quick move that took him completely off guard. He twisted his arm and forced him to the ground as he applied more pressure. The youngster groaned in pain.

Plaatu and Brad found themselves surrounded by five other similar-sized youths and they were every bit as defiant as the first.

"Git your hands off him!" barked the largest of the group. He too was wearing a vest and they all had baseball caps on their heads. He made a move in the direction of Ryan and seemed bent on helping his fellow gang member.

'I really don't have time for this shit," said Brad as he reached under his coat and withdrew a 9 millimeter Beretta and just let it fall to his side in his hand. "You boys really want to push the issue?" he asked menacingly.

They all glanced down at the blue-plated pistol and for the first time showed some hesitation.

Plaatu just watched the scene play out. He never felt like he was in any danger but he was content to let Ryan and Brad handle this as it was their turf. They were probably accustomed to dealing with this sort of thing.

Ryan continued pushing down hard on the boy's twisted wrist, then he took the slim-jim out of his hand.

"I'm only going to tell you this once," he said through clenched teeth. "I don't care who else's car you mess with in this city, just don't ever mess with mine again. Do we understand one another?" He twisted even harder as the boy cried out in pain. Ryan thought he heard a bone pop in the boy's arm but he wasn't in a very sympathetic mood.

"OK! OK!" the boy shouted. "I hear ya!"

Ryan let him up as the boy grabbed his twisted wrist and tried to rub away the pain.

"Now take off!" Ryan warned.

The boy rejoined the others and they began heading for the parking lot exit, several of them still cursing under their breaths.

"Go mess with the governor's car," shouted Brad, "useless sons of bitches."

"I can't believe we were that age once," remarked Ryan. "Were we punks like that?"

"Shit no," said Brad. "We would never have backed down in a situation like this."

"Do you always carry a weapon in your travels?" asked Plaatu. The tone in his voice suggested a certain disdain towards firearms.

"In this country, it's almost a matter of necessity," said Brad. "You've never lived in Connecticut my alien friend. Sometimes it's a damn jungle out here. I told you before I don't like guns and I hope I never have to use it, but it never hurts to be prepared."

Actually, Plaatu was pretty well-versed as to the crime situation in 21st century United States. He had conducted an extensive amount of research during the previous few days on his way to Earth and his conclusions were anything but uplifting. At present, the US had the highest per-capita crime rate and prison population of all the industrialized nations on the planet. What he couldn't understand is how the country with the reputed highest standard of living and the most wealth also have the highest population of disenfranchised citizens. It was a huge paradox in his mind but its solution would have to wait for another day. Plaatu was prepared to help this planet's inhabitants in any way he could, but he wasn't a magician.

The three men climbed into the SUV and Ryan started the engine. Plaatu chose to sit in the rear seat this time to give Ryan and Brad the chance to converse about the parking lot incident more easily. Something told Plaatu that it wouldn't be the last time they would face such a situation.

"Well, let's hope the rest of the day goes better than it started," he thought to himself.

The trip to the pond took just 8 minutes as traffic was much lighter than usual. "Everybody must be sleeping in," said Brad.

Ryan turned the vehicle off the main road and it rolled down an asphalt incline that emptied out onto a small public beach area. There was trash strewn everywhere. The beach was never particularly clean for that matter but Brad didn't remember it ever being this disgusting. There were discarded beer cans, wine bottles, trash bags and even a few dirty diapers in full view.

The men got out and Plaatu brought his case down to the edge of the water, seemingly oblivious to the debris.

"This is downright embarrassing," Brad whispered to Ryan.

"Kids must have been hanging out here last night like we used to," said Ryan. "We never left the place like this though, damned pigs."

Plaatu put the case of materials down and began walking around the edge of the pond. It was only about a mile across and other than the access road leading down to the beach area, it was completely surrounded by trees. There was a jogging path that wound its way through the trees which were still covered with leaves but they were slowly withering in the autumn air. The foliage around Frog Pond was not as colorful as it had been in years past, thought Ryan. But then, not every year brought with it the same results. The area had not received much rain over the course of the previous summer and unusually dry conditions still prevailed.

Brad began leisurely walking around and kicking items of trash off to the sides of the road. There were some pretty important people coming and he was genuinely angry about the condition someone had left the beach the previous night. But not angry enough to pick up other peoples' garbage. That was definitely above and beyond the call of duty.

Plaatu took a sample of the brownish-green pond water and tested it with one of the agents he had brought with him. In a few moments the contents of the small beaker he was using turned a bright orange.

"Yes," he said to himself. "This should work just fine. This water is downright repulsive. I wouldn't let my worst enemy drink this water. People actually swim here?"

"We used to," said Brad sheepishly. "Why?"

"Are you feeling any side effects?" joked Plaatu. This water has more forms of bacteria in it than just about any water I have ever tested."

"Now he tells us," said Ryan.

"So you are saying I should think twice abut casting my fishing line and trying to catch us something for dinner tonight?" asked Brad.

"I would recommend you stay as far away from this pond as possible," answered Plaatu, "at least until I finish my demonstration."

Plaatu removed another beaker from his case and removed the cap. He poured a few drops into the contaminated water, then watched as the orange color slowly disappeared. In a few moments, he was holding a crystal clear vile of what appeared to be pure water.

"So you can make water change colors?" joked Ryan. "That should really impress them."

Plaatu didn't take offense. He was getting used to the dry sense of humor his camping associates had been exhibiting and knew that it would be best not to take them too seriously. It was pretty obvious that they didn't take each other very seriously either.

Pleased with the results of his first pre-test, Plaatu closed the case and again walked to the edge of the pond.

"How deep would you say it is?" he asked the two men.

Brad took three folding chairs out of the SUV and set them up a few feet away from the edge of the water. Then he thought about what Plaatu had said a few moments ago in regards to water quality and moved the chairs back about twenty feet. He sat down and sipped from a cup of coffee he had brought with him.

"It's not very deep at all," answered Ryan who sat down next to him. "But it has a steep drop off about thirty feet out. Where you are standing, you could probably walk out ten feet or so and only be up to your knees."

Plaatu put his hand under his chin and continued to stare at the placid water. Liquid always had a very calming effect on him. On his home planet, the water supply was not quite equal to that of Earth's. For that matter, few if any planets could match the ratio of land to water that Earth enjoyed. That was what made it such a valuable commodity in the galaxy. Golon did have large sized lakes however, and he still could remember frolicking in the waves when he was a child. He was an excellent swimmer and felt very much at home in the water.

There was no way in hell he would even think of going swimming in this muck though.

"I'm going to take a walk around the pond," he said as he headed for the jogging path. It was a work day and it did not appear as though anyone was using it at that time. He found the entire area to be quite picturesque and tranquil. As he reached the beginning of the jogging path he pondered for a moment that if not for the near toxic condition of the water, it would be a great place to spend some leisure time.

"Don't go getting lost on us now," said Brad chidingly.

"You really can't get lost if you stay on the path," added Ryan. "It circles around and comes back out behind us. Just stay on the path and you won't have any trouble."

Plaatu was gone for about thirty five minutes when the two men saw him approaching from the near side of the pond behind them. His timing couldn't have been better because a large black van was just pulling down the access road. It was the congressional delegation.

After the driver pulled alongside Ryan's SUV, eight individuals got out and approached the three men.

Ms. Randell was out in front, dressed in a nicely tailored gray pants suit. Her striking blonde hair was down this time though and it fluttered gently in the breeze as she walked.

"Be still thy heart's desire," said Ryan softly to himself.

He and Brad walked over to greet them just as Plaatu emerged from the trees. She shook hands with Ryan, then Brad and Plaatu.

"I trust you all slept well?" she asked timidly, trying not to return Ryan's unyielding gaze.

"Very well, thank you,' answered Plaatu, completely oblivious to the dynamics of the moment.

In a completely business-like manner, she then began the introductions. It was clear that Ryan's infatuation would, at least for the moment, remain unrequited.

Accompanying her were the two other congressional members from the previous day, Stevens and Hall. She had also invited Dr. Stan Fitch from the Environmental Protection Agency. Next to her was Dr. Kristine Goudy from the Food and Drug Administration. She had to include law enforcement and national security so John Foley, who was the district chief for the FBI accompanied them. Joseph Kerrins was sent to serve as Secret Service representative and finally Steven Manning was with them from the State Department. He was there to personally represent the president and would report immediately to the White House once the demonstrations were concluded.

"I hope you don't mind," she said, directing her comments to Plaatu, "but I tried to get a cross section of the various agencies that will have to be involved in anything we decide to do after you finish here today. I'm sure you would have likewise invited members of law enforcement if you were in my shoes and someone approached you claiming they were from another world."

Plaatu just smiled. He wasn't the least bit taken back by the presence of Kerrins and Foley. Humans were a very suspicious species and he would have been surprised if they had acted any differently.

"No offense taken," said Plaatu. "Why don't we begin, shall we?"

Plaatu directed the group down to the water's edge. As they lined up so that they could all see him clearly, Plaatu addressed them as a teacher would address a group of students on a field trip.

"My purpose here today is to convince you all, on a very small scale mind you, to some of the benefits of accepting membership in the Coalition. My hope is that if you leave here sufficiently convinced, you will grant me an audience with the leading representatives of the world. My message is not for a few, but for everyone on your planet."

Brad and Ryan were content to stand a few feet behind the others. They would never admit it openly but they did feel just a bit intimidated in the company of such high-ranking officials. It didn't take long for Ms. Randell to glance back over her shoulder to catch Ryan staring down at her ass. He was so engrossed he didn't even realize he had been caught red-handed until Brad nudged him in the ribs. Randell just turned her head forward and smiled wryly.

Plaatu removed a vile from his case and held it up in front of the gathering.

"Your planet is experiencing potential catastrophic issues," he continued. "You have already begun discussing them in public forums. Global warming, pollution, viral outbreaks for which you have no cures, overpopulation. Unfortunately, while you continue to debate the issues, my readings indicate that some of these problems are already past the point where humanity can deal with them effectively utilizing your current technology. I intend to show you just a few of the advancements that could benefit your planet through shared technologies with other members of the Coalition."

Plaatu kneeled down and filled a beaker with pond water.

"If you look closely at the body of water before you, you will notice that it is impossible to see the bottom even where the water is only a foot deep. This is indicative of high concentrations of harmful bacteria that can adversely affect not only the life forms that exist in the pond, but any life forms that come in contact with it. Humans swimming for example or birds in search of food."

He poured the beaker of contaminated water onto the beach. Then he removed another from his case containing one of the agents he had brought with him. He lifted the cap and emptied its entire contents into the pond.

"This anti-bacterial solution could virtually purify all the drinking water for your entire planet. Not only will it purify the water, it will stimulate growth resulting in greater numbers of healthy fish and other sources of food."

"How does it work?" asked Dr. Goudy with mild curiosity.

"It is a remarkable substance called Zadon," answered Plaatu. "It is both a catalyst and a replicant. Once the correct combination of target bacterial agents are formulated and identified, this compound can be designed to attack and convert only those harmful agents which are then turned upon other unhealthy hosts until the entire body of water is completely free of all harmful elements. In just a few short moments, this body of water should turn from its current distressful state to crystal clear liquid. You will actually be able to see the bottom no matter where you are standing or how deep the water might be."

As the others continued to gaze out over the pond, there appeared to be no change at all.

"How long did you say it would take?" asked Dr. Goudy? Her tone was dripping in skepticism which she was clearly making no attempt to conceal.

Then the water turned a darker shade of black and something popped to the surface and was floating about 20 feet out from the shoreline. It was a large, apparently quite dead, fresh-water trout.

"They stock this pond, did you know that?" asked Brad who was now standing at the far end of the group.

"Every once in a while you get one or two that were probably a bit sickly to begin with," added Ryan. They were vainly trying to break the tension but another fish floated to the surface and just bobbed atop the water in a lifeless state. Then another and another until petrified fish dotted the surface of the entire pond.

"Is that supposed to happen?" asked Brad nervously.

"Ickeymay," muttered Ryan in Brad's direction. It was a word they both used to describe any event that was not going as planned.

Plaatu just stared out over the water looking completely dumbfounded. The pond water was so dark it was beginning to take on the appearance of crude oil. It was as if the chemical reaction that was supposed to take place was being completely reversed. Instead of attacking the harmful bacteria, it appeared to be stimulating it and causing the pollution levels to increase.

Congresswoman Randell turned to Ryan with a look of alarm.

"Are you sure about this guy?" she whispered in a very harsh tone.

Ryan just shrugged. He had seen the vile of nasty orange water turn crystal clear. Maybe it just wasn't strong enough to handle the whole pond. Then again, maybe Plaatu just wasn't a very good chemist.

"I don't understand it," Plaatu muttered to himself. "The test worked perfectly. There is no reason for this to be happening."

"Well, you did accomplish one thing here today Mr. Plaatu," said Dr. Fitch of the EPA caustically. "You have just given my agency another toxic site to clean up." Fitch turned to walk towards the van. "I've seen enough," he added in disgust.

Ms. Randell rushed to stop him. It was time for damage control and that task fell to her.

"Wait Dr. Fitch," she implored. "Let's not be so hasty." She turned back towards Plaatu and the others. "Perhaps the process just takes a long time with this pond. It was pretty nasty to begin with. What else did you want to show us?"

She was barely holding things together at this point and Ryan could sense her distress. It wasn't her fault of course, by now the pond was giving off the appearance of something out of the Paleolithic Era. This must have been what the tar pits looked like he thought to himself. His congressional contact needed some help and the other two House members didn't appear to be willing to come to her aid. Typical politicians, he thought to himself. Never willing to stick their necks out for anything or anyone.

"Hey everybody," he said in a loud voice, "Let's not be so quick to rush to judgment. Plaatu has come a long way to talk to us, how about giving him the benefit of the doubt? There is more at stake here than you know."

"Like what?" said Kerrins? He had been standing back with that typical law-enforcement type; you're guilty until proven innocent look on his face since he got there. Ryan would have liked to walk right over and wipe that smug look off his face with a right hook. But that would have only made matters worse. Instead, he disregarded his remark which he hoped would tick him off even more.

"We have other places to visit," said Ryan. "Why don't we proceed to our next destination and give Plaatu a second chance. He deserves that, at the very least."

It was as if the proverbial Sword of Damocles hung over the entire delegation and Brad really felt badly for Plaatu. This really hadn't gone according to plan.

"Let's just pack up and head over to the research facility," he said trying to spur them on. "I'm sure things will go much better there. This pond should have been condemned anyway."

"Please," said Ms. Randell again. "We really should hear him out. Let's get back in the van and see this through."

The seven others in her party began walking towards the van where the driver was waiting inside. As they all got in, Ryan and Brad walked over to where Plaatu was still staring out over the pond.

"Jesus," said Brad, "what the hell happened?"

"If you were trying to convince us not to go swimming here again," added Ryan, "you did one hell of a job."

"Something is not right here," said Plaatu in an angry deliberate tone. "There is absolutely no scientific explanation for what just happened. I performed the test, you both saw it. There is some devilry at work here and I am going to find out what it is."

"Well," said Ryan, "let's come back and explore that later. I hope your next trick is a bit more convincing or this show is going to have a very short run."

Plaatu packed up his case and the three men headed for the SUV. Ms. Randell was standing near the drivers' door and took Ryan aside.

"They reluctantly agreed to see one more demonstration," she said softly. "But this better be convincing. I still haven't been able to win their confidence in regards to his claims to be from another planet. If he wants a bigger audience, he had better have one hell of a trick up his sleeve. Either that or I hope he is planning to land his space ship on the White House lawn again."

"Look," said Ryan, "I'm sorry I've put you in an awkward position. But this guy is genuine, you have to trust me. Meet us at the facility and keep your fingers crossed." He turned to leave, then he pivoted back towards her. "Oh, about that other thing," he said, a bit flushed, "I hope you didn't think I was staring at . . ."

"Forget it," she snapped, cutting him off abruptly. "Just make sure this next display doesn't end in disaster the way this one did or it will be the last ass you ever stare at!" She turned sharply and walked towards the van.

"Woof!" remarked Brad. "That wasn't very romantic now was it?"

"Up yours," snapped Ryan as he, Brad and a very puzzled looking Plaatu returned to the SUV.

The two vehicles pulled up the access road and away from the pond leaving behind a lot of very unhappy fish.

Ms. Randell had called ahead to the research facility to inform the director that they would be stopping by. Nitco Inc. was already under contract with the United States government for a number of projects so they were accustomed to occasional visits from government representatives.

Upon their arrival, a young researcher by the name of Theresa led them to one of the laboratories where Plaatu could have access to a variety of lab specimens. He had been grumbling during the entire fifteen minute ride to the lab. After the 'pond massacre', Ryan wasn't sure if he was going to be able to regain his focus and pull this off.

As they walked into the laboratory, there were a number of open work stations for Plaatu to choose from. The workers had been instructed to toil elsewhere throughout the facility for the period during which they congressional team would be present.

Plaatu put his case down on a metal table at the nearest work station. He glanced around the room at the wide range of research equipment on display, most of which appeared to be very primitive in nature, at least by his standards. Then he gazed up at the bright fluorescent lights and for a moment had second thoughts about pursuing his present course of action. His mind was still reeling with confusion after the failure of his first demonstration. "Am I jinxed all of a sudden?" he thought to himself. He simply had to regain his composure. There was far too much at stake here. He asked Theresa to bring him a cancer-stricken specimen for his experiment. He informed her that the more infected the specimen the better.

As the group gathered round the work station, Brad and Ryan stood back and tried to gauge their moods. A slight hint of formaldehyde hung in the air. The three members of congress as well as the two doctors in the group and the state department representative seemed willing to give him this second chance. FBI agent Foley looked a bit more dubious but of the entire group, Kerrins really stood out. He had a smirk on his face, as if he was harboring some strange underlying animosity towards something or someone. Ryan couldn't put his finger on it but this guy gave him the creeps.

Theresa returned with a small plastic case containing a medium sized white mouse. It scurried to and fro inside the case like a possessed ear muff. It was frantically looking for a way out, no doubt painfully aware from previous observations that when any of his relatives were carried off by a human in a white coat, they didn't come back.

She set the mouse down on the table and waited for further instructions. Brad thought she really looked very petite and irresistibly attractive in her lily white lab coat and long flowing jet black hair. He felt a tinge of lust rush over him as he watched her assume a posture that sent a very clear signal that she was fully prepared to do whatever she was asked. She noticed his gaze and smiled at him tersely but her eyes were like daggers so he averted his stare. "Standoff-ish huh? What a shame," he thought to himself. "I bet she'd be a knock out in one of those little French maid outfits."

Plaatu gathered his wits and prepared to perform his second demonstration.

"Ladies and gentlemen," he said in a far more reserved tone than he had displayed when the day began, "it is common knowledge that cancer will claim millions of human lives in the decades ahead. Your best attempts to find a cure for this scourge have failed. The Coalition can offer you cures for many such illnesses, something that will enhance the quality of life on your planet immeasurably. Would you mind assisting me?" Plaatu asked Theresa.

"Of course I won't mind," she answered politely. "What would you like me to do?"

Brad sighed imperceptibly.

"Now who's the pig?" whispered Ryan. He had an uncanny ability to read Brad's mind, perverse as it could sometimes be during moments like this.

Plaatu loathed rodents and there was no way he was going to actually touch one of these things if he could help it.

"I assume you have tested this little creature and have established it is heavily infected by cancer cells?" he asked.

"Oh yes," answered Theresa. "I can say with complete confidence that this mouse is in the last stage of cancer development."

Plaatu removed a vile from his case, then handed it to Theresa.

"Would you mind administering a dose of this serum for me please?" he asked politely. Ryan couldn't be sure but he could have sworn he saw Plaatu's hand shaking ever so slightly. His stomach muscles tightened with the realization that Plaatu was not brimming with confidence and his lack thereof was becoming contagious.

Theresa picked up a syringe and pierced the top of the vile Plaatu had handed her. She withdrew a small amount of the serum, then reached in with her gloved hand and deftly grabbed the mouse around his mid-section.

"Is there any way you could use an eye-dropper to deliver the serum orally to the specimen?" asked Plaatu. While he may have loathed rodents, needles made him downright squeamish.

"Of course," she responded. She put the mouse back in the case and closed the lid. The mouse scrambled about even more frantically than before. Brad feared the little guy's heart would give out from a panic attack causing Demonstration Part Deux to go down in a ball of flames just like the first. Theresa prepared a dropper she picked up from a small rack of laboratory instruments and filled it with the serum. With a bit more difficulty this time, she again clutched the mouse and began squeezing drops of the liquid into the rodent's mouth. It struggled fiercely to resist but she was very experienced at this and eventually, it reluctantly ingested the serum, then she placed the mouse back in the clear container and closed the lid to prevent him from climbing out.

"This will only take a few moments," said Plaatu. "This particular serum enters the blood stream quickly and immediately begins attacking the cancer cells. It is so remarkably effective, we have actually cured members of certain species who were in the very last stages of demise."

Ryan and Brad weren't paying any attention to Plaatu. Their gazes were fixed directly on the table and the little mouse that was running around the cage as if someone had just lit its tail on fire.

"I don't think he likes it," whispered Brad.

"Do you have an inexhaustible supply of these serums?" asked Ms. Randell trying to keep the atmosphere upbeat and of a positive nature.

"Absolutely," answered Plaatu. "More importantly, our medical leaders can work with you and instruct your people in how to prepare the serums at your existing facilities like this one." Plaatu casually glanced around the room. "You would need a few updates to your current level of technology however," he added, trying not to sound overly elitist.

Plaatu looked down at the case and the mouse had stopped his frantic movements.

"It is time to see how effective the serum is," he announced. "I think he is ready to be tested."

Theresa once again removed the mouse from the case but she had no problem corralling him this time.

As she lifted him into the air, her expression remained completely unemotional. "Ready to be tested did you say?" she muttered to Plaatu. "I think he's ready for the morgue. This little guy is dead as a doorknob."

"What!" exclaimed Plaatu. "Why, that's impossible!"

There was stunned silence throughout the room. Brad turned to Ryan and whispered softly, "Can you spell Ickeymay? Or better yet, exit stage left?"

Plaatu slammed the cover to his case and seemed on the verge of a meltdown. Dr. Fitch from the EPA and Ms. Goudy from the FDA were the two standing closest to him. The sound of his case slamming shut startled them to the point where they began to back away.

"It's OK," said Ms. Randell. "Perhaps he was just too far gone for the serum to work." Her attempts to minimize the damage were completely futile. The looks on the faces of the other observers said it all. For Plaatu, it was clear that they were not going to allow him a third strike before calling him out. Two misses were quite enough for these umpires.

Kerrins stepped forward and confronted Plaatu.

"I'm sorry Ms. Randell," Kerrins said in an authoritative tone. "I have instructions from my superiors to take this individual into custody in the event his credibility is called into question. I'd say what I've seen so far would classify as discreditable."

"What do you mean, you're taking me into custody?' protested Plaatu. Three more men in suits walked menacingly into the room and moved towards him. Brad and Ryan rushed towards them to block their path.

"Hey! Wait a minute!" said Brad in a loud voice. "No one is taking anybody into custody. This man has done nothing wrong."

One of the three men grabbed Brad by the arm and forcibly moved him out of the way.

"Stand aside everyone," the man ordered. He reeked of Old Spice which assailed Brad's nostrils almost to the point of nausea.

Brad violently tore away from his grip and stood his ground. He looked ready to bring this confrontation to the next level but Ryan pulled him back knowing nothing constructive would come from an all out free for all.

"I wasn't told about this," said Agent Foley. He stepped forward in an apparent attempt to assume command.

Neither was I," added State Department representative manning. "On whose authority are you taking this action?"

"On the authority of CIA Director Miles," said Kerrins. "Now, come with me Mr. Plaatu," he demanded.

Plaatu glared at Ryan and Brad with a look in his eyes as if he had just been handed over to the Romans.

"Where are you taking him," asked Ryan firmly. "We have a right to know."

"We're taking him to CIA headquarters in Virginia," Kerrins said defiantly and the four men led Plaatu out of the room.

Brad and Ryan approached the others who were standing around looking every bit as dumbfounded as they felt.

"Did you know anything about this?" Ryan asked Ms. Randell in an angry tone. The fire in his eyes and the level of intensity in his voice took her off guard. She hadn't been convinced after the failure of both experiments that Plaatu was in fact who he claimed to be but there was no doubt from the look in Ryan's eyes that he believed in him unequivocally.

Congressman Stevens stepped in to defend Randell from what he perceived to be an unfair attack. "Hold on there Mister," he demanded, "If it wasn't for her, we wouldn't even be here."

"No, it's alright," she said looking Ryan straight in the eyes. "I would never do anything as deceitful as this. I will look into this and trust me, I'll get to the bottom of it. We kept a very tight lid on this right up until the moment we met you at the pond. The CIA is the last group I would want to see involved in anything."

They were approached by Agent Foley.

"I'll see what I can find out," he said reassuringly. "I realized things didn't go as planned and I'm still not convinced of his authenticity, but there was no need to go off the deep end like that. It's not as if the guy came off as being a threat to national security for chrisakes." He turned to Randell. "What do you know about this Kerrins guy?" he asked her. "I never met him before today."

Randell thought about it for a moment. For that matter, neither had she. She brought Manning into the conversation. Being from the State Department, he surely would know something about him.

"I never met the guy," said Manning. "I just placed a call to the head of the Secret Service to send an agent and assumed Kerrins to be the person they assigned to the job."

"You're all kidding me, right?" asked Brad. "What kind of operation are you people running here? Don't you screen people anymore?

Theresa was quietly conversing with Congresswoman Hall as well as the two doctors. Their level of alarm seemed a bit less heightened and at one point Theresa glanced down at her watch as if out of concern she might miss lunch. Ryan turned back to Ms. Randell. She genuinely appeared to regret how the situation had digressed so badly so he softened his tone. "Please keep me apprised of what is going on," he asked. "I would really appreciate it."

"Don't worry," she answered, "We won't let anything happen to him."

The government delegation left the lab leaving Ryan, Brad, Theresa and a lifeless mouse to ponder the situation although the mouse probably wasn't doing all that much in the way of pondering anything.

"Are you sure he is dead?" asked Brad.

Theresa lifted him slightly off the table, and then dropped him. He landed with a thud. He didn't move.

"He's as dead as he's ever going to be," she announced. "Sorry. I wish I could tell you otherwise."

"Well, can you do an autopsy or something?" asked Ryan.

"You want us to do an autopsy on a dead mouse?" she said, noticeably bewildered.

"Well how else are you going to know what killed him?" said Brad impatiently.

"He was full of energy, then I gave him some drops," she said sharply. "Now he is dead. That should give you some hint."

"Look," implored Ryan, "humor me OK. Do some tests or whatever you people do and just see if it was definitely the serum that killed him. Can you at least do that?"

She sighed heavily as if she was being asked to perform the seven trials of Hercules.

"We'll bring you some fresh fish for your efforts?" said Brad. "Do you like fresh water trout? We know where you can get a whole slew of them not too far from here."

"No, I hate fish," she said. "But I will see if I can figure out if that stuff he gave him had anything to do with what happened."

"Thanks," said Ryan. "I owe you one."

He and Brad started walking towards the door. Brad stopped in his tracks, then he turned and retrieved Plaatu's case which had been overlooked in the confusion.

"Do you think we should just blow Plaatu's cover and lead them to his ship?" asked Brad. "That will convince them that he is telling the truth."

"Not unless he wants us to," said Ryan as they exited the lab. "I already feel like we let him down, I don't want to compound the issue by giving up his ship to the military unless he feels it's the right time. For now, let's head back to my place and give Mikey and the others a heads up."

"I wish you hadn't stopped me from popping that guy," said Brad as they descended the stairs. "Smug, smelly son of a bitch he was."

"He was a big smug son of a bitch too," quipped Ryan. "In case you didn't notice. How do you know he wouldn't whip your ass?"

"One never knows does one," said Brad. "That's what makes your average every day confrontation so intriguing. No one knows who is going to come out victorious until it is over."

"Well don't be too disappointed," said Ryan. "You still might get your chance. Something tells me this is far from over. Something smells awful fishy here and I don't mean Frog Pond."

They exited the building and headed for the car.

CHAPTER SIX

When congresswoman Randell returned to her office in Hartford, there was so much unopened mail on her desk she thought she had become an annex of the United States Postal Service. The in box was overflowing and there was a large bag of unopened mail sitting next to her credenza on the floor.

"What is all this?" she asked her executive aide in alarm.

Philip Agnetta could only shrug his shoulders. He had been traveling back and forth to New York during the past few days so the responsibility of monitoring incoming mail was not his bag. Junior staff members were familiar with the policy of sorting, classifying, and opening pertinent mail so that it didn't pile up. What often sounds great in theory doesn't always pan out in practice however. Someone was shirking their responsibilities and he was determined to find out who it was.

"Didn't you hire a new girl last week to help with the mail?" Randell asked as she continued to fill a sack with various sized envelopes.

"Yes, we did," answered Agnetta innocently. "Trained her good too."

Randell handed the heavy bag to him and said, "Well, tell her to put her talents to use and begin going through this stuff. That should keep her busy for a few months."

Agnetta struggled under the weight of the bag, then hoisted it onto his shoulder and carried it out of the room.

"Now I know how Santa Claus must feel," he said under his breath as he closed the door behind him.

Ms. Randell took a seat behind her desk and pushed a button on her intercom system to contact her secretary in an outer office.

"Yes, Ms. Randell?" she heard her secretary say.

"Could you get me General Carl Koopman of the Joint Chiefs of Staff Please," Randell asked.

"Right away ma'am," came the response.

It was time to call in a favor. She had contacted the General's office the previous day and asked them to conduct a thorough search of the White Mountains in the hope that they could locate Plaatu's ship and prove beyond any shadow of a doubt as to his authenticity. Randell had gone to bat for Koopman the previous year when congress was debating whether or not to severely reprimand him over what came to be known as the "Island Affair." As a newly-appointed member of the Armed Services Committee, Randell had lobbied hard on his behalf and had virtually saved his ass in the process. Confidence in Koopman's abilities was on the wane after the botched policing operation on the island of Guam in the South Pacific.

The incident had a strangely familiar ring to it. Some students had put in a desperate call to the US Embassy that they were being held hostage by hostile terrorists. The navy and marines, under Koopman's orders, had dispatched three destroyers and seven smaller support vessels to rescue the students in a "Granada-like" mission . . . The ships remained in the area for two weeks during "negotiation" sessions when it was discovered that the call for help was nothing more than a hoax. The large contingent of military personnel enjoyed a rather nice vacation in Guam at the taxpayer's expense.

One of the smaller support ships, the frigate USS Sheridan had been stolen and was still reported as missing in action. No sailors were aboard at the time claiming they were all performing "undercover" anti-terrorist surveillance work at a nearby resort. The incident was a colossal embarrassment to the highly-vaunted United States military.

Agnetta returned in a few moments. He was generally accepted by Randell and her office staff as reasonably competent but he was still a bit of a dweeb. She had no choice in hiring him. His father Matthew was the CEO of Mellon Bank, one of her biggest campaign contributors. Agnetta had his share of detractors who privately referred to him as Mellon head but it could have been worse. His uncle Joe was a district manager for the A. B. Dick Company.

"Many of those envelopes I just carried out of here have checks in them," he reported matter-of-factly.

Randell stared at him for a few moments with a blank look on her face.

"And these checks are made out to . . . are you going to tell me?" she said impatiently.

"UNICEF, of course," he said with a smile. "It looks like you got one hell of a response from that 'feed the world' campaign you launched last month." He stood there fidgeting with his tie, quite pleased with himself. Agnetta knew no boundaries when it came to modesty and style. He went out of his way to find the most outlandish ties he could find and proudly wore a different one to work every day. This morning's number featured likenesses of Moe, Larry and Curly in their classic golfing outfits.

Randell sat back in her chair and smiled. "Well what do you know? There are some good people left out there after all. You just have to know where to find them I guess and that's not always easy."

The intercom indicator beeped. She depressed the answer button.

"Yes?" she said.

"General Koopman on line one," she heard her secretary say.

"Thank you," answered Randell. She glanced up at Agnetta. "See that those checks get to the proper destination, would you Philip? Oh, and call Langley and check on the well-being of our Mr. Plaatu also. I want to make sure he is alright."

"Sure thing," he responded and he turned and left the room.

Randell pushed line one. "I certainly wouldn't want to keep the good General waiting," she thought to herself.

"Carl," she began, "how did you make out?"

Koopman had a commanding voice but his tone could sometimes be mistaken as aloof or merely disinterested. Randell had gotten used to it during her previous encounters with him but some people really just plain didn't like him, perceiving his demeanor as one of pure arrogance.

"Well," he said, "we found your ship for you. A helicopter spotted it during a fly-over at about nine this morning."

"You have absolute confirmation that there is a space ship, not of this planet, on the ground in the woods up there?" she asked excitedly. Something within her was still having difficulty accepting the fact that she was personally involved in what could very well be the first recorded incident of contact with life from another world. She almost felt as if she was having an out-of-body experience. Things like this just don't happen everyday. She remained completely oblivious to the fact that prior to her being born, Plaatu had already made first contact. Distorting the true and accurate details of that visit to the world was no easy task for the United States government. He had in fact landed on US soil so like it or not, it was their job to manufacturer the biggest lie the world had ever been collectively fed. It required an enormously large spoon. He had after all, stopped every electrical impulse on the planet for a solid half hour but the UN merely explained it away as the result of never-before-seen levels of solar activity. The sun is without question the go-to object whenever government officials can't explain something. Due to its enormous size, makeup and constantly fluctuating nature, it has served as the perfect scapegoat throughout human history for explaining away forces that we simply lack the intelligence to understand. It was a testament to the incredible naiveté of the masses. There were to be sure, small pockets of hardcore diehards who refused to accept the UN's spiel, but they had over time been written off as "conspiracy theorists'.

During the 1960's the clamor over whether or not unidentified flying objects had visited Earth grew to such an uproar, the government was forced to launch an investigation in an attempt to calm public hysteria. The result was the infamous "Project Blue Book", an investigation undertaken by the United States Air Force. Hundreds of sightings and reports were investigated and carefully examined in an effort to answer once and for all, the public's unyielding curiosity over the existence of UFO's. The final conclusion, according to the Air Force was that there simply was no concrete evidence that UFO's existed. Then they closed the book on the subject.

"We have concrete confirmation that a craft was sighted," answered the General. "I never said where it came from. It's just sitting there on the ground. It doesn't look like it is in a hurry to go anywhere. As a matter of fact, we think it is abandoned but I wouldn't try to move it. It's pretty big and we would have to clear a large section of trees. That's National Forest up there and the environmental wing nuts would go bonkers."

"I don't want to move it," said Randell. "But I would like you to send a small contingent of military personnel to guard it. Do it quietly, under the cover of darkness. I do not want to instigate a media circus up there."

"No offense here congresswoman Randell," said Koopman, "but we're spread pretty thin right now with this Iraq and Afghanistan thing. I suppose we could send a small contingent of the National Guard to keep an eye on it."

"If that is all you can spare that will have to do," she said, "but please keep it quiet for the time being."

"No problem, we've got you covered. I'll get back to you once the units are in place."

She heard the phone click from his end, terminating the conversation. "What an odd duck?!" she thought to herself. He has just received word that a space ship has landed on Earth and he acts like it's just another day at the office.

"What are these military leaders smoking nowadays?" she muttered to herself in amazement.

Agnetta burst back into the room. He looked uncharacteristically riled up.

"Langley doesn't know anything about this Plaatu guy," he blurted. "They never heard of him and don't know what we're talking about."

"This is getting weirder by the minute," she muttered to herself. She picked up a pitcher of water and began walking around her spacious office to see to her assortment of plants. Agnetta knew that the only time she did this was when she was totally befuddled. It was a deliberate act to distract anyone else who may have been standing in the room from the fact that she had absolutely no clue what the hell was happening. She was a very sensitive woman. She detested 'dumb blonde' jokes and took them very personally. She was driven by an intense sense of pride that demanded that she give every appearance, at all times, that she was in complete control, even during moments like this when she was in fact baffled beyond clueless.

"Was this all a whacked out Hollywood publicity stunt?" she thought to herself. "Dead fish, dead mice, secretive secret service agents, a man claiming to be an alien? And what about this Kerrins character? She had never met him prior to today but her office had received clearance from one of his superiors at the White House. This was getting to be a bigger problem than she had been accustomed to dealing with. It was time to call in the cavalry. She needed more resources at her disposal to find out what the hell was going on. Could the campers be involved in this deception? "If this all turns out to be a lavish prank, I will hang them by their testicles," she thought to herself. Agnetta watched quietly as a sadistic grin formed on her face.

"Philip," she said finally. "I want you to set up a meeting with the Secretary of Defense and his entire staff. See if they can make it this afternoon. Tell them to be prepared for something that is literally out of this world."

"Yes ma'am," he answered.

Randell picked up the phone to dial Ryan. It was time for him to come clean.

Plaatu had been whisked away in a black Lincoln continental. As he was forced into the back seat of the car, the foolishness of his approach to this entire mission hit him like a blast from a plasma pistol. What made him think he could soft-shoe his way into putting himself in a position where he could address humanity en-masse? Appeasement had rarely worked for him in the past in similar situations, what made him think a dignified, intelligent, considerate approach would work with a species as notoriously irrational as humans?

He cursed himself for coming on this mission without Bort. He cursed himself for leaving his ship unarmed and for putting his life in the hands of total strangers. More than anything he cursed himself for returning to this planet which had caused him so much grief the first time he had visited here. Life is like walking down the streets of a city, he once read. Some streets turn out to be relatively pleasant. They might have quaint little shops and inviting places to grab a leisurely bite to eat. Then there are other kinds of streets where muggers lurk and one could easily end up being the victim of an ass whooping. Those are the kinds of streets you don't want to go down again.

There were four armed men in the car, one on each side of him in the back seat, the driver and Kerrins was in the front passenger seat giving the orders. Escape would be a tricky assignment under the circumstances. The two men sitting on each side of Plaatu were much younger, much bigger and he could only presume, much stronger than he was. There was a plexi-glass petition separating the driver's compartment from the rear seat. It was partially open in the center. His mind swooned with confusing thoughts and if there was anything Plaatu didn't like, it was a prevailing lack of clarity.

"Why hadn't the experiments worked?" he kept asking himself. "There was absolutely no reason for them not to."

He was very familiar with the chemical agents he had used and he had seen them perform effectively countless times before. It was simply outside the scope of known physics for them not to function along normal parameters.

Those were issues that had to wait. Right now he needed to focus on the predicament at hand. Once they had left the facility, the car headed in a north by northwest direction. Upstate New York, Plaatu guessed.

He watched as Kerrins leaned over and said something to the driver but he couldn't hear it through the petition.

"I thought we were going to Virginia?" Plaatu asked. He continued to watch Kerrins closely. He seemed unusually tense for someone in his position.

"We are," answered Kerrins. "We're just taking a route around New York city to evade traffic."

"This is pretty far out of the way," remarked the man to Plaatu's immediate right. "It's the middle of the day and traffic isn't usually that heavy."

The man's cologne was overpowering. As Plaatu sat there breathing in the unpleasantness of his situation, the mosaic that was increasingly taking shape in his mind with the word 'retirement' stamped on it seemed more and more appealing.

"Excuse me," said the man to Plaatu's right, "Did you hear what I said? This is going to take us far out of the way and it is not necessary."

Kerrins turned and glared at the man through the glass. It was an ugly glare, a nasty menacing glare, one that said quite clearly that if you open your mouth again I'll rip your eyes out. It silenced the man immediately as Kerrins did, in fact outrank him.

"Have you guys worked together before?" asked Plaatu, still sensing a general lack of cohesiveness from the four men.

"Agent Daniels, agent Crawford and I have worked together," answered the man to Plaatu's left. "But I never worked with this hot head before," he added softly, motioning towards Kerrins.

Plaatu noticed that the driver was perspiring heavily. It wasn't as if it was particularly hot inside the vehicle. He discreetly leaned forward and glanced over the seat, trying not to attract Kerrin's attention. Kerrins was holding a weapon that was aimed at the driver's rib cage. The weapon was clearly not of this Earth. Plaatu's entire body tensed with alarm.

"Not exactly secret service issue," Plaatu said to Kerrins as he leaned back in his seat.

Kerrins now focused his menacing glare on Plaatu. "Very observant," he snarled.

The car was traveling on a long wooded road and Kerrins glanced in both directions to scan for any witnesses.

"Pull over right here," he ordered the driver. The car pulled onto the soft shoulder of the road and stopped.

"Get out!" Kerrins barked at the two men in the back seat on either side of Plaatu. He was now pointing the odd looking pistol in their direction.

"What the hell is going on here?" said the man to Plaatu's left.

"I said get out!" Kerrins snarled. "Don't make me repeat myself."

The two men opened their doors and stepped out of the car. Kerrins turned back towards the driver as the two men slammed the rear doors shut.

"Now drive," he said. "I'll tell you where to go."

As the car began its forward motion again, Kerrins leaned out the window and with remarkable speed and accuracy, fired an energy blast at both agents, striking each of them squarely in the chest. They both dropped to the ground like limp rag dolls.

"They're just stunned," said Kerrins. "I don't want them giving our position away."

Plaatu feared that they were not 'just stunned'. The fog began to clear in Plaatu's head. How could he have been so easily fooled?

"That's a Tilatin sidearm if I'm not mistaken," he said. "And I can only assume you are in fact a Tilatin surgically altered to appear human."

"Very good Mr. Plaatu," said Kerrins. "Not that it matters."

"What's a Tilatin?" asked the driver nervously. He wanted no part of this. He had only recently been appointed to field duty and was still considerably 'wet behind the ears'. He had never been called upon to fire his sidearm in the line of duty and was not yet sufficiently hardened nor seasoned enough to handle a situation like this.

"Just keep both hands on the wheel and you'll survive this journey," said Kerrins. "I would have dropped you at the side of the road with the other two if I knew how to drive one of these things."

"So you sabotaged my demonstrations, didn't you?" asked Plaatu.

"Maybe," said Kerrins, purposely intending to be evasive. It was clear that the Tilatin was a bit on edge. The gravity of his situation, having already abducted a member of the CIPF was obviously weighing heavily on his diminutive mind.

Plaatu's confidence was returning now that he was at least certain of what he was dealing with. His mind had been so preoccupied with the failure of his demonstration efforts that he momentarily lost touch with who he was. He wasn't a chemist, nor was he a professional diplomat. He was a member of law enforcement and it was time to start acting like one once again.

"I don't think I have to remind you of the consequences of interfering with a member of the CIPF?" Plaatu said. Then again he thought, he wouldn't find himself in this situation in the first place if he hadn't been so careless. It was just another vivid example of the fact that he was slipping. Call it age, call it burn out, call it whatever, but he was definitely not as sharp as he once was. The reality of that unpleasant truth continued to gnaw at his conscience like a ravenous beast.

"I'm not worried about that," said Kerrins. "No one is ever going to know about any interference."

"You have other plans then?" probed Plaatu. He had dealt with Tilatins before and knew from experience they loved to talk about their schemes, even when it meant they were tipping their hand. It would be an understatement to suggest that they were not the brightest stars in the intellectual galaxy.

"We need this planet," said Kerrins. "We need it badly, and we will take it how ever we can. Humans are merely turning it into a celestial cesspool anyway so we are going to take it while it is still livable."

"You mean the way you turned Tilatin into a cesspool?" asked Plaatu.

Kerrins just scowled at him. Tilatin was in fact, on the verge of becoming the most noxious floating rock in the galaxy due to a number of environmental offenses committed by its inhabitants.

"Spare me your holier-than-thou morality," said the Tilatin. "We bought our way into your high-minded Coalition with ease. We are all just predators out here you know. Oh sure, we put up facades, your Coalition being one example. We establish enforcement agencies, we mandate laws and proclamations but when you shake it all out, what tumbles to the ground is the inescapable truth that when we want something, we will do whatever it takes to get it. I've studied Earth history, perhaps not at length as you have, but I have learned two lasting lessons. They are every bit as predatory in nature as we Tilatins, a very commendable trait I might add. But this annoying tendency to relate everything in terms of Gods and deities is really quite humorous. Only this Darwin character seems to have stumbled on the true nature of life throughout the galaxy. The strong overcome the weak and that is the way it always has been and always will be. You just happened to be in the wrong place at the wrong time."

"What do you mean?" asked Plaatu.

"You're going to become a victim of this tragic affair that will come to be known as the Coalition's attempt to reach out to humanity which will end in total failure. Not wise of you to travel without your metallic sidekick eh? Our operatives informed us that Bort was not with you. You will have been shot dead by a human. We are going to incite a world war and once the humans destroy enough of one another, we will come in and mop up. Re-colonization, my friend. It's a wonderful loop-hole in the Coalition's highly touted rules and regulations. Very exploitable."

The driver noticed that Kerrins was not wearing a seat belt. The strange looking weapon was now resting in his lap as he had relaxed his guard while divulging this master plan of his to Plaatu. If he had any hope of regaining the upper hand, it was now or never.

The car was traveling at about 55 miles per hour. The two lane road was deserted as they had reached the mid-state section of New York, far from the more populated areas further south. He glanced in his rear view mirror to make sure no vehicles were directly behind him. Then he jammed his foot down onto the brake pedal. The car skidded for what seemed like an eternity to Plaatu as he was thrown forward into the back of the front seat. The Tilatin's head slammed off the windshield so hard it caused it to shatter. The car came to a stop in a ditch with the front of the vehicle listing to the right. The agent went to draw his gun from its shoulder holster but it was already too late. The Tilatin raised his weapon and fired. The energy blast struck him square in the right shoulder as he slumped forward onto the steering wheel.

Plaatu regained his balance and saw the man was unconscious and probably dead from the blast. Not many victims survived a direct hit from such a weapon.

"Poor fellow," he thought to himself. "I could have told him that the Tilatin's have the hardest heads in the galaxy. It is nearly impossible to incapacitate them by hitting them there."

"Insolent fool!" cursed the Tilatin. His head was bleeding slightly but it wouldn't for long. Their blood was like sludge and would coagulate in seconds, closing the wound.

"Now what?" asked Plaatu? His entire body ached after being thrown forward but fortunately he had struck the padded part of the seat which cushioned the blow.

The Tilatin was still seething. They were generally lazy creatures by nature and the thought of having to walk a great distance was probably causing him a good deal of angst.

"Get out damn you!" he hissed. "Fortunately, our ship is located not too far from here. We had no problem evading the primitive human tracking systems as you did."

Plaatu opened the door and stepped out as another car rolled to a stop back up on the road.

"Hey!" a man yelled down to them, "you guys OK down there? Want us to call for some help?"

The Tilatin climbed out with difficulty because of the bad pitch at which the vehicle had settled.

"No, we're fine!" said the Tilatin. "No need. Just go on your way."

The vehicle remained for a moment as if the driver wasn't sure what to do. Then it slowly began to roll forward again.

"Ok," said the man in the passenger seat. "Whatever you say."

The car drove off and was soon out of sight. They were headed in the direction of the two fallen agents and Plaatu hoped they would notice them and call for assistance. He only hoped they were still alive.

"So," said Plaatu. "You're going to kill me here and claim the human is responsible, is that it?"

"Not yet," said the Tilatin. "My commanding officer will want to speak with you first. You know us better than that. We always keep a trump card in reserve in case all else fails. Start walking. Through the woods that way."

Plaatu glanced back into the vehicle at the driver.

"What about him?" he asked. "At least let me see if he is still alive."

"Forget him," said the Tilatin. "He doesn't matter. Soon their will be many more just like him. I wouldn't be so concerned with one puny human if I were you."

"You Tilatins," said Plaatu in contempt. "You have so little respect for other life forms. Who did you bribe to gain entry into the Coalition? It must have taken a very large sum."

"I don't get involved in such matters," he answered. "I just do what I am told. Now move!"

Plaatu proceeded in the direction in which the Tilatin was motioning with his pistol. The woods were dense but not so much so as to impede his progress. This could work to his advantage. He needed to find out what they were up to on a larger scale and the only way to learn that was by speaking to this lower ranking Tilatin's superior officer. He could only hope that it was not already too late to stop them before they inflicted wide scale damage.

Brad and Ryan stopped on their way home to pick up some more coffee from their neighborhood coffee shop, "Dandy Dan's Coffee Emporium'. They were both coffee junkies of the highest order and blatantly ignored the recommendations of the surgeon general that all Americans cut down on their daily caffeine intake. Brad had remarked on more than one occasion that when he died, he wanted to be buried with a three pound bag of ground coffee beans, preferably Colombian Supreme. Donuts would be accepted as well. It even said so right in his will.

The teenage youths were back in greater numbers when Ryan's SUV pulled into the parking lot next to their apartment building. As he looked for an open spot to pull into, the juveniles noticed him and began heading towards the exit. Apparently he and Brad had left a lasting impression but they were still amazed at the audacity these youngsters displayed.

"Ballsy little bastards aren't they?" remarked Ryan as he threw the shifter into park and prepared to get out. He could have called the cops but they would take hours to get there for something as trivial as a vandalism complaint. How times had changed. When he was young, the neighborhood kids rarely engaged in anything more unlawful than playing football in the street. Every once in a while someone would bounce an errant pass off a nearby parked car. The police would be called by the irate owner and on one occasion, the men in blue drove a few of the older boys around the block in the back of a squad car under the guise that they were taking them off to jail. It scared the bajeezes out of them. While it may not have been sufficiently traumatizing enough to discourage them from going back and playing football in the street, it did have an unexpected side effect. It motivated them to work twice as hard on their passing accuracy so as not to hit any more parked cars.

This current generation was completely different. Playing football and hockey in the street had been replaced by video games and computers. High tech electronics cost big money and the only way these imaginative youngsters could afford their addictions to high priced toys was to steal whatever they could whenever they could.

"Whatever happened to respect for authority?" Ryan thought to himself.

The two men walked upstairs to Ryan's apartment and waited for the arrival of Mikey and the others. Ryan had called them earlier on his cell phone and suggested that they meet at his place to discuss the troubling new developments. Brad placed Plaatu's case on the kitchen table. He heard something softly beeping inside but when he went to open it, he realized that it had no latches. He examined it more closely and as he studied it from every angle, there didn't appear to be anything that was holding the top and bottom lids in place. No hinges, no latches, no outward sign of any means of entry whatsoever, just a built in handle for carrying purposes. "Damndest thing I've ever seen," he muttered, scratching his head.

"Try waving your hand over it somehow," said Ryan. "I could have sworn I saw Plaatu do that and the sucker opened right up for him."

Ryan heard a loud knocking at the door. It had a rhythmic quality to it, as if someone was trying to tap out the melody to a song. Only Chris knocked like that, he thought to himself. He opened the door and the other members of the now ill-fated camping trip were standing in the hallway.

"You lost him already didn't ya?" said Spike as the four men walked into the living room and sat down. As they settled into the plush velour padding of the couch and companion love seat, Brad came in from the kitchen with a tray of steaming cups of coffee. He set the tray down on the coffee table and began handing them to each of the men.

"I know you don't like yours too strong," said Brad as he handed a cup to Tommy. "So I took the liberty of watering yours down with a little paint thinner. I didn't think you would mind."

"Gee thanks," gushed Tommy. "You guys are swell to me."

"So what the hell happened this morning?" asked Mikey. "Can't we leave you two alone for five minutes without you screwing something up?"

Ryan was still pondering the events of the last forty eight hours. It was almost surreal and he kept hoping that someone would just pinch him and wake him up from this bizarre dream he found himself floating in. He conveyed what had transpired to the others but as he rehashed the strange events verbally, it didn't make it any easier to unravel the reasons why it had ended the way it did.

He continued to struggle with his thoughts. In previous years, the six men had embarked upon their annual camping outing under the same types of conditions. There was always a war going on somewhere, people were starving somewhere in the world in large numbers, the stock market rose and fell, it was all nothing more than the status quo of human affairs, no different than the annual spectacle of the leaves of the trees turning colors, then dropping lifeless to the ground. They were all cyclical occurrences that had been a constant throughout his life ever since the day he first became aware of his existence. He was not unmoved by human suffering, he just felt powerless to do anything about it beyond the relatively small boundaries of his personal life.

With human population levels now surpassing six billion, it only stood to reason that some were not going to have enough food to eat. Compounding the problem was the fact that the highest birth rates were occurring in areas that could least afford to sustain them. Amidst all the complex issues humanity had been grappling with for centuries, humans had always proceeded under the assumption that we are alone in the seemingly limitless vastness of space. In the span of just two days, that long accepted illusion had been completely shattered in the eyes of Ryan and his friends. They didn't discover this through the artificial, emotionally remote window of his television set. It had walked right up to him and tapped him on the shoulder. Plaatu wasn't just some flat two-dimensional image; Ryan couldn't just turn the channel and block it out of his mind hoping the government or the Red Cross would respond to yet another human dilemma. Fate had brought them together and like it or not, he had become embroiled in something unlike anything he had ever contended with before. It was quite literally beyond his imagination to think that something like this could happen to him and his friends while engaged in something as seemingly insignificant as an annual camping trip. What are the chances he kept asking over and over again in his mind?

"Now I know how Judas must have felt," said Brad remorsefully when Ryan had finished bringing the others up to date.

"Oh, come on!" barked Ryan in frustration. "We didn't cause this to happen. How the hell could we have known that his demonstrations wouldn't work? That was all his idea."

"He's in the hands of the government now," said Tommy. "It's out of our control. Once the CIA and FBI get involved, you don't think they're going to allow us any access to what is going on. We're just a bunch of pee-ons to them."

"That's *Mister* pee-on to you," snapped Chris.

"Well, I'm not going to just sit here and wash my hands of this," said Brad. "We have his case. I don't have a clue how to open it to see what is beeping inside but I say we go looking for him."

"Have you tried a hacksaw?" asked Mikey.

"No I didn't try a hacksaw," said Brad sharply. "How would that look? 'Here's your case back Plaatu. Hope you don't mind that we broke into it while you were away.' That would go over real big with him I'm sure."

"Besides," added Tommy. "I doubt a hacksaw would work if that case is made of the same metals his ship is."

The phone on the kitchen wall rang loudly.

"Is there a fire in the building?" shouted Chris.

"Stow it!" said Ryan as he rose to answer it.

"You had to see the look on Plaatu's face when everything started going wrong," said Brad remorsefully. "I really felt bad for the guy. There was nothing we could do though. As soon as those agents showed up, they just took right over."

The men sat quietly for a few moments immersed in introspective thought. A noticeable cloud of helplessness hung over them and was causing varying degrees of indigestion and consternation. Ryan's voice could be heard from the kitchen but they could not make out who he was talking with or the nature of the conversation.

When he returned to the living room the expression on his face was enough to indicate that it probably wasn't a call from the state lottery informing him he had just won a large sum of money. His eyes sharply darted from side to side as if he was looking for the answer to an unsolvable riddle. He began mumbling to himself. It sounded like he was arguing with an unseen entity in the room.

"What is it?" asked Brad finally.

Ryan was still groping for words, his face contorted in a mass of confusion and anger when he finally blurted, "What the hell is going on here?"

"Jesus man!" said Spike, "get a grip on yourself."

"That Kerrins guy may not have been who he claimed to be!" Ryan said finally, directing his comments at Brad. "That was Randell and she is really pissed at us. She thinks there is some skullduggery going on here."

"What's a skullduggery?" asked Tommy softly.

Ryan ignored him. "She thinks that we're part of it. She doesn't know where Plaatu is or who those guys were that took him. She did say the military had found his ship in the woods. Then I got pissed at her for accusing us of being involved in something shady and for searching for his ship behind our backs."

"What is skullduggery?" asked Tommy again. "Is that like buggery on the high seas cause if it is . . . ?"

Mikey stood up and assumed a posture of authority. They all knew that when he assumed this stance, whatever he said next was not to be trifled with, nor contradicted. It would be a complete waste of time. Mikey wrote the book on stubbornness and blind determination.

"I'm tired of sitting around asking questions," he said firmly. "We don't know where he is and the government doesn't know where he is either but we DO know where his ship is. I say we truck our asses up there and wait for him. He has to return there and if he can't, it is only safe to assume whoever he is connected to will show up there looking for him."

Mikey gazed around at their faces and waited for a response, fully expecting unanimous agreement.

"I don't agree," said Spike resolutely. "That won't accomplish anything."

"Why don't we contact thee news outlets?" asked Chris. "This is bigger than us; we're not used to dealing with events of this magnitude. I mean come on, who are we trying to kid?"

Brad stood up to claim the floor. "No, forget about it. The longer we can keep the news hounds from picking up his trail the better. They are nothing more than a nuisance and will only turn this into a three ring circus."

"Hold on one minute?" said Spike. He went into the kitchen and grabbed the case, then he returned to the living room and placed it on the coffee table. "Let's have one last crack at this thing." He banged on it from every angle. Then he picked it up and began shaking it violently to no avail. He dropped it on the floor and jumped up and down on it like a madman. Convinced of his own futility, he picked it back up and set it down on the table, still breathing heavily.

"Are you through?" asked Chris. "Because that wasn't very scientific if you don't mind my saying so."

"That is one tough case," said Spike, still trying to catch his breath.

Brad went to put his cup down on the table right next to the case. As soon as he let go of it and pulled his hand away, the case effortlessly swung open revealing its contents.

"How the hell did you do that?" asked Spike in total frustration.

"It's a skill like anything else," quipped Brad, not willing to admit that he had no clue how that just happened.

They proceeded to explore the contents of the case. Much of it was completely alien in nature. There were several small vials neatly stacked in latched compartments. There were a number of small metal devices and finally, what appeared to be some sort of radio transmitter. This little rectangular box was the source of the intermittent beeping they had heard. It had a directional arrow and it was pointing northwest.

"Hey, this is a tracking device of some kind. I'm sure of it," said Ryan. "Maybe it will lead us right to him?"

"Change in plans," announced Mikey. "Forget the ship. Let's see if we can't track him down. Don't defy me twice in a row because you know how that annoys me."

"Brilliant!" exclaimed Tommy.

"Alright," agreed Ryan. "Let's pack up Mikey's van and my SUV. It will be more comfortable than crowding into one vehicle. Let's go north and see where this thing leads us. Mikey is right, anything beats the hell out of sitting around here. If we want answers, we're going to have to go out there and find them."

In just under a half hour, the two vehicles were fully loaded with camping gear and provisions, to last them a week if necessary. As Ryan climbed into the driver's seat, Brad joined him on the passenger side. The other four would go in Mikey's van. As Ryan started the SUV, he glanced around the parking lot and noticed there were no youths lurking about.

"I can be an intimidating son of a bitch, can't I?" he said with a smile.

"I tremble in your presence," said Brad. "Now drive will ya?"

CHAPTER SEVEN

The woods became increasingly more dense as Plaatu and the Tilatin continued to weave their way towards their destination. Plaatu had been watching the signs along the highway from the backseat of the car and guessed that they were in the Otsego region of New York, northwest of New York City. It was not an easy hike as they were forced to cross two waterways and hilly terrain that proved to be more challenging than the Tilatin had anticipated. There was little conversation as Plaatu's captor wasn't the least bit pleased with his situation. He stayed a few yards behind Plaatu with his blaster pistol at the ready and chose to speak only when giving a direction or to curse the Tilatin Gods for sending him here on this assignment. Like the White Mountain National Forest where Plaatu chose to land, this area was a vast and protected region of woodlands. The likelihood that they would encounter any life forms, other than the assorted flora and fauna indigenous to this part of the country was highly unlikely. It was extremely rare for humans to come here this time of year as the summer tourist season had ended weeks earlier.

Plaatu was in relatively good shape for a man of his age. Despite his muddied boots and soiled uniform which had suffered a few tears along the way due to the occasional thorns he had to fight his way through, it gave him time to think and re-evaluate his situation. It had only been 72 hours since his conversation with Em Diem during which they discussed the details of the mission. It was almost funny to Plaatu to think that fixing a faulty transmitter could turn out to be such a full-blown disaster. In all his travels and encounters with life forms of all shapes and sizes, the two that had distinguished themselves in his mind as the most irrational had been the Tilatins and humanity. How ironic that these two should be thrown together like this in a contest that could very well determine the future of this planet. Plaatu had no idea how this crazy adventure was going to turn out, but he was determined to see to it that its present inhabitants emerged intact and in possession.

The captive and captor came to an area where the decaying trees and rotted limbs on the ground became entangled like an impenetrable spider web of shrubbery. As Plaatu struggled to find his way along, he heard a loud thud behind him. He turned sharply and found the Tilatin struggling to regain his feet after falling into a ditch. He stared for a moment, looking for the opportunity to disarm him.

"Enshway da! Nik ta toi te!" cursed the Tilatin in his native tongue as he regained his upright position.

"Are you alright?" asked Plaatu in a completely unconcerned tone that lacked the slightest degree of sincerity.

"I'm fine!" snapped the Tilatin as he brushed himself off. His grey Pierre Cardin suit was anything but. He was covered with mud and dirt from the bottom of his shoes to his thighs. His elbows weren't looking all that much better.

"Aren't you glad we came this way?" asked Plaatu cheerfully. "I'm rather enjoying this hike. I just love the outdoors don't you?"

"Just keep going," the Tilatin snarled. "Laugh now while you can. Your time will come."

Plaatu began walking again as the Tilatin plodded closely behind, occasionally stopping to check the directional locator device he carried in his hand. Dark clouds were beginning to form overhead. A low pressure system had been stalled over the region for days and had been causing unusually high amounts of rainfall for this time of year. It was a bit raw and dank as they continued weaving their way forward. Plaatu spotted a white-tailed deer in the distance. The two men were making no attempts to conceal their presence and as soon as the deer glanced up and noticed them, he sped off in the opposite direction.

"Why is it that every creature I encounter on this planet runs the other way when approached by a humanoid?" he pondered. "Most peculiar."

Finally, after what seemed like an hour of trekking through the woods, Plaatu spotted a ship up ahead in a clearing. As he drew closer, he could make out its details more clearly. It was a Tilatin ship alright. A smaller scout ship he guessed. They usually carried three or four man crews with them. Their design was not all that much different from his ship, other than the propulsion system they utilized. They were saucer shaped but there were two hydrogen powered engines with exhaust cylinders mounted to the back part of the saucer. They were ink-black in color, as if their hull had been covered with nothing more than a primer coat of paint. It had the traditional "wedge-like" protrusion added to the front, a throwback to the earlier days in Tilatin history when they were well-known for ramming their enemy's ships as a last resort. With the improvements in shielding that most crafts now employed, such maneuvers were archaic but these devices still remained on many Tilatin vessels.

"Crude looking crafts," thought Plaatu, "but they were designed more to intimidate rather than be aesthetically appealing."

Thoughts of escaping had been dancing in Plaatu's head since they abandoned the car. He knew full-well he could have outwitted this Tilatin dullard with relative ease but he had decided against it. He needed to know more details of their reckless scheme before planning any exit strategy. They were not just going to gun him down. Tilatins were generally believed to be one of the dumbest species currently sitting at the Coalition dinner table. They were nevertheless, fully aware of the consequences that would follow if they were found guilty of recklessly taking the life of a CIPF officer. There were still a few details they needed to learn from him in regards to who knew he was here and who was monitoring his activities before proceeding with any executions. He could use this to his advantage.

As they walked out into the clearing and approached the ship, there were three other Tilatins standing together watching their approach. The one in the middle wore the garb of an officer with his blood red cross sash and silver emblem on his chest. Plaatu recognized him immediately from an earlier encounter.

"Zuf Pada, I presume," he said with utter loathing as he stopped a few feet in front of him. Pada just smiled, revealing a mouthful of rotting teeth. Tilatins were also known for terrible dental hygiene and Plaatu had seen better choppers on baboons.

"I am flattered commander," answered Pada as he stood defiantly with his hands behind his back. His hair was slicked back except for a thin strip down the middle of his head which stood up slightly as if it were lacquered. It looked shiny and greasy and relatively disgusting.

"I had to dispose of three humans along the way," said Plaatu's walking companion. "We may want to consider moving the ship tonight."

"Well done, Zippa," said Pada. "The important thing is that we have destroyed the good commanders' integrity with the humans. They'll never trust you now Plaatu."

"I'm going to get out of these wretched human clothes and into my uniform," said Zippa.

"You're name is Zippa?" asked Plaatu sincerely. "What is your last name?"

"Pagnoneetswatayentilly," said the Earthly-attired alien, "not that it matters." Tilatins had notoriously long names.

"It must be quite a chore remembering such a lengthy name," said Plaatu.

The Tilatin raised his pistol as his face filled with rage. "I don't know what you are implying but I don't like it. I've been forced to spend more time with you than I cared to lawman. Don't push your luck."

"Gentlemen!" interrupted Pada as he stepped between them. "We may differ on Coalition policy in regards to this planet but we can still be civil to one another can't we? At least for the time being." The other two Tilatins continued to train their blaster pistols on Plaatu.

"We'll finish this discussion later," hissed Zippa as he walked up the metal stairs and entered the ship.

"He's a bit hot-headed," said Pada turning back towards Plaatu. "It wouldn't be wise to provoke him. He has no love for you CIPF types."

"And you do?" said Plaatu.

"I am a diplomat at heart Plaatu," said Pada. "You should know that from our last engagement. You do remember that infamous meeting before the High Council?"

"Like a bad hangover," answered Plaatu as he continued to size up the two other Tilatins who were standing dutifully off to the side ready to act if necessary. They were both very large individuals and the scowl on their faces was enough to convince Plaatu that they would fire without hesitation if ordered to do so. "You were advocating for re-colonization of a planet in the Tau Ceti system. Ever since you Tilatins were granted membership you have done nothing but attempt to exploit this obscure policy to your own advantage."

Plaatu wasn't even aware of the policy until that very meeting just three years earlier. He did some reading up on the extreme measure known as Proclamation 33, which was only meant to be applied when a planet was practically in its death throws. The Tilatins, since the day they were granted full membership, had been trying to convince the Council that the time frame for employing the measure should be re-evaluated. It was common knowledge that the entire Coalition of Planets was increasingly aware of the limited number of healthy planets that existed within the immediate vicinity of the galaxy. They were still branching out and searching for new and suitable worlds but the process was costly and time consuming. Every step was being taken to safeguard those planets that were already under the Coalition's sphere of influence. Over population was a common problem not exclusive to Earth and many planets were dealing with this and other troubling issues.

In Plaatu's mind, the real debate centered on the "worthiness" of a given species to continue to occupy a particular planet. History had shown that in the past, whenever the Coalition hesitated to intercede, several key planets became unlivable due to a number of reasons. Contamination and out-stripping the planet's ability to replenish its natural resources were the most common maladies. The Tilatins had tried to make a case for re-colonization of the seventh planet in the Tau Ceti system and had been denied. Plaatu correctly assumed that they were now going to approach the Council again in regards to Earth but they needed to create conditions which would strengthen their case. They had much to work with as they pondered ways in which to weave their treachery.

Earthlings were definitely guilty of many offenses against their planet's eco-system. Pollution was choking the water supplies; global warming threatened to cause catastrophic climate change, not to mention nuclear proliferation which Plaatu found heinously unforgivable. They were wiping out numerous species of birds, fish and mammals while driving many more to the brink of extinction. This planet was not, however, on the verge of being rendered uninhabitable. By Plaatu's estimation, that dire condition would not be reached until at least another one hundred years or so.

Pada motioned to his fellow Tilatins to lower their weapons and relax their stance. It didn't make them look any less like brainless thugs to Plaatu but at least they were no longer pointing their weapons at him, having placed them back in their holsters obediently.

The fourth unwelcome visitor to the planet re-emerged from the ship in his Tilatin uniform. He was carrying a container of liquid and when he stepped off the ladder and planted his feet on the ground, he drank from it heavily as if to mock Plaatu.

"You a little thirsty after that long walk?" he asked sarcastically. He drank again, and then stared at Plaatu with renewed defiance.

"Not really," answered Plaatu smugly. "We 'lawmen' as you put it are trained to go long periods without requiring nourishment." There was no way he was going to give any indication to this celestial grub worm that he could get to him. "I bet it is going to hurt when they put your face back the way it was. I hear that those surgical species altering procedures can be very painful."

The procedure actually required little more than flattening out the thick wrinkles Tilatins have on their foreheads and filing down the ridge of bone and skin that runs over the top of their heads. A little human hair works wonders to cover up the procedure quite nicely.

"We Tilatins like pain," he answered.

"Enough of this," said Pada. "I grow weary of this fruitless banter." He repositioned two chairs for him and Plaatu to seat themselves. Plaatu took advantage of the opportunity. He was determined not to show it but he was weary from the morning's events. His anxiety levels continued to escalate with every passing moment. No planet he had ever visited had caused him more bad luck than this one did in just two relatively short visits. He might as well have been sitting there naked as he was unarmed and surrounded by four extremely unlikable characters. One look around the clearing in which they had chosen to land their ship told him everything he needed to know about their living habits. There was trash strewn everywhere, they had made no attempts to respectfully dispose of their waste materials. Tilatin males had peculiar eating habits to begin with and were not known for tidying up after dinner hour. Plaatu looked off to the grassy area behind the ship and noticed the carcass of a large brown bear. It must have come nosing around and had paid the ultimate price.

"Vile creatures," he said in disgust. "Was it absolutely necessary to kill that animal?"

"Calm down," said Pada as he sat across from Plaatu on a metallic chair. "That unwelcome beast was conducting himself in a threatening manner. Would you deny us our right to defend ourselves?"

Plaatu would have liked nothing better than ringing Pada's neck but caution is often the better part of valor. They weren't going anywhere and he needed to act in a cooperative manner for the time being but beneath the surface, his blood was beginning to boil.

"Let's get serious shall we?" Pada continued. "I do not want to have any problems with you Plaatu, I can assure you. Disposing of you, which I will do without hesitation if necessary, would be a somewhat messy business. I am well aware you have friends in high places and to be frank, I respect life and would never kill anyone or anything unnecessarily."

"Tell that to your friend over there," said Plaatu. "He left three dead humans in his wake."

Zippa looked at him with a sadistic grin and continued to watch the conversation intently.

"Well," said Pada with an equally repulsive smirk, "I'm sure he would not have acted so rashly if it was not absolutely necessary."

Plaatu looked at Pada with scornful disbelief. He acted as if the lives of those three men meant absolutely nothing. Plaatu had learned through years of experience that few beings died without leaving behind broken hearts and too many mourners. In his travels, he had been forced to look into the eyes of far too many children who's father's and mother's had been tragically snatched away before their time. Plaatu had many dislikes throughout the galaxy. None were more contemptible than beings like Pada who seemed to have absolutely no respect for the life of another. He made a mental note to himself that if he did succeed in getting safely back to his ship, he was going to see to it personally that these Tilatins never saw the light of day again.

"Here's the thing," said Pada leaning forward on his hands. "Zippa here wanted to extinguish you and blame it on the humans. I am a bit more forgiving than he is. I would like to make you an offer. You could make our job so much easier if you would simply support our case when we address the Council upon our return. We already received permission to take a closer look at this planet, so long as we did not interfere with your mission. If you would simply testify to the dire conditions that exist here and support our request to re-colonize, we can remain friends and you can go on with your career. We will reward you handsomely of course which should provide a very nice retirement for you in the not too distant future. I am not oblivious to your situation. I have learned that you are contemplating taking a nice long rest. We can enhance your financial situation quite nicely. Why do you care about these human bugs anyway? From what I have heard, they have not been very nice to you old boy."

Plaatu continued to scan the area for escape routes. The Tilatins must have taken a page out of his book in picking this site. Most campgrounds in the Northern United States were unoccupied this time of year. Their ship, like his, could easily evade radar and travel at will under the cover of darkness. They were equipped with engines that ran every bit as quietly as his cruiser. They had picked a camp site in New York knowing full well that he would be forced to contact the leaders of this planet through the United Nations which was headquartered there. As his present dilemma rolled around in his mind, he wondered if there were other species involved in this devilry ass well.

For a fleeting moment, Plaatu debated the offer he had just been presented. He had been serving in this capacity for a very long time. During his entire career he had never taken a bribe, never accepted any graft or played one party against another for his own personal gain. On occasion, he would help himself to a few tidbits that a particular planet had to offer such as pilfering a few bags of coffee beans while flying over the Andes in South America but that was as far as it ever had gone. He was considered among his peers as a man of honor and above reproach.

All of which added up to a very conservative pension once he retired from the force. He would be able to live on it, but he would certainly not regard it as living in the lap of luxury. He had put his life on the line many times in the line of duty and had scant little to show for it. He couldn't deny that the offer had a certain allure.

"How much are we talking?" Plaatu asked, trying to buy time. Might as well know what is at stake, he thought to himself. Hell, if the Tilatins wanted to they could have dropped him right there and buried him in the ground with the unfortunate quadruped lying out behind the ship.

"I knew he had a price," said Zippa who was standing a few feet behind Pada. "You CIPF types all have a price."

Plaatu clenched his fists and struggled to restrain his urge to lunge at him and wipe that repulsive grin off his face.

"You can name your own price," said Pada. "After all, we are talking about a planet that is teeming with natural resources here. The water rights alone would be worth a fortune."

Plaatu lowered his head and feigned as if he were pondering this enticing chance at easy money. The look on Zippa's face was all he really needed to focus on in coming to a decision however. How could he even think about selling out to scum like this? Besides, these dimwits couldn't even comprehend the possibility that if Plaatu wanted to, he had access to any number of sources that could provide him with a very comfortable retirement. He didn't need Tilatins to extort graft; such opportunities were plentiful throughout the galaxy to anyone unable to resist such temptations. What he did need was time to discover what the hell they were up to in their diminutive albeit moderately imaginative minds.

"Ok, so what are we talking about here?" he asked. "What is it you intend to do and where do you need my help?"

Pada smiled broadly then stood up and began slowly pacing back and forth in front of Plaatu. It was time to reveal their master plan and apparently he needed to move in order to stimulate more blood flow to his brain.

"We have already contacted the necessary parties down here who are willing to help us carry out our plan," he began. He stopped in his tracks for a moment and glared down at Plaatu. "I know you and your council friend have been trying to deceive the other member planets as to this world's true condition. I presume you had good intentions but we have had operatives down here for years working secretly among the humans."

Plaatu's expression turned to one of surprise, then he tried vainly to suppress it.

"Yes my friend," said Pada smugly. "You may have even met one of them already, besides Zippa here of course."

Plaatu was growing increasingly angry with each new revelation this mission was throwing his way. "Damn, how could we be so sloppy?" he thought to himself. "So what do you intend to do?" he said aloud. "I'm so glad you asked," answered Pada as he began pacing again. "We intend to exploit the biggest single issue currently causing so much conflict all over this planet. These humans with their primitive religious beliefs have been warring with each other for years. Muslims and Christians have been committing atrocities upon one another for centuries. It's perfect. We have already made deals with a select group of Muslim terrorist fanatics who have agreed, with our help of course, to smuggle a bomb into the General Assembly of the United Nations. It will result in total chaos. Then we will carefully detonate more explosives strategically around the globe in order to incite another world war. Hopefully it will turn out like the previous two this planet experienced in the last century. If they choose to revert to using their nuclear arsenals, it could make matters very messy. Such an exchange would render the planet inhospitable for decades before anyone could re-colonize it. With a little luck, they will stick to conventional weapons only and annihilate the vast majority of themselves. Then we should have no problem convincing the Council that we be given the right to re-colonize. The surviving humans should make a tremendous source of cheap labor for us."

"When do you intend to pull this off?" asked Plaatu. His mind began to reel with thoughts of how his mission was spiraling totally out of control. It was as if he was caught in a black hole and couldn't get out. How could something as ridiculously simple as repairing a transmitter turn into threats of a world war? It was becoming so convoluted it was almost laughable.

"Tomorrow at precisely noon time," said Pada. "The General Assembly is scheduled to meet over some insignificant issue and one of our Muslim contacts will smuggle the weapon into the building and detonate it right inside the main chamber. The poor simpleton is already drooling over the thought of having his way with these 72 virgins they think await them in the afterlife. What complete fools. It will be a beautiful thing. You see Plaatu, you can think whatever you wish about us. These humans are every bit as devious and corruptible as we are. It's a shame they chose not to join the Coalition. If they had, not only would they have served as worthy adversaries in time, but they would have also saved their planet. Now we intend to take it. It is not a, pardon the pun, completely alien concept. Humans have employed a doctrine they refer to as 'Manifest Destiny' in their past which is no different than what we intend to do. How does that Earthly expression go, what's good for the goose is good for the gander?"

I must be getting soft in the head, Plaatu thought to himself. Some of what this despicable creature just said is, in fact, true and accurate. He almost has me convinced that this isn't such a bad idea. These human cretins had, he couldn't forget, shot him three times.

"So, are you with us or not?" asked Pada hopefully. "I'm giving you a chance here Plaatu. I respect your position. You are a man with a well-earned reputation. I feel you deserve better than the bear."

"How magnanimous of you," he said with a hint of aplomb. A device on Plaatu's belt buzzed softly.

"What was that?" Pada asked in a mild tone of alarm.

"Just a direction finder," said Plaatu quickly. "The battery is low." He stood to his feet as the sound of a car engine approached from the dirt road leading into the park.

Pada and the other Tilatins peered in the direction of the approaching vehicle. They didn't seem to know what to make of it. Something in Pada's mind told him there was no need for alarm. On the whole, he held humanity in very low esteem and the thought that they could actually pose a legitimate threat to him never even crossed his mind. He ordered Zippa to watch Plaatu as he walked towards the edge of the clearing. A blue passenger van accelerated towards them at a high rate of speed, then abruptly screeched to a halt, raising a cloud of dust and debris. Four men jumped out and began shouting like a band of rowdy tourists. It was Mikey, Chris, Tommy and Spike. Plaatu feared for their lives but on another level, he was equally glad to see them.

"Hey!" screamed Chris. "Are you guys shooting a movie up here?" He glanced over at the Tilatin ship. "Great props!" he exclaimed.

The four men continued to slowly walk towards the Tilatins in an unthreatening manner. Zippa moved to within a foot of Plaatu and jammed his pistol into his lower back. "Say one word and I fire," he hissed.

Pada and the other two Tilatins closed ranks and blocked the advance of the men. They had no idea what to make of them. Their behavior was highly irrational but they didn't seem to be anything other than curiosity seekers.

"Gentlemen," said Pada. "I'm afraid you have entered a restricted area. You should get back in your vehicle and leave at once." He really didn't relish the thought of more bodies piling up behind his ship and preferred to just send them on their way.

Tommy and the others lined up directly in front of Pada and the two Tilatin guards. Plaatu and Zippa were standing just a few yards behind them.

"Where are your cameras?" asked Tommy in a far-too-juvenile tone. Mikey cringed slightly as he feared he would blow their cover.

"Hey," said Mikey quickly," we just happened to see your ship and thought we could get a glimpse of a movie set. We meant no harm."

"No harm taken," said Pada but he was losing his patience. "The other members of our movie crew are on break so like I said, it would be best if you got back in your van and left this area. I mean now gentlemen!" The two Tilatin guards placed their hands on their pistols and prepared to draw their weapons. Plaatu knew that once they did, they would not hesitate to fire. If the four men didn't turn in a matter of another few seconds, he would have to watch helplessly as they were all executed right before his eyes. He had no doubt whatsoever that the Tilatin pistols would be set to kill and not merely stun.

Mikey glanced into Plaatu's eyes. It was clear that their new-found alien friend was an unwilling participant to this standoff and was being held against his will. That is all he needed to know.

The Tilatin guards began to draw their weapons. Plaatu's heart nearly leaped out of his chest. Zippa felt his captor's body tense right through the point of his pistol which he now dug deeper into Plaatu's back.

"Ok!" Mikey said loudly as he snapped his fingers in the air. "Let's do it!"

The sound of two gun bolts being pulled back rang out from behind the Tilatins. They collectively turned slowly around to find Brad and Ryan aiming rifles at their heads.

"Move again and you'll be breathing out of a new air hole!" said Ryan in a menacing tone. Plaatu took advantage of the situation and deftly grabbed the pistol from the distracted Zippa and wrenched it out of his hand. Then he delivered a state of the art, CIPF trained blow to his midsection that lifted the Tilatin off his feet. His knees buckled as he collapsed to the ground where he writhed in pain and struggled to regain his breath.

"That was for the three humans you left dead on the road," he fumed. Plaatu switched the pistol's setting to stun and fired two blasts striking both of the guards squarely in the chest. They sailed through the air landing in the bushes in a heap. "And that was for the bear!" Plaatu shouted.

"Bear?" said Ryan softly, turning to Brad. They had not yet noticed the fallen beast laying out behind the ship.

"I don't even want to know," said Brad, never taking his eyes off of the only Tilatin still standing.

Pada stood rigid, wide-eyed and relatively speechless. It had all happened so fast he seemed unable to grasp his quickly-regressing situation. Plaatu walked briskly over to Ryan and Brad.

"Gentlemen," he said with a broad grin. "I can't tell you how happy I am to see you. But never point your weapons at their heads. If you shoot them there it will only make them mad."

Tommy and the others could see that Pada was not carrying a weapon so they grabbed him under the arms and escorted him towards Plaatu.

"Easy humans," no need for roughness," Pada protested. They all stood in a circle around the Tilatin who all of sudden appeared much smaller in stature.

"Lucky for you we found that tracking device in your case," said Mikey. "It led us right to you."

"We got a phone call that those agents hadn't taken you where they claimed to be taking you," said Brad. "We figured we owed you a rescue attempt at least. We do have an image to uphold you know."

Plaatu looked around at each of the men. He had only known them for a few days and yet they had just risked their very lives for him. Not for glory and not for monetary gain. They did so simply because they felt it was the right thing to do. Pada had been correct when he accused humanity of being every bit as devious and corruptible as Tilatins. But there was a dichotomy at work with these humans that was not found on Tilatin or many other planets throughout the galaxy. Humans were multi-dimensional. They could be the most ruthless, evil beings in the galaxy one minute, and in the next they could exhibit the most honorable of qualities. It was in Plaatu's eyes, their most endearing feature. He simply never knew what to expect when interacting with them.

Plaatu turned to Pada. It felt good to be back in charge and back on course and if it was the last thing he did, Plaatu was absolutely determined not to lose control of this mission again. "I'm going to call for more CIPF involvement down here," he began. "You and your friends are going to be detained and I will have one of my fellow officers pick you up here. I don't know what made you think you could get away with this crazy scheme of yours but you will have to answer for your deeds. You Tilatins never learn. Treachery is a risky business and it comes with very severe consequences which I assure you, you and your friends here will soon discover."

Plaatu turned to Mikey. "Gentlemen, do you have any rope in your van?"

"Sure do," answered Spike who was still beaming at their successful intervention.

"Good," said Plaatu. "If you would be so kind, could you tie these four up as efficiently as you can? Tommy, could you fetch my case for me please?"

"Sure thing," Tommy answered as he ran off in the direction of the van.

"Now," said Plaatu, "if you men could drag those others together for me I would appreciate it."

The men complied and as the four Tilatins were huddled together, Plaatu stunned Pada and Zippa into unconsciousness. Then they were tied with so much rope Mikey began chuckling at the result. "What if bears wander onto the site?" he asked in a moderately concerned tone. "They'll be at their mercy."

"Well," said Plaatu, "that would be fitting now wouldn't it."

"What do you mean?" asked Chris. The men still had not noticed the bear carcass.

"Never mind," said Plaatu not wanting to depress them by pointing it out. "Shall we go my friends?"

"Where to?" asked Ryan as he hoisted his rifle over his shoulder.

"Back to where it all began," said Plaatu. "I need to get to my ship before all hell breaks loose. I'll explain on the way."

CHAPTER EIGHT

Mikey's van and Ryan's SUV reached the access road to their original camping grounds in just under four hours. It was now late afternoon and the autumn sun was beginning to set behind lingering clouds. As they pulled off of Route 27, they were stopped abruptly by the sight of a road block made up of two large military trucks. If Ryan's request to Congresswoman Randell was being taken seriously that Plaatu's presence there be handled discreetly, they wouldn't know it by this welcoming committee. Mikey was in the lead vehicle and he rolled to a stop with Ryan's SUV directly behind him. A heavy-set guardsman wearing Corporal stripes approached the van with a swagger that was right out of a John Wayne movie. He was bulging around the midsection and his stride was more of a waddle. He had an M-16 slung over one shoulder but he was not carrying it in a threatening manner. The other guardsmen on duty just mingled about half-hazardly.

"Is that Gomer Pyle I see standing over there?" muttered Chris from the rear seat.

"Stow it Chris," hissed Mikey as the soldier approached.

"Good afternoon gentlemen," said the corporal in an authoritative voice. "Where do you think you're going?"

Some thing told Mikey that it didn't matter how he responded. Whether it was sheer intuition or just plain cynicism, his hunch told him it wasn't going to make any difference to this yahoo. He might as well just say 'to grandma's house we go" because he was pretty sure there was no way this soldier was going to allow them to proceed any further. He did not want to raise any suspicions however, so he felt it wise to at least engage the Corporal in conversation.

"We were going to do a little camping," responded Mikey. "What is going on?"

"This road is closed and the area is off-limits," replied the Corporal. "Environmental issues I've been told. You guys are going to have to find some other place to camp out for the night. I'm sure there are lots of other places up here?"

Mikey glanced over at Spike who was riding 'shotgun' in the passenger seat. For a moment it was as if they spoke to each other telepathically that it would be an absolute waste of time to remain here. When a member of the United States military is given an order, he was required to carry it out without deviation. That's why they call these things road blocks instead of "intermediary negotiation stations." Block being the operative word here.

"Do you mind if I step out so I can commiserate with my friends behind us?" asked Mikey turning back towards the guardsman. 'I'll just be a minute."

"I don't mind if you talk to 'em," responded the corporal, "But I don't want no comizeratin going on around here. Not on my watch." He stepped away from the van. Mikey got out and walked towards Ryan's SUV. As he approached, Brad saw Mikey giving that trademark raised eyebrow look which told him that all was not well in the garden.

"The buck stops here," said Mikey as he reached the vehicle. "They're not going to let us pass."

"I knew we shouldn't even have pulled in," said Ryan. "Our friend in congress seems to have blown the whistle on us. There are probably military personnel crawling all over this friggin' place. And to think I actually had the hots for her."

Plaatu leaned forward in his seat and tapped Ryan on the shoulder. "Is there any other way in?" he asked.

"There is a narrow dirt road that I know about but it doesn't matter," said Ryan. "They probably have your ship surrounded by now. I can't believe she did this to us."

"This is really getting out of control now," said Brad from the passenger seat.

"Do you think they would accept a bribe?" asked Mikey.

"Like what?" asked Ryan. "Are you carrying a bundle of money that I don't know about?"

Mikey glanced into the back seat at a Dandy Dan's box. "How many donuts have we got left?"

"Is he serious?" asked Plaatu.

"They're national guardsmen for chrisakes," said Mikey. "We're not talking Green Beret here. It's worth a try."

Plaatu's communicator beeped softly. "That's odd," he said as he removed it from his carrying case. Mikey glanced towards the van and noticed that Spike, Chris and Tommy had gotten out, most likely to stretch their legs. They were leisurely conversing with some of the guardsmen.

The sun was just about to drop behind the tree line and in an hour so they would lose the daylight completely. "Maybe we should just wait until dark and try and sneak in when they are sleeping," suggested Mikey.

"They don't all go to sleep at the same time like they're under curfew Mikey," said Brad. "They're not the friggin boy scouts."

Plaatu answered his beeper. "Agent Plaatu here, come in," he said. He couldn't imagine who might be on the other end. His small communicator was incapable of receiving signals from outside Earth's atmosphere, only his larger, more powerful on-board equipment was capable of sending and receiving long range transmissions.

"Where the hell have you been?" he heard a voice ask. Plaatu's eyes lit up with excitement.

"Is that you Moov?" he said with exuberance.

"Who else would it be?" answered his friend. "I've been trying to reach you for the past few hours."

"What is your location?" said Plaatu as he leaned out the window and gazed skyward. The sun was a dim orange ball as it peeked through the clouds and continued dipping towards the horizon.

"Who the hell is he talking to?" whispered Mikey to Ryan.

"Beats me, I'm just the chauffeur. Want a donut?"

One of the guardsmen began walking towards the SUV. It was clear that they were becoming a bit impatient. Brad motioned to Plaatu to keep his voice down.

"You better get back to your van Mikey," said Ryan. "Why don't we head over to that dirt road and discuss the situation. I don't like the attention we're attracting here."

"Good idea," said Mikey. He began walking back towards his van.

Plaatu pulled away from the window. "I'm cruising right above you," said Ecko. "I'm at an altitude of 15,000 feet. Where can I land and meet up with you?"

"Stay put for a few moments," asked Plaatu. "We're repositioning and I'll let you know where we are headed. It is great to hear your voice my friend. Things have gotten a bit complicated down here and I could really use your help."

"You've got it," said Ecko. "I won't go anywhere until I hear from you."

Mikey and the others got back in the van and he put the vehicle in reverse. Ryan steered his SUV away from the access road and headed east with Mikey's van close behind.

"That was a fellow officer of mine," said Plaatu. "I am happy to say that things are finally beginning to look up. I was starting to think they couldn't possibly get any worse after seeing the presence of your military. I dealt with them once before and I am not looking forward to doing it again. They tend to be very rigid in their thinking and I have always had trouble dealing with beings who are doggedly stubborn and inflexible."

The two vehicles traveled two miles east, then turned sharply into the woods and proceeded southwest on the old dirt road back towards the camping area. The going was rough as vegetation had been encroaching upon the narrow road for many years. They moved slowly and the ground appeared to be relatively dry in spite of all the recent rain the area had experienced.

"Where exactly is your friend?" asked Brad as the SUV continued to bounce along.

"He's right above us," said Plaatu. "Is there a place where he can land and rendezvous with us away from the discerning eyes of your military?"

"We can stop in another camp site that is within walking distance of your ship," said Ryan. "Hopefully, the military contingent isn't very large and they aren't too spread out."

"This is getting weirder by the minute," said Brad. "I've never seen a space ship in my entire life and now they are showing up in droves. This house has sure gone crazy," he quipped.

"I would have thought you would be used to this by now," said Plaatu. "You're not going to buckle under the pressure on me now are you Brad?"

Ryan just smiled. "There are a lot of things you don't know about my friend Brad here Plaatu," he said. "Remind me to tell you of the time he dressed up as Marylyn Monroe, blonde hair and all."

"We were going to a Halloween costume party," snapped Brad sharply. "I was the biggest hit of the party."

"Yes you were," said Ryan. "But that party was three years ago. Why do you still have the costume hanging in your closet?"

"It might come in handy some day," answered Brad defensively. "Maybe I'll even sell it on Ebay."

Plaatu sat back and watched the interaction between the two men. They seemed to share a relationship much like he shared with Ecko. It was the kind of connection every living thing should have with another, he thought to himself. Friendship is more valuable than gold and he was glad to know that these fine young men who had risked their very lives to help him, enjoyed such a precious bond.

Plaatu took a jelly donut out of the bright pink and white box sitting next to him on the back seat and bit into it. Maybe a sugar rush would help him to contemplate how he should proceed from this point on. It was the seventh donut he had consumed since leaving Pada and the other Tilatins to ponder their fate in the bear-filled woods. A 32-ounce cup of coffee was helping wash them down. He had put his trust in Ryan and Brad when they assured him that donuts were not all that bad for you in moderation. Then a peculiar thought entered his head. They never really clarified what constituted a 'moderate' consumption of the irresistible little round, doughy, sugar-laced confections. He swallowed the first bite, then he paused to stare at the reddish goo that was oozing out of its middle. "I'm probably taking ten years off my life eating these things," he thought to himself. Then he devoured another bite.

Ecko's arrival was a good omen. Just hours ago he was ready to throw in the towel in utter frustration the way the mission seemed to be spiraling out of control. Thanks to the intervention of his new found friends, everything had now done a complete 360 degree turn and a new found sense of commitment filled his entire being. He felt much more confident that this mission could be salvaged now. The Tilatins had revealed that they recruited human terrorists to assist them in their diabolical plot. The exact identity and whereabouts of said accomplices was a conundrum Plaatu would need to solve. They would have to be stopped before irreparable damage was done to the fragile international relations that had existed down here for decades. Then he needed to convince humanity that it was time to join their interstellar neighbors for the mutual benefit of all. "Mere child's play," he thought to himself. "Yeah, right."

Ryan fortunately knew these woods like the back of his hand. As the two vehicles slowly and silently crawled along the bumpy dirt road the windshields and side panels were assaulted intermittently by unyielding thickets and low-lying tree branches. It was as if the vehicles were being forced to run a gauntlet by these majestic woods to determine their worthiness to enter. He spotted a camp site up ahead. As he pulled off the road and onto the grass, he doused his headlights and waved out the window for Mikey to pull up right next to him. He put the SUV in park and turned off the engine, then he quietly jumped out as Mikey's van rolled to a halt.

"Let's keep it down," Ryan said softly as he leaned his head inside the window, knowing full well from prior experience how rambunctious Tommy and Chris could be in these types of situations. "We're only about a half mile from Plaatu's ship and it's bound to be swarming with guardsmen."

As Mikey turned off his engine, the men remained motionless and listened intently. Darkness was falling and the area was eerily quiet. The only sound, other than a gusty northeast breeze gently caressing the trees was the almost imperceptible movement coming from the direction of Plaatu's ship. Noise carried in the woods and it would be difficult to do much of anything without fear of being discovered. The men could only hope that the frequent gusts of wind would help mask their presence. Chris, Tommy and Spike quietly got out and tried to get their bearings. Thick layers of clouds obscured the moonlight making it difficult to navigate.

"I can't see shit!" said Tommy.

"Why are you looking for it?" quipped Chris. Spike tried to stifle laughter but that wasn't always easy when hanging around with these two hobos.

Tommy had always found the woods to be a bit spooky at night. Having grown up in the city, he was accustomed to the ever-present illumination of modern day life. Being out here where there wasn't a street lamp for miles sometimes gave him the heeby-jeeby's. He could still vividly remember his very first camping trip to the White Mountains with his five friends. The first day had passed uneventfully but he was not prepared for how dark it could get once the sun dipped below the horizon. The first time he exited the tent to relieve himself in the middle of the night, he recalled the sensation of having to feel his way around to the back of the tent. The night was overcast, he didn't bring his flashlight for fear of waking the others and there was no moonlight to help guide his way.

As he stood there expelling some of the beer he had consumed earlier that evening, he glanced towards the tree line which was a few feet away. He scanned right to left and nothing seemed out of the ordinary but then, he really couldn't make out much of anything to begin with. He zipped up his fly when all of a sudden he noticed a pair of bright green eyes staring back at him from the ground level just a few feet away. He let out a blood-curdling scream and ran back towards the tent, smashing into its side and causing it to collapse upon the other campers. As the startled men scrambled to find the exit flap of the collapsed tent with Tommy floundering on top of them, total mayhem ensued. After much commotion, Brad finally managed to get the exit flap open and the five men crawled out on their hands and knees to confront the crisis.

"What the hell is it!" shouted Mikey as he tried to calm Tommy who was still trembling.

"Someone was watching me take a leak from over there," Tommy exclaimed in a shaky voice.

Brad and Ryan walked over to the tree line with rifles in hand and peered into the darkness. Brad switched on his flashlight and after a few moments they discovered what had terrified Tommy so. A cat-sized raccoon stared up at them, then slowly moseyed back into the woods. They watched him disappear up a tree, then they turned back towards Tommy.

"It was just a friggin raccoon!" barked Brad. "Haven't you ever seen a raccoon before?"

"You're dead!" hissed Chris, shivering in the cold night air. "Now we have to put the tent up again!"

"I thought it was a peeping Tom or Jason or something," said Tommy meekly. "It could have been a bear too you know."

"Next time I hope it is," answered Mikey caustically. "Let him eat your sorry ass so I can get some sleep. Now go fix the damn tent!" He had all he could do to keep from laughing hysterically. He had to admit, it was pretty funny.

The following evening Tommy made sure to take a flashlight with him when he left the tent to do his business. The raccoon was there again, almost in the exact same spot. Tommy couldn't be absolutely certain but he could have sworn it was giggling at him. The memory of that first camping trip still lived large in Tommy's mind.

Plaatu and Brad stepped out from Ryan's SUV and joined the others.

"I have an idea," said Brad. "Don't we still have that 'Sounds of nature' meditation CD in your van?" We can crank that up to mask any sounds we make while we are setting up camp for the night. Chances are we are going to be here until tomorrow. We should at least set up the tent unless you're planning on sleeping on bare ground out here in the open."

"Good idea," said Ryan. "Mikey, can you park your van against the trees over there facing in the direction of the guardsmen? Your speakers are much better than mine."

"No problem," said Mikey. "I'm on it."

He pulled the van over and inserted the CD. He started it at a very low volume, then slowly and delicately increased the volume until he thought it would be sufficient to mask their movement.

The soldiers who were assigned to guard Plaatu's ship were just mulling around. There were 15 of them, all members of the New Hampshire National Guard, and they were positioned in the clearing surrounding the ship. They had not brought any armored vehicles and were only equipped with M-16's and small side arms. There were two half-ton military trucks that appeared to be their only means of transportation. As they sat around a make shift fire and busied themselves with a variety of activities trying to stave off the boredom, the sound of the CD began reaching their ears. The soldiers all stopped what they were doing simultaneously and looked in the direction where it was coming from.

"Wow, that's weird huh," said one of the men who was sipping a cup of hot chocolate. "It's like all the nocturnal bugs and wildlife just woke up at the same time."

"Humph," the man next to him grunted in agreement. They all returned to their duties and seemed completely unalarmed.

Convinced that the CD had not aroused any suspicion, the campers quietly busied themselves putting up the tent. Plaatu contacted Ecko again. The site they had chosen was more than large enough for him to land his ship well beyond the scrutiny of the guardsmen. CIPF cruisers were equipped with specially designed engines that ran so silently they could not be heard from more than a few dozen yards away. As Ecko's ship began to descend, Ryan and the others stood off to the side where the vehicles were parked near the tree line. They looked up in awe as the saucer came into view at an elevation of about three hundred feet. The soft pulsating hum of the engines preceded it as it floated effortlessly down to the ground. Ecko chose to land with the three tripod legs extended to keep the ship in an elevated position as he wasn't sure there was enough room to extend the ramp. Once the craft was stable, the engines stopped and the campsite went completely silent again except for the sound of the nature CD wafting in the air.

"That was amazing!" whispered Chris. He continued to stare at the ship as if in a trance, unable to turn away.

"This is one camping trip I don't think we'll forget any time soon," said Spike.

The men continued to stare as the hatch opened and a metal staircase lowered to the ground. Plaatu approached the ship and in a few moments Ecko came walking down the steps. As he reached the ground, Plaatu embraced him warmly. Ecko was taller than Plaatu, much more broad-shouldered and noticeably more imposing. His dark, bushy hair gave the impression that he was much younger than Plaatu, but he was completely human-like in his overall appearance. As they moved towards the gawking campers, Plaatu seemed to be beaming from ear to ear. It was obvious that he felt a tremendous sense of relief to be in the company of a long time friend once again.

"Gentlemen," said Plaatu, "I'd like you to meet a close associate of mine." He went around the group and they each in turn shook hands with yet another being from a distant world. His hand shake was firm and commanded respect. It was almost too much to assimilate for them as the reality of meeting so many extraterrestrials in such a short time seemed to overwhelm them.

"Did you . . . have a nice trip?" stammered Tommy. For a moment he felt silly. "What do you say to an alien who just landed?" he thought to himself. He had never been in this position before. When he first came in contact with Plaatu, he wasn't aware that he was a non-Earthling.

"It was pretty uneventful actually," said Ecko. "Relatively quiet compared to most. This is still an area that doesn't come under the jurisdiction of my agency so there really isn't much traffic up there."

"My friends," said Plaatu nervously. He seemed a bit anxious all of a sudden. "I don't want to appear rude but Ecko and I need to talk privately for a few moments. Would it be too much trouble to prepare something to eat for him while we discuss a few issues?" He turned to Ecko. "The food down here is simply marvelous," he gushed.

"Sure," said Brad. "Go do your thing and we'll discreetly rustle up some grub."

"Rustle up some grub?" chuckled Mikey. "Ride 'em in, ride 'em out, Rawhide."

Plaatu and Ecko had no idea what they were talking about and didn't seem to care as they walked over to the stairs of Ecko's ship and disappeared inside.

"Rustle up some grub?" Ryan repeated. "How hokey is that?"

"Are we going to start nitpicking everything we say now," snapped Brad as they quietly began unpacking some of the food supplies. "It's not like we're in the presence of British Royalty or something for crying out loud. They're just aliens from another world. Happens everyday right?"

"If they were British Royalty," added Spike, "I'd be adding a little arsenic to the stew."

"Leave the British alone," said Ryan. "They're the only allies we have left in this world."

Mikey got a small fire going, making sure that the vehicles blocked the line of sight between them and the soldiers. There was certainly a sufficiently wide swath of trees separating them but he didn't want to take any chances. "After all," he had remarked. "These are National Guardsmen you know. You remember Kent State don't you?"

"You're a sick boy," said Spike in response. "Just don't start throwing rocks at them and everything will be fine."

Chris and Tommy walked around Ecko's ship and talked softly to themselves. They were like two little kids who had just been given a new toy. They periodically touched various parts of the large craft which seemed to satisfy their insatiable curiosity. Tommy was carrying a small flashlight but was careful to angle the beam towards the ship and down towards the ground. The underbelly of the ship was remarkably smooth and there were no openings whatsoever. There were no exhaust vents, no intake manifolds, and no visible evidence that it even had engines at all. It was identical to Plaatu's ship but they were apparently capable of landing with or without the three metallic support legs. While Plaatu's was laying flat on the ground, Ecko's was suspended which allowed them to walk underneath it. As an electrician, Tommy was completely baffled by the technology. He just scratched his head and shrugged. Both he and Chris would have loved the opportunity to crawl around inside the ship's internal workings to see what made it go.

Brad and Ryan stood quietly near Mikey's van and listened for any activity from the guardsmen. They chatted softly and sipped coffee as they glanced over at the two younger men trying to unravel the secrets of Ecko's ship.

"So the big question is," said Brad softly, "How do you think this is all going to end?"

"I haven't the slightest clue," answered Ryan pensively.

He glanced around at the scene unfolding before him. The campsite was laid out like an eerie mosaic with dimly lit specters moving quietly in the darkness. The air had an almost spooky feel to it and the presence of the spaceship simply made it that much more difficult to absorb. He thought about his parents for a moment back home in Connecticut. They were probably sitting in front of their television sets at this very moment watching "Wheel of Fortune" followed by a half hour of 'Jeopardy', totally oblivious to the fact that humanity was about to be confronted with an unprecedented challenge. Our species had always suspected we were not alone in the universe. He imagined that discovering the answer to that riddle, while truly profound, would not be overwhelming once the initial shock had passed. The realization that our planet was being coveted by species more advanced than us however, beings that were prepared to wipe our species away like a strong wind blows away a swarm of locusts was bound to cause widespread panic. Ryan wasn't sure how Plaatu and Ecko were going to proceed but something told him that this crazy saga he suddenly found himself embroiled in was about to reach an epic climax. Emotionally, he knew that he and his friends needed to prepare themselves for that.

Mikey and Spike put the finishing touches on a quick pot of Beef Stew and fresh bread. They didn't dare grille up any fresh meats as the smoke would surely have been seen by the guardsmen. They were just about to serve when Plaatu and Ecko emerged from the ship and rejoined them at the small campfire.

"That smells delicious!" said Ecko as he took a seat next to Tommy. He dwarfed him in size and for a moment, Tommy felt terribly insignificant. It was hard enough to compete with his human peers, now he was being forced to accept the unpleasant reality that he would have to compete with out-worlders as well. "That's gonna suck," he thought to himself as Mikey handed him a bowl of stew.

"It's not home-made, just Dinty Moore," Mikey said, "but it's gonna have to do."

The group of men dined in an awkward silence for a few moments. The nature CD continued to emit an unceasing symphonic assortment of native nocturnal sounds which languidly filled the air around them. The difficulty of adjusting to one alien guest was intimidating enough. Now there were two. Then again, the silence could have been something completely innocent and unpretentious. Perhaps the stew was satisfying their appetites quite nicely and the ambiance of the moment simply didn't require any conversation. Perhaps the tranquility of their surroundings further enhanced the flavor. The White Mountain National Forest did have an almost spiritual magnetism about it that many visitors found simply irresistible. Whichever the case may be, for the present at least, their souls were at peace.

Their moment of peace did not last for long. They could always count on Chris to drop a bomb in one way or another.

"I don't know about you guys but that CD is starting to get on my nerves," he said.

"Suck it up," said Ryan. "We need to leave it on for the time being. I don't want to give our position away."

"Quite right," whispered Plaatu. He threw his cardboard bowl into the fire just as they had done after their previous encounter. It burst into flames and lit up the entire camp site.

"Oops," he said meekly. They all sat deathly still and listened to hear for any increased activity. All remained quiet and they breathed a collective sigh of relief.

"Sorry about that," said Plaatu. "I didn't realize they too were that flammable."

"New rule," said Mikey. "Only throw shit into the fire during the daylight hours."

"Got it," said Plaatu. "Now, let me fill you in on our intentions. Ecko and I discussed the situation at length. There is a minor change of plans. I suggest we all get a good night's sleep tonight. There is no longer any need for me to sneak into the camp site to gain access to my ship. I am going to march over there in the morning and walk right in."

"Are you sure you can handle that many guns?" asked Spike.

"I won't be going alone," answered Plaatu. "There is little cause for worry but I would still much rather deal with them in full daylight. I would appreciate it if you could refrain from doing anything to attract their attention until at least dawn. Then I am heading for New York. If I don't intercept whoever it was the Tilatins bribed to inflame the situation, this could get very ugly rather quickly."

"What about the Tilatins?" asked Ryan. "They could have been eaten by bears already."

"I doubt that very much," interrupted Ecko. "Trust me, one whiff of a Tilatin and these bears you speak of wouldn't go near them."

"If they are even still there at all," added Plaatu. "If they managed to get loose, they are on the run now. I escaped and I know about their scheme. They are either still tied up on the ground in which case Ecko here can go and take them into custody in the morning or, they are high-tailing it back to Coalition space to do some serious damage control. They don't want to do anything to jeopardize their membership. They need the Coalition far more than we need them."

"So what can we do?" asked Brad.

"I was hesitant to ask you," said Plaatu thoughtfully. "I have already imposed upon you men more than I have a right to."

"Hey," said Mikey, "Who's imposing? If the very fate of our planet is at risk, how could we possibly do any less?"

"That is how I hoped you would respond," said Plaatu. "It is clear to me that you are men of honor. I commend you."

"No need to," said Ryan. "We are the ones who owe you a monumental debt of gratitude. You aren't even from this planet and you have been sticking your neck out in our best interest. Tell us what you need and we'll do our best to get it done."

"The transmitter I left here years ago may be malfunctioning," said Plaatu. "My original purpose here was to repair it and leave without incident. While things have become a bit more complicated, I may still need to call upon the service of that device which has other functions built into it. I need you men to go up there and check on it for me. It is buried about twelve feet beneath the ground but someone has unknowingly erected structures on top of it. I can show you how to perform the check-up. It is done by employing a remote hand-held device and you will have to be standing a few meters above it to recalibrate it if necessary. Do you think you could do this?"

"Sounds easy enough," said Mikey. "I'm a mechanic; it shouldn't be all that difficult." He was very confident in his mechanical abilities and was well-schooled in the world of tools. Spike was painfully aware however, that Mikey also had a tendency to be just a tad overzealous on occasion. He vividly remembered each and every incident where Mikey had bitten off more than he could chew, resulting in a cluster fudge of mega proportions that then required Spike's assistance. Like the time he got bored with one of his previous vans and decided to take a Sawzall to it and turn it into a pick up truck. Spike had warned him against it but to no avail. The job required so much time to complete that Mikey decided to scrap it instead and buy a new van.

"Shouldn't be all that difficult?" repeated Spike. "Famous last words," he chuckled.

"I would ask Ecko to do it but not only does he have to go check on the Tilatins, he will also have to thwart operations elsewhere on your planet that are linked to the danger at the UN. I had the opportunity to briefly tap into the Tilatin ship's computers and I now know the two other locations where they intend to strike. Besides, he would also attract attention." The men all stared at Ecko. He looked every bit as human as Plaatu did. He was a might larger but other than that he appeared to be perfectly normal.

"You don't look all that unusual to me," said Brad. "What makes you think you would stand out in a crowd?"

Ecko set his bowl down on the ground and held his hands out in front of him. He spread his fingers wide for all to see.

"I'll be a son of a bitch," said Mikey. "You've got six fingers on each hand. You really are an alien! No offense of course."

"None taken," said Ecko. "Actually, it is normal for beings on my home planet to have five digits on each hand just as most humanoids do. It was a birth defect but you would be amazed at how handy that extra digit can be."

"Once you have completed this task," continued Plaatu, "I should not have to call upon you again. You can either wait for me here or head home and turn on any news channel. The secret will be out soon enough. And this time, your government won't be able to hide the truth from the people of the world."

"Do you have the coordinates for the transmitter?" asked Brad.

"Yes," answered Plaatu. He held up a cigarette pack-sized silver box. "This hand held tracking device will lead you right to it."

"Then we're all set," said Ryan. "Tommy and Chris, why don't you guys very quietly clean up the pots and dispose of the trash. Mikey and Spike, you two can go with Plaatu and learn how to use the repair device he is talking about. Brad and I will map a route to the transmitter."

"Wait a minute!" protested Chris. "Why can't we do the mapping and you guys do the dishes? I can't even remember the last time you guys cleaned up. This is a democracy you know. We're not in friggin' Cuba?"

"Yeah," added Tommy feeling momentarily empowered. "Why do we have to do the dishes all the time?"

"Cause I said so!" snapped Ryan with a menacing glare.

Tommy and Chris hesitated for a moment, unsure if they should push the issue. Then they looked at the two aliens and chose, out of respect to comply.

"Well, seeing as how you put it that way," said Chris as he got up and began picking up the empty bowls. Tommy picked up a trash bag and held it open for him. "We really do get along reasonably well some of the time," he added glibly.

Plaatu smiled to himself. He was really beginning to like these men. There was something about them that was just so refreshing, undeniable and truly noteworthy, something that was in short supply throughout the galaxy at least in his experience. They were in a word, genuine.

He and Ecko returned to the ship and retrieved the repair tool. They still remained unwilling to allow the men entry to the ship. As much as Plaatu would have liked to let them go aboard and look around, he was, and always had been a creature of duty and responsibility.

Mikey, as expected, picked up the user-friendly workings of the device with relative ease and after a half hour or so, he was confident he could perform the task. When it came time for the men to turn in for the night, Mikey shut off the nature CD. He forgot to slowly fade out the volume so it would not be noticeable. After he turned it off sharply, he cringed for a moment and listened intently.

A half mile away the private who had first detected the sound when it was activated earlier noticed the sudden silence right away.

"Damn!" he said to his fellow guardsmen. "They must all go to sleep at the exact same time too. That's pretty amazing huh?"

"Small minds are easily amused," muttered the sergeant as he sat by the fire whittling a car out of a piece of wood. The incident passed without fanfare.

Soon the six campers were tossing and turning in their sleeping bags and they found it difficult to fall asleep inside the tent. This time it wasn't merely the effects of Tommy's unceasing flatulence that was keeping them awake. "Dinty Moore farts are the worst," Tommy mumbled to himself at one point. They were each in their third decade of life and had individually experienced enough adventures to fill a respectable sized novel. Nothing they had ever done however could even come close on the Richter scale to the seismic effects of the last few days. They were unaware that their collective thoughts shared a common thread. Each of them was wondering to himself what future camping trips would be like. They contemplated the possibility of whether or not there would even be any future camping trips. How could their lives possibly go forward without unimaginable changes in the way in which they went about their daily existence? How would this affect their jobs? How would it affect their families? Each of the men had a mother and father who they had, up until now, kept completely in the dark as to what was transpiring. They weren't sure how to breach the subject without frightening them. Each wanted to approach them in person. One doesn't just pick up the phone and say, "Hi mom, sorry I haven't called in a while but I wanted to tell you I've been hanging out with an alien for the past few days. And be prepared because pretty soon there are going to be lots of other aliens running around down here too."

How would their parents react? How would the rest of the world react? What would these new aliens look like? The more their imaginations ran amuck with the possibilities, the more mind-boggling the thoughts became.

They increasingly tossed and turned until Mikey just couldn't take it any more.

"I vote that Tommy sleeps in the van!" he blurted in utter frustration. "I can't breathe in here!"

"No shit!" added Chris. "Somebody open a friggin' vent! I don't care how cold it is outside!"

Tommy just giggled from inside his sleeping bag.

CHAPTER NINE

Tommy was the first to roll out the next morning. It was just after seven AM. He unzipped the tent and stepped out into the cold dawn air trying not to wake the others. As he walked over to the tree line the grass was saturated with morning dew. The sun was shining brightly overhead though and it wouldn't be long before the early morning moisture evaporated back into the air.

He had to relieve himself so he stepped up to a tree and unzipped his trousers. There was a beer can hanging on a branch to his left about three feet away. As he visually scanned the tree line, he noticed that there were other beer cans hanging on branches at intervals of a few feet apart. As he watered the grass, he thought it odd that so many cans would be hung in such a fashion. He didn't remember Brad or Ryan doing any target practice the previous night so maybe they had been left there by an earlier group of campers. He zipped up his fly and was just about to turn back towards the tent when a brilliant beam of light came out of nowhere. In rapid-fire succession, it vaporized the cans leaving behind nothing more than little puffs of smoke.

"Jesus Christ!" he shrieked as he turned to run back towards the tent. As he did he looked in the direction of Ecko's ship and there was a huge metallic looking man standing in front of it. He unzipped the tent and recklessly dove inside, landing squarely on top of Chris who was still bundled up in his sleeping bag.

"We're being invaded!" Tommy shouted as he scrambled for cover. The others jumped up one by one and darted out of the tent. As they stood there squinting in the dazzling early morning sun, they strained to see what it was that had caused Tommy to possibly soil himself and wake them so abruptly.

Plaatu and Ecko were standing a few feet in front of the ship in full uniform but there was something else with them.

"What the hell is that!?" stammered Mikey. They were all unsure of whether to retrieve their primitive weapons, hide in the tent or run for their lives. The 'thing' standing next to Plaatu had to be at least eight feet tall. It appeared to be humanoid in shape but it looked like a walking suit of shiny armor. It had a face plate and at present, it was completely rigid, as if it were standing at attention.

"Gentlemen," shouted Plaatu in their direction. "There is no need to be alarmed. Come this way if you would, I want you to meet someone."

"This is getting weirder . . ." said Mikey but Ryan cut him off in mid-sentence.

"Don't even say it," he interrupted. "This can't possibly get any weirder."

Chris poked his head back inside the tent. "Get your candy ass out here," he commanded to Tommy who was still hiding under a blanket. Tommy got up slowly then poked his head out and asked, "Is it safe?"

"How the hell do I know," answered Chris. "But it is bound to be interesting."

Tommy hesitantly exited the tent and rejoined the others as they began walking towards Plaatu. If they were on edge the night before in the presence of two aliens, it couldn't come close to the reservations they were feeling at that moment as they approached the large metallic monster. They stopped a few feet in front of Plaatu and Ecko but none of them were able to speak. They just stood there staring up at this incredible hunk of, what now appeared to be a mechanical man.

Plaatu sensed their extreme trepidation and for a moment, he felt a tinge of remorse. This was a great deal for these men to grapple with considering all they had been asked to endure over the previous few days.

"My apologies my friends," he began. "I did not intend to frighten you. I'd like you to meet Bort. He is my companion on most missions when I am patrolling Coalition space. He was in for maintenance and Ecko was nice enough to bring him along. He is a member of our robot corps and he is part of the reason why we have managed to abolish wars on our planets. They are given complete authority over us in matters of aggression and they act with complete impunity when necessary. He will not harm you, I promise." Plaatu paused for a moment to gauge their reactions. "Unless of course you misbehave in any way," he added with a wry smile.

Tommy approached Bort with extreme caution. As he stood next to him, he felt like a circus midget as the enormous robot towered over him. He softly tapped on his metallic arm. It was like tapping on a block of solid steel. There was no give to it at all and he felt sure that even if all six of the men tried piling on top of him, he wouldn't budge an inch.

"He almost fried me like a Perdue chicken!" Tommy stammered.

"I'm sorry about that Tommy," said Ecko. "I can assure you, you were in no danger. Bort is as accurate as your best snipers with his energy beam. I was testing him out and Plaatu had given me the idea of using some of the discarded beer cans from last night. He said they made good targets. I was trying not to wake you gentlemen."

"He is one big bastard," said Brad. "Is it really necessary to construct them that large?"

"If they were our height," said Plaatu, "I doubt they would be quite as intimidating. There function is to discourage wrong-doing. Making them appear so formidable helps drive home the point, wouldn't you agree?"

"I wouldn't want to bump into him in a dark alley," said Spike. "Not without a tank under my ass."

"A tank wouldn't help you in that situation," said Plaatu. "There is really nothing in the known universe capable of stopping him. We made sure of that."

"Well, then I am glad he is on our side," said Ryan. "He is on our side isn't he?"

"Yes," said Plaatu with a smile. "He is."

The men seemed a bit more at ease now which made Plaatu feel a whole lot better. He needed to be more careful in the future. With all that he had seen in his lifetime, and the innumerable crisis he had been embroiled in not to mention the myriad of life forms he had encountered, his nerves were more conditioned to dealing with the unknown. These men had never been any further than the comfy confines of Earth and were unaccustomed to dealing with anything that appeared even remotely alien. In many ways, humans were of a hardy stock but at the same time, they could also be very, very sensitive.

"I am going to retake my ship," said Plaatu. "Then I am heading for New York. Ryan, do you think you could contact your friend in congress again?"

"Sure, I'll give her a call on our way up to check on the transmitter. I'll tell her to expect you at UN Headquarters."

"That would be fine," said Plaatu. "Please remind her that I'll be arriving in slightly different fashion this time around and it might be a good idea to clear the plaza of any annoying protesters."

Ryan just chuckled. "I understand."

Tommy continued to marvel at Bort's size and framework as if his eyes were just unwilling to accept his very existence. "Hey Plaatu," he said, "You're not going to hurt those guardsmen are you?"

"Not if I can help it," he said. "Something tells me they'll cooperate with us and there won't be any need for violence."

"Alright, let's boogie," said Mikey. "We can grab coffee and breakfast at a drive-through place on the way. We've got work to do."

"We can leave the tent right where it is,' said Spike, "and come back and get it later."

"Good luck gentlemen," said Ecko. He shook hands with Plaatu and re-entered his ship. He was off to check on the Tilatins that had been bound and left in the woods of New York. Plaatu began walking towards the road leading to his ship. "Bort! Baringa!" Plaatu said over his shoulder. The robot immediately began moving to fall in behind him. Ryan and the others just stared up at him in awe as he walked silently and effortlessly without the slightest hint of gears, machinery, or any sound of internal mechanisms. They couldn't imagine what made him go but he was one, well-oiled machine.

The men returned to the tent and grabbed their toiletries. Mikey filled some large pans with fresh water so they could at least wash up, shave if anyone wished and brush their teeth before departing. They weren't sure who they might bump into along the way but it was always a good idea to appear as minimally frightening as was humanly possible.

"Boy I sure would like to be there to see the look on those guardsmen's faces," said Tommy as he pulled on a wind-breaker. A breeze was kicking up and the air temperature couldn't have been more than forty five degrees. The men heard a soft hum and as they turned to look, Ecko's ship was lifting off and quietly ascended into the clear blue sky.

"Look at that thing go!" muttered Chris in total amazement.

"Un-freaking-believable!" added Tommy.

"We might as well get used to scenes like this one, huh?" said Brad softly. "I have a funny feeling alien air traffic is going to increase rather significantly in the days ahead."

Plaatu had thoroughly briefed Mikey on how to re-calibrate the transmitter and from the way he described the procedure, it certainly sounded like a relatively simple task. Mikey was well aware however that Murphy, the most famous of Irish philosophers, was a wise old man, and Murphy's Law specifically states in no uncertain terms that whatever can go wrong, will go wrong. The men finished their preparations and within moments the vehicles headed out towards the highway via the back road they had taken coming into the campground to avoid the guardsmen. After a quick stop for "sustenance" at Dandy Dan's, they headed northeast. By the time they finished their coffee, the two vehicles were already proceeding slowly up Sleepy Ledge Road where the resort was located. As they approached the recently constructed ski facility, the area was relatively quiet. There were several cars in the parking lot but ski season had not yet begun so it was not filled to capacity. Most, if not all of the occupants had come for the annual foliage display. When all the environmental ingredients fell into place, it could be well worth the effort. The New England region featured some of the finest autumn colors on the planet and people would come from all over the country to bask in its unique splendor.

Elsewhere, Ecko had arrived at the co-ordinates Plaatu had given him but the Tilatins were nowhere to be found so he returned to orbit leaving a slew of UFO sightings in his wake. He and Plaatu had discussed this the night before. Both agreed that there was no longer any need to sneak around in sheer mode. Alien visitors would soon be coming for dinner so the Earthlings might as well get used to it. Then he laid in new co-ordinates for Beijing and Moscow where the terrorist acts were scheduled to take place. Disarming the devices would be an easy task since they were both stationary and Plaatu had given him the exact locations. Deactivating them remotely from his ship by using the proper frequencies would be child's play since they were set with timers and were not being detonated randomly by suicide bombers. Plaatu had far and away the more daunting of the two assignments.

Ryan and Mikey pulled the two vehicles into adjacent parking spaces at the lower end of the lot. Chris and Tommy had once again traveled in Mikey's van and had been bantering back and forth in frivolous rhymes during the entire twenty minute ride. Mikey and Spike bribed them, cajoled them and finally outright threatened them if they didn't stop but it was simply futile. Once the two got up a good head of steam, it was tantamount to a verbal avalanche of painfully poor prosaic gibberish.

After the men exited the vehicles, they paused for a moment to enjoy the view. The parking lot was south of the Resort's main lodge. It faced away from Mount Washington which rose to its 6,223 foot summit just to the northwest of where they were standing. It was currently shrouded in clouds and was not clearly visible.

There was a steep ledge at the lower edge of the parking lot. It descended to the Kangamangus Highway which passed east to west at its base 1000 feet below. There was a rest area at the bottom and this area was a very popular starting point with climbers who found the steep ascent up "The Ledge" to be a formidable challenge.

"Maybe we could attempt it someday," remarked Brad as the men stared over the aluminum railing which separated the parking lot from the top of the ledge.

"I'll certainly give that thought all the consideration it is due," mused Ryan as he stared down at the traffic traveling along the locally famous highway. From his vantage point, the cars and trucks looked like 'Matchbox' toys.

"Before you do though," added Tommy, "Could you make me the beneficiary on your life insurance policy?"

"Come on," interrupted Mikey, "We've got work to do."

He turned on the directional indicator and waited for a signal. He looked up and the main lodge was slightly off to his left. It was a large brown wooden structure with a patio deck that wrapped around the entire building. Smoke billowed from a red-brick chimney in the center of the roof and it was apparent that the fireplace was being well fed.

"What happens if the transmitter is right under the lodge?" asked Spike as he looked down at the indicator.

"We're in luck," said Mikey. "It's pointing to the east of it. Near those units over there."

He pointed at a line of condos that rimmed the parking lot. Above and behind them built into the side of the hill was another group of units. Each building had eight units and each unit was two stories. The style and décor was strictly "Old New England" with clapboard construction but the reddish paint was already fading badly from the harsh winds that prevailed throughout the area. It was obvious the builder wanted to maintain the ambiance of the region but the entire resort appeared to be badly in need of a new paint job. As Mikey began walking towards the units, the indicator continued to point in a straightforward direction indicating that he was going the right way. Spike accompanied him while the others stayed with the vehicles, feeling that it would not be wise to attract unwanted attention by moving as a pack.

As Mikey and Spike reached the first building, the indicator pointed slightly to the left so Mikey continued to follow it trying to be as discreet as possible. Some occupants emerged from a unit to his right. There were two adults, probably a married couple with two young children in tow. They conversed cheerfully among themselves as they headed for the lodge, perhaps for a late morning breakfast. They gave Mikey and Spike little more than a passing glance.

He continued walking around the first building and approached the units behind it. The parking lot was well paved and made it that much easier to ascend the hill. As he stood in front of the second building, only a few of the units appeared to be occupied. He stopped in front of the first door and felt comfortable that this was where the transmitter was buried.

"This is it," said Mikey softly. He handed the indicator to Spike and turned on the device Plaatu had given him to perform the re-calibration test.

Plaatu felt reasonably sure the device was working properly but he needed to be certain. That is why he had asked the men to undertake the assignment. Mikey angled the device down at the ground and watched the various indicator lights to take an initial reading. He was familiar with the signals he would have to achieve to determine if the device was working efficiently. He turned a few control knobs trying to get the various signals to align but as he turned to controls to both extremes, they simply would not line up.

"This isn't working," he muttered in frustration. "Did I say it or didn't I?' he asked Spike. "Murphy's friggin' law! I knew this sounded too easy."

Spike remembered something Plaatu had said that if the device didn't work from outside the building, it may become necessary to enter the structure in order to get closer. Mikey looked up at the windows of the unit. Of the eight units in the building it appeared only three were occupied. This just happened to be one of them.

"Just our friggin luck," he muttered. "Come on." He and Spike began walking back towards the vehicles to discuss the situation with the others. As they arrived, Brad, Ryan, Tommy and Chris were just sitting around with the side doors of the van wide open. It was breezy and downright chilly but the sun continued to shine brightly overhead. It was gradually warming the air and all in all, it was a rather splendid morning to be hanging out in the White Mountains.

"We've got a problem," said Mikey. "We have to get into the unit to get this done. I have to get closer and that is the only way I can do it."

"So," said Brad, "knock on the door and ask them what's for breakfast. People are very hospitable in this part of the country."

"You know I'm not good at that kind of stuff," protested Mikey who under certain circumstances could be notoriously shy. "One of you guys knock on the door. Tell them you're from the phone company or something and that we have to check out the service."

"You wimp!" said Tommy. "I'll do it. Just follow me. I'm an electrician and I know the lingo." He began walking towards the condos.

"Should I trust him?" asked Mikey. "Is this going to come back to haunt me?"

"It's quite possible," answered Ryan, "But even if it does, it should at least be entertaining." He smiled that devious smile of his and Mikey just shuddered.

"Chris," said Mikey, "you stay here. Anytime you two are together I get heartburn. Plaatu made it pretty clear that making sure this thing is working properly was pretty important so I don't want to screw this up."

"I have that effect on many people," Chris answered proudly.

"I'd go with you guys," said Brad, "but I haven't showered since yesterday."

"Neither have we!" said Spike. None of them had the opportunity to shower that morning having slept out in the woods again. They had been able to wash up out of pots and pans but that had been the extent of their personal hygiene levels.

"Yes," said Brad, "but I have personal standards to uphold. And they are much higher than any of you."

Mikey just shrugged. His sense of humor was on the wane. It was still early, they were functioning on drive-through coffee and donuts, he hadn't had time to even warm up the water they had used to wash up earlier. Now he was being put in a position where the success of this mission was totally dependant on Tommy's persuasive abilities to carry it off. Not a rosy picture to say the least.

"Let's go Spike," he said in disgust. "I just want to get this over with before matters get any worse."

He and Spike turned and began walking back towards the unit. Brad, Ryan and Chris stayed with the vehicles once again and went back to enjoying the view.

"Twenty bucks says they screw this up," said Brad softly.

"You're on," answered Ryan. "I have a lot more confidence in Mikey than you do apparently. Some friend you are."

"It isn't Mikey I'm worried about," chided Brad.

As Tommy reached the door of the unit and knocked on it loudly, he was filled with a sense of resolve and determination not to screw this up. He sensed a collective lack of confidence in his abilities from his comrades and saw this as a golden opportunity to make them eat crow.

He heard Mikey and Spike approaching from behind him. He carefully went over what he would say in his mind as he waited for someone to answer. "Hi, sorry to bother you today," he recited in his head. "I'm Tom and I'm with the phone company. We are going through the units checking on the newly installed fiber optic phone lines to make sure they are working properly. Would it be alright if we just took a few readings and we'll be on our way?" Yes, he thought, that sounded like a good angle to approach it from. Piece of cake. "Get in, get out. What a great philosophy with which to approach such an assignment."

He heard the doorknob turning. He cleared his throat, raised his head and thrust out his chest in an effort to look convincing. The door swung open and Tommy's jaw dropped. He just stood there, his mind a complete blank as the words he had carefully gone over and over vanished into nothingness.

Mikey and Spike had stopped about 15 feet away and were waiting for him to speak and try to gain them access. From their vantage point, they could not see who had answered the door.

"What the hell is he doing?" whispered Spike as he continued to watch the speechless Tommy.

"Can I help you?" said the incredibly attractive young lady standing in the doorway with nothing more than a towel wrapped around her. She had long flowing auburn hair and a figure that was causing Tommy's mind to experience a complete meltdown.

"Uh . . . uh . . ." stammered Tommy.

She smiled at his dilemma; no doubt she was use to such male reactions.

"Are you lost or something?" she asked playfully.

"No! No!" blurted Tommy, "Of course not!" He laughed awkwardly and shifted his weight from one foot to the other, then back again. "I'm from the phonatell company . . . I mean telephone company and I'm here to check your fibers."

"Excuse me?" she asked, still smiling.

"No, no," stammered Tommy. "I don't mean *your* fibers. I'm sure your fibers are just fine, or at least they look fine from here." He struggled to regain his composure. "I meant the phone fibers. In the phone. Inside the wires . . ." He gulped helplessly.

Mikey and Spike couldn't take it any more and walked up the three stairs to the small landing where Tommy was fidgeting and gesticulating awkwardly. They could now see why he was making such an ass of himself. Mikey stared down at her long shapely legs and found it difficult to speak as well. One of them needed to get a grip and that duty fell to the oldest of the three.

"Excuse me, ma'am," said Spike in a slow deliberate tone, "we're out here from the phone company and we need to take some readings from inside the units. We won't be long but would it be alright if my associate here came in and checked out your service. We don't want to make you nervous so my speechless friend here and I can wait outside."

The men heard other voices from inside the unit. They were young female voices.

"Who is it Kerri?" someone yelled down from the second floor.

"It's just some guys from the phone company," she yelled. "They need to check the phones!"

Mikey heard footsteps running down the stairs. The door swung wide open and now there were four young vixens standing there staring them straight in the eyes. It was like a dream come true. They were all scantily clad and apparently didn't seem the least bit ashamed to be seen thusly attired.

"Phone company guys huh?" said the first girl. She had a look on her face as if she was gazing upon a member of the opposite sex for the first time in her life. The three men just stood there as if they were collectively pondering the amazingly remote odds that they would find themselves first in the company of aliens, and now in the company of four goddesses. All in one camping trip no less.

"Pinch me will ya?" whispered Mikey to Spike.

"Well come on in!" said Kerri. "Do what you have to do. Don't mind us, we're just up here on a long weekend break from work. We are nurses at New Hampshire Medical."

The men walked in and she closed the door behind them. The other girls escorted them into the living room where Spike and Tommy sat down in the plush blue sofa chairs next to the couch. The room was a mess with various items of clothing strewn about. There were empty bags of Cheese Curls, discarded beer cans and a half-empty bottle of Chardonnay on the coffee table. It was clear that they had been partying heavy the night before but they sure didn't seem to be sporting any hangovers as a result of it.

Kerri introduced her three friends as Karen, Jenny, and Michelle, then she escorted Mikey to the kitchen wall phone. He thanked her and suggested it might be a good idea if she went and got dressed. Oddly enough, an overwhelming sense of fatherly instincts began to replace his initial impulses of lust and desire. His conscience told him that if she was his daughter and he found out that she had let three strange men into their unit this easily, he would have been furious. They were fortunate indeed that on this particular occasion, they had granted access to three honorable men. They might not be so lucky next time.

He could hear the other girls conversing and giggling among themselves as they entertained Spike and Tommy. Kerri took his advice and went upstairs to put on some clothes. As he glanced down at the alien device and began adjusting the controls, the intoxicating fragrance of her perfume lingered in the air and made it difficult for him to focus on the task at hand. "Snap out of it!" he hissed. He manipulated the controls again and this time, they immediately fell into alignment. He was standing right over the transmitter and in the matter of a few moments, the device softly beeped and all the indicators read normal. From what he could see, the transmitter had been correctly re-calibrated and for all intents and purposes, should work properly if Plaatu's instructions were correct.

Mikey turned off the device and breathed a huge sigh of relief. He looked around at the spacious kitchen. The units were very large; and the living room had a Cathedral ceiling. They were designed with east-west exposure to maximize sunlight and they were definitely bright and cheerful. But boy, he thought to himself, are these girls sloppy. The sink was full of dirty dishes even though there was an under counter dishwasher in the unit. If this was how their apartments looked, someone should read them the riot act. Then a thought came to his head. The job was done, or at least it appeared to be judging by the readings. There was nothing else they could do to double-check it so it was now out of their hands. Plaatu was on his way to New York so both he and planet Earth for that matter were in fate's hands now for better or for worse. So why not try and make the best of the present situation? The nearest showers available to them were four hours south in Stamford at their homes. Except for those right upstairs. "Never pass up on a good opportunity," he thought to himself. Besides, spending a bit more time in the company of this unit's occupants seemed far more alluring than hanging out with aliens. All this save-the-world stuff was beginning to get very stressful.

He walked into the living room where Tommy, Spike and the three girls were still laughing and talking light-heartedly. Tommy still had that same look on his face like he had just woken up on Christmas morning. Something inside Mikey's mind did a complete 360 degree turn. As he gazed around at the three ladies, none of them appeared to be more than twenty five years of age. He again re-confirmed in his mind how fortunate they were that he and his two phone company impersonators were not sexual deviates or worse yet, serial killers. These girls were far too naive and far too trusting. They were wearing nothing more than teddies which left very little to the imagination. Mikey was in many ways a typical male. He enjoyed a healthy display of cleavage as much as the next guy. In this day and age however, these women would be wise to show far more caution.

Kerri rejoined them and was more appropriately dressed in dungarees and a UNH sweatshirt. Her delicate feet were still exposed however and the casual attire did nothing to take away from her innate beauty and irresistible sex appeal. Mikey's eyes met with hers for a few moments but then he tore away from her mesmerizing gaze and interrupted the light-hearted discussion.

"Ladies," he began. "I've finished what I needed to do and I just want to say thanks. This is going to sound totally crazy but we have been working around the clock due this deadline we are under, do you think we could bother you to use your showers for a quick refresher? I know it probably sounds suggestive but I promise we will be in and out of here in no time."

Tommy and Spike both stood up and looked a bit unsure of Mikey's request.

"No, that's OK," said Spike apparently a little uncomfortable with the idea.

"Nonsense! It's alright," gushed Kerri. "We've all showered already. Help yourselves."

"Oh, alright," said Tommy. "As long as you girls don't mind?"

A few moments of awkward silence followed as the girls waited for the three men to move, not realizing that they were collectively wrestling with the conundrum of who would go first. Mikey solved the issue.

"Tommy," he said calmly, "why don't you go first. I have to call the others on my cell phone and let them know what we are doing."

"No problem," said Tommy shyly as he brushed by the three girls who were sitting on the couch and prepared to head upstairs. Mikey dialed Brad on his cell phone when all of a sudden there was a knock at the door. Kerri went to answer it as Mikey heard Brad pick up on the other end.

"What's up?" he heard Brad say. "You guys done yet? I'm getting hungry again. Maybe we can grab some chow in the lodge before we head out of here."

Kerri returned to the living room with a puzzled look on her face.

"Hey," she said, "how many of you phone guys are there? There are three more at the door saying they need to get in here." She lowered her voice. "They look really weird though."

Mikey glanced over as three figures appeared in the hallway just inside the front door. An alarm went off in his head. They were still in the shadows and he couldn't make out their features but he was certain they were not Ryan, Brad and Chris.

"Well!" said the man in front of the other two larger men who stood dutifully behind him. "We seemed to have interrupted a little party."

They were all dressed in bright red ski parkas, blue ski pants and white stocking caps with New England Telephone emblems on them. They were so obvious it was laughable. But Tommy, Spike and Mikey weren't laughing. Kerri noticed the look of alarm on Mikey's face and immediately became frightened. It was as if the folly of her actions had finally coalesced in her consciousness. The clarity of their situation hit her as if someone had just dropped a building on top of her.

"What the hell is going on here?" she asked nervously. The other three girls noticed her state of alarm and it was contagious.

"Yes," said Zuf Pada with a devious grin as he stepped out into the light. "What is going on here?"

Mikey was still holding his cell phone and the connection was still open. He could hear Brad shouting for a response on the other end of the signal.

"Ickeymay," is all he could mutter as he closed up the phone and glared at Pada.

"It would appear that masquerading as telephone employees is very much in vogue this time of year," said Spike sarcastically.

"What do you want?" asked Mikey angrily as Tommy and Spike moved into position to assist if necessary. The two larger Tilatins behind Pada remained unyielding and were as imposing as ever.

Kerri stood a few feet away from Pada and was severely regretting having ever opened the door to any of them. The tension in the air persisted for a few moments more when she was compelled to act.

"I'm calling the police!" she blurted as she moved towards the phone. She never made it.

Pada swung his right hand violently, striking her square across the side of her face and sent her careening into the living room wall. The other three girls shrieked in alarm as Kerri crumpled to the floor.

Tommy's face filled with rage. "You bastard!" he cursed as he lunged for Pada. He was too slow however as the Tilatin withdrew his pistol from beneath his jacket and fired an energy blast that hit Tommy square in the mid-section. It lifted him off his feet and he went sailing over the couch like a crash test dummy. Spike and Mikey immediately reacted but their threatening moves were met with his pistol being aimed in their direction stopping them dead in their tracks.

"Now give me the transmitter," snarled Pada. "I know why you're Golonian friend wanted you to perform your little re-calibration errand and we're going to undo it. I've got some rather large fireworks planned for your little planet and I don't want your friend Plaatu to spoil the fun."

The two Tilatin guards moved menacingly towards Mikey and one of them extended his hand. Mikey had little choice. He reluctantly handed over the device.

"Stick it where the sun don't shine," he said in defiance. Then he went to assist Kerri who was still unconscious on the floor. Spike rushed to check on Tommy who still lay motionless behind the couch.

They were both still breathing but Pada's blow had opened a small gash on Kerri's cheek. A thin trail of blood trickled down her face. Mikey glanced up at the three girls who were standing off to the side, frozen with fear.

"Do you have a first aid kit?" he asked, ignoring the glare of Pada and the other Tilatins.

"Keep your weapons trained on them," Pada ordered the guards as he took the re-calibration device and switched it on. He watched the readings intently, then he moved towards the kitchen.

Outside in the parking lot, Brad closed his cell phone and just stared off into space for a moment. Ryan and Chris watched him intently, then Ryan waved his hand in front of his face as if Brad was in some sort of trance.

"Hello?" said Ryan in a frustrated tone. "What gives? What is taking them so long?"

Brad looked directly into his eyes. "Ickeymay," he said softly. "I think we've got problems."

CHAPTER TEN

Plaatu proceeded in the direction of his ship with Bort following closely behind. The sun continued to warm the air and as he glanced from side to side at the trees that lined the road, the varying colors dazzled his eyes. It may not have been the best foliage display the area had ever offered up but it wasn't very often in his many travels that he had beheld such a beautiful sight. He stopped for a moment. Bort did as well. As he stared up at the bright yellow ball in the sky through his protective glasses and felt its warm radiant glow upon his face, he was momentarily transfixed. The proximity distance of Earth from its sun was probably the most significant reason why no other planet in this solar system seemed to be teeming with life the way Earth was at that precise moment in time. There was a balance of nature here that Plaatu had not experienced very often. All the necessary elements seemed to be perfectly aligned allowing countless forms of life to flourish. It offered just the right combination of chemical agents, proper temperatures and gravitational pull to support a vibrant and healthy eco-system in which millions of life forms could survive and multiply. In Plaatu's mind it merely strengthened his resolve that such a planet simply had to be protected at all costs.

There wasn't another soul in sight. He knew the guardsmen were just around the next bend but at that precise moment, he found himself lost in the sensation that if nirvana truly did exist anywhere in the galaxy, this certainly could be it, or the closest thing to it. A gentle breeze was blowing causing the branches of the trees to sway to and fro, as if they were waving him on. No rest for the weary, they seemed to be whispering. Another crisis needed to be addressed. No time to stop and smell the roses. A planet's fate hung in the balance. Millions of lives were at stake yet again. How long had he been doing this? When was it all going to end? He so wanted to just sit down and stay there forever, soaking up the intoxicating ambiance this area of the universe was laying before his senses. Let somebody else deal with the turmoil, his mind pleaded.

He glanced up at Bort, standing dutifully at the ready once again. He had become like an appendage to Plaatu and his absence had its consequences. Plaatu never felt fear when Bort was by his side. There simply was no bodyguard in the known universe better equipped to deal with just about any situation than Bort was. For a moment, Plaatu envied him. He was a machine, totally incapable of feeling the myriad of emotions Plaatu found himself wrestling with. He was immune to fear, anxiety, frustration, all the things that plagued most humanoid species. But like everything else in life, this too was a double-edged sword. He could never feel joy, love, and contentment either. He was merely about function and efficiency.

Plaatu saw Ecko's ship lift off and knew the guardsmen would see it as well. He needed to get moving again. The proverbial turd was about to hit the fan. "Once more into the breach, eh old friend," he muttered to Bort. "Isn't that how that poem goes . . . ?"

Bort just stood motionless like a metal statue, awaiting further instructions. Plaatu placed his hand on his shoulder as if he was in need of reassurance that this increasingly more complicated conundrum he had become embroiled in would turn out alright. He glanced off in the direction of his ship and pondered his next move. There was no need to overly frighten these men. Perhaps he could convince them to leave the area in their own best interest. He instructed Bort to stay close at hand but out of site in the initial moments.

They began walking again, their footsteps crunching softly on the gravel-covered road beneath their feet. As they rounded the bend in the road, Bort moved obediently off to the soft shoulder and remained out of sight as Plaatu approached the clearing. One of the guardsmen spotted him and alerted the others. They all moved to intercept him just as Plaatu entered the campsite. His ship was a few dozen yards away directly in front of him. A uniformed man with a safety mask was attempting to gain access with a blow torch.

"That won't do you any good," said Plaatu in a loud voice. Several guardsmen now stood directly in front of him but their weapons were pointed downward. "That's a refreshing change," he thought. A few others were positioned around the perimeter and a large truck blocked the entrance coming in from the highway.

"You can't be out here," said a soldier wearing sergeant stripes. "This area is off limits to civilian personnel. I'm afraid you're going to have to leave."

Plaatu just smiled and continued to watch the man with the blow torch in his futile effort to get into the ship.

"Gentlemen," said Plaatu, looking directly at the guardsmen. "I would appreciate it if you would allow me to re-enter my cruiser so I can be on my way. I have an important engagement at your UN headquarters in New York."

The guardsmen seemed a bit confused for a moment, understandably unable to recognize that they had an alien in their presence.

"Did you say 'your cruiser'?" asked the sergeant.

"That's right," said Plaatu matter-of-factly. "I am its pilot and I really need to be on my way."

"Hey! You're that space guy!" blurted the corporal who was standing just a few feet behind the sergeant.

Plaatu just chuckled. "Yes, my good man, and time is of the essence. Now please, sergeant, move your men away so that my robot and I can continue our mission."

"What robot?" asked the corporal.

The sergeant was hesitant for a moment. He wasn't the least bit convinced of Plaatu's sincerity. He was assigned to guard the ship and something in his troubled mind told him that if he just let some guy who claimed to be its owner take possession of it, there might be serious consequences with his superiors.

"Now hold on there cupcake," he said smugly. "I don't know who you are but I gotta check in with command before I do anything." He turned to his subordinates and ordered them to watch Plaatu closely.

As they raised their weapons and moved to follow his orders, the sergeant began walking towards the back of the truck where the platoon's radio equipment was located. He had only taken a few steps when the campsite erupted with energy blasts that came at the soldiers from all sides. Plaatu instinctively retreated backwards and crouched to the ground as each of the guardsmen was systematically blasted into unconsciousness. He remained crouched, his mind filled with uncertainty as he saw three other figures approaching from different directions. They were the only three men still standing but they weren't wearing army fatigues.

"We were wondering when you were going to show up," said the largest of the three men as they stopped a few feet in front of Plaatu. "Zuf Pada would like to have a few words with you."

Plaatu rose to his feet slowly and glanced down at the side arms they were carrying. They were Tilatin blasters all right. These were three different Tilatins than the ones he had dealt with the previous day meaning another ship was on the ground somewhere.

They kept their pistols trained on him and they seemed to be enjoying his dilemma.

"You Tilatins are beginning to annoy me," Plaatu said caustically as he surveyed their clothing. The Tilatins were dressed in hunter's garb with denim trousers, John Deer caps and plaid long-sleeved shirts." Masters of masquerade, you buggers. For your sakes, those pistols had better be set on stun. If any of these men die, you will live to regret it."

"Is that a threat?" asked the lead Tilatin smugly. "I really don't think you are in any position to threaten anyone."

"Bort! Baringa!" snapped Plaatu in a boisterous tone.

The Tilatin's jaw dropped and his face took on the look of someone who had just had a cattle prod rammed up his butt. The other two Tilatins took on similar expressions and began to slowly move away from Plaatu. An energy beam vaporized the blasters in their hands almost simultaneously. Bort's metallic visor then lowered and he stopped a few feet behind Plaatu.

"You were saying?" said Plaatu with a wry smile. They remained rigid and unwilling to speak. "Hold that pose for a moment would you?" he said as they obediently stood motionless under Bort's watchful stare. Plaatu checked the pulse on the sergeant. He was still alive, as were the other soldiers he tended to. He breathed a sigh of relief, then he walked over to his ship and lowered the entrance ramp. He hurried inside and returned with a small hand-held device. One by one, he pressed the device into each of the guardsmen's arms and they slowly regained consciousness. As each of them stood up, they glanced around the campsite trying to comprehend what had happened. At random intervals, each guardsman's gaze came full circle and then stopped abruptly upon the huge metallic robot. In a few moments, they were all just staring up at him, their minds collectively filled with confusion.

Plaatu addressed the sergeant. 'Don't let him frighten you," he said in a comforting tone. The sergeant rubbed his arm where Plaatu had administered the stimulant, then he rubbed his chest where he had been stunned by the blaster. He still looked groggy as he leaned over and picked up his M-16 rifle.

"What the hell is going on here?" he snarled with as much authority as he could muster. He had all he could do to keep from booting his breakfast.

Plaatu would have liked to stay and chat but time was a commodity in short supply at the moment. He needed to be on his way.

"I don't have time to explain," he said, "but I would appreciate it if you would take these three vermin into custody for me and hold them until I return." There were holding cells on Plaatu's ship but babysitting three Tilatin prisoners was something he would rather avoid with so much uncertainty that lay ahead. He ordered Bort to follow him and began walking towards the ramp.

"What'd they do?" asked the Sergeant. "Are they the ones who knocked us out?"

"Affirmative. They're aliens," said Plaatu, "and nasty buggers too. Watch them closely."

Plaatu stopped briefly at thee top of the ramp and waited for Bort. He glanced over just in time to see the sergeant haul off and belt one of the Tilatins right in the chops. The alien's head lurched back but it had little effect. The other soldiers had their M-16's trained on them so he dared not retaliate.

"Not in the head!" yelled Plaatu. "Aim a little lower."

The sergeant wound up and nailed the lead Tilatin right in the mid-section. He buckled to one knee and didn't get up.

"Hey thanks," yelled the sergeant.

Plaatu followed Bort into the ship. Then he retracted the ramp and the hatch closed behind him. In a few moments the cruiser lifted gently off the ground and began to ascend. As it climbed higher and higher, the guardsmen were completely mesmerized as they followed its upward ascent. It served as a perfect diversion for the Tilatins who scurried off into the woods completely unnoticed.

As Plaatu's ship reached an elevation of ten thousand feet, he laid in the necessary coordinates which would guide his ship to New York. Then he quickly washed up and donned a fresh uniform. The trip would only take a matter of minutes which would get him there well in advance of whatever the Tilatins had planned. The exact point at which the event would take place however was still a bit of a predicament. Plaatu knew it involved the United Nations general assembly chambers but it was a large room in a large building sitting on a very large track of land. He heard Pada say it would happen around noon but he would need a bit of luck if he was going to successfully prevent a potentially catastrophic incident from occurring.

"Aircraft approaching," announced his computer as his ship continued in a southwestern direction.

"Identify," he ordered, not the least bit alarmed.

"Four United States Air Force F-16 fighter jets on an intercept course," said the computer. The main viewing screen switched on and Plaatu watched as the jets appeared in the distance. They were still many miles away and they would never be able to out-maneuver his ship, but as he continued to watch them, they moved into what appeared to be an attack formation. "Humans,"

Plaatu muttered to himself with amusement. "Shoot first and ask questions later. They are so predictable." Then the pilots fired their weapons just as he suspected they would. The Am-Ram missiles followed his ship's heat signature and began to close on their target. Plaatu sat back in his command chair and exhaled heavily. "Always the aggressors," he said in a remorseful tone. "Computer, all stop."

His ship hovered in the air and within a few seconds all four missiles found their target. They exploded harmlessly against his ship's outer hull with a loud thud, then the four jets rocketed past him. Plaatu could only imagine the looks on the faces of the pilots as they whizzed by the undamaged ship. As the jets turned to make another run, Plaatu ordered the computer to descend quickly and proceed back on course. By the time the jets finished their turns, Plaatu could see the UN Building on his main viewer. The ship continued to descend and the jets broke off their pursuit. He knew they wouldn't risk another attack at a lower altitude for fear of harming civilians on the ground.

It was 11:25 AM. He only had 35 minutes or so before the Tilatins carried out their objective.

Plaatu fully expected that there would be a welcoming committee of some sort waiting for him once he reached UN plaza. As his ship continued to descend however, the scene materializing on his main viewing screen caused the hairs on the back of his neck to stand straight up. His request that Ryan contact Congresswoman Randell to inform her that he would be coming and to keep it discreet apparently got lost in the translation. Granted, the words discreet and New York rarely collide in the same sentence but it looked like a full blown circus had come to town. His nerves continued to twitch as his ship lowered to an elevation of five hundred feet. He was directly over the plaza now and as he instructed his on-board computer to set down, Plaatu watched as spectators began to clear the area. They shrewdly recognized that if they didn't surrender their position, there would be a relatively good chance they would be crushed under the ship's belly. In a few seconds, Plaatu felt the soft thud of his ship making contact with the unyielding cement surface of the plaza. The engines shut down and for the moment, it was completely quiet inside his ship. Outside however, it was anything but. An almost-carnival atmosphere filled the entire plaza as thousands of spectators awaited the appearance of this visitor from another world. He had no idea how news of his coming got out but he wasn't the least bit happy about it. Up to this point, Plaatu had tried the quiet approach to this mission. That was now a fleeting memory. His nerve endings continued to tingle as he prepared to exit the ship. Maybe this was the approach he should have taken right from the start. Perhaps by being more direct and assertive, he would have been finished with his mission and on his way home by now. "Then again," he thought to himself, "maybe I am getting a little sick and tired of second guessing myself."

He rose to his feet and walked slowly towards the exit hatch. As his ship's ramp lowered to the ground, the noise from the multitude of people surrounding his ship suddenly assaulted his ears. The sun was shining brightly over head so he donned a pair of tinted glasses and ordered Bort to accompany him as he walked down the ramp. As soon as he became visible, a tumultuous roar erupted from the crowd. It was so loud, he stopped in his tracks for a moment. "They have been watching far too many movies," he muttered as he gathered his strength and continued down the ramp. Bort was directly behind him.

As he reached the ground, there was a contingent of military representatives waiting to greet him. Plaatu scanned the perimeter of the plaza. Sure enough, there was a strong military presence, armored vehicles, soldiers and enough hardware to make him more than a little nervous. They were attempting to display a non-hostile appearance, but Plaatu knew better. The F-16's he had encountered only a few moments earlier were anything but non-hostile.

Bort stopped next to him and remained motionless as a high ranking member of the welcoming committee walked towards Plaatu. The crowd surrounding the plaza continued to voice their excitement and if not for the cement barriers that had been brought in to keep them at bay, Plaatu was sure they would rush his ship in zealous curiosity.

A line of flagpoles rimmed the front of the building and the flags of all the nations fluttered in the wind as Plaatu continued to weigh the situation. An enticing aroma hung in the air all around him. As he tried to scan the crowd nearest to him in an effort to discover its origin, his eyes locked onto a food cart with a sign on the front of it that read "Jose's Sausage, Pepper and Onions."

"Mr. Plaatu I presume," said the front man for the group. It was General Carl Koopman, decked out in his dress blue uniform with ribbons and medals adorning his upper chest. He had a shit-eating grin on his face as he glanced up at Bort in amazement. "Is he a friend of yours?" Koopman added, insinuating he would like to be introduced to the metal giant. As supremely confident as he was trying to appear, he really had no idea what to make of him.

Plaatu immediately didn't like this man. He reeked of a disingenuous air that almost caused Plaatu to gag. "This is my traveling companion," said Plaatu with little enthusiasm. "His name is Bort."

"I see," answered Koopman, still grinning broadly. "Well, would you accompany me inside the building? There are some people who are looking forward to speaking with you. It will be much quieter inside." Koopman turned as if to escort Plaatu towards the front door but Plaatu hesitated. The crowd was still wildly exuberant and Plaatu was acutely aware that the level of military hardware in evidence was completely over the top. His entire body was filled with an overwhelming sense of apprehension and he just couldn't shake it off. He wasn't going to go anywhere until he felt that he had a much better grasp on the situation. He needed to gain control, even if that meant wrestling it away from the good General.

"Would you mind instructing your military vehicles to leave the area?" Plaatu asked in a deliberate tone.

"Aw, don't worry about them," said Koopman smugly. "It's just a precaution, that's all. They have strict orders not to fire unless absolutely necessary."

"I see," said Plaatu. "Just like the F-16's I just encountered during my descent?"

Koopman's facial expression became flushed as if he had been caught staring down his secretary's blouse. "I don't know about any F-16's," he said awkwardly. "I'm an Army man myself."

"Of course," Plaatu replied curtly.

Koopman's tone of confidence and bravado didn't appeal to Plaatu one bit. It was obvious this high-ranking dolt had no control over the situation as the entire plaza was nothing short of a semi-contained melee. There were far too many soldiers, too many weapons and too many noisy onlookers for Plaatu's liking. He was getting too old for this kind of nonsense and he was not in the mood for primitive human shenanigans. As he glanced around at the rowdy onlookers, the TV cameras, the brightly colored signs with colorful phrases painted on them like, "welcome to Earth" and "Take me with you", he was reminded of something. While he actually liked some of this planet's inhabitants, there were far too many of them and some could be downright annoying. His patience was wearing thin.

"Bort, badabinga," he said in a commanding tone. Bort took three steps forward and his visor slowly raised. Koopman stepped away not sure what to make of it. He stared up at Bort as if frozen in his shoes, then Bort began to fire. The first vehicles to be vaporized were the three M-1 Abram's tanks that were directly across the plaza near the front of the building. As the tank's inhabitants scrambled to exit through the hatchways, the three enormous metal vehicles began to glow brighter and brighter, then they were gone. A

hush fell over the crowd as they collectively tried to unravel in their minds
what that meant to them. Then they began to panic. Bort began to fire at the
various machine guns mounted on the backs of Jeeps and finally he focused
his unstoppable beam on the small arms that lesser ranking soldiers were
carrying. In what seemed like a matter of just a few seconds, there wasn't
a single member of the military who retained a firearm. They all just stood
there with their mouths hanging open as if they had been stripped naked and
buried up to their chins in the desert sand.

"Bort barada nikto," ordered Plaatu.

Bort's visor lowered and he resumed a motionless position.

The crowd began to flee in terror as shouts and screams came from every
direction. Even the traditionally undaunted camera crews turned and ran for
their lives. Bort was an imposing figure and his ability to disarm such a large
military presence so effortlessly convinced even the bravest of reporters that
it may not be wise to hang around. Plaatu just stared at Koopman during the
entire episode. The general's smug look had quickly changed to one of awe
and self-doubt as onlookers scurried off in every direction.

Then it became very quiet. Plaatu could now hear the distinct sound of
the flags flapping in the breeze and he found it to be very soothing.

"Now," he said calmly, "that's better isn't it?"

Koopman and the other officers standing a few yards behind him just
stood there, not quite sure what to do next. Plaatu was eminently more
comfortable now and was ready to enter the building.

"Shall we go?" he said as he began walking towards the entrance. Koopman
fell in line behind him but he kept a safe distance.

The entrance checkpoint at the UN building had been busier than
usual that morning. An important vote was to be considered by the General
assembly and virtually every member nation had a contingent of delegates
present for the occasion. The six security personnel assigned to monitor the
metal detectors were swamped and as Plaatu's ship arrived on the plaza, the
commotion and noise combined to present them with more activity than they
were accustomed to handling. Just as the Saudi Arabian representatives arrived
there was a commotion just outside the sliding glass doors that led into the
building. The disturbance drew two of the security agents away from their
stations. The Saudi's were already a bit spooked by the size and frenzy of the
crowd and were very much on edge. Pandemonium broke out as several of
the Saudi's began to shout and attempt to rush through the metal detectors
to get away from the noisy crowd outside. Before the remaining four security
agents could restore control, two men had slipped past them unnoticed and

had disappeared down the hall. One of them was carrying a brown leather suitcase in his right hand.

Brad, Ryan and Chris stood motionless in the mid-day sun; each trying to unravel in their minds what kind of situation might be waiting for them inside the condo unit. "Ickeymay" meant only one thing. Mikey and the others were in trouble and things had not gone according to plan. They could only assume that Mikey was not in a position to elaborate on their predicament or, he would have . . . elaborated on their predicament.

Brad stared at the ground as a myriad of thoughts entered his mind. The past few days had been anything but predictable. Just when they thought their involvement in this crazy escapade had come to an end, they got dragged right back into it. This was supposed to be the end of the trip, the roller-coaster ride was supposed to have come to a halt and let them off. Instead, here they were facing yet another crisis.

Ryan quickly pondered the events of the last few days in detail. As he did, he endeavored to ascertain who might want to prevent them from carrying out Plaatu's instructions to re-calibrate the transmitter. On the surface the task certainly seemed harmless enough. What could be so important about a simple transmitter? "All it does is send signals right?" he thought. "It's not as if it was some sort of powerful weapon like a death ray or photon torpedo. Who would be the most likely suspect at this precise moment in time that would benefit most from deterring them from completing this assignment? Then it dawned on him. He glanced up at Brad and Chris with a look of alarm. To his surprise, they had seemingly come to the same conclusion as he did.

"Tilatins!" he muttered ominously.

"Tilatins!" repeated Brad.

"So what do we do?" asked Chris anxiously.

Ryan looked inside the van for ideas. The rifles were definitely out of the question as they would be much too obvious. The sight of three unkempt men striding through the parking lot with menacing looks and sporting firearms could potentially frighten onlookers and incite them to contact the authorities. Then he noticed the bag of softball supplies he had from the previous week's games. He removed three of the aluminum bats and handed one each to Brad and Chris.

"Remember," he said. "Plaatu told us never hit them in the head; you'll only make them mad."

The three men turned and began walking towards the condo and the reckoning that surely awaited them within its walls. It was time to lay an ass-whooping on some aliens. They assumed their game faces as they continued across the lot, their hearts thumping faster and faster with every step. As they passed the main lodge, Brad noticed that the bust of a bull moose hung over the front door.

"Hey!" he blurted. "I have an idea."

Inside the unit, Mikey was tending to Kerri's wound under the watchful gaze of the two armed Tilatins. Zuf Pada had gone into the kitchen. Tommy was still unconscious but Spike had carried his limp body and laid him gently on the couch. Jenny had asked permission to fetch a wet washcloth to place on his forehead and the Tilatin guards had grudgingly granted her request. As she sat next to him, gently daubing his forehead, Kerri began to regain consciousness. She opened her eyes slowly and Mikey greeted her with a warm smile.

"Are you OK?" he said in a compassionate tone. Pada had not held back when he struck her and Mikey had really feared for the worst when he saw her fall to the floor. He breathed a huge sigh of relief now that she was coming to.

Kerri groaned and tried to sit up against the wall. Mikey held her gently and helped her gain a sitting position. He had placed a bandage under her right eye and it had successfully stopped the bleeding.

"Try not to move too much," said Mikey. "You had a nasty cut there and you lost a little blood."

Pada walked back into the living room and was still holding the re-calibration device. He looked around the room at the others with scorn and contempt.

"Let your friend Plaatu try and activate it now," he said with an ugly grin.

Mikey clenched his fists and tried to control his rage. Every bone in his body wanted to lunge at the loathsome Tilatin and pummel him to within an inch of his life but the two Tilatin guards made the odds simply impossible. His mind reeled with anger as he struggled to determine a course of action when he heard a knock at the door. The expressions on the faces of the three Tilatins changed to one of concern. Pada moved to answer it, then backed off and softly ordered one of the guards to respond to it instead. He ordered the other guard to carry Kerri out of the hallway where she wouldn't be seen. "If any of you cry out, you all die!" Pada hissed in a venomous tone.

"Worthless coward," Mikey thought to himself as he watched the guard open the door. His vantage point from the hallway gave Mikey a clear view of who was knocking and as the door swung open he saw someone standing there with the bust of a moose over his head. As angry and enraged as he was, he had all he could handle trying to refrain from breaking out in laughter. Judging by the man's height, he knew it could only be Chris.

"Hello!" Chris blurted in a muffled tone. "I'm from the White Mountain National Forrest Foundation. We are collecting contributions to protect the endangered Beluga Moose of North America in this area, would you like to contribute?"

The Tilatin guard was completely stupefied and turned to Pada for direction. Pada walked towards the front door feeling reasonably sure that the moose headed human posed no threat when Chris lunged forward antlers first and drove them into the chest of the Tilatin guard. It hurt Chris more than it did the Tilatin but it did catch him off balance and opened enough room in the doorway for Brad and Ryan to rush in with bats flailing. They moved so quickly Pada was slow in getting his pistol out of its holster. It was now five to three and Mikey took advantage of the improved odds by lunging for Pada. He tackled him to the ground as Spike moved to intercept the guard who had carried Kerri out of the hallway.

Jenny, Karen, and Michelle escaped to the kitchen out of harms way as the living room erupted into a full-fledged, old fashioned donnybrook. The Tilatin who had answered the door was the first to be confronted as Brad wound up and slammed him in the mid-section. The guard buckled over and before he had time to recover, Ryan followed with a blow to his upper back knocking the wind out of him. He dropped to the floor with a thud and remained motionless.

Spike didn't fare very well as the other guard swung his arm squarely into his upper chest and sent him sailing over the coffee table, but not before he was able to grab the pistol from his belt leaving the Tilatin weapon-less. Mikey and Pada were wrestling in the hallway so Chris, having removed the bust piled on to assist. That left Brad and Ryan to confront the remaining guard. As they entered the living room they put some distance between them. Now they could come at him from both sides. They squared off for a few moments, each sizing up their attack. It was clear each was hesitant to commit to the first blow for fear of missing the target. Then the guard glanced towards the kitchen out of the corner of his eye. There were hostages there that he could put to good use. A devious gleam came to his gaze but Brad had postured long enough. He took a step to his right and raised his bat knowing full well that the Tilatin would have to defend against the blow giving Ryan the chance to thwack him from his opposite side. The strategy worked as the Tilatin ducked under the blow but was momentarily vulnerable. Taking his cue, Ryan had already raised his bat and as the guard tried to regain his center of balance, Ryan buried his aluminum club into his mid-section. It sounded like he had struck a bag of wet sand and this Tilatin was obviously made of sterner stuff than the first. He doubled over but was still more than game for the fight. He grabbed Ryan's bat on the recoil and yanked it out of his hands but before he could do anything with it, Brad caught him right in the throat with a vicious swing. The guard went rigid for a moment as his huge frame reacted to the blow. Brad nailed him again, this time square in the gut and he dropped to the ground like a felled tree.

"He was one tough hombre wasn't he?" said Ryan, still breathing heavily.

Mikey had let loose on Pada, landing solid punches to his jaw that would have knocked most men senseless. In his rage however, he had forgotten that Tilatins have unusually strong chops and Pada was still quite capable of fighting back. He caught Chris with a kick to the mid-section that sent him hurtling down the hall. Then he rolled over and caught Mikey with a body blow that staggered him enough to force him to relax his grip on the Tilatin. Pada jumped to his feet and upon seeing Brad and Ryan approach menacingly, he reached for his pistol. Realizing it had fallen to the floor during the scuffle, he scurried out the front door.

"Son of a bitch!" fumed Mikey as he slowly got to his feet and tried to catch his breath.

Chris, Spike, Ryan and Brad joined him in the hallway. Chris and Spike were panting heavily but not seriously hurt. Tommy still lay motionless on the couch.

"Don't worry," said Ryan. "I'm sure Plaatu and Ecko will track him down easily enough. What happened to Tommy?"

"Pada nailed him with his stun gun or whatever those things shoot," answered Spike. "We better get him and Kerri to a hospital."

Mikey surveyed the floor of the condo for a few moments. Then he began to look around, searching under furniture and in every corner. A Tilatin blaster was there but that's not what he was looking for.

"He took the re-calibration tool," said Mikey.

"So what?" asked Brad. "Didn't you do your thing already?"

"Yeah, I did," said Mikey. "But Pada took it from me and I think he undid what I . . . did."

"Shit!" said Spike. Then he paused for a moment as a look of confusion came over his face. "How significant is that anyways?"

"I don't know," answered Ryan, "but I got the distinct impression that Plaatu felt it was relatively important that this device buried under the ground be working properly. I think that means that we had better chase down the swine and get it back from him. What time is it?"

Brad looked at his watch. "It's 11:30," he said.

"That means we have one half hour to find him in these woods and get back here," said Ryan.

The three women emerged from the kitchen, still visibly frightened. They looked down at the two Tilatin guards still lying motionless on the floor. They glanced up to catch Ryan, Brad and Chris ogling them in their dainty little teddies causing each of them to blush.

"You haven't introduced us to your friends," Chris said to Mikey.

Mikey introduced Brad, Chris, and Ryan to the three ladies, then walked over to where Tommy still lay motionless on the couch.

"They won't be regaining consciousness anytime soon will they?" asked Jenny, pointing towards the Tilatin guards.

"If they do," said Spike, "Shoot them with this." He handed her one of the three blasters they had confiscated after the melee. "It should do the trick quite nicely."

"Alright," said Brad. "Here's the deal. Ryan, Mikey, Spike and I will head out after Pada. He can't be far. Chris, why don't you and the ladies here get the van and take the wounded to the hospital. Then we'll meet you back here."

"Got it," said Chris and he headed for the parking lot to retrieve the van.

Karen and Michelle helped Kerri into a chair. She still appeared to be a bit groggy but her gaze was no longer glassy and distant. Mikey placed his hand on Tommy's forehead. It was cold and clammy. His complexion was white as chalk and his breathing was nearly undetectable. Mikey's heart sank as he felt for a pulse. He found one but it was dangerously weak. An overwhelming pang of guilt possessed him as he recalled the numerous occasions where he had badgered Tommy unmercifully.

"You hang in there," he said, his voice shaking. "Don't you go quitting on me."

"We'll look after him and Kerri," said Jenny softly. Mikey gazed into her eyes and saw genuine compassion. "Thank you," he responded humbly.

Once outside, Mikey scanned the woods behind the condos feeling reasonably sure that Pada would take cover there. Mikey still had the tracking device with him and to his pleasant surprise he discovered that it worked for tracking the re-calibration device as well. "That Plaatu thinks of everything," he mumbled. As he scanned the readings and triangulated the signal, it pointed directly northeast. He smiled broadly at the other three men. "Let's go get him."

Ryan glanced over his shoulder before following Mikey, Brad and Spike into the woods. He was more than a little relieved that the ruckus inside the condo had not attracted any unwanted attention. The resort was far from filled-to-capacity but noise tended to carry up here in the mountains. "These condos must have been built with exceptionally good insulation I guess," he chuckled to himself, then he followed after the others.

Plaatu walked at a steady pace across the plaza and noticed another contingent approaching him but this time they were dressed in civilian attire. On closer inspection, he recognized Congresswoman Randell and the US ambassador Joseph Henderson but he did not recognize the others. They met about twenty feet from the front door and Plaatu looked at his wrist indicator. Time was growing short.

"Mr. Plaatu," said Randell as she and the others stopped a few feet in front of him. "Please let me apologize for your harrowing experience the other day. We had no idea that agent was not what he claimed to be. I'm just glad you are alright."

Plaatu's first reaction was to lambaste the lot of them for being so inept, not to mention the less-than-cordial greeting he had gotten from the F-16's. He knew that would accomplish little to nothing however. He needed to get into the building and put himself in a position to foil whatever the Tilatin accomplices were planning. He could always chastise them later which he fully intended to do.

"No problem," he said tersely, "now why don't we go inside. I would like to address the General Assembly at once." Whatever Pada was up to, Plaatu was reasonably sure he would target the largest audience he could so chances are that would be the members from all nations which would be gathered in that room.

"Just a moment," interrupted ambassador Henderson, "we can't just barge in there and take over the meeting. We need to follow proper protocol and ask if the members will allow you to speak. A vote must be taken and tallied, then an agenda drawn up . . ."

Plaatu cut him off. "Mr. Ambassador, if you don't escort me immediately to your General Assembly chambers, I can assure you, you may not live to draw up any more agendas."

Henderson just gave him a puzzled look.

Randell immediately picked up on the sense of urgency in Plaatu's tone. She was in full agreement that the time for talking was at an end. It was time to listen to this man from another world. It was impossible to doubt him any further as his ship and quite formidable looking metallic friend were quite visible and in living color just a short distance away.

"Plaatu," said Randell with a smile, "There is someone here who would like to say hello. Please allow me to introduce Senator Robert Benson." A grey haired man with gold wire-rimmed glasses stepped forward out of the group and approached Plaatu. As he did, he extended his hand in friendship and smiled warmly. "Hello Plaatu," he said, with a tone of genuine affection. Plaatu responded with indifference. His patience was wearing thin and he failed to grasp the need for more superfluous introductions. The man's eyes were filled with warmth and adulation however. There was something different about him. It was as if he knew Plaatu, his expression was in such great contrast to the others that Plaatu couldn't help but take notice.

"You probably don't remember me" the man said thoughtfully. "I don't blame you. It has been a long time."

Plaatu eyed him up and down and in fact had absolutely no idea who this man was. He was torn between barging past these so called dignitaries that were deterring him from a very important objective, and engaging in conversation with this man who seemed so sincere and determined to make his acquaintance.

"I'm Bobby," he said with utmost affection. "You stayed at my house the first time you came here so many years ago. I took you to meet Professor Barnhardt remember?"

An alarm went off in Plaatu's head that rocked every nerve ending in his body with the resonance of a cathedral size church bell. The encounter the man was referring to re-formed in his consciousness.

"Bobby!" Plaatu shrieked as he lunged forward and hugged him firmly. Something about the embrace brought a deep level of meaning back to his senses. Up until now this trip had felt so completely unfamiliar to him. There was so little evidence of the world he had visited fifty years earlier, so much had changed that he hardly even recognized the landscape. Seeing Bobby again and the memories of their previous visit was the first sensation he had felt that brought any degree of nostalgia and connection to that fateful encounter. Plaatu felt a tremendous sense of warmth and relief. Up until now, he had been put in a position of convincing so many people of his credibility and authenticity that he repeatedly found himself in the dubious position of having to trust total strangers. That would no longer be necessary; they couldn't possibly doubt him now. Bobby would once again advocate on his behalf just as he did all those many years ago.

"I'm really sorry I didn't come sooner," said Bobby, his face beaming with joy. "I didn't become aware of your presence until last night. I knew you would come back eventually. The government tried to cover up your last visit but I never forgot."

Plaatu was still smiling when the realization returned to him that he needed to get into the building.

"Bobby," he said firmly, "I must get into the General Assembly chambers before noon. Don't ask me to elaborate please, just help me would you?"

"By all means," answered Bobby, "follow me." He took Plaatu by the arm and guided him towards the entrance. "Stand aside everyone!" Bobby ordered as they walked through the sliding glass doors and approached the security station. Congresswoman Randell followed close behind with Ambassador Henderson. They were all scanned and cleared for admittance by the guards. Plaatu was allowed to retain the array of alien looking objects contained in his flight-suit style uniform only after Bobby vehemently vouched for him. They proceeded quickly down the hall to the first elevator bank. Bobby pushed the up button and they waited for the doors to open.

"Did she say you are a Senator?" asked Plaatu.

"Yes," said Bobby. "I represent the sate of Maryland. You were the one who inspired me. I was so taken by your visit and the reason you came here that I felt I should aspire to try and put myself in a position where I could really make a difference in the world. I just can't believe I'm standing here with you again."

"How is your mother?" asked Plaatu.

Bobby lowered his head slightly. "She passed away seven years ago. Cancer took her. She never forgot you even though, over time, her thoughts became confused about your visit. The governments of the world did one hell of a job brainwashing the people of Earth that your visit was a publicity stunt. They almost had me convinced."

"I'm very sorry to hear about your mother," said Plaatu sympathetically. "She was a fine woman."

"Thanks," said Bobby. "I miss her very much." He paused for a moment as if lost in thought. Then he spoke again. "Professor Barnhart died a number of years back as well. I often think about him and how, when I was a boy, I thought he was the smartest man in the world."

"He was indeed a remarkable human being," said Plaatu thoughtfully.

Congresswoman Randell walked down the hall and joined them as they waited for the elevator.

"Have you two been catching up?" she asked pleasantly.

"A bit," said Bobby. "I just wish I had known about you sooner," he said with a stabbing glance towards Randell and Henderson who just appeared after having difficulty yet again at the security checkpoint. Security was so tight at the politically volatile building that even Henderson had to go through the metal detectors just like everyone else. Most of the guards knew him but he was occasionally flagged whenever there was a new employee on duty.

The elevator doors opened and they hurried inside. Randell pushed the number four for the General Assembly chambers and the doors closed behind them.

"I'm sorry Bobby," said Randell defensively. "I really didn't know you were acquainted with Plaatu or I would have told you sooner." She turned towards Plaatu. "You sounded so urgent out on the plaza," she said, "Is there any danger here that we need to know about?"

"I think you should put your security people on high alert but I doubt if there is much they will be able to do," said Plaatu, trying to conceal his complete lack of confidence in their human abilities to deal with such a crisis. He reached in his pocket and removed a small electronic device. He switched it on and watched as the power indicator read fully charged.

The elevator doors opened and they hurried down the hallway to the General Assembly room. As they entered, the large, oval-shaped chamber was filled to capacity with representatives of all the nations. They were collectively bantering with one another and dressed in a wide assortment of indigenous garb. The entire room was colorfully adorned with crimson seats, Lavender curtains against the walls and navy blue carpeting throughout. As Plaatu scanned the chamber for anything out of the ordinary, he quickly surmised that finding a terrorist in the room would be next to impossible at this point. But that didn't matter. As long as his camping friends carried out their assignment, there would be no reason to worry. All his hopes lay with the hand held device he clutched by his side.

"Ok, we got you here," said Randell rather curiously. "Now what?"

Plaatu looked at his time piece. It was 11:55. He had made it in time. But for what?

Pada had a five minute head start on the others but to his disadvantage, he was not as familiar with the terrain as Mikey and the others who had been camping and hiking in these mountains for years. Tilatins had physical attributes that may have exceeded those of humans but eyesight wasn't one of them. On more than one occasion, Pada would head in a direction that he felt reasonably sure would lead him back to his ship that was sitting just a mile or so from the resort, only to find he was heading in the wrong direction. The sun was directly overhead so it was difficult to gauge which way was

East or West. As he continued to wind his way along the rough terrain, his footsteps crunching on the dried fallen leaves could be heard from a good distance away. Mikey and the others had formed a skirmish line and were moving towards him while stopping every few yards to listen for his location. In a few moments, Pada could be seen struggling to ascend a ridge about a hundred yards in front of them. Once they made visual contact, it was time to close in and apprehend. He had dropped his blaster during the scuffle in the condo so the odds were four to one. Should be a piece of cake, Mikey thought. "But if I had to describe the past few days in terms of cake," he mumbled to himself, "it would be most definitely devil's food.

Pada could now see the four men closing in on him. He cursed them and frantically tried to scramble up the ridge. Rocks and tree stumps jutted up from the ground through the layers of fallen leaves and caused him to trip and fall repeatedly. Mikey and Spike branched off to the left to cut him off while Brad and Ryan approached from the rear. Just to be on the safe side, they were still carrying their bats. They waved them at Pada every time he glanced down the ridge at them hoping to spook him in to dropping the re-calibration device. So far, the ploy wasn't working.

Mikey and Spike had managed to gain the higher ground as Pada increasingly became disoriented in the unfamiliar surroundings. As they approached him, he turned and reversed direction but he pivoted so hastily, he lost his footing and tumbled down the steep embankment. He landed with a thud just a few feet in front of Ryan and Brad. As he struggled to regain his footing, they were on him.

"Hold it right there dirt bag or I'll knock you right out of the park!" shouted Ryan and he took up a Tony Gwynn-like stance within striking distance of the beleaguered Tilatin.

"Nicely put!" said Brad as he mimicked his stance on Pada's other side. They had him cornered and as his head darted from side to side, his breathing became heavy and frantic. Sweat began to drip down his face as he glared at them like a cornered rat. For a moment Brad sensed he was preparing to make a run for it so he tensed his muscles and prepared to swing. Mikey and Spike were descending towards them which just made Pada even more antsy. Then the Tilatin's expression changed from one of intense panic to a sadistic grin. He scanned the ground for the nearest rock. It was right in front of him so he quickly raised his arm over his head. He was holding the re-calibration device high in the air and before Brad and Ryan could react, he brought it crashing down upon the rock with all his strength.

Ryan and Brad just looked at each other with stunned bewilderment.

"Did he just smash what I think he smashed?" asked Brad.

"That would be a correct assessment of the situation as I see it," answered Ryan.

Then they noticed Mikey out of the corner of their eyes lunging at their prisoner.

"ARGHHHHH!" he screamed as he slammed into the Tilatin like he was a tackling dummy. They both went crashing to the ground and Mikey landed on top. He began pummeling the Tilatin's head once again with a fury his friends had never witnessed before.

"Not in the head!" yelled Spike as he arrived a moment later, but Brad and Ryan knew nothing would be accomplished by laying a beating on Pada. They put their emotions aside and rushed to restrain Mikey. They dragged him off of the astonished Tilatin who appeared genuinely impressed with Mikey's level of intensity and the ferocity of his attack.

"My goodness," said Pada as he sat up and stared at Mikey. "You really don't like me at all do you?"

Mikey struggled to pounce on him again but Brad would have none of it.

"Enough already!" he said, holding him back. "We need to get back down and re-set the transmitter. We only have a few minutes!"

Mikey was still enraged but he knew Brad was right. He took a deep breath and walked over to where Pada had smashed the device upon the rock. As he picked it up, he hit the on switch. The device didn't look damaged but the indicator lights were dead. He again switched the device on and off repeatedly but there was no activity.

"Damn!" he shouted as he turned to the others. "It's not working. What are we supposed to do now?"

"You're supposed to die," sneered Pada, "just like every other miserable inhabitant on this planet."

Brad wound up with his bat and clobbered the Tilatin right on top of his noggin. Pada fell backwards but got right back up again and shook it off.

"What the hell did you do that for?" asked Ryan.

"I don't know," answered Brad in utter frustration. "It just seemed like the appropriate response."

UN chief John Billingsworth brought the assembly to order with several very forceful whacks of his gavel. He was an austere man with thinning hair who unlike many of his colleagues, refused to cover his exposed cranium with a cheesy hairpiece. His demeanor was gruff and borderline obnoxious but anyone who was placed in a position of trying to control this type of crowd couldn't possibly succeed conducting themselves otherwise. It was a conclusion he arrived at quickly upon being appointed chairman nine months earlier. His first week on the job had proven to be one of the most chaotic in General Assembly history. Out of sheer naivety, he tried to approach the position with dignity and expected the same from the members. That was his first mistake. It only took him a week to realize that expecting them to conduct themselves in a civilized manner was like asking a pack of starving hyenas to form an orderly, straight line for dinner. He soon learned to scoff at the term "dignitaries" and privately came to refer to the members as "squawk boxes with legs."

The room eventually softened to a controlled din as members took their seats and waited for the meeting to begin. Plaatu again scanned the room but saw nothing out of the ordinary. There was only one other entrance to the room and it was on the other side of the large hall. The several emergency exits only opened outward so if anyone tried to gain access, Plaatu had a 50-50 chance that they would have to do so through the exact point where he was currently standing, right inside the main entrance. He checked his time piece. It was just after twelve noon. As he and Bobby stood off to the side with Randell and Henderson, Billingsworth began his introductions and proceeded to take the role call.

"It isn't very often that we get this kind of turnout," whispered Bobby. "You picked a good day to address them. I'll go inform the chairperson that we have a very special visitor who would like to address the assembly." Bobby had no idea that Plaatu's presence there was multi-faceted. He was completely unaware of the impending danger and Plaatu saw no reason to cause him any undue anxiety by divulging details of what he knew.

Bobby began descending the stairs towards the table where Billingsworth was seated. Congresswoman Randell stood behind Plaatu and unaware to the Golonian, she was watching him intently. Henderson had one hand in his pocket and was picking his nose with the other. The poor man was completely unable to appreciate the gravity of the situation and was eminently agreeable to letting others assume responsibility for whatever was about to happen.

As Bobby reached the lowest landing, he walked over to Billingsworth and began whispering in his ear as the collective assembly broke out in a chorus of jumbled conversations. Patience was anything but a virtue when it came to the General Assembly. On any given day, there was enough tension in the room to power the Space Shuttle.

Billingsworth glanced up at Bobby with disbelief. Then he gazed up in the direction of Plaatu with an equally annoying look of chagrin.

"I'm not kidding!" Plaatu heard Bobby exclaim in frustration. The grumbling coming from every corner of the room increased as the members shouted for an explanation as to what was going on. Billingsworth began pounding his gavel on the table but it was obvious that it was going to take more than the usual twenty or thirty whacks to restore order this time.

Plaatu just chuckled to himself. Their behavior was very much in character, he thought to himself. Humans had previously proven to be very irrational creatures but oddly enough, he found it almost endearing in a macabre sort of way.

"Embarrassing, isn't it?" said Randell in an icy tone from directly behind Plaatu.

He glanced over his shoulder to catch her leering at him as if he was a delectable plate of pork chops. He found it very odd but before he could evaluate whether it had any ulterior significance, there was a commotion just outside the door.

"You cannot go in there with any kind of case," he heard a security guard say as he tried to restrain a man in a white Islamic-style robe. The man burst past him and charged down the stairs to the main floor. As he did he began shouting "Islamic Jihad! Islamic Jihad!"

The man raised the case over his head. Plaatu had assumed correctly. The Tilatins plan was for one of their accomplices, masquerading as a terrorist to smuggle a "dirty bomb" into the United Nations and detonate it. "Dirty bombs" were at the top of the country's most feared catastrophes and such a threat had been anticipated for months. It made perfect sense. No one would suspect alien involvement in such an attack.

Plaatu was one step ahead of them. He depressed a button on the small hand-held device he had brought with him, then waited for all the electrical current in the room to come to a complete halt, just as he had done for one half hour to the entire planet, precisely at noon during his previous visit fifty years earlier. The transmitting device he had buried in the ground that he had instructed the campers to re-calibrate had a two-fold purpose. It tapped into Earth communication signals and relayed them to Coalition listening devices, allowing them to monitor Earth's progress, or lack there of. It also was the focal point for disrupting electro-magnetic signals and could emit a dampening wave that could bring every electronic function on the planet to a standstill. It was incredibly sophisticated and could be programmed to allow essential services and functions to continue such as medical establishments and planes in flight. The portable device Plaatu was carrying received the dampening signal directly from the master transmitter and was designed for smaller areas such as the chambers he was presently standing in. Plaatu knew that it would prevent the bomb from detonating since the device would need to be triggered electronically.

Plaatu stared up at the ceiling lights and waited for them to go out, indicating the dampening field was working.

The lights didn't go out. They remained on and were shining as brightly as when he first walked in. Plaatu frantically pressed the button again but nothing happened. He stared down at Bobby with complete disbelief.

"Nice try," he heard a woman say. It was Ms. Randell's voice coming from behind him. Now why would she say something like that, he thought as his mind swooned with conflicting messages.

The white robed man was running down the stairs faster than he should have. The delegate from the tiny Island of Samoa who was sitting in an aisle seat deftly stuck out his leg and tripped him. The would-be mad bomber went sailing head over heels as the briefcase went flying high into the air. The entire gathering seemed to hold its collective breath in disbelief as the case began to descend towards the floor but Bobby caught it in mid-air as adeptly as an NFL wide receiver. Assuming it could be a bomb, he started running back up the stairs to take it out of the building. All hell broke loose as other delegates set upon the fallen white-robed deliveryman and began pummeling him mercilessly. Some of the delegates who were also wearing white robes and presumably from Middle East countries came to his defense and a full-fledged brawl broke out. Billingsworth violently banged his gavel but no one could hear it over the raucous din.

Plaatu could do little but stand back and watch as the chaos escalated out of control.

Mikey and the others raced back down the ridge and left Pada sitting on the ground. He had no weapons and would pose no immediate threat to anyone. Dragging him along with them would only have slowed them down. Mikey hoped that the reason the re-calibration tool wasn't working was because they were simply too far away from the transmitter. When they reached the condo, the four men rushed inside. As they entered the living room, they were greeted by Chris, Tommy, Kerri and the other women sitting calmly sipping coffee. Tommy and Kerri appeared to be completely unharmed.

"Refreshments anyone?" asked Tommy with a wide grin. He held up a plate full of chocolate chip cookies.

Mikey and the others glared at them in total confusion. As they stood there trying to catch their breath, they remained speechless, completely unable to fathom what was going on.

"I don't get it!" blurted Mikey finally. "I thought you took them to the hospital?" he said in Chris's direction. Then he looked at Kerri's cheek and the bandage he had placed there was gone. The wound was completely closed.

Brad looked around at the floor. Everything had been put back where it belonged. There was no sign of the altercation that had taken place just minutes earlier. Then something else dawned on him.

"Where are the two Tilatin goons we knocked out?" he asked, still wide-eyed as if he had seen a ghost.

"They're in good hands," said Chris with that impish grin of his. "Have some tea."

A few more moments of silence passed when Ryan simply couldn't take it any more. This may have been Tommy and Chris just being Tommy and Chris but there was just too much at stake for this kind of drivel to continue any further.

"What the hell is going on here!?" he screamed. He heard someone in the kitchen. Then he saw a figure appear in the doorway and walk towards them. His jaw dropped as he recognized the newcomer. It was Ecko Moov.

"Good day gentlemen," he said cheerfully. "Nice to see you again."

When Bobby reached the top of the stairs, Plaatu grabbed his arm.

"Wait a moment!" he said nervously. Bobby complied but he couldn't imagine why Plaatu would want to prevent him from disposing of something that was quite possibly capable of blowing them all to smithereens. Plaatu guessed that the case's initial bearer possessed the detonator. Judging by the beating he was suffering on the chamber floor, it was safe to assume that he was in no position to activate it but what if someone else was holding it and waiting in the wings? He raised his little device once more and depressed the activation button. This time the lights in the hall went completely dark. The hall filled with shouts and screams but in a few moments, the battery operated emergency lights went on emitting enough light to allow safe movement. Plaatu opened the briefcase and disarmed the device carefully as Bobby watched in amazement.

"Your little device didn't work the first time," he heard Randell say from a few feet away. "How did you fix it?"

"Always have a back-up plan," answered Plaatu as he eyed her suspiciously.

A swarm of security personnel rushed into the room and in a few moments, they managed to restore order to some degree. Two of them ushered the beaten man with scuff marks all over his previously Lilly-white robe out of the chambers.

"We found his accomplice hiding in a janitor's closet," said one of the guards. "We'll handle it from here."

The noise level in the room slowly diminished as Billingsworth resumed slamming his gavel upon the defenseless table. Delegates slowly returned to their seats, many of them still boasting that they had delivered the fiercest blow during the assault on the hopelessly outnumbered terrorist. Plaatu felt reasonably sure that the plot had been foiled so he switched off the dampening field and the lights in the room returned to normal. He breathed a huge sigh of relief as calm was restored.

"Did you know about this?" asked Bobby, still trying to catch his breath.

"I knew there was a risk that something would happen," said Plaatu, "but I wasn't one hundred percent sure of what it would be. I am sorry Bobby. I wish I could have told you more but I didn't think it necessary to frighten you."

Ambassador Henderson approached them. He had been hiding behind the curtains when the ruckus broke out.

"I'm sure glad you know what you're doing," he said. Plaatu paid him little attention as he slowly gazed around the room once more.

"Still on guard huh?" asked Bobby. Plaatu locked eyes with him. For a moment, his thoughts drifted back to their previous encounter. He had grown quite fond of the boy. He represented many of the qualities Plaatu admired most in humans. His untainted innocence, his willingness to help, the love and respect he displayed towards his mother, the memories still lingered in Plaatu's mind. It gladdened his heart to know that Bobby had, at least from what he had observed in the past few moments, grown up to become such a fine man.

Plaatu smiled at him warmly, then said, "No, I think everything is alright now." He looked around at the delegates and thought about what he would say to them, then he glanced down at Billingsworth who was still pounding his gavel. The sound of thwak-thwak-thwak resonated throughout the entire hall. As Plaatu continued to stare, a bright flash lit up the room for a split second and was gone. The room went ominously silent as a hush fell over the chambers. Plaatu watched in alarm as Billingsworth collapsed flat out on the floor, his gavel still in his hand.

"Always have a back up plan, eh Golonian?" he heard a woman's voice say from the shadows. He turned sharply to his left. Congresswoman Randell was pointing a Tilatin blaster directly at him. Before he could react, she blasted the dampening device out of his hand.

"You won't be needing that," she said with a grotesque air of confidence. The briefcase was at her feet. "I took the liberty of re-arming it. I hope you don't mind."

Plaatu's hand throbbed with pain. The blast did not strike it directly but it was close enough to cause severe discomfort.

"I want all security personnel out," she snarled. "Right now!"

After the security guards exited as ordered, several delegates tried to make a run for the exit doors. She dropped each one of them with a level of firing precision that even impressed Plaatu. There was silence again.

"If you want to end up just like them try and leave!" she shouted to the remaining delegates as her voice echoed loudly, then faded away. She turned her attention back to Plaatu. "I give you a lot of credit Plaatu," she said. "You have earned quite a reputation in the CIPF. I'm truly impressed. You and your Council friend have been proceeding under the false notion that your attempts to keep this planet's existence a secret were successful all these years. How wrong you are. We have had operatives down here for years planning and plotting. How unfortunate that your career will end on a planet that will soon become the new home of the Tilatin civilization. If it wasn't for you, we would have never found this beautiful place. We owe you a tremendous debt of gratitude."

"If you detonate that thing," said Plaatu, "you'll die as well. You won't be around to enjoy this 'beautiful place' as you called it."

"My spirit will return in the form of another," she said smugly.

"Blast!" Plaatu thought to himself. He had forgotten for a moment that Tilatins are re-incarnationists. While they were unafraid to die, it wasn't 72 virgins that they believed would greet them in the here after, it was another life back here in the corporeal world as another person. He needed to employ a new tactic.

Randell removed a small device from her pocket. Plaatu could only presume it was the detonator. She flipped it open and placed her finger on the trigger.

"See you in the next life," she said with a sadistic grin. Bobby winced and grabbed Plaatu's arm. For a brief moment time stood still as all eyes in the room remained transfixed upon Randell's right hand.

She depressed thee trigger as the entire gathering gasped in unison. Nothing happened. She pressed it again and again but it was clear the device simply was not functioning.

Plaatu exhaled heavily. "It would appear that the Tilatin gods are not with you today," he said.

"Maybe," she answered smugly. "And then again, maybe not."

An ungodly sound rang out from Plaatu's left. It was an ear-piercing shriek unlike anything he had ever heard before. As he turned, he saw Ambassador Henderson charging towards the exit with his arms flailing wildly as if he was on fire. It was such a bizarre sight, Randell relaxed her guard for just a moment and moved to avoid his wild gesticulations. As she did she tripped over the briefcase and lost her balance. Plaatu saw his chance and didn't hesitate. He lunged for her left hand and tried to snatch the blaster away from her. She landed with a thud but she retained control of the weapon. She quickly assumed a sitting position where she could shoot from. She fired as Plaatu tried to roll out of harms way. The blast struck him square on his upper right side. He collapsed to the floor and his body went limp.

Bobby stood in stunned silence looking down at his long lost friend lying wounded on the floor. His mind reeled with confusion. "This is madness," he thought to himself. "What in God's name is going on here?" There were people with bombs, guns and detonators, it was all too much for him to assimilate. Then he saw Randell rise to her feet. Their eyes locked for a moment and Bobby knew exactly what she intended to do. He lowered his head and charged her midsection, tackling her to the ground. His speed and agility took her completely by surprise and the blaster slid out of her reach. Bobby rolled to his left and firmly grabbed the pistol. He jumped to his feet and trained it on Randell.

"Hold it right there!" he said angrily. "Don't even think about it!"

Henderson had disappeared down the hall but all the commotion had attracted the attention of the security people as they returned en masse. Several of them stood in the doorway for a moment not quite sure what to make of the scene.

Then Bobby took command. "Arrest this woman," he ordered. "And call the medical technicians to get up here right away!"

Two of the officers ushered Randell out of the chambers while Bobby went to Plaatu's aide. He knelt down by his side to check his breathing. It was slow and steady but his pulse was very weak. He gently rolled him over onto his back. Then he instructed one of the officers to pick up the briefcase.

"Handle that with care!" he snapped. "Get it to the bomb squad right away."

CHAPTER ELEVEN

Mikey quickly brought Ecko and the others up to snuff on what had transpired in the woods. He also had some explaining to do with Kerri and her nurse-mates as to why they had lied their way into their condo in the first place. Fortunately, the four ladies were remarkably forgiving. Ecko thanked the campers and prepared to head out the door to begin his pursuit of the other Tilatins. He reminded Tommy of how fortunate he was that the pistol that sent him hurtling over the couch had been inadvertently left on stun. Such Tilatin oversights were very rare indeed. Ecko began his search where Mikey claimed to have left the Tilatin leader. It wasn't long before he found Pada wandering aimlessly through the woods and took him into custody. He escorted him to his CIPF star cruiser which was positioned about a quarter mile from the Tilatin ship. Then he locked him up in the holding tank with the two Tilatin guards he had found in a rather groggy state on the living room floor of the condo. The fourth Tilatin who had masqueraded as the FBI agent had remained behind with their ship per Pada's orders but he had apparently wandered away from the craft for reasons unknown. All Ecko found for remains was a few articles of tattered clothing. He could only presume he had been eaten by bears. Ecko knew there was a second ship involved but they would just have to wait. He lifted off to rendezvous with Plaatu in New York. He would have liked to take a few of the campers along but Ecko, like Plaatu, was a creature of unyielding duty. He quickly reminded them that it was simply against the rules to allow non-member species access to Coalition technology. Besides, Mikey and the others were pre-occupied with their sensually-captivating new-found friends.

The campers didn't even resent the fact that Plaatu had put a back-up plan in place when he asked Ecko to keep an eye on them in the event they were unable to re-calibrate the transmitter. Anyone else may have construed the act as demonstrating a total lack of confidence in their abilities but under the circumstances, they completely understood. After all, the fate of an entire planet hung in the balance. Ecko was able to complete his assignments in Beijing and Moscow in just over an hour giving him more than enough time to return to assist the campers if necessary. He returned in time to set things right with the back-up re-calibrator he had in his possession and they were completely grateful. He had revived Tommy and used some of his "miracle cream" on Kerri's wound to boot so how could they possibly be anything but appreciative.

As Kerri and her nurse-mates busied themselves in the kitchen putting together some soup and sandwiches, Brad and Ryan furtively watched Mikey quietly standing in the kitchen doorway casually studying Kerri's every move. It was obvious he was smitten by her and they knew that when Mikey fell for someone, he fell hard. He was without question the undisputed champ in the "World's biggest pushover" category.

"Hey guys!" yelled Spike who was seated on the couch in the living room. "CNN has live coverage of the UN! You might want to check this out."

Brad and Ryan joined Tommy, Chris, and Spike who were watching the television intently. UN plaza had once again filled with curiosity seekers and the TV cameras were once again back in force. They could see Plaatu's ship where Bort was still standing at attention but there was no sign of Plaatu. They had no idea he was, at that moment, laying badly wounded on the floor of the General Assembly chambers.

"Hell of a week huh?" asked Chris to no one in particular.

Brad and Ryan had brought chairs in from the dining room to accommodate everyone. They sat down and poured themselves a cup of coffee from a butler sitting on the table.

"That's putting it mildly," said Brad. "If you had told me two weeks ago that our annual camping trip would turn into something as zany as this, I would have had you committed."

"Like I said before," added Ryan. "What are the odds?"

"Hey," said Spike, "Out of the six of us, Tommy's the only one who got zapped by one of those guns they were carrying. So how did it feel Tom?"

"All I remember is it was lights out," he answered. "I'm reasonably sure it didn't do any permanent damage though. My brain seems like it is functioning normally."

"That's an improvement," laughed Chris. "I don't ever remember it functioning normally before they popped you."

Tommy grabbed one of the small decorative pillows on the couch and flung it at Chris's head. Chris ducked and it hit Spike square in the face.

"Ooops," said Chris. Spike was unhurt and wisely chose not to retaliate. This was no time for a pillow fight.

"Are you sure you're OK?" Brad asked Tommy again. He vividly recalled the image of Plaatu blasting the two Tilatin guards in the woods of New York. He could still picture them being lifted off their feet and sailing into the bushes. He didn't imagine that it was all that pleasant in the least.

"I think my endolphin levels are a little low," said Tommy trying to sound diagnostic. "But other than that, I still have this dull pain in my chest."

"Uh, that would be endorphins Tommy," corrected Ryan. "And I seriously doubt if your levels have been affected adversely in any way."

"Do you think we'll get medals or anything?" asked Tommy as if Ryan's remark hadn't even registered.

Mikey walked in from the kitchen carrying a tray of food.

"I've got your medal right here," he quipped. "This is the closest thing you're going to get so smash a sandwich in your pie hole and be grateful. Besides, all you did was get knocked out. We did all the heavy lifting." Privately, Mikey was overjoyed at the sight of Tommy's remarkable recovery. Outwardly, he wasn't about to show it and stubbornly intended to maintain the status quo. Something in his mind told him that if Tommy ever discovered how truly fond Mikey was of him, he would lose the upper hand for good.

Kerri and the other women were right behind Mikey and took the remaining open seats. Karen, Jenny and Michelle had previously gone upstairs and changed into more suitable clothing much to the disappointment of the six male admirers.

"Oh, that's mean," cooed Michelle in response to Mikey's remark. She sat down right next to Tommy. "I thought that was very brave of you to do what you did."

Tommy blushed slightly. It was more blind rage than anything else but he was willing to accept her assessment of it being an act of bravery.

"That's what I always told him," said Chris, "when in doubt always lead with your head."

"Alright," interrupted Brad as everyone helped themselves to the finger sandwiches, "pipe down for a minute so I can hear what's going on."

The CNN reporter on the TV was having a tough time holding back her long jet-black hair in the unyielding wind as she struggled to deliver her report.

"The breeze is really kicking up here," she began, "as we await word of what is going on inside the building. The man who came out of the space ship you see behind me entered the building almost thirty minutes ago and no one is being allowed inside. The building is in complete lock down and reporters are prohibited from getting anywhere near it."

"Then I guess we'll just have to wait won't we," said Ryan as he bit into a tuna on wheat.

"Ah yes," added Tommy, "the old waiting game." He didn't want to admit it but he did feel just a tad foolish at having gone down so easily. His conscience kept reassuring him though that no one could have withstood that blast.

Mikey looked at Kerri who was sitting next to him and said softly, "So, are you sorry you ever opened the door this morning?"

Kerri had indeed been shaken up by the whole experience. Now that they had reached a calmer moment, she was able to absorb it all. She still had some reservations but as she glanced around the room, these did seem like good men. "The jury is still out," she said with a smile. "I'll let you know when I get to know you a little better."

The medics arrived and Bobby relinquished his position next to the fallen Plaatu. As he rose to his feet, he saw other members of the medical staff attending to Billingsworth and the fallen delegates who had attempted to leave the chambers. With the chairman down for the count, someone needed to address the remaining delegates as many of them were visibly upset and preparing to leave. There was nothing more he could do for Plaatu except allow the technicians to see to his care so he descended the stairs and assumed the chairman's seat. He switched on the communications system and addressed the gathering.

"Could I have your attention everyone," he began in an authoritative tone. As he spoke, many of the delegates picked up their ear pieces to tie into the main translator. "Could everyone please return to your seats and allow the medical people to do their job. We still have important business here today so I ask you to please be patient and do not leave the chambers. We are reasonably sure that the danger has passed so there is no need to panic."

Bobby watched as the delegates slowly began returning to their seats. There was a certain genuineness and sincerity in his tone that seemed to convince them that this was not a time for petty squabbles and unrealistic demands. A sense of calm and willingness to co-operate seemed to permeate throughout the entire chambers. It was so pronounced that even Bobby was mildly surprised by the effect his words had on the gathering.

He returned up the stairs and as he reached the top, Plaatu was sitting up under his own power but his eyes were glassy and his gaze was almost hypnotic.

There was a technician on both sides of him and as Bobby approached, Plaatu looked up at him with a look of recognition.

"Bobby," he said weakly, "how nice to see you again." It was clear that his strength was in short supply as he continued to breathe slowly and tried to clear his head.

Bobby knelt down next to him and felt his hand. It was clammy and twitching slightly. All of a sudden this man from another world who had made such a lasting impression on him all those years ago looked so much older and terribly frail. Bobby could only imagine what Plaatu had been through during the decades since his last visit. Something in Bobby's mind became furious that the governments of the world had done everything they could to discredit this being who had traveled all this way with nothing but good intentions.

"We need to get you to a hospital," said Bobby caringly. His heart was heavy seeing Plaatu like this.

"No!" said Plaatu with an effort. "I came to deliver a message today and it is important that I do so. I should consider myself lucky that she had the blaster set on stun. She probably assumed we were all going to die in the explosion anyway so she never bothered to check the weapon setting."

He struggled to get to his feet. The two technicians held him by the arms and help steady him. Plaatu reached into one of his uniform pockets and removed a small cigarette-sized device. He held it to his mouth and inhaled deeply. A mist of condensed air streamed from the device into his lungs and his eyes immediately grew wider. In a matter of seconds, he was able to stand without assistance and his breathing seemed much stronger.

"What the heck was that?" asked Bobby with surprise.

"Just a Golonian based stimulant," Plaatu answered. "It is almost like injecting pure adrenalin into the blood stream but much more potent."

Plaatu took several deep breaths and seemed to grow stronger with every one. "It won't last long however so we need to act quickly. Would you mind escorting me to a position where I can address all the delegates?"

"Of course," answered Bobby. He led Plaatu slowly down the stairs to the speaker's podium under the watchful gaze of the entire room. Everyone was clearly teeming with curiosity as to this strange man's identity. As Plaatu reached the podium, he put his hand on Bobby's shoulder. "Thank you my boy," he said softly. "Or should I say thank you my man." Bobby just smiled affectionately. Then Plaatu gathered his strength and gazed around the hall. For a moment it seemed almost surreal to him. Here he was once again in a room full of total strangers, aliens to him no less. Yet, they were all sitting in an orderly fashion and fully prepared to let him speak. It was rare that he received this level of understanding and cooperation during his previous experiences with non-member planets. He cleared his throat and began to speak.

"Good people of Earth," he began, "My name is Plaatu. I was born on the planet Golon which is millions of miles away but in many respects, it is not so unlike your world. My people share some of the same qualities yours do. I have traveled here once before although it almost seems like a lifetime ago. I have had the privilege of watching your planet develop both through first hand observations and through historical records. I have seen the very best and the absolute worst in your species. I have not encountered another species in all the universe that possesses the incredible depth that you possess for both good and evil."

Plaatu's hands gripped the sides of the podium more tightly as he struggled to steady himself. Bobby could see this was putting a tremendous strain on him. Though he was not exhibiting any outward signs of injury, whatever that weapon was that had put him down for the count clearly packed a tremendous wallop. Bobby remained close by his side to assist if necessary.

"I was sent here by a coalition of your planetary neighbors to warn the people of Earth that if they continued on their present course of building bigger and more powerful weapons, there would be severe consequences," Plaatu continued. "It has become painfully clear to us that you have ignored our previous warnings. By doing so, you have aroused attention from some alien species that, if left to their own devices, would invade and re-colonize your planet without hesitation. In the process, they could wipe out humanity the way you eliminate an unwanted colony of ants. There are those in our council who believe that Earth could be a tremendous asset to our Coalition and others who believe that your influence could damage us irreparably but that is a paradox we are willing to entertain."

Bobby watched as Plaatu's demeanor suddenly changed. Up until now, it was clear that he was attempting to draw upon every ounce of strength he possessed to appear as statesman-like as possible. He had been standing perfectly erect with his head held high. As Bobby watched helplessly, Plaatu's shoulders drooped and his posture became bent and slightly hunched over. It was clear that Plaatu could not hold it together much longer.

"You have no idea," he said in a tone that was now more imploring than commanding. "You reside on the most beautiful planet in the galaxy. I have never seen so many remarkably exotic and fascinating life forms as I've seen here. From out in space, Earth appears like a floating blue gem in a sea of darkness. I sometimes find it appalling how shamefully you humans take it for granted."

He paused for a moment once again. Bobby grabbed his arm to steady him. "Do you need another dose of that stimulant?" he whispered.

"No," said Plaatu weakly. "It is not meant to take repeatedly, it is far too potent."

Plaatu steadied himself once more. The room full of delegates sat in total silence, mesmerized by what they were hearing, still struggling to accept the authenticity of the dire warnings his words conveyed.

"I'm afraid it is too late for you now," Plaatu said. "There will be no more ultimatums. You no longer have any choice. You must agree to join us in peace and immediately begin dismantling your stockpiles of nuclear weapons."

A smattering of protests resonated around the room.

"Or face utter annihilation!" shouted Plaatu.

The room erupted in a hail of shouts and angry barbs as the delegates reacted to what they saw clearly as a threat.

"Who are you to intimidate us?" yelled the delegate from Pakistan as he jumped to his feet.

"This is an outrage!" the delegate from France chimed in.

Plaatu wasn't surprised. He fully expected such a reaction, knowing full well from past experience that the best way to get under a human's skin is to confront them with threats and ultimatums. For the first time, Bobby saw Plaatu smile. Then he began speaking again.

"Ladies and gentlemen!" he said loudly and the ruckus gradually subsided. "I am not sure if you fully grasp what we are offering you here. There are many benefits to becoming a member of the Coalition and all we ask is that you curb your aggressive tendencies. Now I put it to you. Is that so much to ask?"

The grumbling began again but this time it was much less hostile.

"Look at your planet!" continued Plaatu. "As we sit here in the relative comfort of this building, millions of your inhabitants are starving to death. Your population is expected to double in the next fifty years, you simply won't be able to feed them all with your current technology. You continue to squabble over which is the 'One True God'. We have learned to believe in one creator and have outgrown the urge to kill indiscriminately because one group's beliefs just happen to differ slightly from another's. You have ignored my previous warning and have amassed enormous stockpiles of nuclear weapons that are sitting in the ground like ticking time bombs. Disease, famine, global warming, we can help you eradicate many of these ills. I am not here to invade your world; I am merely here to offer you an opportunity for a better future. I would strongly recommend that you embrace this opportunity immediately. If you resist I can assure you that the alternative will be far less palatable."

The hall went silent as the delegates pondered the very large plate of philosophical cuisine Plaatu had just presented them. In his heart, he knew full well that the prospect of inviting aliens down here in large numbers was a difficult one to digest but they really didn't have any choice.

Plaatu saw Billingsworth approaching him with the aid of a technician. Plaatu's heart was gladdened that he and the other victims of Randell's marksmanship were not seriously hurt.

"Mr. Plaatu," said Billingsworth, "I have been listening carefully to your message. Why don't you let me take it from here. As you said we really don't have any choice so I don't see where there will be all that much trouble bringing this to a resolution. Will you remain here to guide us as to what happens next?"

"I'm afraid not," answered Plaatu remorsefully. "But there will be others coming soon enough. You might as well tell the people of the world to get used to it. Your umbrella of isolation and secrecy has been stripped away whether you like it or not. You're not alone out here and this might be a good time to break out the welcome mat."

"I understand," said Billingsworth.

"Bobby," said Plaatu, "would you mind walking me outside? I need to return to my ship."

"Of course," answered Bobby and he and Plaatu began ascending the stairs. As they did the room remained deathly silent as the full weight of Plaatu's words hung heavily in the air. When they were half way up, a smattering of delegates stood up and began to applaud. As the two men continued up the stairs, the applause increased until the entire room was cheering and shouting in appreciation of Plaatu's efforts. They may not have liked everything he had to say but it was clear he had gone to great lengths to bring them this message. Each of the delegates apparently felt that in itself was well deserving of an outward display of collective appreciation.

There was mayhem out in the hallway as security personnel tried to maintain control. Randell had been taken into custody but Plaatu knew that he would have to escort her off the planet. He was mildly angry with himself for not recognizing her as a Tilatin but they were getting better and better at disguising themselves.

A short, heavy-set security officer walked up to Plaatu. He was holding something in his hand. It was a small detonator just like the one Randell had been holding. The red alert signals went off once again in his head.

"Now what?" he snapped as the officer held it out to him.

"Ambassador Henderson dropped this as he ran screaming out of the chambers," said the officer. "Not to worry though. I just got word they successfully de-activated the bomb."

Plaatu took the device and it all became crystal clear to him. "Of course," he mumbled. "Henderson must be working with her and it was his job to detonate the bomb if her device failed but he didn't have the guts to see it through. Apparently he doesn't have the same level of faith in the after-life as Randell does."

"I'll be damned," said Bobby.

"We almost were," chuckled Plaatu. "You had better locate Mr. Henderson and take him into custody as well," said Plaatu, turning back towards the officer.

"I'll put the word out sir," he responded, then he turned and headed down the hall.

Plaatu placed the device in his pocket. In all, he counted six Tilatin operatives who were apparently in on this scheme. But could there be more? He and Bobby took the elevator to the lobby. As they stepped out onto the plaza a great roar went up in the crowd. The rubber-neckers were back in force and Plaatu stopped in his tracks, appearing to be unwilling to contend with the thunderous mob. Bobby motioned to a group of New York's finest to clear a path for them across the plaza. The reporters and cameramen were beginning to surge towards them.

It was sheer pandemonium as they began pushing their way through the crowd. Plaatu yearned to be back inside his ship. He despised large gatherings and for a moment, he felt terribly alone despite being in the midst of thousands of people. It was at that precise instant that he knew in his mind that his decision to call it quits once and for all was the right one. No more missions, no more endless trips across the galaxy. He had simply had enough. More than anything else in all the universe, he just wanted to go home.

The crowd tried to press ever closer. Plaatu felt the protective circle of police officers getting smaller and smaller. Bobby struggled furiously to keep the cameras and reporters at bay. The noise level reached a fever pitch and Plaatu thought for sure they would be trampled in the madness. Then a shot rang out from somewhere in the crowd. People began screaming and running in all directions. Bobby pulled Plaatu to the ground, not sure if he had been hit. The several police officers vainly scanned the crowd trying to see where the shot had come from when they heard another shot ring out. "Kill the alien!" someone yelled. As the crowd continued to disperse in all directions, the officers spotted a man in a long black coat holding a pistol about ten yards in front of them. They raised their service revolvers and the forward-most officer yelled, "Drop the gun!" They prepared to fire if the man did not immediately comply. The shooter brazenly ignored the order and raised his pistol again in total defiance. The lead officer's finger began to apply pressure to the trigger of his revolver when he saw a beam of light strike the man squarely in the back. As the officers watched in disbelief, he began to glow. There was a slight hissing sound in the air as the gunman grew brighter and brighter causing the officers to avert their gaze. Then he was gone. The only thing that remained was a faint scorch mark on the ground where he had been standing.

The officers looked off in the distance towards Plaatu's ship. The visor on Bort's head slowly lowered to its closed position. A hush went over the multitude after seeing the man executed right before their eyes. An eerie calm ensued as everyone just stood and gawked at the huge motionless man of metal. Bobby helped Plaatu to his feet and gently held his arm to steady him.

"Are you alright?" he asked nervously.

Plaatu had not been hit but as he glanced off to his right, he saw the body of a young boy lying motionless on the ground. A sobbing mother knelt over him and caressed him in her arms. He ran to the boy and felt his pulse but he could sense no flow of life-giving plasma through his veins. Blood oozed from a wound in his neck. Plaatu's heart sank as he looked into the mother's eyes. She sobbed uncontrollably as she looked back at him. Her gaze seemed to be begging him to bring her boy back but there was nothing he could do. The resuscitation chamber in his ship that had once prolonged his life was designed only for members of the Coalition. Human physiology was not programmed into its memory as of yet so the device would be totally ineffective.

"I'm so sorry," he said softly. He looked up to see Bobby standing over him. He motioned to some medical personnel to assist the grieving woman.

"Do you see Bobby?" asked Plaatu remorsefully. He rose to a standing position again. "This is why we created our corps of robots. One of the most important duties of any civilized society is to protect the innocent."

Bobby just stared up at him. This reunion with his childhood friend had not gone anything like he had hoped.

"Do you see their faces?" Plaatu continued, motioning to the crowd. "Look at them. There isn't a single person on this plaza who won't think twice about committing a violent act for fear of arousing Bort's ire. That is what your planet has to look forward to. You may not agree with the concept completely but the fact of the matter is there are presently over two million of your inhabitants who are incarcerated. Your prison systems are bulging at the seams. On my home world of Golon we have one prison. We maintain it as a museum to remind us of what life was like before we came to our senses. We haven't reached total perfection but I can tell you with utter certainty the quality of life that awaits your planet is far superior to what you are experiencing currently. Just imagine what your world would be like with no more innocent victims. Fear of punishment, Bobby. It's what keeps most humanoids in line." He sighed heavily and closed his eyes. "I think I will retire to my ship now."

As he and Bobby again began walking towards his ship, the reporters and cameras slowly converged on them. The officers interceded but they were much more apprehensive this time.

A buzz went up in the crowd as spectators began pointing frantically up towards the sky. Another ship was descending towards the plaza and as it did the crowd began to pull away. The ship landed quietly right next to Plaatu's, then its engines disengaged. Plaatu knew it was Ecko and a wave of relief surged through him. He was still woozy and welcomed the presence of his friend and fellow officer.

Bobby and Plaatu followed the wedge of police officers that was pushing their way through the crowd. As they reached the halfway point on the plaza, Ecko's ramp lowered to the ground and Plaatu saw his friend emerge from the hatchway. He and Bobby walked a few steps further, then Plaatu glanced up again. Two more figures proceeded down the ramp behind Ecko. Plaatu strained to see in the bright mid-day sun as he wasn't aware that Ecko had anyone with him on his ship when Plaatu went aboard it the previous night. It hardly fazed him in the least. He was tired and nearly overwhelmed with fatigue and the aftereffects of being stunned by the blaster. Nothing was registering at this point.

"Are those friends of yours?" yelled Bobby over the crowd which was shouting again at decibel levels that would make most rock groups envious. Plaatu was mere yards away and as he strained to see who was with Ecko, the face of the person on the right became clear. It was his council friend Em Diem. He saw him wave in his direction and was sporting a huge smile. "How in god's name did he get here?" thought Plaatu in total confusion.

His spirits gained new found strength as he hastened his pace to greet him. Em Diem was blocking his view of whomever the third person was who was standing behind him. As Plaatu finally reached the bottom of the ramp, he embraced Em Diem warmly.

"How did you get here!" he shouted with genuine contentment.

"Ecko had relayed to me two days ago that he suspected you might encounter some difficulties with these Tilatin buggers so I thought I should pay you a visit," said Em. "I hopped on board one of those state of the art super-fast little shuttles and voila. Here I am. We linked up in orbit where my ship is still positioned. My crew is watching the store." Then he looked intently into Plaatu's eyes and took him gently by the shoulders. "I brought someone very special with me," he whispered thoughtfully.

Em stepped to the side to reveal who it was that had descended the ramp with him.

A middle-aged woman in a white Coalition-issue pants suit stepped forward out of the shadows. The bright sunlight reflecting off the silky sheen of her uniform gave her an almost angelic glow.

"Hello father," she said affectionately as she gazed up into his eyes.

Plaatu's knees almost buckled as Bobby and Ecko grabbed him by each arm. He gazed at her as if staring at an apparition, his limbs seemed unable to move.

"Nara," he muttered, then he threw his arms around her and drew her close to him.

"Oh father," she said as her eyes filled with tears. She hugged him like she had never hugged him before. Ecko, Em Diem and Bobby just watched and each man had all he could do to remain dry eyed himself.

"I missed you so much," Plaatu whispered in her ear, still holding her tightly. "I never want to be apart from you again."

"I missed you too father," she replied. "We have so much to catch up on."

Their arms unlocked but Plaatu felt it difficult to let go of her. He needed to return to his senses though and see to some introductions.

"I'm so sorry," he gushed, "Bobby, these are two dear, dear friends of mine. Allow me to introduce you to fellow officer Ecko Moov and Council member Em Diem."

"How do you do," said Bobby politely as he shook their hands.

"And this," said Plaatu with enormous pride, "is my daughter Nara."

"It's a pleasure ma'am," said Bobby warmly.

The police were having a difficult time keeping the reporters at bay so Ecko and Plaatu thought it wise to re-enter their ships and seek quieter surroundings. As Plaatu glanced off in the direction of the street, he saw a line of military vehicles approaching. Koopman had apparently gone for reinforcements. Plaatu just chuckled to himself.

A shout of alarm went up behind Plaatu from one of the police officers. They turned just in time to see Henderson scurry by them flailing his arms like a mad man. A small army of security personnel were in hot pursuit.

"This is getting really crazy," said Plaatu as he moved to escort Nara into his ship. Ecko and Em Diem hurried up the ramp of their ship and readied for lift-off. As Plaatu reached his cruiser, he ordered Bort inside. As soon as the spectators saw him move, they scattered like buzzards. Plaatu began walking up the ramp with Nara, then he stopped abruptly. He turned sharply and saw Bobby standing at the bottom of the ramp. Plaatu walked back down and faced him.

"I can't thank you enough for all your help. I will be seeing you again my friend but we really have to leave now. Your mother would be very proud of you Bobby. I want you to know that."

Bobby smiled at him broadly. He never thought beyond his wildest dreams that he would ever see Plaatu again but here he was, standing on the plaza of the United Nations building with him at a turning point in human history. It was almost too much for him to handle. He embraced Plaatu, then stepped away.

"On your way!" he shouted, "before it gets any zanier. We'll be in touch!"

The two ships lifted off almost simultaneously and were soon out of sight leaving behind an army of disappointed reporters and a sea of startled faces.

That evening, Mikey and the other campers decided to spend one final night in the woods before heading back to Connecticut the next morning. Darkness had fallen and as they huddled around a glowing campfire, they sat in stunned silence. The magnitude of all that had happened over the course of the week was beginning to hit home now that they finally had time to sit quietly and digest its many truly fascinating intricacies.

They had watched the events play out on UN plaza in the company of their nursing friends. Each cheered wildly when the television cameras transmitted the image of Plaatu emerging from the building as he struggled to weave his way through the crowd to get back to his ship. They were horrified as they witnessed the shooting incident and the plight of the fallen boy. They were relieved to see Ecko land his ship and come to Plaatu's aide but remained in the dark as to who the other parties were that Plaatu had embraced. Judging by the look on Plaatu's face however, all seemed to go reasonably well.

The men had said their goodbyes to Kerri and the others but they made plans to get together for dinner in a few days. Mikey still had a slight gleam in his eye and although his five comrades had refrained from ribbing him about it out of respect, he knew their self-invoked 'oath of solemnity' wouldn't last forever.

Chris had his five inch portable TV on his lap and he turned the channel to CNN once again as they all listened intently to the continuing coverage of the day's events. The news that Randell and Henderson were not of this Earth and working with the Tilatins came as a real shock, especially to Ryan since it was his idea to approach her in the first Place. That tid bit of information didn't go unnoticed.

"Do you believe that?" said Mikey with mild incredulity. "Who knew?"

"No shit!" said Spike. "They have been walking around down here for years and no one could even tell." There was a long moment of silence, then they each began sizing up one another with their eyes.

"While we're on the subject, how do I know you're not an alien?" asked Brad turning to Ryan sitting next to him.

"Well how do I know you're not an alien?" he shot back.

There was another moment of tense silence, then all eyes turned towards Tommy.

"Hey!" he exclaimed defiantly. "Don't look at me!"

They all laughed and turned their attention back towards the inviting ambience of the camp fire.

"Well," said Ryan, "the world is going to have to get used to lots of aliens coming down here now. I just hope their as friendly as Plaatu."

Mikey gazed languidly up at the stars. It was a view unlike any they could find in their hometown of Stanford. Up here, far from the city lights, the night sky came to life with a clarity only found in places like this. They didn't need a telescope up here to appreciate the depth and majesty of the universe. All the constellations were breathtakingly visible. On a clear night, the number of stars evident to the naked eye was virtually limitless.

"I wonder where they are now." Mikey said softly as the fire continued to pop and hiss.

"No idea," answered Spike. "Probably half way to where ever it is that he calls home I guess."

Their tone was a bit somber. It was as if they were unable to accept the fact that their involvement in this incredible event was now at an end. They had not been able to be there at the UN. They had been relegated to watching it from afar on a television set no less. Granted the company they shared made it eminently more enjoyable but as they sat around the campfire, far from the excitement and commotion no doubt taking place in New York, a feeling of profound emptiness permeated the air.

"It would have been nice to be there," said Tommy as he stretched out his legs and rested is feet on the rocks that rimmed the campfire.

"What's the matter?" asked Chris. "Do you feel cheated?"

"I don't know," answered Tommy, "I just feel like no one has any idea of the part we played in all of this."

"And that's just how I like it," said Mikey. "I don't need the attention. There's probably no money in it so why put ourselves in a position where we are set upon by the media and hounded relentlessly? I don't need it and I don't want it." He drank heavily from the can of Coors light he was holding in his hand.

"Mikey's right," added Brad. "There is nothing to be gained by it but aggravation. We know in our hearts and minds that we did what we could and that is all that is really important. Let this remain a secret amongst us, a bond if you will that we can share for the rest of our lives."

"Yeah," added Chris, "kinda like the Dead Poets' Society."

They all turned and stared at him with mild disdain.

"The Dead Poets' Society?" they repeated in unison.

"That is so lame!" said Spike with a chuckle.

The camp went quiet again except for the CNN broadcast softly emanating from Chris's small TV.

"Why don't you shut that off Chris?" said Mikey softly. "I think I've had enough CNN for one day."

Chris switched off the television and placed it on the ground. An owl hooted softly in the distance. The night air was crisp and clear and as they sat there soaking up the great outdoors, the soft glow of moonlight lit up the forest.

In a few moments, Tommy had dozed off. His head was tilted to the side and he was snoring softly. What he didn't know was that his shoes were beginning to melt on the hot rocks they were resting upon.

"Should we tell him?" asked Chris softly.

"Nahhh," said Mikey. "He'll realize it soon enough."

"You're really cruel, ya know that?" laughed Brad as he hurled an empty beer can softly at Tommy's head. It glanced gently off his temple and his eyes flew open.

"What the . . ." he mumbled as he sat straight up. He sniffed the air and looked around. "What's that smell?" he snarled.

"Ah, that would be the smell of your shoe leather beginning to burn," said Chris.

Tommy yanked his feet away from the fire. "You assholes," he snapped, "you would have let me fry wouldn't ya?" He jumped to his feet and began stamping them on the ground. "Brand new boots too," he said in disgust. The others couldn't contain their laughter.

Then Ryan glanced over towards the opening to their campsite. With a look of alarm, he jumped to his feet.

"Who the hell is that?" he said nervously.

The others rose to their feet as well and turned in the direction Ryan was pointing. A very large figure was standing at the edge of the campsite where it met the access road. He wasn't moving but whoever it was, he was huge. The campers were not easily frightened men but there was just something about being confronted by someone lurking out of the darkness in the deep woods that triggered a certain level of primal fear. As they continued to stare, the figure began walking towards them at a slow but deliberate pace.

"I don't like this," said Tommy, his voice rising.

The campers began retreating to the other side of the campfire so as to keep it between them and the intruder.

"Brad," whispered Ryan, "get the guns just in case."

Brad made a move towards the van but was stopped dead in his tracks by a voice that boomed out of the darkness to their left.

"That won't be necessary my friends!" they heard in a familiar tone. It was none other than Plaatu. He appeared out of the darkness and approached the men with a broad smile.

"Scared you didn't he," he said gleefully. Bort came to a halt about ten feet away where the campers could now make out his metallic features.

"Scared isn't the word," said Tommy. "I think I need to go change my undies."

"I couldn't resist," said Plaatu. He was dressed in a flight suit similar to the original one he had worn when they first met. "I couldn't leave without at least saying goodbye," he said warmly, "and also to say thank you. I am deeply indebted to you all."

"Think nothing of it," said Mikey. "We seen our duty and we done it."

"Do you have time for a quick brewski or a cup of coffee?" asked Chris. Something about seeing their new found alien friend again made it difficult to let him go. Secretly, none of them wanted their association to end.

"I'm sorry but I must be taking off," said Plaatu. "I landed in my favorite spot so I could surprise you. There is someone I want you to meet though."

Another figure appeared out of the darkness, but this time it was a female.

"My friends," said Plaatu, "I would like you to meet my daughter Nara."

She stepped forward into the light of the campfire and the men momentarily found themselves speechless. She was very beautiful and dressed in a soft-colored tunic and knee-high boots. Her hair hung loosely around her shoulders and she carried herself with grace and an unmistakable air of confidence.

"It's a pleasure," she said sincerely. "My father has told me much about you in the past few hours. I get the sense that you were a tremendous help to him for which I am grateful as well."

"The pleasure was all ours," said Ryan humbly.

"So where will you be heading?" asked Spike.

"I am going home my friends," said Plaatu. There was an unmistakable tone of resignation in his voice. "I have missed many years with my daughter and I have some serious catching up to do. I am hanging up my robot and space ship and going into retirement. But rest assured, I will try and make it back here for a visit. If successful, I will most definitely look you men up."

"Life is going to change immeasurably down here now isn't it?" asked Ryan in an almost melancholy tone.

"Yes it is," answered Plaatu. "But like everything else that goes on in this amazing universe of ours, some of it will be positive and some of it will be not so positive. I like to refer to it as growing pains. Earth will be alright now. The Coalition, although far from perfect, has enough positive elements to assure your assimilation with your celestial neighbors will go relatively smooth. The greatest immediate benefit to your planet will be, for the first time in half a century, you will be freed from living under the ominous threat of nuclear proliferation."

"Do you really think the governments of the world are going to just dismantle their billions of dollars worth of nuclear stockpiles just because your Coalition tells them to?" asked Mikey.

Plaatu just smiled. "Oh, they'll dismantle them alright. If they don't, the scare Bort just threw into you is nothing like the scare he will unleash upon your planet. They'll comply, I can assure you."

Tommy was scurrying around picking up beer cans. Then he went to the edge of the tree line and hung them on branches in a straight line. They glistened ever so slightly in the bright moonlight.

"One more time," he said returning to the group. "Just one more time and I'll never ask you for anything again, I promise."

Plaatu smiled broadly and turned towards Bort. "Bort, badabinga!" he said.

Without hesitation, Bort walked a few feet where he had a clear line of sight towards the trees. Then the campers watched in amazement as his visor went up revealing the diamond-shape light in his head. They watched in awe as Bort's energy beam vaporized the cans in a rapid fire sequence that lit up the entire camp ground. His visor closed and the campers cheered and clapped their hands.

"I gotta get one of these!" shrieked Tommy.

There was an awkward pause in the conversation and it was clear that the campers were having difficulty with the finality of the moment. Plaatu felt for them and wished there was some way he could help them with the transition back to their normal lives. To Plaatu, this was just another day at the office but to the six men who had been so willing to help him, this past week would no doubt serve as the most eventful of their entire lives. How does one top this?

"I'll tell you what," he said finally. "I give you my word I will pay a return visit and since Earth will be a member of the Coalition by then, I'll have Ecko give us a ride around the solar system. That should give you something to look forward to."

"Thanks Plaatu," said Brad. "That would be awesome."

"It's the least I can do," said Plaatu. He stepped forward and extended his hand. "Good bye for now my friends."

They each shook his hand and then said farewell to Nara as she, Plaatu and Bort walked back towards his ship. In a few moments, the three figures disappeared beyond the trees and were gone.

The campers resumed their seats in silence. A few moments later Plaatu's ship appeared overhead. It hovered for a moment, then soared off into the night sky and disappeared.

The overwhelming feeling of emptiness returned as they sat there staring once again at the colorful blue and orange flames flickering before them. Spike got up and grabbed a few more pieces of chopped wood and gently placed them on the fire. It was obvious that they would not be turning in for the night any time soon.

"Anyone need another beer while I'm up?" he asked.

"Yeah," said Mikey, "that sounds good," but his attempt to sound upbeat was strained and unsuccessful.

Spike walked over to the cooler and grabbed a round of beers. Then he handed one to each of the men and resumed his seat. A chorus of cans being popped open filled the air, then they drank in subdued silence. The atmosphere grew more melancholy with every passing minute until it became almost funeral-like. Brad refused to allow it to sink any further.

"Alright!" he shouted. His voice jolted them all to attention. "Enough of this morose shit!" He rose to his feet. "Everybody stand up!" he ordered.

The men grudgingly rose to their feet.

"I propose a toast!" he said, holding his beer can out in front of him. "Here's to one hell of an adventure, and to many more to come!"

"Here! Here!" added Ryan, thrusting out his arm. They all tilted their cans back and took long swigs of their icy cold ales.

"Ahhhhhh!" said Chris. "Das good!"

"And here's to bumping into some really hot looking nurses when you least expect it!" said Spike.

They all drank again.

"Chris!" barked Brad, "turn on that radio and crank up some tunes damn it!"

Chris leaned to the ground and grabbed his boom box which was sitting next to his lounge chair. He switched it on and the sound of the Pretenders filled the air.

"Welcome to the human race with its wars, disease and brutality.

You with your innocence and grace, restore some pride and dignity in a world of decline."

"And here's to Chrissie Hynde for being so hot and such a great singer," said Ryan. He was interrupted by a rumbling sound off in the distance. They all listened for a moment to what appeared to be the sound of several vehicles approaching from the highway. Chris quickly turned off the radio.

"Who the hell could that be?" asked Brad. "Nobody comes up here this time of year."

Mikey picked up a pair of night-vision binoculars and scanned in the direction of the approaching vehicles. As they drew closer he could make out that there were four vans and each had large lettering on the side panels. He strained to read them through the trees.

"C-N-N . . . A-B-C . . ." Mikey said. Then it dawned on him. "Those are television crews!"

"How the hell can that be?" asked Ryan. "Hardly anyone knows we're even out here?"

"This place has sure gone crazy," mused Spike.

The vans continued rolling directly towards them as the campers struggled to unravel this new mystery.

Then one by one, all eyes turned towards Tommy who was twitching nervously.

"Tommy!" shouted Mikey in anger.

Tommy threw up his hands in utter resignation.

"I'm a victim of circumstance," he gushed innocently.

Plaatu had one more task to complete before heading home. He laid in coordinates for the South Pole. As he and Nara sat side by side watching the main viewing screen, Plaatu pointed out the many interesting sights along the way. The vast Amazon basin and Andes Mountains of South America stretched beneath them as they hurtled towards their destination. Nara was fascinated by the myriad of life forms that call this part of the planet home.

As the ship reached the designated coordinates, Plaatu zoomed in on the Emperor Penguins still huddled together under the protection of the thermal heat device. The blizzard had passed and the weather had moderated considerably so Plaatu felt it wise to return them to their native conditions. He ordered the on-board computer to retrieve the device. As it did, the penguins began to squeal loudly in disapproval.

"Sorry," Plaatu chuckled. "But I can get in a lot of trouble for that." As the ship ascended and disappeared into the atmosphere, he left behind a penguin uprising.